D0475974

YA Smith
Smith, Charles R.
Chameleon

WITHDRAWN

$16.99
ocn164570339
1st ed.   09/24/2008

CHAMELEON

CHARLES R. SMITH JR.

CANDLEWICK PRESS
CAMBRIDGE, MASSACHUSETTS

To Mom and Dad

This is a work of fiction. Names, characters, places, and
incidents are either products of the author's imagination or,
if real, are used fictitiously.

Copyright © 2008 by Charles R. Smith Jr.

All rights reserved. No part of this book may be reproduced,
transmitted, or stored in an information retrieval system in
any form or by any means, graphic, electronic, or mechanical,
including photocopying, taping, and recording, without prior
written permission from the publisher.

First edition 2008

Library of Congress Cataloging-in-Publication Data
Smith, Charles R., date.
Chameleon / Charles R. Smith, Jr. — 1st ed.
p.   cm.
Summary: The summer before starting high school in inner-city
Los Angeles, fourteen-year-old Shawn grapples with his first
experience of love, the complicated bonds of friends and family,
and the reality of street gang violence.
ISBN: 978-0-7636-3085-0
[1. Coming of age — Fiction. 2. Inner cities — Fiction.
3. Summer — Fiction. 4. African Americans — Fiction.
5. Los Angeles (Calif.) — Fiction.]   I. Title.
PZ7.S6438Ch 2008
[Fic] — dc22   2007027963

2 4 6 8 10 9 7 5 3 1

Printed in the United States of America

This book was typeset in Mendoza.

Candlewick Press
2067 Massachusetts Avenue
Cambridge, Massachusetts 02140

visit us at www.candlewick.com

When I discover who I am,
I'll be free.

—*Ralph Ellison*

ONE

"YA MAMA SO TALL, she tripped on the curb and hit her head on the sun," Lorenzo spit out between sips of pineapple soda and bacon-and-sour-cream chips.

"Ohhhhhhh!" me and Andre shouted. Our hands formed megaphones over our mouths to broadcast our pleasure at Lorenzo's well-crafted bag.

Trent scooched his narrow butt closer to the edge of the step, then turned up toward Lorenzo, seated above him, and said, "Oh, you wanna bag? All right, then . . . lemme see . . . Ya mama so fat, she . . . Ya mama so fat, she stood over me and the sun disappeared."

"WEAK!" Lorenzo crunched into Trent's ear.

"Trent . . . that *was* weak," Andre said from the sideline between basketball chest passes aimed at Billy Dee Williams on a faded Colt 45 malt liquor poster.

The small patch of real estate between Trent's All Stars held his attention. He swished his purple quarter water back and forth on the concrete with his thin hands. A blood-burgundy Cadillac Brougham bumping bass thumps stopped at the light in front of us and caught Trent's eye.

School was out for the summer, but Mama still dropped me off at my aunt Gertie's house in Compton. Summer meant lazy days filled with soap operas, TV game shows, and Aunt Gertie's frequent alcoholic blackouts.

This summer would be different. In a few months I'd be a freshman. In high school. No more junior high! But right now I had three months to kill, and in Compton, with nowhere to go, that's an eternity. At least now that I was older, Mama had loosened up on me a bit and let me hang out more with my boys.

By ten a.m. every day except the weekends, we could be found outside Pop's Liquor Store off Wilmington Avenue doin' what the cops call "loitering" — shootin' the breeze and letting the wind carry our thoughts into the day. The sun was always bright. The air was always hot. And we were ready for anything.

"Trent, you still with us?" Lorenzo said after a swig of soda.

"Yeah. I'm thinkin', I'm thinkin'."

"See, that's your problem, Trent: you think too much," Andre bounced.

"Yeah, baggin' is all about the quickness. Reaction. You gotta be quick or you will be broken down," Lorenzo said.

Trent's eyes darted between the concrete and the Cadillac.

Green light. The bass thumped into the distance and bounced an idea into Trent's head. His eyes lit up.

"All right, wait . . . all right . . . I got one. Hold on. . . . Ya mama so black, they marked her absent in night school."

"Ohhhh! There you go, Trent, that was a good one," I said, giving him a soul clap.

"Yeah, Shawn. That *was* good. That's because I said the same thing just a couple of weeks ago. Remember?" Lorenzo said.

"Is that where I heard it from?" Trent asked.

"Yeah . . . that's where you heard it from," Lorenzo said. He stood and dusted bright golden chip crumbs from his black tracksuit, then crumbled the empty bag of chips into a ball. His white Adidas heels inched up into a half jump shot aimed at the brown wire trash can.

"Three, two, one . . ."

Brick.

"Dang!"

Lorenzo stretched his thick arms to the sky, exposing his round Buddha belly under his sweatshirt.

Trent finished off his last purple swallow. Andre stopped passing the basketball to Billy Dee and started weaving it between each leg, bounce-bouncing a nice little rhythm. Until I stole it from him.

"What we gonna do now?" I asked.

What are we gonna do today?

Same question. Different day. This was always where the spark was struck for the fire that would become that day's story.

"Let's play some ball," Andre said.

Trent and Lorenzo came off the steps to join me and Andre. We each took turns shooting our trash into the garbage-can goal.

Trent: "Three, two, one . . ."

Brick.

Andre: "Three, two, one . . ."

Swish.

Dang. I wish he missed once in a while.

Me: "Three, two, one . . ."

Brick.

Trent took the ball from me. "They got courts over at Bunche," he said.

"Nahh . . . too much glass," Andre sneered.

"How 'bout Carver?" I said.

"Nahhh . . . the Mexicans take over the court at this time of day."

"What about MLK?" Trent said.

We stood in a circle, each facing out. Pop's is on the dividing line between Crip blue and Piru red, or what I like to call the DMZ. My dad taught me that in Vietnam, DMZ meant demilitarized or neutral zone. That meant no trouble. But if we headed east, Pirus. West, Crips. This was always the biggest decision of the day. We didn't wanna be in the wrong place at the wrong time. Planning helped.

"I don't know about MLK. When I was there last time, I saw some Crips hanging out near the handball courts shootin' dice. But then my brother told me that he saw some Pirus playing ball there one time, so I don't know," Lorenzo said.

'Zo's shoes pointed north as he tugged at his thick waistband.

"How 'bout DuBois?" I said.

"Man, they ain't got no nets on those creaky rims," Andre said.

He stole the ball from Trent and rocked it side to side.

"Yeah, that's why it'll be empty," Lorenzo said.

He stole the ball and took off in the direction of DuBois.

"I swear, Andre, you act like every court has to be the Forum," I said before hustling after Lorenzo.

Andre brought up the rear.

"It ain't that. That court just sucks," he said.

And that's how it was. Yeah, DuBois's court sucked, but we'd rather deal with rickety rims than trigger-happy gangbangers.

TWO

"**COLOR CHECK**," Lorenzo shouted.

The four of us looked ourselves over from head to toe.

Trent: White shirt. Green shorts. White socks with yellow rings around the calf. White All Stars. Cool.

Lorenzo: All black sweat suit. Doesn't he ever get hot in that? White Adidas with black stripes. Cool.

Andre: Yellow Lakers shirt. Black shorts. White socks with yellow rings. White Ponys with a black stripe. Cool.

Me: White shirt. Blue shorts. Blue shorts! Dang!

"If we going anywhere, Shawn, you better change your shorts," Lorenzo said.

I knew he would say that.

"I'll be all right, man. They're dark blue. They look black."

Trent took the ball from Lorenzo and said, "Come on, Shawn, you remember what happened to Andre that one time."

Did I remember? How could I forget?

Rewind to last year, first day of summer vacation. Andre decided to wear his brother's new basketball shorts. His brother is in the navy, like my dad was, and everything in the navy is blue. So he was wearing blue shorts when we decided to go to MLK. That's our favorite park because it was the biggest and the rims actually have nets. Anyway, it was the first day of vacation, and we were just happy to be out and playing ball, so we weren't even thinking about a color check.

Everybody was busy just doing their thing when four gang-bangers rolled up on the court, laughing, carrying forties, and choking on weed smoke. Their red All Stars, polos, and dangling bandannas let us know they were Pirus.

"Wuzzup, blood?" one of them said.

My mouth widened as my eyes narrowed in on fat red rollers curled into his permed hair. Fresh-pressed black Dickies drooped beneath his boxer shorts, which glowed white on his jet-black torso. Skull and skeleton tattoos screamed from his skin. A red bandanna dangled from his back pocket alongside a golf club that had been broken in half. The club end stuck straight into the air and jammed him in the back. His left hand gripped his crotch while his right hand clutched a forty-ounce of malt liquor covered by a brown bag. He strolled up to the four of us, tugged on his crotch, and spoke again: "I said . . . wuzzup, BLOOD!"

My mouth closed and my eyes blinked. I swallowed hard, then managed to squeeze out, "What's up?" with Trent and Lorenzo.

The three of us hovered near the basket while Andre shot free throws behind us.

40-Ounce called out to Andre, "Ay. Navy . . . come here! Navy! Come here, Navy!"

Andre clanked the free throw as he heard the request. We turned and locked eyes with him to tell him not to move.

"Don't look at them! Ay! I'm talking to you!" 40-Ounce pointed his brown bag toward Andre. "Come here!"

Andre dropped the ball to the ground and headed toward us. Slowly.

40-Ounce shook his head and raised his voice. "Uh-uh . . . bring yo' ball."

MLK, a favorite park of all the neighborhood kids, quieted its buzz of activity as all eyes fell on the four of us, surrounded by red Pirus. Double-Dutch ropes swung by schoolgirl hands stopped skipping. Kickballs bouncing off schoolboy feet stopped flying. The distant sound of an old man playing checkers, shouting, "King me!" to his opponent, broke the silence.

Like four vulnerable black checkers, we stood waiting to get jumped by red.

"You heard me," 40-Ounce called.

One weed-choker added, "Come on, li'l man. We ain't go do nothing. Just wanna talk to ya."

"Come here, podna," 40 said. "Lemme ax you a question."

Andre stared at his sneakers and shuffled over with the ball on his right hip. He tried to keep some distance between him and 40, but 40 claimed the space and stood right next to him. The brown bag shifted from 40's right hand to his left. His right arm swung, fatherly, over Andre's shoulder.

"What's yo' favorite color?"

"Purple," Andre said without hesitation.

"Purple!? Ain't that kind of a faggoty color?" 40-Ounce said, shaking Andre's shoulder in mock jest.

Andre squeezed the ball between his hands and replied, "I ain't no faggot. I like the Lakers. So purple is my favorite color."

"So if purple is yo' favorite color . . . why are you wearing those?" 40's bottle pointed down at Andre's navy shorts.

"Oh, these. These are my brother's."

Andre's left hand began to rub his waistband front to back, back to front. His right hand, his shooting hand, clutched the ball at his side. Each skinny digit caressed each ridge and dimple.

"What set yo' brother roll wit'?" 40 spit into Andre's ear. His left hand reached back to the golf club in his back pocket to shift its position against his back.

"Come on, Doc, let's play some ball," Laugher #1 said. He took a long pull on the joint, then offered some to 40.

"Naww, I ain't done wit' Navy yet."

So the other Pirus surrounded a bench near the court to watch, and the joint made its way around the circle.

"Ay, Doc, swing that 40 over here," Laugher #2 shouted.

"I don't remember any of y'all puttin' in on this," 40-Ounce said, looking over at them. "Besides, I told you, I ain't done here yet." His tattooed arm remained draped like a shackle around Andre's shoulder, to whom he returned his attention.

40's words spit quicker. "Look here, podna. Let me ax you this. . . . Are you disrespecting me?"

His eyes filled with fire and flamed onto Andre's face, up close and personal.

"Nah, man. I don't wanna disrespect nobody."

"Wearing those shorts *is* disrespectful to me. How you go come up here in *my* park, in my hood, and disrespect me like this?"

In one swift motion, he dropped his arm and shifted the bag from left to right. His left hand plunged past his waistband and into his checkered boxers.

Andre jerked.

Booming bass crept into our eardrums as a candy-apple-red Chevy Impala glided by. Its speakers carried the beat away to another block as the other Pirus picked up the chorus to Parliament's "Flashlight."

Dah dah dah dee

Dah dah dah dah dah dah daaaaaaahhhhh

The hot air pressed down on us.

The three of us looked at Andre and tried to use the Jedi mind trick to tell him it was gonna be cool, but Andre stood still as a statue.

"Relax, man. My nuts just itch," 40 said, scratching and laughing.

The bag remained swaying in his right hand while his funky scratch-hand made its way around Andre's shoulder and dangled in front of his nostrils. Then 40 took a swig of his brew.

Andre stepped away from the funky fingers.

"Look here, podna. Gimme yo' shorts," 40-Ounce said, no longer laughing.

"Huh?"

"You heard me. Gimme yo' shorts." 40 stood large over Andre and glared down at him. Spit rained from his lips when the next sentence exploded from his mouth. "Did I st-st-stutter? You heard me—TAKE OFF THE DAMN SHORTS, HOMEY!"

That answered Andre's question all right. Weed-Choker and Laughers #1 and #2 sat and watched. Weed-Choker dug into his pants and pulled out a plastic baggie filled with brown, dusty weed.

"Who got the Zig-Zags?" he asked.

The hyenas began looking in their pockets.

"You got papers, Doc?" #1 called out.

"Man, don't you see I'm busy?"

"Ay, look here, Navy. You better give up the shorts. 'Cause he go get 'em one way or another. Catch my drift?" #1 said, now serious.

Andre stood center stage, his brother's navy shorts hanging on him like a flag about to be captured. He tried to negotiate again.

"Ummm, my brother gave me these shorts, and I don't see him but once in a while, so I really can't give 'em to you."

Andre tried to step away.

40 pretended to listen, then a sinister grin crept across his face as he hoisted his pants quickly, then screamed, "J-Dee! Ant-Dog . . . GRAB THIS FOOL!"

The two Laughers sprang off the bench so fast, it looked like they were on speed instead of weed. Laugher #1 grabbed Andre's arms and head and put him in a headlock while #2 grabbed his legs. The ball bounced to someplace safe. Trent rushed to help Andre while me and Lorenzo moved in to back him up. Before we could blink, 40 reached in his back pocket and swung the cut-down club on Lorenzo. 'Zo ducked out of the way, but it slammed into the meat of my back and knocked me to the ground. MAN, THAT HURT! I got a face full of dirt as Weed-Choker rushed over and planted a heavy red All Star into the pounded flesh of my back where I had just been whacked.

Andre was locked in tight by the Laughers while 40 held his club inches from Trent's and Lorenzo's wide-eyed faces.

"Now see what y'all made me do! I didn't want to have to use this, but y'all made me do that. Just back on up, let me get them shorts, and we'll be Kool and the Gang," 40 said.

Weed-Choker's jeans drooped far below his butt, now exposing most of his boxers. I tried to wiggle free from the foot but only got a mouthful of dirt as it pressed harder.

Andre squirmed in the arms of the Laughers while 40 strolled over and yanked the shorts off in one quick jerk. He dangled them from the handle end of his club and twirled them around in circles.

"See, that wasn't so hard now, was it, Navy?" He laughed.

The Laughers dropped Andre as quickly as they had rushed him. His bright cotton tighty-whiteys glowed among a sea of bloodred.

"You lucky yo' underwear ain't blue or we woulda took those too, homey," one of the Laughers said.

Andre got up slow and tried to pull his baggy T-shirt down as far as it would go.

My back got lighter, so I stood up too. I dusted off my body and my pride and made my way toward Andre. Lorenzo and Trent were huddling close, trying to shield him from all the eyes in the park.

40 stood proud like a victorious general, admiring the captured shorts spinning on his club.

As we turned to leave, Trent grabbed the ball from the grass, and once again 40 spoke up.

"I'll take that ball too."

"Ay, man, that's my ball," Lorenzo said, stepping closer.

"Was I talking to you, fat boy?"

40 snatched the ball, then raised his club high.

"You don't want no more of this, do you?"

Lorenzo stepped back.

40 threw the shorts over his right shoulder, then bounced over to the bench where the other Pirus had sat down.

"I got some Zig-Zags in my back pocket," he said.

And that was that. The Pirus continued their party as we walked out of the park. Young girls laughed and pointed at Andre in his underwear. Young boys whispered among each other, knowing the same could happen to them at any time. A pair of gray-haired men playing checkers shook their heads and continued playing. Battered, bruised, and broken, we got out of Dodge with our confidence bubbles burst.

Staring down at *my* dark blue shorts, I replayed that scenario in my mind — only in my replay, each of us whipped up on one of the Pirus: *Lorenzo snatched the red off them. Trent shut the hyenas up. Andre poured the forty over 40's head, and I whupped him with his cut-down club while I screamed, "See what you made me do. I didn't want to have to use this, but you made me do that. You made me do that!"*

Judging by the fire in my boys' eyes, I wasn't the only one remembering and changing the ending of that movie.

Yeah, I remembered that day. I remembered it well. How could I forget? Piru red was branded into each of us forever.

THREE

MY BRAIN WAS BLAZING, memories tightening my back and marinating my mouth with the taste of dirt. The breeze caressing my scalp did nothing to cool my thoughts.

"Come on, Shawn, let's go change your shorts. Your auntie's house is on the way," Lorenzo said, slapping me on the back.

Unfortunately he was right. My watch ticked ten minutes to noon. That meant ten minutes to Aunt Gertie's favorite soap opera, *All My Children*. That meant that a pint of the brown stuff had already been polished off.

How could anybody drink that crap in the daytime?

How could anybody drink that stuff period?

"Shoot! You know what? . . . I forgot, I don't have any extra shorts at my auntie's house. . . . Mine are all at my house," I said.

"I don't know how you do it, Shawn. Going back and forth and everything. I would get too mixed up," Andre said. He paused at the curb.

My house is about twelve miles away, in Carson, but with nobody there to watch me, Mama always drops me off at Aunt Gertie's before work and picks me up after. I go to school here and spend most of my time here, so I hang with my boys whenever I can. It's a lot of back and forth between Carson and Compton, but I always know where home is.

Red light. We stopped. Stood still. Waited. Gray Cadillacs, red DeVilles, blue Impalas, burgundy Regals, and primered Pintos paraded past us in a procession of traffic. Lorenzo tugged at his waistband, the ball between his legs. Trent tied his Stars. Andre scraped gum from his Ponys with a sharp stick. My nostrils twitched at the scent of burnt hair and fried fish floating on the breeze.

"So what now?" Andre said. His right foot scraped against the concrete like a baseball batter digging his cleats in for a pitch.

"You got some shorts that'll fit me?" I asked Andre.

"You know I live back the other way, Shawn."

It was bad enough that Auntie might be drunk, but worse if she was passed out. The fellas still don't know about her, but I think they gettin' hip to me, because in all the years we've known each other, they still haven't been there. I always manage to come up with some excuse. I don't want them to see the bottle or hear the slurred words as she repeats the same stories over and over and over again:

"I'm glad he's gone . . . thas right . . . I'm glad. . . . He wadn't goo' fur nuthin'. . . . No, he wadn't. . . . That goo'-fur-nuthin' durrty dog . . ."

I still haven't figured out who "he" is.

I didn't want them to see her limp body sprawled across the couch, hand clutching an empty glass. I didn't want them to smell the stench of the whiskey-splashed carpet from days past, memories lost, and fights forgotten. I didn't want them to hear the constant moaning or the endless drunken sighs.

"What about you, Lorenzo?"

"I know your skinny butt is not asking me to borrow some shorts. Shoot, you and a twin could fit into a pair of my shorts, skinny as you are, Shawn."

"Why can't we just go back to your auntie's house, Shawn? It's right on the way," Trent said. "You've gotta have something there you can wear."

Because. Because. My life has doors. Doors hide things. And that was a door I didn't want to open.

I tapped the Walk button. This light is always slow.

"Ay, Shawn, is that Marisol?"

Across the street a young Mexican girl about our age headed into the Tamale Hut. Lorenzo nodded her way.

"Where?" I said, darting my eyes around the intersection. Marisol. My savior.

She was at ten o'clock. The Tamale Hut. Clear jellies on her feet. Sunshine-yellow pedal pushers on her legs, a flower on the lower right pant leg. White blouse. Long black hair caressing her butt, with a butterfly clasp pulling the hair out of her face.

Yup. Marisol.

Her slow, easy stride carried her inside, where she was joined by two of her friends, Passion and Ivy. *Mare-ee-solll.* Just the syllables coming out of my mouth made my heart skip a beat. We went to school together, and I had it bad for her. I wanted to learn Spanish because of her. It might have been the hair or . . .

Lorenzo elbowed Trent in the ribs and nodded again toward the Tamale Hut.

"I feel like gettin' a tamale," he said.

"Awww, man. Let's just go to the park. I ain't trying to deal with Passion and Ivy," Andre said.

Lorenzo grabbed me around the neck.

"Come on, Trent. I *know* Shawn is hungry for some spicy Mexican food. Huh, Shawn?" he said.

Andre snatched the ball from Trent. "I thought we was gonna play some ball?"

Trent tapped at the Walk button with excitement, then did a little dance on and off the curb.

"Come on, you guys."

Lorenzo tugged on my left arm.

"Yeah, Shawn. What you got to be afraid of?" he said.

Plenty. But anything that'll keep me from my auntie's house is fine by me. Even if it did mean I might make a fool of myself.

Marisol Rodriguez. Yes, she was fine. But better than that, she was cool. She was even finer because she was cool. Most girls that are fine know they are fine and act all conceited and stuck-up. But the ones that are fine and don't quite know they are fine are usually cool. Real cool. This was Marisol. We been going to school together since Head Start, and for as long as I can remember, she's had that long, jet-black hair of hers. Sometimes she wore it in a ponytail. Sometimes she twisted it up. Most of the time she just let it cascade down her back like a waterfall.

Our neighborhood is a pretty good mix of blacks and Mexicans. Almost equal. Everybody'd gotten to know each other over the years in school, and me and Marisol became friends. Not close friends, but friends. The first time I heard her speak Spanish to a friend of hers, I asked if she could teach me something. I didn't think she would teach me "I love you" right off the bat, so I started with the basics: cuss words. From there we moved on to the alphabet, then numbers, then the real touristy stuff. Things like:

Hello.

Hola.

How are you?

¿Cómo estás?

I'm fine.

Estoy bien.

Where is the bathroom?

¿Dónde está el baño?

What time is it?

¿Qué hora es? (Which really means "What hour is it?")

My name is . . .

Me llamo . . .

Yes.

Sí.

No. Which is still "no," just with a hard accent.

I had her repeat that one because it formed her lips into a kiss. I think she was on to me, though, 'cause she only said it a couple of times. I mean, how hard is it to say "no"?

What I really wanna say is: *You are so beautiful, I want to brush your long flowing hair and taste your hot-sauce lips.*

But not yet. Right now I can barely say "*hola.*"

The light changed and we booked it across the street. Lorenzo made a beeline for the Hut. I brought up the rear except for Andre, who was bouncing the ball. Trent got behind me and pushed me inside.

"Come on, Shawn. You look hungry. Ain't you hungry?" Trent asked.

Not for food.

Marisol, Passion, and Ivy noticed Lorenzo right away when he stepped through the door, and they all started talking. Andre stayed outside bouncing circles around each leg. Right hand: dribble-dribble right, dribble-dribble back, dribble-dribble between legs, switch. Repeat with left hand. He'd gotten good enough that he could wink at me and Trent as we crept inside.

The Tamale Hut. It was also in the DMZ, and since it was on the way home for almost everybody, it was always jumping on afternoons during the school year. The door dinged open onto little wooden tables with orange benches scattered across a small room. Bottles of Cholula hot sauce sat next to Tabasco and salt and pepper as the condiments of choice. Miguel, the owner, had been bangin' the bell there for as long as we could remember.

Ding-ding: "*Número ocho.* Tamale platter. Strawberry soda."

Miguel was cool too. His son went to our school a few years ago, and Miguel was nice to everybody: blacks, Mexicans, whoever. Plus his food was good. But the hot sauce he put on the table was a monster! The first time Lorenzo tried it, he poured it on like it was salt or something. Shaka-shaka-shaka. Shaka-shaka-shaka.

"Lorenzo, man, you gonna burn your tongue. Why don't you taste it first?" I said.

Shaka-shaka. Shaka-shaka-shaka. Shaka. Shaka-shaka.

"See, that's the difference between me and you, Shawn: you too careful for your own good. Me: I'm an adventurer, an explorer," Lorenzo said.

When the tamale touched his lips, his tongue leaped from his mouth. His nostrils flared, and his eyes became a faucet for his tears.

"You all right there, Marco Polo?" I asked.

"Water! I need water! Miguel . . . *agua, por favor! AGUA!*" Lorenzo had screamed before rushing the counter like his drawers were on fire.

See, there's a difference between being an adventurer and being stupid.

"What's up, skinny Shawn?"

Passion's voice snapped me back into the present.

Her thin black frame plunked down next to me, across from Trent. Lorenzo was already up at the counter.

"Oh, and hi, fool!"

Trent rolled his eyes and looked at me. I knew that look.

But Passion Jackson is a good friend to have. If somebody was to curse any of her friends or bad-mouth someone who's done something good for her, then she is their personal pit bull. She'll defend your name like it was hers. Get on her bad side, though . . .

One time during PE she got mad at Trent because he almost hit her with a softball. It was an honest mistake, because everybody knows that Trent can't throw too straight. So the ball comes flying in a little too close to her face. Well, that was just *it*. Passion sucked her teeth, shook her head, rushed the mound with the bat, and started swinging at Trent. Me, Ivy, and Lorenzo jumped in, and ol' girl just would *not* stop. Good thing Trent was fast, 'cause he ran away from her when she got too close with the bat. Ever since then she thinks Trent is out to get her. Trent thinks she's crazy. Shoot, if I had a girl rush me with a bat, I would think she was crazy too.

"So what y'all up to today?" she asked.

"You know. Same ol', same ol'. Play some ball. Hang out . . . you know," I said.

Her eyes narrowed in on Trent.

"Yeah, I know . . . a whole lotta nothing as usual."

"Don't start with me, Passion," Trent said.

"Don't start with *me*, little boy," she said, rolling her eyes and neck at Trent.

"Come on, now. You guys are worse than cackling hens," I said.

As Trent and Passion exchanged evil eyeballs, I wandered my eyes over to Marisol. Mare-ee-sol. *Te amo.* I love you. *Te quiero mucho.* I want you. Oooh, you look good today. How you say that?

"So what's up with Marisol these days?" I asked Passion.

"What you mean, what's up with Marisol?"

"He's asking you if she got a boyfriend, thickhead," Trent jumped in.

"Shawn, please tell me Dumbo here didn't say what I think he just said. I *know* he didn't call me no thickhead!" She stood and hovered over Trent.

"Passion, sit down. And calm down," I said.

This girl. Man. I don't know how her family puts up with her. I guess when you have six brothers and sisters, you gotta find some way to stand out.

"Come on, Shawn, everybody knows you got a thing for my girl. Why don't you just talk to her? She ain't with nobody right now, but" — she motioned at Marisol sitting between two older guys— "as you can see, that could change at any time."

"Who's that?" Trent asked.

"Shoot, I don't know. Pro'ly some Marshall boys," Passion said, taking her seat.

"For real?" Trent said.

"Is it true what they say about Marshall?" I asked Passion. I knew a couple of her brothers and sisters went there.

"Is what true?" she snapped.

"Come on, thickhead. You know what he mean. Do they be wilding out like we hear or what?"

Aw, Trent, "thickhead" again? This boy was one tamale short of a combo platter.

"What you say? I *know* you didn't just say what I thought you said. Right, Dumbo? Those words didn't just come out of your nasty little mouth, did they? You did *not* just use your little pea brain to step to me, did you?" Passion said. Her eyes bored holes into Trent.

Here we go again.

"You know, I should just take some of this hot sauce and splash it in your ugly mug. That'll shut you up once and for all. I'm trying to sit here and talk to my *friend,* but your stank behind keeps *interrupting* me."

Passion lived up to her name. All eyes were on us for a moment.

"Trent, be cool. Can we just sit here for a little bit and have a conversation?"

"Whatever, Shawn." And just like that, he got up to join Andre outside.

Thurgood Marshall was the high school we would be going to in a few months, and we all had heard stories. Some had relatives there. Some, like me, didn't. That's what happens when you're an only child.

Passion cooled her fire.

"My older brother Vonnie told me that one time in his world civ class, this Crip comes in all blued up, right, and then starts talking loud and cursing the teacher out, right?

But when the teacher tries to send him to detention, the Crip pulls out a blade twice as long as my longest finger and straight rushes the teacher. Nobody moved, but security came running when the teacher screamed and yanked the Crip off him before he could do any damage. Vonnie said he ripped the teacher's pants and took a slice out of Africa on the map, but as they dragged the Crip out, he was all like, 'I'm go do to you what I did to Africa, homey!'"

A fly could've flew in my mouth the way it hung open. Crips pulling knives on teachers? Is this what I have to look forward to?

"You all right, Shawnie-Shawn?"

"Ah yeah. I was just getting ready to yawn."

"Yeah right. Looked like your heart was about to jump through your chest. I know the Crips and Pirus got y'all spooked."

"I'm not spooked. I was just thinking about high school and how it'll be different from junior high. That's all."

"Oh, it's gonna be different, all right, but from what my brother tells me, the principal has the school on lockdown now with the 'pink slip.'"

Her bright white tank top touched her seat back as she folded her arms.

"The 'pink slip'? What's that?"

"What's up, guys?" popped into my ears from behind. Who said that?

Marisol. Uh-oh. She took Trent's still-warm spot on the bench.

Right in front of me.

Sit up straight. Be cool. Pretend you don't see her. Dang, but she's fine. That hair. Those eyes. Those lips. Those lips . . .

"Marisol, can you believe Shawn here ain't heard of the 'pink slip' at Marshall?" Passion said, thumbing my shoulder.

"It's not like everybody has brothers and sisters that go there," Marisol said.

Her big, beautiful oh-so-lovely eyes met mine before she spoke again. "I can't believe you haven't heard about it, though, Shawn."

She rested her oh-so-lovely chin on her oh-so-lovely left hand while she pushed her oh-so-lovely hair back with her oh-so-lovely right hand.

Sigh.

Don't look in her eyes. You won't be able to talk if you do. Remember?

Look around. Where? The counter. Behind her. Yeah. Hmmmm, today's special is the tamale combo with one tamale, Mexican rice, and a Jarritos soda. Ohh, I love Jarritos, especially *tamarindo*.

"All right. I don't know what it is. So sue me. Is somebody gonna tell me, or are we just gonna sit here talking about how Shawn don't know what the 'pink slip' is?"

"It ain't no big thing," Passion said. "It's a permission slip they send home with you on the first day of school so the principal can paddle you if you act a fool."

"Oh, that slip. I thought you was talking about something else."

"Yeah, right. 'Something else.' You don't even know what the paddle looks like, do you?" she said. Her arms crossed and she stared me down.

I threw it right back at her, though.

"Do *you* know what it looks like?"

"Well . . . I've never seen it, but I heard it's real long with all these holes drilled into it. My brother told me Principal Simms has assemblies when it's time to paddle so everybody can see what happens when you act out," Marisol said. Her eyes met Passion's, then shifted over to mine.

Look away. The counter! How much is the combo? $3.95. Dang . . . didn't it use to be $2.95?

"All right, so I haven't seen it. But I heard the same thing. I also heard that it's about as wide as my hand and about as long as your fool friend Trent's bony legs." Passion pointed her eyes and right thumb at the window next to us.

Lorenzo must have already gotten his tamale and left. He, Andre, and Trent were on the other side, fogging it up with their hot breath. Three big mouths sucked and squeaked against the glass.

Lorenzo banged at us.

"Uh-oh, y'all, Shawn is talking to Marisol now. Watch out!"

Passion rolled her eyes, grabbed her drink, got up, and left. Leaving me and Marisol. Alone.

Wait.

Wait.

Don't go. The fellas were still on the other side of the window, their twisted faces no longer silent.

Trent started in: "Shawn and Marisol sitting in a tree, k-i-s-s-i-n-g . . ."

"Ah, I gotta go."

I slid from the booth to muffled chants of . . .

"GO, SHAWN . . . GO, SHAWN . . . GO, SHAWN . . ."

Marisol waved as I stumbled out.

"See you later, Shawn."

I pushed past Passion and Ivy, then turned to see Marisol smiling at me as I rushed out the door.

Wait, was she smiling at me . . . or laughing?

Hot air hit my face as my name hit my ears.

"GO, SHAWN . . . GO, SHAWN . . ."

I snatched the ball from Andre and hustled toward the intersection.

"Shawn. Hold up. Where you going?" Andre said, chasing me down.

Lorenzo huffed his way over and took the ball from my hands.

"I know you ain't mad about Marisol," he said.

Trent strolled over and slung his arm around my neck.

"Come on, Shawn, you know we was just messing with you. You act so serious about her. You need to relax. We was just having fun," he said.

"Did it look like I was having fun with you guys clowning me?"

I snatched the ball back.

But it's hard to stay mad at these guys because that's just the way it is. We always have each other's backs. But still. Marisol? Dang!

"Looked like you were having a good time to me. Sitting there acting all serious, knowing you can't even look her in the eye," Lorenzo said.

Bass beats from overworked car speakers serenaded us as we hustled across the street to continue our stroll.

How does he know I can't look her in the eye?

"Can you blame him? Marisol does have some pretty eyes. Kind of greenish blue with . . ." Andre started.

Hold up . . .

"What you doing looking at her eyes?"

Lorenzo joined in, "And that hair, man . . . umm. That hair is something else! Reaching all the way down to . . ."

"Y'all better stop. Right now. I'm serious."

My forehead felt like a hot tamale.

"Look at you, Shawn. All serious. Again. See, we was just messing with you," Trent said, pushing one shoulder, "again."

Lorenzo bumped the other and added, "But only because you make it so easy."

FOUR

FORWARD. Our sneakers scuffed the sidewalk in the direction of DuBois. Storefront sights and sidewalk sounds mixed with each bounce of the ball.

Liquor store. Chinese takeout. Check cashing. Church. Fish-fry shack. Fried chicken shack. Mexican food. Bar. Barbecue shack. Liquor store. Check cashing. Barber shop. Market. Chinese takeout. Church. Beauty parlor. Liquor store.

"Ay, y'all see that?" Lorenzo said.

His fat finger pointed in the direction of a woman squatting behind a large Dumpster about half a basketball court away. Shards of broken green glass dusted her tainted pink fur coat while Fatburger wrappers hung on the hem for dear life. Her head swiveled away from us for privacy.

"Aw, man, I don't wanna see that," Trent said. He brushed past me to turn the corner.

Andre bounced the ball faster. "Man, that's nasty. Taking a crap in front of everybody," he said, more to himself than the rest of us.

Lorenzo cupped his hands around his mouth and shouted, "Why don't you go someplace else to do your business!"

She shouted back, telling him to go do something with himself that made us cup our hands to our mouths and shout, "OOOOOHHHH!"

"She told you," Andre said.

"Shut up, 'Dre. I don't care. That's nasty, man. Have some respect for yourself. For real. Y'all just too scared to say anything."

"You think I haven't seen that before? Man . . . if I had a nickel for all the weird stuff I done seen out here, I'd have enough money to buy each of you guys about three mansions," Trent said.

I can say the same: women hiding behind Dumpsters; men dropping their drawers to passing traffic; junkies swaying in their walk, fightin' gravity with twitchy hands; teenage girls wildin' out on each other, scratchin' faces with way-too-long fingernails; grown men gettin' whipped with extension cords in the street by their much bigger wives. And of course the war between the red and the blue.

That thought turned my mind from Dumpster squatters to the coming school year. What's it gonna be like? I'd heard a lot about Marshall, but I didn't know what to believe. Or who. I trusted Passion, but what did she really know? I mean she's going there for the first time just like me.

What am I gonna study?

Will the four of us have classes together?

Do they have French? Or just Spanish? I know some Spanish, but I wanna learn French so I can go to France someday. Dad's been there and said I should go when I'm older.

How big are the classes gonna be?

How often do teachers get swung on with a knife?

Is the "pink slip" for real?

"You guys ever heard of the 'pink slip' at Marshall?" I floated to the wind.

About four steps in front of me, Andre weaved the ball between his legs while Trent tried to steal it from him. Lorenzo stood staring at a poster of a caramel-colored Colt 45 malt liquor girl when his ears picked up the question.

"What? My eyes were occupied by Ms. Thang right here so I didn't catch everything you said. Did you say something about a pink slip?" Lorenzo replied.

He peeled his eyes off the faded poster and rested them on me. I nodded.

"Yeah, I know all about that. My brother Dayshaun brought his home a few years ago, and my mama signed it with a big smile on her face." His eyes recalled that memory on the ocean-blue screen above our heads. "She hoped Principal Simms could knock some sense into that rock-hard head of his," he continued. "Believe it or not, he never got the paddle. But some of his 'bangin' friends did."

"Is it true about the assemblies and stuff? I heard he has them just to paddle the knuckleheads," I told him.

"From what I hear. Who told you that?" he asked. His wide body stopped to block my path.

The words came out of my mouth before I could stop them: "I was talking to Passion and Marisol at . . ."

"Marisol, huh?" he said. A grin spread across his face.

He moved, so I followed. Our sneakers were on autopilot as we crossed the intersection and strolled south. DuBois was only a block away.

Lorenzo finished giving me the lowdown on "pink slip" assemblies and the slip itself. First of all it had an official name: "Permission Form to Discipline." It was handed out the first day of school and had to be returned by the end of the week. I was surprised to hear it didn't have to be signed. But, he said, most parents did sign it because they felt if they couldn't knock some sense into their hardheaded child, maybe Principal Simms's paddle could by smacking their behind in front of the whole school.

But the last words out of his mouth made the most sense: "If your mama is signin' the pink slip and she got a smile on her face . . . then you must be a knucklehead. You don't get smacked for shooting spitballs at the teacher—you get smacked for swinging knives at the teacher."

Passion's story popped into my head.

Yeah, that made sense. Unfortunately, it made perfect sense. But still. How much fun is it gonna be going to a school where on the first day the first thing you get is a form saying my mother gives my principal permission to whack my butt in front of the whole school?

FIVE

"**MANNN, SHAWN,** next time can you please remember to wear some shorts that ain't blue?" Andre said. "I hate playing on these rickety rims," he added in disgust as his first shot bricked off the backboard at DuBois.

"Yeah, you lucky ain't nobody even here 'cept us. A couple of 'rus show up and it'll be last year all over," Lorenzo said, chasing the rebound.

"I know, I know, but what y'all want me to do?" I shrugged. "I told you I don't have any shorts at my auntie's."

Even if I did, I definitely wouldn't take them there; I'd rather deal with the possibility of Pirus than a definite drunken auntie.

"Don't even sweat it, Shawn," Trent said. "We got plenty of time to figure something out. The day's just getting started."

"Speaking of which, let's get this game started," Andre said, tossing the ball to Lorenzo. "It'll be me and Shawn against you and Trent."

"No, no, no, no, no. It's always you two against us two. Let's switch it up. Let's start with me and Shawn against you and Trent," Lorenzo replied.

"Whatever. You gonna get dusted either way. I'll just let it be with Shawn first," Andre said. He stepped back to swish a shot from the top of the key.

"Don't I have any say in this matter?" Trent asked.

"No," we said in unison.

Trent is probably the weakest player of all of us, but he plays hard D and doesn't call ticky-tack fouls. Lorenzo, on the other hand, calls all kinds of fouls. You would think the biggest player on the court would be causing more fouls than calling them, but nooooo. If any of us even brush him the wrong way: "FOUL!" Otherwise he uses that big body of his to get rebounds. He may be big, but he can jump with the best of us. Andre is a whole different story. Where do I start? The boy can play. Period. Whenever we play in a pickup game, whoever guards him shows no respect for his jumper by giving him too much space. That's when he splashes it in their eye. Every time. When they finally step up to guard him closer, he crosses them and takes it to the hole. He's almost unstoppable. Almost. That's where I come in. I'm the only one who can stop him. That's why they call me "Lockdown." Because that's what I do: lock you down on D. When I say "lockdown," I mean you won't even touch the ball. But that's on defense. On offense I been working on my jumper with Andre and can splash it from the key now. Not all the time, but if I'm open.

"Straight to eleven. Make it, take it. Check up," Andre said, tossing me the ball.

"Hold on. Do we have to take it back?" Trent asked.

"Only if it hits rim. Then you gotta take it back to the free-throw line. If it hits just backboard, you can put it right up," Andre answered.

Let's go. What you gonna do, Andre? Try to set me up with the crossover and splash the J? I don't think so. All I gotta do is wait till you get low and try to go left and . . .

"Nice steal, Shawn," Lorenzo said.

He parked underneath the basket on the right side and raised his arm for the ball. I lobbed it over Trent's head and cut to the basket hard. 'Zo spun left and dropped a sweet bounce pass to me. Andre played me tight, so I pump-faked to put him in the popcorn machine, then put in the easy layup.

"One–zip, us," Lorenzo said.

He flipped a quick pass into me, and I flipped it right back. 'Zo's silhouette bounced near the top of the key with Trent bouncing around him. I cut back and forth across the court until he made his move. Dribble left, dribble right. 'Zo charged to the basket like a bull, but Trent stepped in front of him and got knocked onto his back.

"Foul!" Lorenzo shouted.

Trent jumped up and shouted back, "What? You gotta be kidding me! I'm the one on the ground, and you calling a foul on me? I know you don't think you getting the ball back, because that ain't about to happen."

I sighed. This was gonna be a long game.

"I'll let it slide this time, but next time you foul me, Trent, you better respect my call," Lorenzo said.

"Respect your call? Are you serious? I'm the one who should be yelling foul, not your Buddha belly," Trent shouted. Again.

"Come on, you two. Can we get this game going, please?" Andre said.

We scored. They scored. Lorenzo called more fouls, and finally the game was over. We had taken it 11–9, and we all hit the fountain for a quick break. Andre went back to swishing shots as the rest of us wandered over to a bench on the side of the court. A handful of people were sprinkled throughout the park, including two older men in fedoras playing dominoes on a bench.

A little girl with a rainbow of barrettes in her hair squealed in a swing pushed by her father.

A honey-colored toddler wearing only a sagging diaper ran around, chased by his young mother.

A tall, slender man in an all-black Chinese outfit practiced karate kicks on the green grass beneath one of the larger trees. He reminded me of a black Bruce Lee. . . . WAAAA-TAAAAAAA.

If I could fight like Bruce Lee, I woulda took it to them fools in red last summer.

When 40-Ounce said "Gimme yo' shorts, podna!" that's when I would've pounced into action.

With Andre surrounded by four Pirus and Trent and Lorenzo held from behind by two of them, it was up to me. I dropped from the sky, landing in front of the two holding Trent and Lorenzo.

"WAAAAAA-TAAAAAAAA!"

40 stood inches from me as I approached. He took a swig from his brown bag and snorted. "'Sup, homey? That supposed to scare me or something?"

We stood eye to eye. My knuckles cracked. This was gonna be fun.

"You . . . messed with my friends. That . . . was a mistake," I said.

Calm flowed through my body like a waterfall as I stared into his eyes.

"Man, Shawn, quit screwing around. Take these fools out!" Lorenzo shouted.

"I . . . will count to three, at which point . . . annihilation . . . of you and your crew will begin, soon followed by . . . humiliation," I said.

"Are you serious, homey? I know you ain't serious walking all up in my park with that Chinese waiter's outfit thinking I'm go be scared of you or something. Come on, now! What yo' wannabe behind need to do is bring me an order of shrimp fried rice, some garlic chicken, two egg rolls, and what else? Ay, anybody else want anything?" he shouted.

The Laugher holding Trent shouted, "Some spare ribs too!"

"With extra sauce!" Lorenzo's captor added.

40 took another swig and smiled. "You heard them. Some spare ribs too. With extra sauce." He then clutched his crotch and chugged down more brew. His already-sagging Dickies shimmied down his boxers as he laughed himself into hysterics.

"Look here, podna, you say you gonna count to three—well,

here let me do it for you and save you some trouble," he said with a smirk. "One. Two. Three."

When his teeth appeared after he said "three," I head-butted 40 and sent his brown-bagged bottle crashing to the ground. He reached in his back pocket for his club and swung. I ducked to the ground and swept his feet out from under him.

"Andre, Trent, Lorenzo . . . DUCK!" I shouted.

They did. I popped up as quickly as I went down and snapped kicks at the heads of two of the hyenas, dropping them to the ground. The third tried to get cute by ducking also, so I front-flipped over him and back-kicked him in the back. I spun on him and played rat-a-tat-tat on his back.

My boys hustled behind me as the Pirus jumped up. I didn't think. I reacted. My limbs flowed through each Piru like water. My feet cut through them like a hot knife through butter. My fists slammed into them. I leveled them all like a hurricane in a trailer park, then stopped to admire my handiwork.

Moans and groans replaced the taunting cackles of the one-time comedians ordering takeout.

"Chinese waiter, huh?" I screamed over 40's snaking body on the ground. "Spare ribs, huh? Spare this!" My right foot smashed into his ribs. "And don't forget your fortune cookie." I slammed the other side. "Andre, come here."

A big smile spread across Andre's face as he stared down at those who once stared down on him.

"Lorenzo . . . Trent . . . come here."

The four of us towered over the bloodred thugs. I approached 40 from high and stooped to his level. "Now see what you made me do! I didn't want to do that, but you MADE me do that. I didn't wanna have to whup up on you, but you brought that on yourself." I stood, then shouted, "You have just suffered annihilation, now . . . HUMILIATION! Lorenzo, Trent, Andre! Grab their pants!"

The moans and groans of the fallen increased in volume as the fellas rounded up the fresh-pressed, once-sagging pants. It's not like they'll miss them, the way they were hanging off their butts.

"Get up!"

All of them creaked to a standing position. The laughter that was once turned on us now fell on them.

"Now get out!"

They slithered out of the park in checkered boxers barely hidden by bloodred shirts, their feet guiding them in even bloodier-red sneakers. The fellas slapped me on the back, and applause filled the park.

My thumb brushed across my nose and I reentered reality. I jumped off the bench and onto my feet.

"Do you think . . . you can beat me? Come, let's see? Ha-ha-ha-ha-ha-ha-ha!" I said.

"Oh no, not kung fu theater again," Lorenzo said from his spot on the bench.

But Trent had been watching Black Bruce too and responded to my challenge. "Ha! Your skills are no match for mine. You challenge me to a match you cannot win, young kid. En garde!"

He leaped to a fighting position and faced me. His right hand thrust out in a fist, and his index finger curled to beckon me over. Just like Bruce Lee. I sniffed my nose at him. He sniffed his nose at me. I wiggled my eyebrows. He wiggled his. I bounced around on my toes. He bounced around on his toes. Then the noises started.

High-pitched "YIPs," "KIYAIs" and "WAA-TAAs" rang out as Trent and I clashed. He kicked. I ducked. I punched. He blocked. I rolled backward. He rolled backward. We kicked and punched and screamed until we were out of breath. The bench caught us as we collapsed to suck the dry Compton air.

SIX

LORENZO LOUNGED ON HIS BENCH with his eyes closed and his belly pointed to the sun. He loved to take catnaps, and we loved to mess with him whenever he did. I motioned to Trent, then pointed at Lorenzo. I pressed my finger to my lips to keep quiet. He smiled, on the same page as me. He plucked a long blade of grass from beneath the bench and touched it across Lorenzo's face. Lorenzo's hand flew up like he was shooing a fly away. Trent then brought the blade up to his left ear and plunged it in, wiggling it around. Lorenzo snorted and leaped to his feet, trying to shoo the "fly" from his ear.

"You know I hate when you guys do that," he said. His hand still brushed at his ear.

"If you didn't sleep all the time, we wouldn't do it," Trent said.

"Come on, guys. Let's run it back," Andre shouted from the court.

Since Trent and Andre lost the first game, we kept the same teams. When they won, we would switch. That was the rule. This kept it even and interesting. Me and Lorenzo made a good team. I played good D on Andre, 'Zo crashed the boards, and we passed it when the other was open. So we also won game two. They finally beat us in the third game, 11–8, so we switched teams. We don't play more than three games in a row with the same team anyway because we agreed that three games was about all we could take playing with Trent, win or lose. This became known as the "Trent rule."

We ran until we couldn't run anymore, then dragged our bodies to the shade of a tree. Andre rested the ball under his head on the grass. Trent leaned against the trunk. Lorenzo lay on his back with his hands under his head, and I sat Indian-style, plucking and tossing blades of green grass into the soft breeze.

DuBois just might have the freshest grass around: nice and thick and green. MLK just might have the worst: dry and thin and brown. It makes your butt hurt because there's nothing under it except dirt. My butt felt good on this grass. I could melt into the green.

"I'm hungry," Lorenzo announced.

"So what else is new?" Trent replied.

"Don't start with me, Trent," Lorenzo shot back. "Don't make me break out the bags on ya." He lay on his side.

"Bring it on, Buddha. What you got?"

43

'Zo bolted upright and exposed his white teeth.

"Ya mama so fat, her blood type is gravy!" he said.

"OOOOHHHH!" me and Andre shouted. Our hands flew to our mouths as always.

Lorenzo was going for broke from the giddyup. As always.

"Come on, Trent. What you got?" Andre asked.

"Hold on. Ummm. Lemme see. Ummm . . . ya mama so fat, they found a small family hiding in her armpits."

"What? I don't think so, Trent. Why do I even bother with you? You not even in my league. I'm a star on the varsity. You ride the pine on JV.

"But seriously, y'all," he continued, "I *am* hungry."

He hoisted himself up and stretched his thick arms east and west. We did the same minus the arm stretch.

"What time is it, Shawn?" Trent asked.

"About a quarter to three."

Since I'm the only one with a watch, I'm the official time-keeper. Mama gave it to me for my birthday last year 'cause she got tired of me strolling into Aunt Gertie's late and using the lack of a watch as an excuse.

"Where should we go?" Andre asked.

"Anybody got any money?" I added.

We turned our pockets out to reveal nothing but the insides.

"Ain't this a blip! We ain't even got a dollar between the four of us," Lorenzo said. He sucked his teeth and tucked his pockets back inside.

"I don't know about y'all, but I need to get something in my belly before I faint."

"Who lives the closest?" Andre asked.

We definitely ain't going to Auntie's. I'd rather starve than go there.

Trent broke into a smile and said, "I have an idea."

A couple of blocks away, he told us, was a street scattered with pomegranate trees. He walked this one block all the time and said one particular house had a bunch of trees in the backyard. We could hop the fence and pluck as many pomegranates as we wanted.

"I don't know, Trent. Pomegranates?" I said.

"Ay, it sounds like a plan. I just want to get something in my belly. Let's go," Lorenzo said.

His sneakers started strolling, but Trent held him up.

"Wrong way. Follow me."

We headed out of the park opposite the way we came in. The hum of activity was gone as we passed empty swings and tables on our way out. The tree that once shaded Black Bruce practicing his kicks now shaded untouched green grass. We carried our hunger and laughs on our path to pomegranate heaven, leaving DuBois empty and silent.

We teased, taunted, snickered, and chuckled our way to the front of a lime-green house with pink trim.

"This is it. There's a whole bunch of trees in the back," Trent said.

Our eyes stared at the house the way thieves stare at a bank.

"How do we get back there?" Andre asked.

"That fence looks pretty big," Lorenzo said as Trent walked up to it.

"I don't know, Trent. We could get into trouble if people see us trying to get back there," I said.

Luckily the fence was shaded by a tree so we couldn't be seen looking in. I swiveled my head around the block for eyes that might be watching us. I caught a few cars, but most of the driveways were empty. The last thing we needed was someone calling the cops, thinking we were trying to rob the place.

"Lorenzo, come here and hold out your hands to put me over the fence," Andre said, walking toward Trent. His eyes remained fixed on the trees behind the fence.

"I don't think so. I wanna go over there too, and if I hold you up, that means I gotta hold up everybody else," Lorenzo said. Like an angry child, his arms folded up and he stared us down.

"Come on, 'Zo, that's the only way. We'll hop over, grab as many as we can, then hop back," Andre said.

"Yeah? And how you gonna get back over, Einstein?" Lorenzo said, unfolding his arms.

He looked at Andre. So did Trent and I.

"Hold on, hold on. I have an idea," Trent said. "You see that car?"

In the driveway sat an old Chevy Vega body on four cinder blocks. Cobwebs covered the axles, and flat-gray primer hid most of the rusted brown frame. It was parked right in front of the fence and definitely wasn't going anywhere anytime soon.

"If we can get on the roof of that car . . ."

Lorenzo didn't let him finish. "Trent, you are a genius!"

He booked it over and began to climb. The car groaned beneath his weight and wobbled on the cinder blocks the moment he stepped on the hood.

"Hold up," I said. "How do we get back? There ain't a car on the other side, is there?"

Trent and Andre looked at me, then we all looked at Lorenzo.

"Relax, I see some crates over here that we can use," he said, peering his head over the fence.

"Be careful, man. The last thing we need is to have this car fall off the blocks," Andre said as Lorenzo stood tall on the roof before jumping over the fence with ease. When we heard him say it was cool, we followed, retracing each other's footsteps so the car wouldn't rock or tip.

I was the last over. Lorenzo was already stuffing his pockets with pomegranates when my feet hit the dirt. I looked around to check out the surroundings. In a far corner of the backyard, a doghouse with a large opening caught my eye. It had the same peeling lime-green paint as the house and baked in the sun.

"You guys see a dog?" I asked.

No answer. I started plucking the fruit and filling my pockets as fast as I could, swiveling my head around the whole time. If there *was* a dog, I didn't want to meet him.

Andre and Lorenzo stuffed their pockets while Trent stacked a pile of wooden crates on a trash can to hop the fence back to the other side. The sound of a rattling chain yanked me around.

"Shawn, watch out!" Lorenzo shouted.

His pomegranate-filled palm pointed at the white bow-legged pit bull racing my way. I turned to race back to the fence, blinded for a hot second by the sun sparking off the dog's silver-studded collar.

Get to the fence. Get to the fence.

Shoot! How do I get over?

The crates Trent was on! Where are they?

The barking got louder.

There they were! Up on the left. Lorenzo, a few feet in front of me, hopped over. A loud crash, a couple of thuds, and assorted cries of "OH NO!" came from the other side.

Gotta go! Gotta go! my brain shouted to every muscle in my body. I glanced back to see the dog closing the gap. I leaped onto the pile no problem. Pomegranates dropped from my pockets as I raised my hands to the fence. One of the fat fruit globes plunked him in the head, making him yelp and leap toward my feet as I hoisted them up. Then sharp fangs cut through the canvas of my left sneaker and broke the skin on my ankle.

OOOWWWWWW!

I yanked my foot free and tumbled onto the car. The dropped fruit was snatched up one by one. The black metal gate on the front door creaked open and a worn voice called out, "Somebody out there trying to steal my pomy-grannies?"

I guess we weren't the first to pluck the prized fruit.

Screams of "Come on, Shawn!" rang out.

Shoot! She's gonna hear them. I glanced down at my left foot. Spots of red colored my sock. A green handkerchief–

covered head poked out of the gate just long enough to search the front yard.

"Get 'em, Lucky! I can't keep these hoodlums from stealing my fruit, but I can keep 'em from coming back," she said.

I hid on the other side of the car and stood when the door closed.

Where is everybody? I swung around and saw three figures turning the corner at the end of the block.

They better not leave me!

I grabbed my pockets to keep the pomegranates from bouncing out and followed. Every time my left foot hit the ground, I was reminded of the memento Lucky left me with. Step-ow-step-ow-step-ow-step-ow. All the way to the end of the block. I pumped the brakes as I chugged around the corner and almost tripped over the three of them on the other side.

Huff. Puff. Huff. Puff. Huff. Puff.

"I need to sit."

I collapsed to join them on the concrete steps of a church.

"Dang, Shawn, he got you good," Lorenzo said.

He fingered the mangled piece of canvas dangling from my sneaker. The high-top part that was once tight on my ankle was now shredded in three parts just beneath a big bloodred dot on my sock.

"Does it hurt?" Trent asked.

"Actually, it feels pretty good. . . . Of course it hurts, man! Look at it!"

" 'Does it hurt?' " Andre mocked Trent.

He shook his head and checked it out for himself.

"Yup. He got you good, Shawn. You lucky you fast," Andre said.

He fished a pomegranate from his pocket and slammed it onto the concrete. The shell cracked open, and he went to work on it. Purple seeds caught the afternoon sun as his thin fingers plucked seeds out one by one. Each seed was picked, sucked, then spit out. I forgot this is what we were after in the first place.

"Ummm, these are good," Andre said.

His teeth turned purple with each suck, and the church steps became a burial ground for the spit-out seeds.

"What should I do? It's still bleeding."

The red dot grew from the size of a dime to a quarter in a few huffs and puffs, even though I put pressure on it.

Breathe.

Inhale. Exhale. Inhale. Exhale.

What were we thinking? Trying to steal pomegranates? In broad daylight? It's bad enough we almost got caught. Now I got this to deal with?

"My house ain't too far. My mom is at work, but my sister might be there. She won't care," Trent said.

"Is your sister still fine?" Lorenzo asked.

Trent was the only one of us who had a sister: Janine. Andre had a big brother, Lorenzo had a couple of big brothers, and me . . . well, it was just me. Janine just graduated from Marshall and was getting ready to go off to college someplace. Her body was in great shape because she was always playing some kind of sport. Plus, she was cute. No, fine. Real fine. And we let Trent know it whenever we saw her. That was the main reason he didn't like bringing us to his house. I had Aunt Gertie's drinking, but Trent had a hot sister. One man's heaven is another man's hell.

"I ain't even about to answer that question, 'Zo. I'm trying to help our boy, and all you can think about is pushing up on my sister? We going there to do what we gotta do and then we leaving," Trent said. His finger and voice wagged at Lorenzo like a naughty child.

"All right, all right. Calm down, brutha man. I'm just playing," Lorenzo said.

"She is fine, though, Trent," Andre added.

The words trickled out between sucks.

Trent huffed and I felt his pain. They helped me to my feet, and we treaded over to Trent's house. Slowly. I leaned on each of them at different times during the journey, and it dawned on me how much walking we do every day, going from place to place. What would otherwise be a quick trip of a couple of blocks now seemed like a trek through the Sahara in snow boots.

"What you gonna tell your auntie?" Trent asked, looking down at my foot.

I wasn't worried about Aunt Gertie. Her memory was usually clouded by the bottle. Mama, on the other hand, was a different story. She didn't miss a thing.

SEVEN

SOFT MUSIC FROM A STEREO drifted in from the back of the house as we stepped into Trent's living room.

Janine must be home.

I still remember the first time I met her. It was only two summers ago when she showed up at MLK to drop something off for Trent. It was hot, as usual, so she had on—man, I still remember it—these tiny little hot-pink shorts with a little cheek showing. I don't remember the shirt 'cause I don't think I ever looked up past her waist. Anyway, she gave Trent whatever it was she came for, and as she walked away, all Andre, Lorenzo, and I could say was "DAMNNNNN!"

We haven't seen her since. Trent made sure of that.

"All right, let's do what we gotta do and get up out of here," Trent said.

Boxes were stacked everywhere, spilling a rainbow of clothes across the floor. Janine must be packing. I wondered where she was going. The pain in my ankle plopped me onto the couch.

"Where'd you say your sister was going to college?" Andre asked, speaking my thoughts.

"UCLA. I told you that," he said. "She's starting to pack now 'cause the girl got a ton of clothes and she wants to start weeding stuff out."

Trent hustled around the house gathering stuff to fix my ankle and shoe. Each time he crossed through the living room, something new was in his hands: scissors, tape, Band-Aids, alcohol, washcloth, a pot of water. When his hands were full, he brought everything into the living room and set it on the floor beside me on the couch.

Andre checked out the assorted pictures of Trent's family scattered around the living room while Lorenzo drifted to the back to uncover the source of the music.

"Lorenzo, what I tell you? Get in here so we can hurry up and get out," Trent said.

It was too late. As Lorenzo sulked his way over to the couch, a door from a back room opened and the music got louder. A sight emerged that put us all on pause.

Trent's sister floated in carrying a tall, clouded blue glass. My pain floated away as I caught a glimpse of her beauty. Bright red toenail polish dotted honey-colored feet moving with ease across the brown shag carpet. Tight calves morphed into powerful thighs barely covered by neon-yellow short-shorts that squeezed hallelujahs from the bottom of my soul.

Her belly button blinked at me from the middle of her narrow waist. I tried to turn away, but like a car crash, it screamed for my attention.

The painted-on matching yellow tank top clung with all its might to her chest, pointing directly at the three of us on the couch. My eyes played peekaboo with the golden cross resting in the hammock of space beneath her face. Jet-black hair blew in the breeze of her movement. Her roll slowed as she noticed us.

"Hi, guys!" she said.

Manicured fingers tickled a beauty-queen wave at us and tickled me in my manhood. Or boyhood. Or teenhood. Or whatever you want to call it. Nonetheless, the pain disappeared from my ankle and reappeared in my shorts. Glad I wasn't standing because I would have to sit for sure.

"Hi, Janine," we released in unison.

Our eyes latched on to her as she made her way into the kitchen.

"Trent, man, you got some water?" Lorenzo asked.

He hopped off the couch and headed toward the kitchen.

"Sit down, Lo-me-o! I'll get it," Trent said.

He stood up and gave us the evil eye, then whispered that we needed to hurry up and go. We followed him with our eyes into the kitchen and listened to him and his sister.

"Janine, what you doing walking around like that?"

"I know my little brother's not trying to tell *me* what I can wear!"

"I'm just saying. We trying to do something, and you're a little . . . distracting."

"And just what is it you guys are doing?"

"None of your business. Could you just hurry up and go!"

"Did you just tell me to 'hurry up and go'? Is that what I heard, baby brother?"

"Look, I just . . . I hate my friends staring at my sister like that."

"Like what?"

"You know. Like . . . that."

"They don't have to stare. I'm just packing up my stuff. I'm not hurting anybody."

Lorenzo responded with a whispered reply directed at our ears: "Oh, yes, you are," he said.

We broke into laughter on the couch. Trent made his way out as we held on to our sides to keep from busting a gut.

"What's so funny?" he asked.

"Nothing, man, just some bags, you know," Lorenzo replied. His laughter disappeared with a few snickers bubbling beneath the surface.

"Here, knock yourselves out," Trent said without a smile, emphasizing "knock" while staring at Lorenzo.

Three different-colored glasses with bright red fluid inside were placed in front of us. Kool-Aid? Janine came out of the kitchen carrying the same.

"So, ahhh, Janine, I heard you was going off to college," Lorenzo said.

The boy was not to be denied. With two older brothers to look up to, he thought he knew a few things about talking to girls. Usually they just laughed in his face, proving he *thought* wrong.

"Well, you heard right."

She stood in the shape of a capital S. Her left hand rested on her out-thrust hip as her right foot shot out to the side.

My brain flashed Technicolor messages in bold letters to my lungs that read: BREATHE! In. Out. In. Out.

The Kool-Aid kissed her black-cherry lips. My heart couldn't take it.

"So where you going?" Andre said. He tried to hide his smile.

"I already *told* you: UCLA," Trent said.

He was annoyed. No, he was mad. So I kept my mouth shut. I was afraid of what would come out if I opened it. Andre and Lorenzo didn't care. They kept talking like he wasn't even there.

"I want to hear it from her," Andre said, his eyes never leaving Janine. The smile was front and center this time.

She was enjoying this. Why else would a future college freshman be making small talk with three scrawny — OK, two scrawny and one large — future high-school freshmen? Maybe she was bored.

"Yes. I am going to UCLA. On a track scholarship, thank you very much. Maybe you guys can come to a meet sometime," she said.

The S stretched its shape as she took another sip.

"I would love to meet with you, Janine. I can tie your shoes for you or something," Lorenzo said.

Trent sucked his teeth in disgust. "Tie her shoes? Man, please."

A network of veins formed a tree on his forehead.

Janine laughed.

"No, that's what a track competition is called — a meet."

Her outfit glowed a brighter shade of yellow from her laugh.

"Good-bye, Janine!" Trent said. He stood and faced her square on.

Her hands raised up as if to say "All right, you win" and she left the room. Our eyes followed her like a cop.

The whole room exhaled, and it was silent for a moment. My heart pulsed right out of my chest.

"So, Trent, the answer to my question is yes . . . a big fat yes!" Lorenzo announced.

"What question?"

"You know . . . is your sister still fine? Although I must say . . . she put fine in the rearview mirror a *long* time ago and is closing in on super-duper-fwoine, with a *couple* of *w*'s in the middle," Lorenzo said.

We tried to keep quiet, but Lorenzo spoke the gospel. Laughter from the pits of our belly replaced the silence as we howled in agreement. Assorted *amens* followed in whispers, and again we were silent. But not for long. Trent's anger sliced through the silence as he leaped to his feet and hurled himself at Lorenzo. He stepped on my ankle as I stood to hold him back, but his mouth still unleashed its assault: "You don't talk about my sister like that. She ain't a piece of meat! You hear me, fat boy?"

Fat boy? Whoa. These two. They always going at it. Maybe we should get all this stuff out now while the gettin' is good. But dang, Trent, did you have to step on my foot?

57

"Trent, calm down. You know we just playing," Andre said. He was now on his feet helping me hold Trent back.

"Naw, Andre. I'm tired of this. I'm tired of you guys 'just playing.' You come up in *my* house, drink *my* Kool-Aid, and talk about *my* sister like that and expect me to be cool with that? Naw, I don't think so."

The muscles in his neck clenched tight, and his eyes bulged out when the words shot from his mouth. His whole body was taut as a rubber band stretched to its limit.

We loosened our grip as his muscles relaxed. He unleashed a long sigh, then dropped onto a chair muttering, "Naw, naw, naw."

The silence returned. His words flashbulbed through my mind in quick bursts.

SISTER.

PIECE OF MEAT.

FAT BOY.

I'M TIRED OF YOU GUYS.

There it was. The truth. In black and white. Spoken as plain as it could be spoken. A familiar frustration echoed from his lips to my ears: *I'm tired of you guys.* Familiar because I've said it many times as I pulled on a blue shirt that I wanted to wear only to pull it off, worrying about being attacked by Pirus who might think I'm a Crip. Familiar because I've said it many times as I told Mama "no" to anything red, worried that the Crips might think I'm a Piru. Familiar because I've said it as my face was shoved into the dirt with a red heel pressed between my shoulder blades.

Yeah, Trent, I'm tired too.

Music drifted in from the back room, breaking the tense silence.

Lorenzo looked down at his sneakers, exhaled, then stood up to smooth out his tracksuit. He eyeballed me and Andre, then reached deep into his pockets. He cleared his throat and leaned over Trent. A fat pomegranate lay in his outstretched paw.

"Umm, Trent, here . . . take this. The whole pomegranate thing was your idea, so . . . take it. I got a bunch more," he said.

Trent eyed the fruit like it might be poison, then looked at me and down at my sock turning redder by the second. It seemed to bring back memories of why we were even here in the first place.

The frost on Trent's face melted as he took it. "Yeah, it was a good plan, huh?"

"I'm glad y'all kissed and made up, but can we take care of this, please!" I said, collapsing back onto the couch, pointing at my torn sneaker and bloody ankle.

How was I gonna explain this to Mama? Keep the shoe and make something up? Or borrow some other shoes and make something up? Either way, I gotta make something up, because I can't tell her what really happened; I can't tell her we hopped a fence to steal pomegranates.

I flexed my ankle, and the pain brought Lucky's fangs back into my brain. Mama is gonna kill me. I can hear her line of questioning already:

"Now, your ankle is red *why?*

"What'd you do today to make that happen?"

Lord only knows what else she'll come up with.

"Trent, what you doing, man? All we need is a washcloth to clean it and a small bandage. Just because it's a lot of blood doesn't mean it's a big hole," Andre said.

He plopped down next to where my ankle rested and took a peek. With one hand he tugged the sticky red-soaked sock down to expose the flesh. A gash about the size of a small paper clip revealed itself in all its ruby-red glory.

"See . . . that's not too big."

"I'm glad you think it's small, but that don't change the fact it still hurts!"

My patience did a Houdini, so I took care of it myself.

I pulled my foot close and went to work. Dad always said if you want something done right, do it yourself.

I peeled the sock off and cleaned the naked ankle with alcohol. I winced in pain. Andre and Lorenzo did too when they saw my ankle jump. Once the wound was cleaned, it was even smaller than it had looked in the first place.

I held up a bandage about the size of my pinkie to Trent's face.

"You don't have nothing bigger than this?"

He shook his head. "That's the biggest we got."

I shook my head, then stuck two of them down to hide the hole. It still hurt, but at least I wasn't leaking a bloody trail anymore. I stood.

"Good as new. You got any white socks I could borrow?"

Trent nodded and headed for his room.

"And get him some more shorts too," Lorenzo added.

He looked at me. And my shorts.

"The day ain't over yet, Shawn, and you *are* still wearing blue shorts."

In the meantime I trimmed the ripped canvas with scissors. So much of it was gone that it now looked more like a low-top.

Janine's door opened again, and we heard a couple of sentences exchanged between her and Trent before he returned. Whatever they were saying came out a lot calmer than last time.

"Here you go, Shawnie-Shawn."

He tossed me the socks and some jet-black shorts, and we were back on the pavement in no time.

Lucky's little gift was still with me as I walked, but this time the pain was dulled when I reached into my pocket and pulled out the prize he had been guarding.

"Let's find some place to go crack these open."

EIGHT

WE TREKKED BACK TO DUBOIS and took over a bench. The park buzzed with activity. A handful of girls scattered here, a handful of boys scattered there. Bunches of both nearby. The old men wearing fedoras and playing dominoes last time had been replaced by old men wearing ball caps and playing cards this time. They slapped the table with gusto between shouts of "I'll take that" and "Oh no, you don't!"

The tree that once shaded Black Bruce now shaded a quartet of pigtailed girls about eight or nine years old practicing hand claps and dance steps. Their slapping hands and stomping feet replaced the quiet calm that Black Bruce had created earlier.

We fished the fruit from our pockets, slammed the hard-shell globes open, and began the ritual of eating fresh pomegranate seeds; pluck, suck, spit, repeat. Our tongues became bright purple as each seed released its juice into our mouths.

Man, the pomegranates were good. I can see why that old lady had a dog; a big tree like that might as well be a grocery store for some folks. Pomegranates may not fill you up, but they'll keep your belly happy for a hot minute.

I checked my watch. It was 4:23. I needed to head to Auntie's soon so Mama could pick me up. I didn't want to be late. Again. Especially with somebody else's shorts on and a torn sneaker. She doesn't always remember what I wear, so I might not have to explain the shorts. The torn sneaker would need a story for sure.

Over the years I've gotten pretty good at making up stories when something like this happens. I don't see it as telling a lie; I see it as protecting my behind. And she just got me these sneakers a couple of weeks ago! I begged and pleaded for the longest time for some white All Stars, and when she handed them to me at the register, she said I better take good care of them. And I did. Until today. Was it my fault a pit bull took a bite out of one of them? OK, maybe it was. At least he didn't get my whole foot. Or better yet, both feet.

"I think I wanna go to UCLA," Lorenzo said. Pluck.

"Aww, not again Lorenzo," Andre said. Suck.

"No, no, no, I'm just sayin' . . . as fine . . . I mean as, ahhh . . . attractive as Janine is . . . imagine how many other girls like her go there," Lorenzo said. Spit.

Janine, Janine, Janine. My favorite color might have to change to yellow. I don't think I've seen yellow glow on anybody else the way it did on her, although Marisol was in yellow today and she was looking pretty fine too.

What is it with girls and yellow?

"Yeah . . . well, you guys only know what you see. I have to live with her and, trust me, she can get on your nerves," Trent said. Pluck. Suck. Before he could spit the seed from his mouth, he added: "Lorenzo, don't start." Spit.

"Anyway," Andre interrupted, "to go to UCLA, you need to have good grades or be good at a sport, and you got neither grades or a game, 'Zo." Pluck.

"Oooh, that's cold, Andre," I said. Spit.

"Cold, but true," Trent said. Suck.

"All right, so I'm not a genius." Lorenzo got defensive, then added, "I'm not a dummy either."

Pluck. Suck. Spit.

He continued his train of thought. "I'm just saying . . . if I could go to a school filled with girls like that, I would be hitting the books harder than this pomegranate here."

Slam. He cracked open his second pomegranate. "Besides, I can too play sports. I'm good at ballin', and when we get to Marshall, I'm going out for the team."

Pluck.

"I might go out for a few other things too."

"Like what . . . a pizza?" Trent said. That got a belly laugh from me and Andre.

He was enjoying this now. He knew 'Zo wasn't going to start on his sister again because nobody wanted any drama, so he took advantage of the situation.

Lorenzo spit out a few more seeds and said, "Ha, ha, funny man. I'm just saying. You know how I'm usually late to school because I oversleep, right? Well, I would have no problem dragging myself out of bed to a school filled with beautiful girls."

"First of all, how you know the school would be 'filled' with beautiful girls? I mean we had some pretty fine girls at our school, but we also had plenty of bag heads," Andre said.

Slam. He cracked open his second one.

"Did you say 'bag heads'?" I asked. Spit.

"Yeah. You know, the girl is so ugly you gotta put a bag over her head if you want to kiss her," Andre said. The words came out of his mouth as easy as if he were saying, "Two plus two equals four. It's a fact."

Slam. I cracked open my second.

"Anyway. Our boy 'Zo here seems lost. Maybe we should pick a sport for him," I said. Spit.

"That's a good idea, Shawn," Andre said, and he stood up. A downpour of empty seeds rained on his sneakers. "Why don't you join the football team, 'Zo?"

"Too painful." Pluck.

"How about baseball?" I said. Suck.

"Too hot." Suck.

"Too hot?" I said. Spit.

"Yeah. They play outside when it's hot." Spit.

"How about wrestling?" Trent said. Spit.

"Too faggoty." Pluck.

"Too what?" I said. Pluck.

"Too faggoty. I'm not lettin' another dude grab me and stuff." Spit.

"How about swimming?" Andre said. Pluck.

"Nahh, he'd sink," Trent said loudly.

That caught us off-guard.

"Ha, ha," Lorenzo sneered, before punching his paw into his third pomegranate.

He had dished it out to us so many times, he should've known payback was coming sooner or later. Andre slapped at the bench while I grabbed hold of him to keep from falling off laughing. "Are you guys done?"

We weren't. He sat alone on the bench as we doubled up in pain around him like cackling hyenas on the hunt. Man, my sides hurt.

Lorenzo spit out a few more seeds before speaking again: "Can we have a real conversation now?"

"I'm just saying . . . if something was going to make me enjoy school more, a bunch of fine girls would be it," Lorenzo said. Suck.

"You sure a Fatburger wouldn't do the same thing?" Trent said. Pluck.

We laughed but noticed how Lorenzo was eyeballing Trent. It was time to back off. He was cool with the swim thing and let it go. But after that, he might break out the bags. And judging how hard he came at Trent last time, it wouldn't be pretty. So me and Andre kept our mouths shut. Trent kept laughing but noticed we were silent and took the hint.

"You can always hit the books," I said.

That squeezed chuckles from Trent and Andre and a "Yeah, right" from 'Zo.

I was probably one of the few people that knew Lorenzo was good with numbers. Actually, he was great with numbers.

Last year in math class he had the oddest way of solving the toughest problems. The teacher always gave him a hard time though because he couldn't explain how he got his answers. Shoot . . . I say if he got it right, who cares how he did it? At least he did it. I knew he didn't cheat because he tried to explain it to me, but when he saw I had no clue of what he was talking about, he stopped and said: "All I know, Shawn, is it works for me."

"Are you serious, Shawn?" Lorenzo said. "You know how smart you have to be to get into college?" he continued.

"Actually, I *do* know how smart you have to be to get into college because my mama works at one, remember?" I told him.

"Shawn, your mama works in the cafeteria," Andre said.

Yes, my mother works in the cafeteria. But it was still in a college, and she did it so she could go there part-time. Whenever she saw any of the black teachers in the lunch line, she asked them about books for me, and I must say, they've turned me on to some cool stuff, books I might not have found on my own. For instance, one day Mama comes home with this book called *Invisible Man*. Not *The Invisible Man*, just *Invisible Man*. It's a novel written by a brutha named Ralph Ellison about a black man during segregation. The story shows how he goes through life treated like an invisible man because white people only see the color of his skin and not him as a human being. In the beginning it was hard to read, but once I got into it, it was pretty funny. Some parts had me rolling as hard as my boys do.

My English teacher surprised me with her reaction when I

told her how much I enjoyed it. She said since it wasn't on the list of books to read, I wouldn't get credit for it. What's that about? I didn't care about the credit, because English is my best subject and I didn't need it. What I did care about were the books we had to choose from. Most of them were written by dead white guys, and the rest were by dead white women. No Ralph Ellison or any other black writers. That killed me. How you gonna teach a class of blacks and Mexicans in Compton and not have one black or Mexican writer on the list? It's not like they don't exist. Then she tried to bring up *To Kill a Mockingbird.* "That's a book that shows white people helping black people," she said.

I wanted to tell her what she could do with Scout and her *To Kill a Mockingbird,* but instead I asked her, "Why can't we ever read about black people helping themselves?" She had no answer. And she wonders why the kids in our class groan whenever she assigns us a book.

So, ever since then I read whatever Mama throws my way. The guys know she's going to school, but that doesn't keep them from busting on me once in a while about her working in a cafeteria.

"Yeah well, she's still going to college," I said, brushing off the sarcasm. "She said a lot of her classmates did all kinds of stuff in high school that helped them get into college. Some played sports; some were class president; some played a musical instrument . . . you know, stuff like that," I said.

"He already plays a musical instrument, Shawn," Trent said. "The skin flute!"

He doubled over in laughter and took us with him. I guess he couldn't resist.

"That's it! Now see what you did? You asked for it, Trent, that's what you did. You had to make me bring out the bags, didn't you? Well, I got something for you."

Lorenzo stood and made his way to the trash can to deposit his mangled pomegranate shells.

"Ya mama so fat, she burped and took out a couple of trees!"

"OOOOOOOHHHHHH!" me and Andre shouted to let Trent know Lorenzo hit his target with a bull's-eye. Like he always does.

"But you know what, Trent? You lucky. I'm a let you off with just one because these pomegranate seeds made my tongue hurt."

My watch ticked closer to the witching hour, so I dusted my seeds away and stood.

"Speaking of Mama, I gotta get to steppin'."

We exchanged handshakes before I took off. As I got up from the bench, Trent called out: "Shawn . . . what you gonna tell your mama about your ankle and sneakers?"

I shrugged and threw my hands up. "I don't know. I'll think of something."

The park voices faded as I left DuBois and the guys behind. My sneakers, one of them half the sneaker it was a few hours ago, steered me back to Aunt Gertie's.

Yeah, I'll think of something, but what?

NINE

SNAPSHOTS from the day flipped by in my head to the rhythm of booming bass bumping out of a rainbow of cars parading down the streets.

Lorenzo bagging. Marisol in sunshine-yellow pedal push-ers. Marisol laughing. Sigh. The fellas' mouths pressed against the window. A pink fur coat dusted with broken green beer glass. The "pink slip." Black Bruce Lee. Blades of green grass. Blue lint balls in empty pockets. A lime-green house. Faded lime-green doghouse. Silver dog chain. Yellow fangs. Bloodred sock. Torn white sneaker. Pink pomegranate seeds. Trent rush-ing Lorenzo. Lorenzo swimming. Laughter. Laughter. And still more laughter.

A smile slid across my face as I looked to the sky. Janine's image snapped into my brain, so I painted her picture on a clear patch of blue. My imagined paintbrush sketched a close-up of the gold cross glowing against the crack of her honey-colored chest. I scratched that image and slid down to her legs, stroking the wide curves of her hips with brushes of bright yellow. Sigh.

"Heyyy, watch it, brutha man!" a steely-eyed, charcoal-colored man well past my age snapped at me. A stringy black goatee framed his words.

I couldn't believe what I was seeing: mint-green colored him head to toe. From the snapped brim of his mint-green fedora tilted across his oil-slicked black hair to the bright green gem in his left ear, from the mint-green toothpick in his mouth to the tight mint-green collar squeezing his razor-bumped neck, from the wrinkles in his baggy mint-green suit draped over his rail-thin frame to his mirror-polished shoes, he was a minty-fresh sight.

A lightning-bolt-shaped scar struck from the gem in his ear down to the left side of his goatee and crackled as he spoke: "Get yo' head out the clouds, brutha man, and pay attention to where you going."

I served up a "sorry." The toothpick plucked a reply from his gold-toothed mouth: "You lucky Larry Luck in a good mood today."

Larry Luck? OK. My eyes followed his peacock strut down the block. Past the barbecue shack. Past the check-cashing place. Past the liquor store. Past the beauty salon to the end of the block, where his green heels stopped. Hot pink heels met him at the light. A dingy pink fur coat rested on top of the pink heels.

Wait . . . is that . . . ? Nah . . . it couldn't be. Shoot . . . it is.

71

The coat belonged to none other than the behind-the-liquor-store squatter we saw earlier. I didn't need to see her again. Or want to. Especially in that nasty coat. It reminded me of all the nasty stuff that was on it: Fatburger wrappers and broken pieces of glass.

I continued on my way. My ankle tingled when I stepped off the curb.

What am I gonna tell Mama? I'll be at Auntie's soon.

I gotta think of a story. Fast.

Let's see . . . I hopped a fence to get our ball and my shoe got caught.

Nah. Which fence was I hopping? And why was I hopping it? That won't work.

Think, Shawn. Think.

Maybe she won't notice the shoe. I mean, it's on my *foot*. It's not like it's my shirt or something real obvious.

Doesn't matter. I gotta come up with something. She'll notice it. She always does.

How about . . . I let Lorenzo borrow my shoes 'cause he didn't have any b-ball shoes and he busted them?

That's funny, but that won't work either. What shoes would I play in?

Shoot. One more block after the liquor store on the corner.

Think. What did we do today? Hang out. Shoot the breeze. Play ball. Or as Passion would say, "A whole lotta nothing!"

Just like every other day.

All right. Where do we spend most of our time? Walking. On the streets. Anything can happen on the streets.

Wait . . . instead of it being an accident, maybe I did it on purpose.

Mama's always getting on my case because I want the latest styles and stuff, so what if this was a new style for sneakers? What if I cut them down like this on my own to be in style?

Yeah. That's good. That could work.

What about the shorts? She probably doesn't even remember what color shorts I had on this morning anyway. Doesn't matter, I still need an excuse just in case.

Let me see. Ummm . . . we were at the Tamale Hut and Lorenzo spilled a soda on my shorts so Trent let me borrow a pair of his that I changed into at his house. His mom is gonna wash them, and he'll get them back to me later.

Sounds good to me. Yeah . . . while I was at Trent's, the fellas busted on me about my Stars not being "in style," so I trimmed them while I was there.

I ran through the story a bunch more times and couldn't find any holes. Looking at it now, you would never know the sneaker was ripped apart by an angry pit bull. Thank goodness. If she found out we were stealing pomegranates . . .

She already gets on my case about hanging out with the fellas, because she thinks they're in some kind of gang. She's only met Lorenzo, and that was a few years ago. It didn't help that he was wearing his big brother's jacket that day with *D-Bone* printed on the back in Old English lettering; like some of the gangbangers wear. Or that the jacket was blue, the color of the Crips.

Back then we didn't know what gangs did, but we knew

they existed. Lorenzo's older brother Dayshaun was friends with a few 'bangers, so we thought it was a cool thing to do. That's why he "borrowed" his brother's jacket that day. It wasn't until a couple of years later that we learned what being in a gang meant.

We had been on our way home from school one day, walking past the back entrance of Carver Park, when we saw five guys in creased blue jeans and assorted blue shirts. Their black faces were hidden by blue bandannas, like outlaws in the old West. Crips. Cut-down golf clubs and garden hose cut into short pipes were their weapons of choice as they took turns inflicting pain on a red-clad body sprawled on the ground. Each swing got a different response: a whack on muscle with the hose pulled out an "unnnh" like a hard punch to the gut, and a swing of the club on bone yanked out a horror-movie scream. That's probably what it felt like for the guy on the ground: a horror movie.

The screams had gotten louder as we got closer. A pair of eyes peeking over one of the blue bandannas caught me and Lorenzo staring and snapped a picture with narrowed eyes. We turned away as he raised his club and were gone before it came down.

By the time we had huffed and puffed our way to the Tamale Hut a couple of blocks away, I knew red and blue didn't mix. So did Lorenzo. Now we knew the difference between the two. They were different, but the same: two colors to be avoided whenever possible.

Aunt Gertie's street was now under my feet as I walked past all the familiar houses on the block. For the most part, it was a quiet and clean street: nice lawns with trimmed green grass, nice cars here and there in each driveway, lots of trees, lots of old folks, and lots of porches.

Miss Johnston, her neighbor a couple of houses down, could always be found on her porch in her chair enjoying the fresh air. Most days she'd be waving "hello" to anyone who drove or walked by. For me, she always had a "Whatchu say there, Mr. Shawn?"

Then there was Mr. and Mrs. Wright, who lived next door to Auntie. They were older and only spoke to me once in a blue moon. Most of the time they just eyeballed me like I'd stolen something or was about to.

On the other side was Miss Bricknell, Aunt Gertie's sworn enemy. I hated seeing her. She was always telling me something like: "That auntie of yours needs to turn down her TV. I can't hear my stories."

It looked like she was sucking on a lemon when she spoke.

By late afternoon, when Aunt Gertie's bottle had taken full effect, she could usually be found in front of the TV cursing Miss Bricknell. "What that old hag really needs is a man in her sorry life. Thas what she needs. Uh-huh. Thas right. She need somebody to warm up that big ole, cold empty bed of hers. Uh-huh. Thas what she needs. She need a man to take the chill off them cold bones of hers. Uh-huh. Shooooot . . . talking to me about . . . my stories and all that other foolish-nesh. It's jus foolishnesh is what it is. Uh-huh." The end of her sentence was punctuated with a wave of her glass and a taste of the contents inside.

Miss Johnston was out front as usual. A white housedress with orange flowers covered her body, and white house shoes covered her feet. Her reading glasses hung on a chain around her neck as she did a crossword puzzle. She was way up there in years, but that didn't keep her from sitting outside every day. She always seemed to have a smile on her face, and a day never went by that she didn't have a visitor.

"Whatchu say there, Mr. Shawn?" came the familiar call. "My, my, my, you are getting big, huh, chile?"

"How you doing, Miss Johnston?"

"Oh, you know, just enjoying the light of the Lord on another glorious day" came her familiar answer. "You tell that auntie of yours I said hey and that the Lord is watching over her, ya hear?"

Said with a smile on her face and love in her heart. As always. Maybe that's why she had so many visitors.

"All right, Miss Johnston. I will."

Miss Bricknell, on the other hand, was the flip side of that coin; she never had any visitors. Aw man . . . is that her? Yup, the sourpuss herself. I caught a glimpse of her in her garden and tried to hurry inside.

The hat on her head spun around as I stepped through the gate. "Shawn? Shawn! I know you see me, boy. I don't know what your auntie is doing in there, but she got all kind of racket coming from inside—the TV, music, and Lord knows what else. I can't even hear myself think. My rosebushes need my full attention, and that auntie of yours ain't helping. You tell her I said . . ."

I didn't wait for the end. I ran up the steps and into the house to run through my story again. I still had time before Mama came to pick me up, which meant I had time to eat something. Those pomegranates were good, but I needed real food.

The "racket" Miss Bricknell mentioned hit me as I stepped through the door. Two talking heads on TV argued while the radio blasted a mix of music and static. It *was* hard to think. My stomach did the thinking for me. Food. I need food.

Where's Auntie?

"Auntie, I'm home!" I shouted.

I searched the house. She wasn't on her regular spot on the couch in the living room, so I checked the kitchen. My nostrils twitched as I recognized the smell. My aching feet stepped from the stained brown carpet to the faded white kitchen floor where, stretched across the dirty tiles, lay Auntie, her bottle on the counter towering over her.

Not again.

I shouted down to her, "Auntie, you OK?"

Her limp body stirred. She lifted her head to look up at me, then swung her head around to find my voice. Her body shifted from an S shape on the floor to a sitting position. Her eyes blinked their way open, and her mouth moved to make sound. Nothing came out.

A couple of breaths later she said, "I told you I didn't wanna hear nunna yo' excuses. I saw you with that . . . that . . ." Her arms started swinging in the air, and she almost hit me in the face.

The second half of her sentence trickled out: ". . . that fat heifer. You get away from me, Avery. Just go. Go to yo' heifer and have her take care of you."

I bent over to pick her up but was waved off with a slap of the hand and a loud "Don't touch me!"

The last words came out in a cloud of alcohol fumes. The bottle on the counter was bone dry, so whatever haze she was in must have been thick.

"Aunt Gertie, it's me . . . Shawn. Come on, now. You gotta get up."

Her thin neck teetered her swirled hair atop her swaying frame. She exhaled another cloud of fumes as she grabbed my right hand to stand up. Her neck bobbled on my shoulder on her way up. We rocked out of the kitchen and into the living room, where I let her plop onto her spot on the couch. Her right hand shifted to support her still-swaying head. A drawn-out sigh exited her mouth, followed by a stream of lip smacks.

"I'm OK. I'm OK," she said, her eyes blinking awake. "Shawnie, get me something to drink, please."

I filled a plastic cup with ice and water and brought it to her.

"What is this? I don't want this. I said something to *drink*."

My neck hairs felt singed from her hot breath as I made my way back into the kitchen. *Something to drink?* There's no more of that stuff, and I wouldn't pour it for her even if there was. I went back into the living room and found the cup and its contents on the floor. I guess her body lost the battle with gravity, because her head was on one side of the couch while her legs hung over the edge of the other.

"Shawn, can you get me some pillows, please," she whispered.

I propped a couple of pillows under her head to make her comfortable, and her eyelids flickered, so I went back to the kitchen.

I scavenged through the cabinets for food. My eyes lit up when an unopened box of powdered sugar donuts appeared before them. I plucked one out and plunged my teeth inside. I made my way to the window and saw the little black sedan I was always happy to see—Mama's car—coming down the street.

I dusted my mouth, licked my fingers, and wiped my hands on my shirt. Then I went outside.

"Hey, baby," Mama said, stepping from the car.

I gave her a peck on the cheek.

"You bring me anything?" I huffed.

"Good to see you too, Shawn. Is that all you think about, boy: food?"

"Naw, I mean, no, Mama, I'm just hungry. That sweet roll you brought me yesterday was so good, I was hoping you'd bring me another one."

"Sorry, baby. Not today."

She stepped away from the car and made her way inside.

"Why's it so loud in there?"

I was so focused on Auntie and getting something to eat, I forgot about the racket.

"Oh, that was Auntie. I'll go turn it off."

I ran back inside, slamming the door, which made Auntie jerk in her sleep. The radio static and talking heads disappeared as I made my way through each room in the house.

When I came back, Mama was shaking Gertie's shoulder. She didn't look too thrilled to find her son being watched by the person who lay passed out in front of her.

"GERTIE! GERTIE! Come on, now." Her voice carried the weight of anger, but it disappeared as she rotated Auntie's worn face into view. She pushed the hair out of her face and smoothed the wrinkles from her dress. Mama lowered her head and said in a calm voice, "Shawn, could you get me a cold towel, please."

"Come on, Gertie. Get up, ol' girl. It's me, Sis . . . Brenda. Come on, now. Time to get up."

When I came back, Mama held Auntie's head in her arms. Gentle kisses brought her back to life. Gertie's eyes blinked. She gathered herself before acknowledging my mother, her little sister. "Hey, Sis. How you doin', girl?"

"I should be asking you that question . . . how *you* doin'?"

"Oh, you know. Same ol', same ol.' Caught up on my stories . . . did a couple of crossword puzzles . . . watched the news . . ." Her words trailed off as she nodded toward the now-silent TV. "You know . . . some poor chile over on Greenleaf today . . . fell out of a window . . . again . . . eighth floor . . . I think. Only two years old too. Ummm-mmmm-mmm. Is a shame, Brenda . . . a real shame, girl." She shook her head as the words stumbled out.

Her hands twitched in her lap as she smoothed her housedress.

Mama looked at me, then back at Auntie. "You do anything else today, Sis? Go outside for a walk, stop at the store, or anything like that?"

"Who you talking to, girl? Of course I didn't go nowhere today. Hot as it is out there? Shooooot! And you know it's hard for me to miss my stories. Especially *All My Children*, with that Erica Kane, ummm-mmmm-mmmm. She is something else. Lemme tell you . . . today . . ."

Mama cut her off: "Looks like you had yourself a little party."

"Aw, Sis, come on, now. You know me better than that. I just had a little tase . . . thas all."

Auntie shrunk down into her chair as if trying to hide from Mama. I been there before.

"Looks like you had more than a taste."

Her eyes flashed to mine. All I could do was shrug from the easy chair. My sneakers stuck out and rocked a rhythm.

"Wellll . . . you know how it is, Sis . . ."

Her eyes drifted around the room.

"Lissen, Sis, I need a favor. . . ."

Mama cut her off again: "How long did that one last you?"

"Come on, Sis, it takes me a while to get through one. Thas why I only get pints. I don't even remember when I got tha las' one."

"Now, Sis, you know I'm not getting you a pint. The last one wasn't even a pint. It was a bottle," Mama said, in the same voice she uses to punish me.

Auntie sucked her teeth and melted deeper into the couch.

"Besides, you know the store is closed," Mama added, using a line I'd heard before.

Auntie's head bobbed with a quiet, "OK, Sis. I unnerstand. I unnerstand."

With each head bob, her eyes flickered and her head inched lower. She jerked up just before it reached her lap. "I made some oxtails and rice if you want to take some home," she remembered. Her hands clutched the couch as she tried to stand. "Lemme scoop you up a plate."

Aunt Gertie and Mama grew up in Louisiana but moved here when Mama was about six. They moved to Compton when Grandpa died so Grandma could find work. Grandma held down a couple jobs, so Auntie did most of the cooking and taught Mama when she was old enough. Mama's loved cooking ever since. That must be why she got a job cooking for a living. The bad part is that she cooks in a college cafeteria and doesn't always get to make certain things the way she wants. Her boss likes what she makes, but down in Louisiana they like their food spicy, and she can't always do that at school. Every once in a while she manages to get in some gumbo or dirty rice or something like that, though.

"Sit, Sis. Me and Shawn will do it."

Auntie sat. Mama stood.

"You wanna watch some TV?"

"Naw . . . I'm tired, girl. . . . I'm a take me a catnap. You help yourself."

Mama stood and kicked my left sneaker, telling me to get up. The dog bite crept back into my ankle as I winced my way into the kitchen.

"So tell me what happened."

"What do you mean, what happened?" I said.

Had she already noticed the sneaker?

"With Sis? Tell me what happened with her today."

I couldn't stand the pain, so I sat.

"How should I know? I wasn't here."

She slid two Tupperware containers from a drawer and zoomed her eyes in on me. Her free hand found her hip. That's not good.

"And where were you today?"

I leaned back.

"Come on, Mama. I hang out with my friends during the day."

She found a large spoon to scoop up some oxtails. Huge chunks of the tender meat dropped into one of the containers. Mmmmm — I was getting hungry just looking at it.

"Doing what?"

I stretched my legs.

"Stuff. Hanging out . . . playing ball. You know . . . stuff."

"Yeah, I know: nothin' — that's what you boys are doing. Listen, I know you are getting older and getting ready to go into high school, Shawn, but it would be nice if you could spend more time with your auntie."

I jumped up.

"But I don't wanna watch soap operas all day and watch her get all . . ." My words trailed off as I sat back down.

"Come on, Shawn, it ain't that bad," she said, avoiding my eyes and splashing gravy on the stove. But her words were about as believable as the shoe story she would soon hear.

The smell of hot food was getting to me, making my mouth water. I slinked over to the stove and pinched some rice from the pot with two fingers. Her hand smacked mine, and the lid crashed onto the stove.

"Boy, get your hand out of there. You're not the only one eating this."

A voice called out from the living room.

"You all right, Sis?"

"Yeah, Gertie. You just rest!"

Tupperware in hand, Mama scooped out enough rice for both of us.

"Look, Shawn, I know it's hard. But she's still my sister and your auntie. Having somebody around would be good for her."

She snapped shut the container and walked up to me. I was leaning against the wall. My arms crossed as I looked over her shoulder.

"You might not be seeing much of her in the near future."

My eyes lit up. Is she gonna finally let me stay alone in Carson?

"Are you gonna stop dropping me off?"

Her eyes rolled and her head tilted.

"I don't think so. At some point, but not for a while."

She grabbed the containers and faced me again. "I'm talking about Sis."

"What about her?"

The containers sat on the edge of the table with Mama's fingers tracing each lid. Heavy breaths heaved her chest in and out. Her eyes darted outside.

"I mean . . . you know . . . she has problems." Mama dropped her head.

I leaned back against the wall, uncrossed my arms, and whispered, "I'll say."

"Don't be smart, Shawn!" she shot.

"Mama, you don't know," I shot back, exploding off the wall. "You only see what you see when you see it. But me, I see it all—all the time, Mama," I pleaded. "*All* the time: on the floor. On the couch. In the bathroom. Cursing at me. Tossing glasses. Asking me the same thing over and over and over and . . ."

She looked outside again and sighed. The floor squeaked as she pulled up a seat.

"Look, Shawn." She swallowed. "I know you've picked her up and dusted her off more times than you'd like to remember." Her eyes darted outside before she added, "I've done it myself off and on since you started school."

"Dannng!"

"What did I tell you about using that word?" she snapped. I didn't even get out my "sorry" before her voice had softened and she added, "It would be nice, Shawn, real nice, if you could spend more time with your auntie. Just once in a while. I'd hate to have something happen to her and nobody be around until it was too late."

Mannn . . . this sucks. What do I say to that? My stomach grumbled, so I pushed off from the wall and pinched more rice from the pot. I was ready to go home. I stood in the doorway between Mama and the living room.

"Can you do that for me, Shawnie?" she said, stroking her right hand across my cheek.

"I can't even bring my friends here. . . ."

"I know, baby, but could you do this for me . . . please?"

The kitchen walls and ceiling grabbed my attention as I avoided answering her. The soft stroke of her hand on my cheek became a gentle but firm grip on my jaw. She coaxed it around to look me in the eye, so I said the only thing I could say: "All right."

TEN

A PECK EACH on Auntie's cheek and we were gone. The streets of Compton zoomed past my eyes as we headed home to Carson. Supermarkets, restaurants, malls, and banks replaced liquor stores, chicken shacks, beauty parlors, and check-cashing places.

A song on the radio filled the uncomfortable silence. Every once in a while I glanced over at Mama, and even though she was sitting next to me, driving, she wasn't in the car with me.

I couldn't believe Auntie had been like that since I was in kindergarten. I'm fourteen now, so that's a long time drinking that stuff. A real long time. My nose hairs burned just thinking about the smell. I couldn't describe it exactly, but I can describe how it feels when you sniff it. Imagine putting a hot pepper up your nose, and then imagine what it does to your whole body.

Earlier this year in health class, we talked about organs and how you can donate them for transplants. The one I remember most was the liver. Mr. Bremelow, our teacher, said the liver is our filter for bad stuff in our body and certain things clog it up. If the liver gets clogged, other parts of the body slow down to help it out. One of the things that messes the liver up most is alcohol, because it makes the liver work so hard. He said that if a guy about thirty years old drank every day for ten years, his liver would be in worse condition than somebody who was seventy years old but never drank. Now that I know Auntie's been drinking hard since I was about five, that story blows my mind even more.

"Mama, how old is Auntie?"

I had to ask twice before she heard me.

"She's eight years older than me."

Why does she do that? I can't remember how old she is.

"And how old are you again?"

"I know you're not asking your own mother that question." Her head turned in my direction, and she smiled at me.

It's hard for me to remember how old she is because she always says something different when anybody asks. Luckily, there's a way that helps me remember: when she had me.

Let's see . . . I think she was twenty-five when she had me. Yeah, twenty-five. And I'm fourteen. So, twenty-five plus fourteen is . . . thirty-nine.

"Thirty-nine?"

I turn toward her. "So Auntie is forty-seven?"

"Bravo, Mister Math. You figured it out. Why do you care how old Sis is?"

I told her what Mr. Bremelow said about the liver. I could see her brain working as I explained what damages the liver and that if Auntie's been drinking hard for so long, then her liver must be in pretty bad shape.

"But she can change that. If she stops now, it would start getting better."

"I know it's bad but"—her eyes darted over to mine—"when you spend more time with her, you can tell her what you just told me and maybe she'll come around."

I tried to keep from sucking my teeth.

"I doubt it. If she's been doing it this long, it's hard to change. How she get like that in the first place?"

Her eyes stared straight ahead. "I really don't know, Shawn. She's still my sister and just to even think of her that way, I . . ." She exhaled. "Let's change the subject. How was your day?"

Uh-oh. The day was cool but had a few not-too-cool moments. Particularly the one that involved a certain pit bull's teeth shredding my sneaker. I don't have to tell her about that now, though.

"I told you. . . . We hung out . . . played some ball. You know . . ." She glanced over at me. "Me and Lorenzo won most of the games."

"You still hangin' out with that Lorenzo? I thought I told you—"

"He's not in a gang, Mama. I told you before—that was his brother's jacket. Besides, that was a couple of years ago."

Her eyes bounced between me and the road as she spoke. "You know I don't like him, Shawn."

"You don't even know Lorenzo. He's cool. All my friends

are cool. If they hanging out with me, they gotta be." I patted my hair like I was The Man.

"Yeah, right." She sucked her teeth and rolled her eyes from the road to me.

At least she hasn't mentioned the shoes.

"What's that purple stuff on your shirt?"

She nodded at me and arched her eyebrows down.

"What purple stuff?"

I glanced down to see the front of my white T-shirt spotted with what had to be pomegranate juice. Uh-oh. How'd I miss that? I better answer her quickly or she'll know something's up.

"Oh, we had a couple of pomegranates earlier. Trent has a tree. Must be some of the juice."

"Oh."

That's it? Auntie must be getting to her. In the past she would've been all over me asking for details and stuff. Why did you go to Trent's? Where does he live? Was his mother home? And so on and so on and so on.

Oil pumps and car dealerships zoomed by, replacing the malls and banks. The smell of rotten eggs drifted in from a nearby factory. Home was getting even closer.

"Mama, you all right? Everything cool at work?"

Her eyes bounced between me and the road. "Everything's cool at work. I'm just tired from being on my feet all day. But speaking of work, one of the professors gave me some more names of authors and books for you to check out."

"You remember any of them?"

I haven't felt like reading much since summer started, but you never know.

"I wrote them down. The list is in my purse. I think one of them was a poet."

"Poetry! You kidding, right? I don't wanna read about birds and trees and love and corny stuff like that."

She laughed. "It's not that kind of poetry. I mentioned that you love music, and he said you would enjoy this poet because his poems sound more like music than poetry."

"He who? I thought that professor was a woman." I started to put my feet up on the dashboard but remembered my sneaker. Instead, I swung my body around toward her to give her the third degree like she does me.

Maybe that's why she was acting so strange.

"So what's up, Mama? You going out with this dude? How long—"

She cut me off before I could even finish. Her eyebrows arched down at me as she made a left turn. "Shawnie, please stop. Just stop. I'm not going out with him or anybody. It's really none of your business, but his name is Professor Hopkins and all we talk about is books. For you. He's one of the nicer professors at the college, and you seem to like what he recommends, so I say 'hey' when I see him. Some of the professors don't say as much as 'boo' to me. They act like they have a stick in their butt and think their umm don't stink."

"Mama!"

"It's true. I don't care if they teach at a college, that don't make them better than me!"

A branch of veins sprouted on her forehead as she spoke. "My mother, your grandmother, God bless the dead, raised me to treat everybody the same, no better and no worse than I would want to be treated."

I shot one of her own looks back at her. "Uh-huh. Is that why you don't want me hanging out with my friends?"

She didn't face me when she said, "It's not the same."

Uh-huh. I got her.

Our house popped into view as we made our way down the hill on our street. I was glad to be home, where I could eat what I wanted, watch what I wanted, and not have to worry about the smell of alcohol drifting through the house.

As we got closer to our house, I saw plenty of kids pedaling around on bikes. There's more kids here than near Auntie's, but since I don't know most of them, I don't hang out with them. My next-door neighbor is cool, though. I'm friends with him. Not like my boys, but we hang out once in a while. His name is Brian, and he's gonna be a junior. He still can't understand why I won't be going to the local high school with him.

"I don't get it, Shawn. Manning is way better than Marshall. Our football team is always in the state championships; the cheerleaders are fine; the teachers are better . . ."

On and on he goes, but I tell him the same thing every time: It's never gonna happen. Mama works closer to Compton, and it's easier for her to keep dropping me off at Auntie's.

"But what about you? You ain't exactly a baby, you know."

Yeah. I know.

I wonder if she's ever gonna stop taking me to Auntie's.

ELEVEN

"SHAWN, SET THE TABLE while I get the oxtails."

Mama grabbed the food from the car while I tracked down the plates, glasses, and silverware for dinner. I found everything except my favorite fork. It's hard to miss because it's the biggest one in the drawer. Dad got it in the navy, and *USN* is etched on the handle. It's been in the house ever since he left and always reminds me of him.

Mama brought the food in and stuck the oxtails in the microwave.

"Am I going to Dad's this weekend?"

"It's supposed to be his weekend."

I stood in front of the counter and glanced over at Mama. I'm about a head taller than her. She returned my glance and straightened her hunched back.

"Boy, you are getting big, huh? Don't think I haven't noticed how fast you're growing."

I walked over and compared our height. Her hair grazed my chin.

"Dang, Mama—" I said, cutting myself off. "I mean—you sure you not shrinking? I'm a whole head taller than you."

"No, I'm not shrinking. You may be bigger than me, but that don't mean I can't still smack your butt. I will always be your mother."

"I know that. How can I ever forget?" I stepped back and found my spot against the counter.

"So am I going to Dad's or not this weekend? I mean, he's not on the road, is he?"

"As far as I know. He didn't mention any trips to me recently, but then again I don't talk to him every day. Why don't you call him and see?"

"Maybe after dinner. I'm starving."

The microwave dinged, so I pulled out the steaming container and hustled it over to the table. Mama grabbed a big spoon and the rice and sat down.

My father, Shawn senior . . . the man I'm named after. My folks got divorced a long time ago, but I still see Dad every couple of weeks on the weekend. Even though I don't see him every day, we're still tight. He's a photographer for the *Times* here in L.A., which means he doesn't have the same hours as most people. He also spends a lot of time on the road. Mama says that's the main reason they got a divorce. She couldn't deal with his funky hours and the fact that he wasn't making much money when they were together, so a few years after I was born, they split up. For good.

They're still cool with each other and talk, and one thing they agreed on was that Dad would still spend time with me. Mama knows he's a good father and wanted me to have a male figure in my life, so I get to see him every couple of weeks — unless he's traveling. Then it changes. That doesn't make Mama too happy because she says it messes with her weekend schedule, but that's a lie; all she does on the weekend is clean the house.

"Shawn, could you get me some water, please?"

My fork was inches from my mouth when Mama asked her question. I exhaled hard, put my food down, and got it. Am I ever gonna get to eat?

"I know you didn't just huff at me, boy."

"I'm hungry and I was this close to finally eating." I held up two fingers about an inch apart to show her how close I was to getting some food in my belly.

"Ummm-hmmm." She laughed and stared me down as she plunged the food into her mouth. Her face lit up with each chew. Auntie must have done a good job on the oxtails.

"MMM-mmm. Sis did it again. Her 'tails are still better than mine," she said, shaking her head with pleasure.

I sat back down and finally tasted my food. I had to agree with Mama; Auntie had outdone herself again. I devoured the food to my belly's content. Happy sounds and slurps from our water glasses interrupted the comfortable silence.

"So, Mama, why did Auntie start to drink?" I motioned toward my glass.

"Oh, Shawn, not this again," she said, swallowing her food.

"I'm just sayin', I don't understand how the same person that made this could . . ." I said, not wanting to finish.

"Well, Shawn, your auntie, my sister . . . has a disease. She can't control it because it's something her *body* wants — it doesn't know how to function without it." With that, she wiped off her mouth and pushed her plate away. "Make sure you take care of the dishes."

Dang! Every time I bring up Auntie, she throws me attitude. She went into the living room and clicked on the TV. Oh, well. I gobbled up a second helping, then cleaned the kitchen. I called out to Mama about the books and authors.

"The list is in my purse, on the counter."

I hunted through the loose change, lipstick, tissue, and pieces of candy until I found what looked like a list of books.

Langston Hughes — poetry — very bluesy, search by name
Native Son — Richard Wright
Go Tell It on the Mountain — James Baldwin
The Autobiography of Malcolm X — Alex Haley

"Is this the same Alex Haley that did the TV show *Roots?*" I shouted to the living room.

She shouted back, "Yeah, that's what he said."

Hmmm. I know he wrote the book *Roots* and they turned it into a movie, but I didn't know he did other stuff. I've heard a lot about Martin Luther King Jr. over the years but not much about Malcolm X. I should check that out. I don't know about the poetry, though. All that "how do I love thee" nonsense . . .

I finished the kitchen and plopped onto the couch to join Mama with the list in hand. My presence jerked her out of a tired nod.

"If I read these books, I hope my high school teacher gives me credit for them. My last teacher wouldn't even give me credit for *Invisible Man,* you know."

Her head spun around. "Really? But I thought you got credit for anything extra."

"Only if it's on the list. And let me tell you, there's mostly white dudes on that list — the rest are white women."

"Really?"

"I'm serious. I called my teacher on it, and she didn't have nothing to say. Just that I wouldn't get credit. Ain't that a blip?"

"Watch your mouth, boy." She eyeballed me. "Hopefully high school will be different."

"I hope so, 'cause if I don't get extra credit, then I might not read them."

She sat up more alert than ever. Her once-nodding-off head now shook her hairdo as she spoke. "What kind of stupid talk is that? Who cares if you get credit for a certain book or not? That shouldn't keep you from reading what you want. Knowledge for the sake of knowledge is better than knowledge for the sake of a grade any day. My parents told me that, and I've always told you that."

"I know, Mama. I'm just saying."

"Besides, a lot of things change in high school."

Here's my chance.

"Yes, they do. Speaking of which, I'm getting older and

bigger every day, you know, and I can't stay at Auntie's forever, so . . ."

I swung my feet off the couch to look her in the eye.

"I know what you're gonna say, Shawn. I know you're getting older and bigger, but you know my job situation. It's still
much easier for me to leave you at Gertie's."

"Yeah, easier for you. But what about me? You saw how
she was today. She's like that every day, you know?"

Her right hand moved under her head, and she lowered
her eyes down at the curlicue pattern on the carpet.

"I know that, Shawn. We've had this conversation how
many times now? And every time I tell you the same thing:
it's easier for me to have you go to Marshall than go to school
here."

"Yeah, easy for you, Mama. But what about me? You ever
think about what I might want?"

"Boy, where is this attitude coming from, huh? I'm too
tired for all this right now."

"I know, Mama, it's just . . . It's not only about Auntie," I
said, catching my breath. "Do you know about the pink slip?"
I sat up and folded my arms across my chest.

"The what?"

"The pink slip. It's officially called 'Permission Form to
Discipline,' and it goes home on the first day of school asking if it's OK for the principal to whack your child in front of
everybody if they act out."

"What do you mean 'act out'?"

"Well, I don't mean shooting spitballs in the back of the
class. More like . . . pulling a knife on your teacher."

"Who told you that? One of your little hoodlum friends? I find it hard to believe that the principal can get away with whacking a child."

"Well, it's true. And no, I didn't hear it from one of my 'hoodlum friends.' I heard it from some girls, as a matter of fact."

She sat up straighter and swung her legs toward me.

"Girls? What girls?" A smile crept over her face. "You never mentioned any girls before, Shawnie. You got a girlfriend you're not telling me about?"

I knew she would say that. Does she think that just because I hang out with guys that I don't even *know* any girls?

"No, I don't have a girlfriend. But I do have some friends that are girls."

That wiped the grin from her face, and she folded her arms and pushed back into her seat.

"And my friends that are girls have brothers and sisters that go to Marshall. Their siblings told them, and they told me all about the pink slip. They told me about the principal whacking students, mostly 'bangers, with a paddle in an assembly so everybody could see. When I asked if he could do that, that's when they mentioned the pink slip. They said you don't have to sign it, but most parents do just to make sure their kids don't act out. Would you ever sign it?"

"Now, Shawn, you should know me better than that. Why would I let somebody else spank my child when I can have the pleasure of doing it myself?" She laughed, patting me on the leg — hard.

"*Ha-ha*, very funny!"

"Besides, my mother always told me to believe none of what you hear and only half of what you see. Now that you're gonna be a freshman, you're gonna hear all kinds of crazy things. I remember when I started Marshall, the seniors told the freshman they had to buy 'elevator tickets' to get to the second floor. Never mind the fact that we didn't even have an elevator in school. Luckily, Sis and my cousins had already gone there, so I knew what to expect and didn't fall for it."

"Yeah, but see? Since Auntie went there, you believed what she told you. How is that different from what the girls told me? They could be telling the truth too."

"You're right. They *could* be telling you the truth. I'm just saying . . . It's basically illegal to spank in school, so I find it a little hard to believe. Although, now that I think about it, I wouldn't be too surprised because of the knuckleheads that go there. Or shall I say, are *enrolled* there."

She emphasized the word "enrolled" because everybody knows the 'bangers spend most of their time hanging out and causing trouble.

One minute I'm talking about going to school here; the next minute I'm telling her about the pink slip.

"So, Shawnie . . . tell me about these girlfriends — I mean 'friends who are girls.' Will I be meeting them anytime soon?"

How did we even start talking about this?

"I'm sorry, Mama, did you say something? I was watching this commercial about minty-fresh breath and didn't catch what you said." Two can play that game.

I relaxed into my seat and kicked my legs out.

"Shawn, what is that?" She sat up straight and pointed at my trimmed sneaker.

Uh-oh. What's the story again? Stall. Shoot . . . what's the story again?

"What is what?" I sat up, pretending to look around while hiding my sneaker.

"Your foot? What happened to your sneaker?"

The story. What's the story? Style. New style. That's right. A cut-up sneaker is the new style.

"What? This?" I pointed to the trimmed part of the sneaker. "This is the style now. You trim one of your Stars until it's real low. I saw these guys on the court today with sneakers cut like this, and my boys told me it was the new style. They call it a Lowrider." Lowrider, that was good.

"Lowrider? Are you kidding me? I didn't spend good money on those sneakers to have you destroy them."

She jumped forward in her seat. "Wait a second. . . . Lowrider? That better not be gang-related. I know the knuckleheads have all of their codes and stuff, but you better not be getting involved with them. For all I know, it could mean you're about to join."

See, she did it again. Maybe the Lowrider thing wasn't a great idea after all. I thought I had every angle covered, but once again Mama proved me wrong.

"Come on, Mama, you know me better than that. These guys we saw playing were older and real ballers. Since they did it, we thought it looked cool and did it too."

She exhaled and sat back. Her feet found their original position on the couch before she spoke again.

gotta go shopping. All I see is mustard, hot sauce, barbecue sauce, and . . . wait a second . . . what's this . . . wrapped in foil? A couple pieces of Auntie's chicken. Oh, yeah. When was the last time she made chicken? Last week? I hope it's still good — sniff — smells good.

Since school is out, I usually stay up late and watch movies. Sometimes I make it all the way through, sometimes I don't. Comedies, kung fu flicks, and Westerns keep me awake. Dramas and love stories knock me out. I flipped through the channels and stopped at an old Clint Eastwood Western. Cool. Which one is this?

A close-up of Clint's squinting eyes and rugged face flashed on the screen but was replaced by an older, uglier face. A dirt-covered face wiped by a dirt-covered arm cackled a laugh, then said: "Come on, Blondie. We'll work together."

Blondie? Wait . . . is that . . . ohhhhhhhh, shoot . . . *The Good, the Bad and the Ugly.* I hadn't seen this in a long time. It's one of my favorites. I propped my feet up onto the couch and settled into the old West. My teeth ripped apart the cold chicken and in a few short minutes it was gone. I turned my attention to Clint and the Ugly.

A gunshot echoed across the desert.

Where'd that come from?

Two red-bandanna-covered faces raced from the general store to the saloon.

Are they shooting at me?

Pale yellow smoke curled from the barrel of the gun at the end of my arm.

Where'd that come from?

The yellow smoke became green.

A voice called out: "Brutha man. Hey, brutha man!"

Bright green tumbleweeds rolled past my feet. Rust-colored desert dust scratched my eyes.

A whisper: "Follow me."

I looked down at my feet to find the desert dust replaced by a brown hardwood floor. Music danced on piano keys. Voices bounced off mirror-covered walls. I swung my head around. No one. The music stopped.

Faces flashed in front of me like ghosts, disappearing before I could make any of them out. A spray of bullets whizzed by my head and shattered bottles of whiskey on the bar behind me. I spun around and found myself in front of a shattered mirror. Two women tied a yellow bandanna over my reflected face; Marisol stood behind me on the left and Janine on the right. I turned around to face them. The echo of their voices lingered as they disappeared with the breeze.

"Come on out, podna! Don't make me come in there to get you." A man's voice echoed through the saloon.

Who said that?

The music started up again. So did the voice.

"Come on out, podna, or I'm coming in."

Where did that come from?

Cherry-red lips planted a peck on my cheek.

"Good luck," the lips said, disappearing again.

Another pair of lips did the same. And said the same: "Good luck."

"Who's that?" I shouted.

I stood in the center of the saloon. The bar began to spin.

Slow. Then fast. Then faster. And faster. My body remained still as the mirror-covered walls reflected me from all sides. With each spin of the room, I grew larger and taller.

"I'm comin' in!" *My voice punched through the swinging saloon doors.*

The room stopped. I tried to run, but gravity tugged on my legs.

"Blondie . . . you in there?" *I heard.*

My body jerked. I jumped up to find myself standing in our living room with the Ugly talking to Clint — on TV.

I must have dozed off. A moment later rolling credits replaced their faces.

I'm tired. I hope that dream finishes itself off when my head hits the pillow. Not the part with the gun and the voice calling me out, but the two pairs of lips kissing me.

Yeah, that would be nice.

THIRTEEN

THE NEXT MORNING found me in the same place as the morning before. Mama had reminded me to spend more time with Auntie as we pulled up, but Auntie had lots of errands, so she sent me out of the house the moment I stepped through the door. Cool with me. So now . . . Same friends. Same dilemma.

"Whatch'all wanna do today?" Lorenzo asked.

"Let's go play some ball!" Andre said.

He would say that. That's all he ever wants to do. Normally, I'd wanna go play too, but last night . . . something changed. I don't know if it was the dream, but a change of scenery would be nice. Once my head hit the pillow, Janine and Marisol reappeared in a dream, but everything was different. I don't remember much because it disappeared the more I tried to think about it. But when I woke up this morning, my sheets were wet. And sticky. That wasn't the best way to start the day, but I didn't think anything of it because I'd had a big glass of juice before I went to sleep last night.

Flashes of the dream popped in and out of my head as Mama drove me to Auntie's. Splashes of yellow mixed with each of the girls' faces while skin-colored body parts paraded through my brain. The harder I tried to remember what happened, the harder it was to remember anything. I gave up by the time Mama dropped me off, but when Lorenzo asked the daily question, Marisol's hair blew across my brain like a wind-whipped flag.

"I love playing ball, 'Dre, but let's switch it up today," I heard myself say. I didn't even know what I meant; I only knew I wanted to do something different.

"What you mean 'switch it up'?" Lorenzo asked.

His dark hamlike fists scavenged through his early morning bag of bacon-and-sour-cream chips. Crumbs flew out of his mouth as the question escaped his lips.

My shoulders shrugged as the question entered my ears. "Man, I don't know. We've played ball every day this week," I said. "It's Friday. I'm just up for a change." My lap disappeared as I stood and dusted off my cinnamon-bun crumbs.

There's always one point in the summer where everything starts speeding up. Somebody goes away to visit family, and before you know it, school's back in.

"That's cool. I don't care what we do. I just don't wanna hang around here all day trying to figure it out," Lorenzo said. "Anybody got any money?"

We reached into our pockets. A pair of rabbit ears popped out of Lorenzo's pants. I was empty too. But Andre and Trent pulled out some wadded-up bills that we counted.

"I got four dollars," Andre said.

"I got a five-spot," Trent said.

"Nine bucks. That's nine more than yesterday," I said.

"Anybody thinking what I'm thinking?" Trent asked.

"What? That nine dollars divided by four knuckleheads is two dollars and change each?" Lorenzo said.

"No, fool! We got enough money to hit the movies. They got a two-dollar special at the theater down on Slauson," Trent replied.

"Aw, man, you mean the one that smells like fried fish?" Andre said, scrunching up his nose.

"Oh, yeah . . . they got a whole bunch of movies there, right?" I said.

"Yup. Mostly kung fu flicks. They got some horror movies and other stuff too. It's early enough that we can pay our two bucks for one and then sneak in to see some others," Trent added.

"Shoot, I'm always up for some Bruce. Stinky fish smells and all," I said, then added, "WAAAA-TAAAA!" I bounced on my toes and brushed my thumb across my nose à la Bruce Lee.

"Oh, here we go!" Lorenzo said.

Billy Dee Williams's eyes followed us from his poster as we peeled away from Pop's. I don't think there's ever been a time when I didn't see Billy Dee's face at some liquor store urging me to buy Colt 45 — "crazy juice" as my father calls it.

As always, we took our shots at our trash can before we headed out.

Trent: "Three, two, one . . ." Brick. "Dang!"

Me: "Three, two, one . . ." Swish. "Oh, yeah!"

That's the first one this week. Maybe this is my lucky day.

Andre: "Three, two, one . . ." Swish — of course.

Lorenzo: "Three, two . . ."

"*Agggghhhhh!* Time's up, fat boy . . . you lost the game!" Trent shouted.

Not with the "fat boy" already, Trent? We haven't even done anything yet and . . .

"Don't start with me, Trent. Not now. Don't make me bag on that water head of yours," Lorenzo said. His heels lifted off the glass-glittered concrete as he arced his trash into the basket.

"Swish! Lorenzo Thomas does it again, hitting the game-winning shot for the Los Angeles Lakers, giving them another championship!" Lorenzo said.

"Dang, Trent. Bricked again, huh? That's all right. I understand. That head of yours keeps you off-balance," he added, slapping a thick mitt over Trent's shoulder.

Lorenzo stretched his arms to the sky, making his belly button play peekaboo, then said, "Hold up. Color check."

Almost forgot. After yesterday I had made sure I was cool this morning.

Lorenzo: Dark green sweatpants. Matching dark green jacket zippered over a faded yellow T-shirt. White Adidas with black stripes. Cool.

Andre: Dark purple shorts. Plain white T-shirt. Plain

white socks drooping low over white Ponys with black stripes. Cool.

Trent: Gray shorts. Pale orange T-shirt with some funky logo on it. White socks and white low-top Stars. Cool.

Me: Jet-black shorts. Gray T-shirt. White socks with black rings. And of course, white All Stars with the left side chopped lower than the right. Super cool.

"We Kool and the Gang?" Lorenzo looked to each of us. "Then let's go."

Trent bounced a beat with the ball, leading the way as we headed west on the DMZ. I dusted off my crotch again and flashes of yellow popped into my head. Man, what happened in that dream last night?

One thing I remember for sure was waking up with wet pajama bottoms. Not soaking wet like just out of the wash. Just wet in the crotch and sticky. Dang. I hope the sheets won't smell. That's the last thing I need is for Mama to tell Dad I peed the bed like a little kid.

"Ain't that right, Shawn?"

Somebody call my name?

Trent said, "Shawn, you even listening? I said, ain't that right?"

We had stopped. Where were we?

Trent stared at me from the curb with the ball on his hip. Andre stood next to him, shaking his head and saying, "No way!"

"Yes way! Bruce Lee could whup Jim Kelly any day!" Trent said. His tongue punched out Jim Kelly's name like Bruce Lee smashing a wooden board.

"Hold up. Bruce is good but—" Andre started.

"Bruce is *good*? Bruce is the best! Period. End of discussion," Trent said.

Are you kidding me? Bruce Lee? Jim Kelly? Who's the best? Is that what we talking about? That's easy.

"I gotta agree, 'Dre. Jim is one high-kicking, hard-punching, Afro-puffed brutha, but Bruce is the man. I mean, come on—*Fists of Fury* . . . *Enter the Dragon* . . . *Game of Death*. He kicks mucho behind in all them flicks," I said.

Trent nodded in excited agreement. The light changed and cars slowed to a stop. A canary-yellow low-riding Impala driven by a slick-haired Mexican hit the hydraulics as we crossed. It bounced into the air as we bounced across the intersection.

Andre picked up his pace to follow Trent and yelled out: "Hold on. I'm telling you . . . Jim Kelly . . ."

On the other side, Lorenzo turned back toward the intersection and bounced his eyes in tune with the lowrider. Up-down. Up-down. Up-down.

"Man, if I had one of them, girls would be begging me for a ride. And I'd give 'em one," Lorenzo said, before adding, "Man, would I give 'em a ride."

His teeth were exposed in a devilish grin.

I could see a movie starting up in his eyes, him starring in the role of the bouncer with a carload of Janines fawning over him.

"Janine, huh?" I said.

The movie shut down and his eyes snapped back into reality. A look of shock replaced his grin.

"How'd you know?" he said.

"With you, 'Zo, how could I not know?" I said.

The grin crept back onto his face as he threw his right paw over my shoulder. "Shawnie-Shawn, Shawnie-Shawn, Shawnie-Shawn-Shawn-Shawn . . . my brutha from another mother—to the end. You know me only too well."

FOURTEEN

"WE NEED TO MAKE A STOP," Andre said.

His words bounced my attention from my imaginary painting on the clear blue sky to the reality of my surroundings. I was working on a portrait of Marisol, in profile, with her hair flowing over her shoulders, down her back, touching her butt. My mental paintbrush was shaping that cute little behind of hers in those tight Sergios she likes to wear when Andre spoke up, making me splash pink paint on her pedal pushers.

"We ain't got time to be stopping. I wanna see at least two flicks, and you about to cut into that, Andre," Trent said. He snatched the ball from Andre and rat-a-tatted a quick dribble low to the ground.

We stood on Andre's street. A residential street. A quiet residential street. The only sounds to be heard came from our loud mouths and the rhythmic bounce of the ball.

"So, Andre, why we stopping at your house? You gonna give us something to eat? Maybe a little something-something for the flicks," Lorenzo asked. His right hand circled his Buddha belly. His tongue circled his lips.

"Naw, man, my brother is supposed to be coming home today on leave, and I wanna see if he's here yet," Andre said.

"Man, you got plenty of time to see your brother. You depriving us of serious 'WAAA-TAAA' time. We ain't got time for this," Trent said. His hands flew onto his hips.

He looked like a kid getting ready to throw a tantrum in the supermarket because his mama wouldn't buy him his favorite cereal: "But, Moooooooomm, I want Cocoa Puffs, not Choco Puffs. That ain't Cocoa Puffs. Cocoa Puffs got the little bird on 'em. That got a big blue-and-white stripe on it, and everybody know the blue-and-white stripe means it's plain wrap. Moooooom, I don't want no plain-wrap cereal . . . It taste nasty. *I want Cocoa Puffs!*"

It looked like he was gonna start kicking and screaming. Instead, his body and hands started shaking, and he lost control of the ball. Lorenzo covered his mouth, hoping to cover his laughter.

"What you laughing at, *fat boy?*" Trent said.

Again with the "fat boy"? Now I know why Passion is always calling him "thickhead." Does he think before he speaks?

"Oh, no, you did not . . ." Lorenzo started.

I stepped between the two of them, and Lorenzo backed off. He was used to this. Andre stepped in, stole the ball, and bounced toward his house.

"Come on, Trent. You know Andre only sees his brother once in a while," I said.

"Fine, Shawn. Take his side. I don't care. I'm outta here," Trent said.

He started in the direction of the theater but stopped. Lorenzo took off to follow Andre. That left me to talk some sense into Trent's thick head—as usual. He does this all the time, and I'm always the one waiting for him. Maybe it's because I'm an only child. Maybe it's because I'm used to this kind of nonsense with Auntie. Maybe it's because I know he would do the same for me.

"Trent, come on. The faster we go see his brother, the faster we can go to the movies."

A busted lamppost loomed over me and Trent and our conversation on the corner. Trent and the block were silent until a heavy door slammed and a dog bark-barked. Lucky's yellow teeth snapped back into my memory.

"Come on . . . I'll tell you what I told Mama about my sneakers."

We stepped inside Andre's house to find Lorenzo searching for the kitchen.

"Dang, Andre . . . all these rooms and no kitchen?"

Andre didn't answer because he was searching the house for his brother, calling his name between door slams. All of a sudden it got quiet, then we heard, "Hey, man, close the door!"—followed by a slam.

Lorenzo ran out of the kitchen and joined me and Trent in the living room. Three pairs of eyes looked to the rear of the house, where the sound came from.

"Sorry" echoed through the hallway.

Andre came running out and huffed, "Let's go, guys. Quick!"

Lorenzo looked at me. I looked at Trent. Trent looked at Lorenzo. The three of us looked at Andre. He looked embarrassed.

"My brother's here. He's just a little . . . ahhhh . . . busy at the moment," Andre said.

"Whatchu mean? Busy doing what?" Trent said.

Lorenzo's belly bounced with laughter. "Not what . . . who. Right, 'Dre?" he said, poking Andre in the side.

The devilish grin once again crept onto Lorenzo's face. He took a step in the direction of the door slam, then went up on his toes like Bugs Bunny does when he wants to sneak up on Elmer Fudd. Andre grabbed his arm and whispered: "I said, *let's go!*"

"Aw, come on, 'Dre. Is your brother in there—you know— doing his thing?" Lorenzo asked. "Don't you wanna at least listen? I know if it was my brother . . ."

"Shhhhhhhhh!" Andre whispered.

Lorenzo must have planted the seed of curiosity because the ice of embarrassment on Andre's face melted. He put a finger to his lips, then led the way as we inched down a mahogany wood-paneled hallway toward our destination: a closed door with sound coming from behind. We passed a bathroom on our right and a bedroom on our left. If the door opened, we would hide in one of them. Within seconds we reached our target and pressed our ears close to listen.

We looked like a scene out of the Three Stooges, only

there was four of us. Lorenzo is the tallest, so he stood and listened up top. Trent is the shortest, so he knelt low to the ground. Me and Andre fought for position in between. Once everybody stopped "shushing" each other, we heard what was going on. Bass beats bumped the blinds on the windows, muffling the sound behind the door.

"I can't hear nothing," Trent said from down low.

"Wait for this car to go by," Lorenzo said.

"Shhhhhh," me and Andre whispered.

The bass disappeared and we heard everything the closed door had to offer.

The bed bumping against the wall. Sheets rustling. Fingernails scratching wood. Wheels squeaking across the wooden floor. Moans. Groans. Some "oh God's" here. Some "yeah baby's" there. Some "yes-yes-yeses" in between. And then: silence.

Lorenzo darted away. Me and Trent followed. Andre stayed, covering his mouth to keep from laughing. He almost fell into the room when the door flew open. His brother stepped out with a sheet wrapped around his waist.

"*Boyyy!* What did I say?"

Andre hopped up, grabbed his ball, and ran out the door. "Let's go!"

Me and Trent swiveled our heads and followed. Lorenzo hustled out of the kitchen, then out of the house, slamming the door behind him. His right hand clutched a sandwich as he raced after us.

"Ayyy . . . wait up!" he shouted between lip smacks.

We booked it up the block until we hit the corner where this whole thing started in the first place and broke into laughter that echoed throughout the neighborhood and probably all the way back to Andre's brother's ears.

"Man, can you believe that? Andre, your brother was doing his *thing!*" Lorenzo said with bright white mayo on the corner of his mouth. A collection of crumbs flew out as he spoke. Ugh — nasty.

"Dang, Lorenzo! Say it, don't spray it. I want the news, not the weather!" Trent said.

"You got some mayo right here," I said to Lorenzo, motioning to my face.

"Your brother don't waste no time, huh, 'Dre?" Trent said.

The chorus of laughter died down until Lorenzo replayed the sounds behind the door: "Yeah, yeah!" He grabbed and clawed at his shirt like a girl trying to rip it off him.

Andre joined in, unable to contain himself: *"Oooooooooooo-ooohhh, yes-yes-yes!"*

Trent jumped in last but not least: "Oh, God!"

Lorenzo: "Yeah!"

Andre: *"Oooooooohhhhhh, yes-yes-yes!"*

Trent: "Oh, God!"

"Yeah!"

"Oooooohhhhhh, yes-yes-yes!"

"Oh, God!"

"Yeah!"

"Oooooohhhhhh, yes-yes-yes!"

"Oh, God!"

"Oh, baby. Oh, baby . . ."

"Will you guys calm down? People gonna think we freaks or something if y'all don't stop," I said.

We were still outside for all the world to see. And hear.

That was the first time I'd ever heard . . . those sounds. I knew what they were doing, but I had to fill in the details with my imagination because I've never actually seen it myself. That didn't keep me from laughing, though. It was still a funny thing to witness, even if it was only with our ears.

"You could learn a few things from your brother, 'Dre," Lorenzo said, calm now.

"You know we gotta stop back in after the movies to check on him. There might be a sequel," Trent said.

Andre slapped Trent on his arm.

"Now *that* was better than Bruce, right?" he said with a big smile.

"Oh, man!" Trent said, wiping the sea of tears from his eyes as he gathered himself and the ball.

We bounced back on our path, Trent leading the way. Each bounce of the ball was punctuated by the sounds of ecstasy repeated from what we'd heard behind closed doors. Lorenzo played the role of the headboard banging against the wall. Trent did his best to imitate a girl's high-pitched voice saying "Oh, God" or "Yeah" in between headboard bumps. And Andre accented it all with sharp stabs of *"Yes-yes-yes!"*

All eyes turned on us as we turned onto the main boulevard. The presence of others had no effect on the sounds coming out of the fellas' mouths. Either their voices grew tired or they got tired of all the stares, because after a few strides, they quieted themselves. Trent fell back toward me, and Lorenzo approached Andre.

"So, your brother teach you anything to help you hook up?" he asked, slinging a mitt over 'Dre's shoulder.

Andre shook his head. "Awww . . . you know. He's always been a ladies' man, so I picked up a few things here and there. I remember back when he was in high school playing ball, he had girls calling the house all the time. I don't remember their names, but I remember their voices. Some were high, some low. All of them sweet. I asked how many he had, and he said he didn't know and didn't care. He said they all wanted him, so he went out with all of them."

"You sure that's all he did? Go out?" Lorenzo asked.

"I don't know for sure, but my mom was pretty strict. He had to be home by a certain time, and he could only go certain places. He might've done it, but he never told me anything about it if he did."

Andre turned back toward me and Trent, stole the ball from Trent, and dribbled between his legs.

Lorenzo slowed his stroll. "Maybe he's playing catch-up for back when he was in high school," he said to no one in particular.

"Nah, probably because he was at sea for so long. I couldn't be on a ship that long. And with no girls—shoot . . . that would drive me nuts," Andre said.

Lorenzo took hungry bites of the sandwich wedged in his paw.

"You still eating that?" I asked.

"I was laughing so hard, I almost forgot I had it," he said, taking a huge bite. "Almost."

A slice of bright pink ham with a bite mark and a thick glob of mayo hung on for dear life between the white bread. Without hesitation, he jammed what was left into his mouth, smacking his lips with each chew.

"Man, Lorenzo, do you have to do that in front of me?" I said. "Turn around or something. I don't wanna see that."

"For real, 'Zo, that's nasty," Trent said.

"Yeah" — Lorenzo chewed — "but not half as nasty as . . ."

Not again. "What? Not half as nasty as Andre's brother doing it, right? Is that what you was gonna say, 'Zo? Huh?"

I picked up the pace, moving ahead of him. A check-cashing place had a line out the door, so I stepped into the street to get around it.

"Must be county day," Lorenzo said.

"What?"

"I said it must be — forget it. Anyway . . . so, Shawn . . . I noticed you haven't been saying much ever since we heard — you know — 'Oh, God. Oh, God. Oh, God,'" Lorenzo said, catching up. His mayo-covered fingertips stained my shirt as he shook my shoulder.

"*Lorenzo*, do you *have* to keep saying that? We on a public street, man. People gonna think you all fruity or something, whispering that in my ear."

"You ain't never heard nothing like that before, have you, Shawnie-Shawn?"

He stepped in front of my path and forced me to stop. Bacon-and-sour-cream chips, ham, and mayo ignited my nose hairs as he got up close and personal. His eyes looked into mine and his breath heated my face.

I looked away to avoid his eyes and his breath. "Naw, I mean . . . yeah . . . you know . . ."

He moved his head around to lock eyes again. "Come on, Shawnie-Shawn . . . spit it out."

"I'm just saying . . . it's just . . . it was embarrassing listening to them . . . you know . . ." I said.

"Yeah, I know! Tell me about it. I can't tell you how many times I've come home to what I *thought* was an empty house only to hear my brother Dayshaun and some girl gettin' down in his room," he said.

We started moving again. Andre stood at the intersection punching the button as Trent dribbled out a beat.

Lorenzo continued. "You know, Shawn, you can learn a lot from them sounds. Most of the time, with my brother, it sounds like he's running. You know, breathing all hard, trying to catch his breath and stuff. That's him. But the girls . . . oh, man! They make all kinds of sounds! Like there was this one girl who sounded like she was in a fight; her voice was all mean and deep and stuff, and she'd scream every once in a while. Then there was this other girl—"

"OK, Lorenzo, I get it."

As soon as the light turned red, Andre shouted: "Hurry up, y'all! It's right over there."

We dashed across the intersection. I scanned the block to get my bearings. Were we in blue territory or red territory?

The movie marquee greeted us on the other side with a bunch of titles I didn't recognize, all misspelled.

"All I know is I'm gonna give her a reason to scream and shout," Trent said, slapping five with Andre.

"Are we on this again?" I said.

"Shawnie-Shawn got embarrassed," Lorenzo said, bumping my shoulder.

I sucked my teeth and folded my arms across my chest. I looked away to avoid the three of them and check out my surroundings. The movie theater was the largest building on the block with a Louisiana Fried Chicken on one side and a Lucky Liquors on the other side. Next to each of them stood stores with no signs on them. Across the street stood Maybell's Beauty Parlor alongside yet another check-cashing spot. A long line snaked out in front of the check casher.

"Can we go inside now?" I said.

"What's the matter, Shawn, you can't handle the sounds of pleasure?" Lorenzo said, emphasizing "pleasure" by raising his voice and eyebrows.

Andre jumped in. "That's cool, Shawn. I didn't wanna hear it myself at first 'cause I was embarrassed too," Andre said, then added, "But I'm glad I did." He and Lorenzo slapped hands and laughed.

Trent was already at the window, raising four fingers to the ticket seller. We followed him inside but not before Andre finished what he started.

"I figure, that's gonna be me someday, so I might as well get a sneak peek while I can. Fingernail scratches, moans, groans, and all," he said, raising his voice at the end.

Lorenzo did him one better and shouted for all to hear, "Yeah, that's gonna be all of us someday — soon. Hopefully *real* soon."

FIFTEEN

"CAN WE GET SOME POPCORN or something with the one dollar we got left? I'm hungry," Lorenzo said.

I didn't see anything for less than two dollars as we walked past the concession stand.

"We can get something when we leave, man," Trent said.

Lorenzo sucked his teeth. Then his eyes lit up and he raised a finger. "I almost forgot—I brought a little something with me."

Master of the Flying Guillotine—or *Flying Gillateen* as the marquee had said—was about to start, so we hustled to our seats. We fought over where to sit, settling on smack-dab in the middle. A couple of heads poked out here and there, but our group of four was the largest by far. I peeled my Stars off the sticky floor and propped them up on the seat in front of me. The fellas did the same.

Lorenzo stuffed his mitt into his sweatshirt pocket and wriggled out something none of us could see. "I brought these," he said, pulling out what turned out to be a fresh pack of Ritz crackers. He put two in my hand.

Is he serious? "Gimme those. I'll help myself," I said.

I grabbed the package from him. He shrugged and looked to the screen. I passed them down, and when they reached Andre at the end, he said, "Lorenzo, you stole these from my house, didn't you?"

Lorenzo gave no answer, and Andre remained silent. He must have not been too mad. The crunch of crackers mixed with the cheesy music on the screen as Master started chopping off heads, cutting a path through the Imperial Army on his way to Lord knows where.

Feet propped up, food in mouth, and eyes filled with action, I exhaled into my seat and relaxed. The fighting on-screen was replaced by talking, so I let my mind wander.

What's Marisol up to today? When's Janine leaving for UCLA? What's Andre's brother doing right now? What am I gonna find when I get back to Auntie's? What's Mama gonna do this weekend? Wait—it's Dad's weekend. I wonder what we're gonna do. By the time the weekend rolls around, he's tired and just wants to relax. At least his idea of relaxing isn't cleaning the house, like it is Mama's. He missed his last visit because he had to work out of town that weekend. San Diego, Santa Barbara . . . one of them Sans. No big deal. He still called me and we shot the breeze. I hope he brought me back something good.

"Lay down your weapon, or we will be forced to use our

authority against you," an imperial guard said, sitting on his horse, wearing a big ol' Chinese triangle hat. His lips didn't match the words coming out of his mouth.

Cut to the guillotine spinning out of Master's hands. Cut to an image of four chopped heads with those funky triangle hats rolling on the dirt. Cut to an extreme close-up of Master's eyes looking around, his head unmoved. Cut to a long shot of the imperial army facing down Master. Cut to the guards' point of view looking at Master. His eyes narrowed. Cut to Master's point of view of the army. About a hundred guards raised their red-tasseled white-feathered staffs into the air and spurred their horses.

"Here comes the big dance," I said.

"You know Master is blind, right?" Trent said, sitting up.

"For real? How you know that?" Lorenzo said.

"I been listening to what they say. Haven't you?"

"Man, I come to the movies to watch butts get kicked and heads get bashed. I don't care about the story."

"Yeah, but that's how you know who's gonna be fighting who, and why," I said.

"*Shhhhhhhhhhh!*" came from a couple of rows back.

I hadn't picked up on Master being blind either. Probably because my mind was wandering.

"I couldn't be blind," Lorenzo said. "I couldn't handle not being able to see all those fine girls in their fine outfits looking so fine."

"Yeah, but you'd still have your other senses . . . like hearing," Andre said, smiling.

I knew what was coming next.

"Lorenzo, don't . . ." I said.

"Don't what, Shawn?"

He clawed at his shirt and started: "Ohhh, ohhh . . ."

I ignored him and focused on the screen.

I couldn't handle being blind. Not just because of the girls, but everything else. No blue sky. No yellow sun. No red sunsets. No green money. No Laker purple and gold. None of that. Just . . . darkness.

"How would you describe a color to a blind person?" I asked.

"What?" Andre said.

"If your friend had been born blind and you tried to describe a color, like, red, what would you say? 'Red looks like fire'? If he's blind, then he don't know what fire looks like, right, so that don't work. What would you do?" I asked.

"Are you serious, Shawn? We sitting here watching an old, blind Chinese dude slicing and dicing heads, and all you can think of is how you describe the color red to a blind man?" Lorenzo said, shaking his head.

It was dark in the theater, but I could still see the confused look on his dark face. More heads in the theater shushed us. We ignored them.

"Master *is* blind, Lorenzo, so it's not like the question came out of nowhere," Andre said, then added, "I never thought about that, Shawn. What does a blind man see in his head?"

"Will you guys be quiet? Master is about to find out who murdered his students," Trent said.

We quieted ourselves and stared at the screen. I tried to

imagine not being able to see Marisol's jet-black hair, Janine's bright red toenails, brown eyes, brown juice—brown juice I could do without.

I tried to replay the dream from last night, but nothing popped up, just more flashes of yellow. Instead, I created a new dream. I brushed Marisol's hair, and with each stroke, her head drooped lower and lower and her eyes closed like she was tired. The soft skin on her neck called to me. Should I kiss it?

"Vengeance is mine." Loud horns leaped from the speakers and the lights came up.

More than a few eyes looked like they wanted vengeance as they focused on us while leaving the theater. We ignored them and looked at each other.

"Y'all ready for another one?" Trent said.

"I don't know if I can sit through a whole 'nother movie, Trent," Lorenzo said. "We outta Ritz and I'm hungry."

"You always hungry, Lorenzo. Just because you got a big mouth, don't mean you always gotta stuff something in it," Trent said, laughing.

Lorenzo sniff-sniffed the air. Here it comes.

"Did I just get a whiff of a bag? Huh, Trent? You wanna get bagged up?" Lorenzo said, smiling at me, then turning his attention to Trent.

Trent lowered his head. He knew what was coming.

"Too late." Lorenzo rubbed his hands together, intertwined his fingers, popped his knuckles, then said: "Ya Mama so fat . . . her blood type is grease!" Laughter howled from the bottom of his belly.

"Ooooooooooooohhhhhhhhhh!"

Me and Andre almost slid onto the sticky floor from laughing so hard. We held on to the torn seats to keep from falling over. The theater was now empty, so we let it all out. Andre stood and did the laughing dance, slapping at his thighs while stomping his feet. I laughed myself backward into my worn and torn seat, sending my Stars into the air.

Trent snickered too. He knew Lorenzo'd got him. Good.

"He chopped off your head with that one, Trent," I said, slapping him on the back.

Andre shouted, imitating a nurse and cupping his hands to broadcast his voice, "Doctor, we need some blood in this woman *stat!*" His voice changed to a man's, and he said, "No, nurse, this woman needs Crisco. Run over to the store . . . *stat!*"

"Get me some chicken and a frying pan *stat!* We can't let this grade-A grease go to waste," Lorenzo added.

"Ooooooooooooohhhhhhhhhh!"

I chimed in with a *"stat"* and rolled back into my seat. The three of us held on to our sides for dear life.

"Anyway!" Trent said.

He bumped past us into the aisle.

"You guys up for another one or not?"

"I could do that again," I said, standing.

Andre asked for the time.

"It's 11:36," I said.

"It's almost lunchtime! I can't make it through another one without eating something," Lorenzo said, rubbing his belly.

Trent was about to open his mouth, but Lorenzo burned his eyes into him. He got the hint.

"Come on, let's at least see what's playing," Trent said, heading out the door.

The stench of fried fish greeted our noses as we stepped into the hallway. Trent led the way, pointing straight ahead and to the left. We crept over, making sure we couldn't be seen, then shuffled into the theater as quietly as four teenage mouths could.

The theater was already dark and like our theater mostly empty. A woman had her back to the camera as it approached slowly. The hum of a chain saw started up. She whipped around and screamed as the chain saw went to work.

"Man, I don't wanna see no horror flick," Lorenzo said.

"What's the matter . . . you scared, 'Zo?" Andre asked, grabbing Lorenzo's back.

"Yeah, right. I came to see butts getting kicked, not some chick screaming her head off," Lorenzo said.

"Yeah, I ain't up for no horror flick. Let's check out something else," I said.

We snuck into three more theaters with silent and swift ease, but all of them had something we didn't want to see. Trent opened up the door on theater number six, and sounds of punches and kicks jumped into our ears.

"This looks good," Trent said.

We groped our way through the dark theater, our eyes glued to the screen, watching an old man guzzle wine, laugh, and stagger his way through a group of men enjoying a meal. The sober men seated didn't think anything was funny. They taunted the old man and pushed him around. One of them snatched what looked like a vase from the old guy's hand and shouted, "You drunken old fool . . . I told you . . . NO MORE WINE!"

Assorted townspeople in assorted Chinese outfits gathered to watch. The old guy tried to walk away, but his drunken laughter and staggering kept him spinning in a slow circle as the men continued their taunts. A waiter ran out of what looked like a bar, carrying a sheet of paper. He thrust it at the old man and wagged his finger, "Not so fast. You still have to pay!"

The old drunk waved the waiter off and staggered away from the bar. A group of men on horses carrying staffs with yellow feathers and red sashes galloped into his path. Imperial guards?

"Aren't those the same dudes from the last movie?" Lorenzo asked. "These guys stay busy, huh?"

Trent shushed him.

A guard whose staff had more feathers and sashes than the others asked, "What seems to be the problem here?"

"Captain, this old drunk refuses to pay his bill," the waiter said, both arms tucked into one sleeve as Chinese waiters always seem to do in the movies. He pulled out a hand and wagged his finger at the old man again. "And this isn't the first time."

"Well"—the camera jumped from a full-body shot of the guard to an extreme close-up of his face—"this *will* be the last time he does." Horns blared and drums thundered.

"Here it comes — fight scene," Trent said.

"Who's gonna fight? Don't tell me this old drunk. He can barely walk," Lorenzo said, folding his arms as if to challenge the old man himself.

A pair of guards hopped off their horses to contain the drunk, but he kept out of their grip, his wine-weary legs dipping him out of trouble each time.

"You see that?" Trent said.

We did. The captain grabbed his staff and thrust it at the old dude's feet, stumbling and swaying and avoiding the staff. He was untouched. And laughing. Two more guards jumped in, but when they swung their staffs at the old man, he fought back. He staggered drunken punches at one guard, one-two, one-two, one-two, one-two, knocking the guard out. The other guard tried to grab him from behind, but the old man fell onto his back, avoiding the grab, rolled backward between the guard's legs, then kicked him in the butt from behind with both feet, all while on his back!

Trent sat up in his seat. "You see that?" He leaned on the seat in front of him, his eyes big as a kid's on Christmas Day.

"Go 'head, old man!" Lorenzo said, leaning on the seat in front of him too.

A tight shot of the captain standing next to one of his men filled the screen. The camera zoomed in closer on the captain's face: *"Drunken style!"*

We looked at each other with puzzled looks on our faces and said, "Drunken style?"

"Is that a real style?" I asked.

"I guess so. Check out the old dude," Lorenzo said, then added in the same voice he'd used when talking about Andre's brother, "He's doing his thing!"

The old guy escaped, punching and kicking his way through the guards in a drunken stagger, swigging wine between fallen bodies. Refreshed from each drink, he wiped his mouth and howled with drunken laughter: "HA-HA-HA-HA-HA-HA-HA-HA-HA-HAAAA!"

Lazy but powerful blows took out guards left and right as he moved with a certain drunken style and grace. I've never seen a drunk move that gracefully.

I snuck a look at the fellas as they focused on the screen. My own experiences with a drunk were much different: no kicking, no punching, no style, and definitely no grace. Just slurred words, staggered legs, heavy sighs, and tears. Lots of tears.

With each drunken movement on the screen, flash-bulbed images and sounds of Auntie blended in my head. Fist to the face—FLASH, *passed out across the floor.* Kick to the head—FLASH, *passed out on the couch.* Open palm to the throat—FLASH, *passed out on the kitchen table.* Fingers to the eyes—FLASH, *high-pitched yells for ice.* Sweep of the feet—FLASH, *crying whispers from spit-riddled lips.* Flying kick to the chest—FLASH, *an empty bottle.*

I've seen Auntie do a lot of things, but I've never seen her howl with laughter like that.

"Check it out . . . the old dude's gettin' away," Lorenzo said, pointing to the screen.

The old man staggered into the mountains, leaving behind a moaning and groaning trail of beaten-up guards.

"All of that *and* he didn't even pay his bill!" Trent said.

"I guess he's the hero, huh?" Andre said to no one in particular.

Yeah . . . imagine that; the hero is a drunk.

SIXTEEN

A WALL OF HEAT replaced the theater's cradle of cool as we stepped outside into the bright sun. The block, once empty, buzzed from a parade of foot traffic and activity.

"What time is it?" Andre asked, dropping the ball to the concrete to rest under his foot.

"LUNCHTIME!" Lorenzo answered, rubbing circles around his paunch as he scanned the block for grub.

"Why you so worried about time today, Andre?" I asked. I'm the one who usually worried about time. The fellas know I can't be late going to Auntie's, so I'm always checking my watch. But they live here, so they don't worry about time like I do.

"I just wanna make sure I see my brother before it gets dark. Once the sun goes down, he disappears like a ghost. And before you know it, he's gone back to the ship," Andre said.

Lorenzo's eyes perked up. His hand stopped rubbing his belly and draped around Andre's neck. "Yeah . . . we gotta make sure we see 'Dre's brother before he leaves," he said.

"Get away from me, Lorenzo," Andre said, ducking under Lorenzo's large mitt. "What's this 'we' stuff? I said I need to see my brother, not you."

Lorenzo placed his right hand over his heart and took a step back, pretending to take offense. "I can't believe what I'm hearing. Here I am trying to look out for a brutha and what do I get?"

Trent jumped in.

"I'll tell you what you get, Lorenzo . . ." Trent started. I knew what was coming when Lorenzo sniff-sniffed the air, so I interrupted, "I'm hungry too. Let's get something to eat."

My eyes searched the block for something, anything that our lone dollar bill could buy. A buck won't get you much in general, but if you're creative, you can find something.

"Let's check out this Louisiana Fried Chicken," Lorenzo said, pointing next to the theater. His sneakers started off in that direction, but the three of us stood still.

Andre tossed his ball between his hands and said, "I don't know, 'Zo. Last time I ate there, I had the runs the rest of the day. Where else can we eat?"

We couldn't be choosy with only a buck between us, but I knew where Andre was coming from.

"Let's just see what they got," Trent said.

We followed Lorenzo out of the shade and into the light. Andre bounced after him with Trent behind. I brought up the rear, but as I stepped out of the cool of the shade, I felt a hand on my shoulder from behind. Who's that? I spun around and jerked my hand up to hide my eyes from the sun. A green silhouette greeted me: "What's up, Shawn?"

It was a girl.

When I realized who was standing in front of me, my eyes grew as wide as the dead dude's right before his head got chopped off.

"Marisol?"

"What's going on?" she asked.

I stepped back into the shadow to rest my hand and eyes. I glanced back to see the door to Louisiana closing as Trent stepped inside. The fellas didn't realize I was missing.

Shoot! Marisol. I can't look at her without my heart hurting, let alone talk to her without sounding like an idiot.

"I'm here school shopping with my mom. She's in the shoe store just up the block," she said, pointing past Lucky Liquors, "but I saw you standing here and wanted to say hi."

She wanted to say hi to me? That stopped my wandering eyes long enough to focus on her outfit. Dotted green toes poked out of clear jellies. Green pedal pushers pushed their way up to a matching green sleeveless blouse. A waterfall of black hair cascaded over her glowing shoulders.

"Your hair is down."

Shoot! Why'd I say that? She's gonna think I was staring. Look away.

"Yeah, I washed it this morning, so I decided to wear it down for the day. I can't wear it the same way *all* the time," she said. Her right hand touched my elbow as she laughed and exaggerated "all."

Nice hands. Her soft touch relaxed my body for a moment. But only a moment. Now what do I say? Think, Shawn. Think.

Wait. Don't think. Just talk.

"It looks good like that. I didn't realize it was that long. When was the last time you cut it?"

What kind of stupid question was that, "When did you last cut it?" Does anybody remember when they cut their hair? Now she's gonna think . . .

"Can you believe I haven't cut it in two years?" she said, running her fingers through her hair. "The only reason I remember is because my brother dared me to cut it before my twelfth birthday. I said OK, but then he said I couldn't cut it again for at least two years. So"—she touched her hair again— "it's been two years and counting."

She tossed it out of her way to the back, then turned around and glanced back at me.

"It is getting long, huh?"

A sea of black flowed down the back of her green blouse, past her shoulders, splashing onto her butt. My eyes pounced on the sight like a cat on a mouse as her hips swiveled the long black strands side to side. Her pedal pushers were just tight enough to see the curve of her butt stretch the green fabric tight. Mother Nature must have been looking out for me because a light breeze brushed the hair aside long enough to reveal her green bottom in full bloom.

Pop! I snapped a mental picture for future viewing.

I wished I was those pants. My heart sped up. I tried to catch my breath. It felt like I was running a race. She repeated the question and turned again: "Don't you think?"

Shoot, I forgot the question. "Don't I think what?"

"My hair . . . it's pretty long now, right?"

Again she tossed her hair. Again I tried to catch my breath.

"Yeah . . . umm . . . it is pretty long," I said, picking up my train of thought.

Now I remember. Hair . . . cut . . . bet. Bet.

"So what'd you win?" I asked.

She shifted her weight to one side. Unlike Janine, her body didn't form into a full *S* shape. It curved. But not like Janine curved.

"What did I win . . . when?" she asked.

"For not cutting your hair? The bet?"

"Ohhhh, right . . . right. Nothing so far. But on my fourteenth birthday, my brother said he'd get me something special."

She's not even fourteen? I'm older than her? I always thought she was older than me.

"You mean . . . I'm older than you?"

Why did I say that?

"I guess so." Her eyes blinked at mine. "When is your birthday?" She ran her left hand through her hair and shifted her weight again. Is she left-handed?

My heart sped up. Speak, Shawn. Answer the question.

"Umm, it was a while ago. Back in January."

"You're not that much older than me. Mine is in a month, so I'll be caught up to you," she said, brushing her elbow at my side.

I tried to think of something to say, but my thoughts were interrupted by the sound of—

"OH, GOD! OH, GOD! OH, GOD!" punctuated with blasts of "YEAH! YEAH! YEAH!"

No! Tell me I didn't hear what I just heard. Tell me my ears are playing tricks on me. Tell me these three fools are not out here moaning and groaning. Tell me they are NOT doing this. Not here. Not now. Not in front of Marisol. Not . . . in front . . . of Marisol!

I spun around, expecting the worst. The image before me was even more embarrassing than I imagined. The fellas stood in front of Louisiana Fried Chicken facing us, a chicken wing in one of each of their hands, huddled together, moaning and groaning. Lorenzo once again clawed at his shirt with his free hand while Trent grabbed at his own sweat-stained shirt. Andre stood in front, circling his hand across the basketball, thrusting his hips and panting like a hot dog between moans and groans.

"Marisol—I gotta go."

I wish I had a flying guillotine to silence them from where I stood.

"I just . . . I gotta go!" I said, backing up.

If I could hear them, I knew she could. I turned around and picked up the pace, their voices getting louder with each step.

As I dashed away she called out: "*Adiós*, Shawn!"

I looked back over my shoulder and paused as she tickled a beauty-queen wave good-bye. Didn't she do that at the Tamale Hut yesterday?

I can't believe they did it again. I didn't like it when they did it before, and I didn't like it now. They changed their tune as I got closer: "Go, Shawnie! Go, Shawnie! Go, Shawnie-Shawnie-Shawn-Shawnie!"

I snatched the ball from Andre and bounced up the block, huffing past their embarrassing chant. Lorenzo tried to grab my shoulder, but I jerked out of his grip and sped up. They followed. I stopped.

"I hope you guys are happy," I said, jerking my hand up to shade my eyes. Andre and Trent flinched like I was gonna hit them.

"Everything was easy-breezy with Marisol until y'all ruined it!"

I dropped my head and focused on the sidewalk, tossing the ball from hand to hand.

"Come on, Shawnie-Shawn . . . we was just bustin' on you. Having fun. You know . . ." Lorenzo said.

"Yeah, I know . . . you meant to embarrass me!" I said. Loud.

"Naw, Shawn. Come on, man, it ain't like that," Andre said.

"We just . . . we saw you and your girl and . . ." he added.

"She's not my girl," I interrupted.

Lorenzo jumped in. "You could've fooled me. The way she was looking at you, smiling at you, touching your arm, running her fingers through her hair, showing you her butt. . . ." He imitated Marisol doing everything he just said: flitting his eyelashes at me, rubbing my arm, throwing his head back with his fingers brushing through his junior Afro, turning around to show me his big backside. I did everything I could to keep from laughing.

You know, she did touch me more than a few times, and she did run her fingers through her hair a lot but—"Hold on . . . what do you mean 'showing me her butt'?" I squeezed the ball with both hands.

Lorenzo continued, "Oh, come on, Shawn . . . you didn't see that? I saw her turn around a couple of times at least. Most girls, and I do mean most, know we check out their beehind, so they try to hide it from us. But not her, brutha man. Uh-uh. She had it on full display, just for you." He nudged me in the ribs and added, "I saw her turn around, looking back at you all sweet-like—"

" 'What do you think of my butt, Shawn? It's nice and round, isn't it?' " Trent interrupted, making Andre and Lorenzo bust up.

I slammed the ball into his stomach, making him cough and Andre and Lorenzo go quiet.

"Dang, Shawn, I'm just saying," Trent said, clutching his stomach and the ball.

"See, Shawn. Look at you. You got it bad for her, brutha man. But the thing is . . . the way she was acting"—Lorenzo shook his head—"she likes you too."

Was Marisol "checking me out," like Lorenzo said? Her smile flashed across my brain more than a few times as I replayed the scene in my head. Her hair swayed a bunch of times too. Hmmmm. She laughed a lot. And smiled a lot too. Maybe he was right.

"I'm telling you, Shawnie-Shawn, she was eyeballin' you,"

Lorenzo said, adding, "Girls usually try to avoid my eyes at all costs."

"That's 'cause they know you thinking about them naked," Trent said. That drew a laugh from Andre, Trent, *and* Lorenzo, who added, "Well, you know . . ."

I never even thought about what Marisol was thinking, standing there talking to me. Didn't she come up to me, even though her mother was up the block? She didn't have to do that. But she did. Didn't she show me her butt—I mean hair—not once, but twice?

I rewound back to that moment: me standing there squinting my eyes from the bright sun, noticing her bright green outfit glowing in the shade. My heart sped up again, and a smile worked its way across my face. Until . . . that sound. My smile disappeared.

"Yeah, but you guys messed that all up with your little show. I told you to cool it with them noises!"

I was mad. Marisol was gone, and I had no idea when I'd see her again.

I scanned the block for her green figure and sighed when the only thing even close was *Lucky Liquors* written in green letters a few feet from where we stood.

We headed up the block side by side. Andre snatched the ball from me.

"Cheer up, Shawn. Life is good if you got girls smiling at you. I almost forgot," Lorenzo said, pulling a silver package from his sweatshirt pocket and passing it to me, "we saved you some chicken wings. You'd be amazed at how many you can get for a dollar."

I unwrapped the foil to find two plump, grease-splattered fried chicken wings. My grumbling stomach did flips at the sight.

The breeze blew my thoughts back to Marisol . . . her smooth shoulders, her fluttering eyelashes, her bright smile, her black hair, her butt—oh, man—that butt.

And then . . . that sound. A man and a woman—"doing their thing"—moaning, groaning, scratching, clawing, and everything else, repeated for the world to hear from the mouths of three loud teenagers. Repeated in front of the chicken shacks. Repeated in front of the liquor stores. Repeated in front of the beauty parlors. Repeated in front of the check cashers and all the storefronts. Repeated in front of the one person I didn't want to hear them: the girl in green with silky black locks. The girl who made me forget red, forget blue. The girl who made me forget drunken sighs, forget slurred words. The girl who made me forget the hot sun and how to breathe. The girl with the nice butt, who showed it to me, twice. The girl who touched me with her smile: Marisol.

Dang!

I tore into the deep-fried flesh like a lion devouring a deer and managed to chew out a simple and plain "Thanks."

SEVENTEEN

HOUSES TOOK THE PLACE OF storefronts as we bounced in no particular direction. No more liquor stores. No more beauty parlors. No more chicken shacks. Just houses. White ones. Tan ones. Brown ones. Green ones. Blue ones. Yellow ones. Pink ones. Pink ones? Who would paint a house pink? I don't think I've ever heard somebody say, "You know, I would love to have a pink house."

I imagined who was in each house and what they were doing as we strolled by. How many couples were "doing their thing"? How many were just sitting there watching TV? How many were passed out on the floor?

"Where we goin'?" Trent asked, terminating his dribble at an intersection.

To our right was MLK. To our left was Auntie's house. Straight ahead was the Tamale Hut.

Lorenzo wiped the sweat from his forehead and said: "It's too hot. Them chicken wings made me thirsty."

"Yeah, my mouth is like a desert," Trent said, smacking his lips.

Trent wiped the sweat from his forehead, making me and Andre do the same. My mouth was dry too, but we were broke, so . . . another problem to solve.

"Well, we outta money, so what you wanna do?" I said.

Lorenzo flapped air under his shirt and spoke again: "You know what? My house is right down here. We could get something to drink and cool off for a li'l bit."

He pointed right. Same direction as MLK.

"Cool with me," dribbled from our lips, and we bounced off. Andre snatched the ball and weaved between me and Trent like we were pylons in his path.

"You going out for the basketball team at Marshall, Andre?" I asked.

Lorenzo led the way, with me and Trent close behind. Andre was a few steps ahead of us, but he drifted back between me and Trent. He wiped more sweat from his brow and answered, "Yeah, either freshman or JV. JV'll be much better, but I might have to start off on the freshman team. I don't know how it works."

"What about varsity?" Trent asked.

"Shoot, I ain't ready for that. Those guys are huge," he answered, tossing the ball between his hands.

"Yeah, but if you're good, you should be able to play for the best team, right?" I asked.

"If I make JV, I'll be happy with that," he replied, then

flipped the question to me, "What about you, Shawn? You going out?"

"I don't know. I haven't really thought about it," I said.

"Come on, Shawn, if I'm going out, you *gotta* go out—you *better* go out. We could be on the same team and everything," Andre said, nudging me with the ball.

The truth is I love playing ball and my skills are close to Andre's. I'm just not sure how good I am compared to everybody else; I would hate to make the team only to ride the pine.

"That's if I made the same team as you. If you make JV and I make the freshman squad, then . . ."

"Listen to you, talking like you a scrub or something. You know you can play, Shawn. I know you can play. You the only one that can check me on D, and I noticed you been splashing more and more J's every time we play," he said, bouncing the ball again.

I can't see myself play, so I don't know; it felt like my J was getting better, but . . .

"I don't know. I might," I said.

"You know, Shawn, if you play ball, you'll get cheerleaders cheering for you," Trent said, nudging me in the ribs from the other side.

That yanked Lorenzo's head around. "Somebody say cheerleaders?"

"Nothing. Nobody said nothing," I said.

I wonder if Marisol would be a cheerleader. She doesn't seem like the cheerleading type, but hey, you never know.

Lorenzo stopped at the end of the block and pointed right. "This way."

These houses were smaller than the ones we'd just passed. Rusted cars sat in front of most of them, and many of the lawns, small as they were, were taken over by tall weeds.

Nothing looked familiar. I don't remember the last time I've been on Lorenzo's block. Everything looked worn-out and old.

Auntie's block has nice houses, nice lawns, nice people — mostly old people but nice. But you can walk to the end of her block, cross over to the next block, and the houses are older and more worn-out, with not-so-nice lawns and not-so-nice people.

I remember walking that direction for a change of scenery one time to meet the fellas, and a bunch of the houses had pit bulls in the front yard. Not all of them, but it seemed like it. All of them were chained up, but they could still run from the porch to the sidewalk and snap their teeth and bark at you. I saw plenty of pooches but no masters and no bodies. No Miss Johnston waving from the porch. No Mr. and Mrs. Wright talking to another neighbor. Not even a sourpussed Miss Bricknell snipping rosebushes. Matter of fact, the only flowers I did see were those white, willowy weeds that you blow on to make a wish.

Compton was like that — one block well kept with old folks waving at you, another block broken down with pit bulls snapping at you.

Bass beats bounced with us as we approached the middle of the block. A pair of speakers sat in a house window across the street, sending out the sound. The house had a porch. The porch was filled with guys all dressed in black passing around a few forties. Weed smoke puffed from the porch and danced through the air.

No red? No blue?

Lorenzo led the way, with each of us in a line close behind. "Awww, shoot!" he said, stopping dead in his tracks, making our train bump into each other and knock him forward.

Trent, the caboose, stepped out of the wreck and asked, "What's up, 'Zo?"

Lorenzo focused on a telephone company van parked in the driveway of what must have been his house.

"Ay, 'Zo, don't your pops work for the phone company?" Andre asked, stepping out of the line.

"Yeah and he's here. He usually comes home for lunch. What time is it, Shawn?"

"One twenty-two."

"Dang, he's usually done and outta here by one."

"What's the big deal, 'Zo? It ain't like you did something wrong; you just going in to get something to drink," I said.

Does he have the same problem I have with Auntie?

He rubbed his belly and said, "The big deal is that my father is always getting on my case about getting a job. And I don't feel like hearing that right now."

"Don't even sweat it, 'Zo. We just going in to cool off. He should understand that," Trent said.

"I hope so. Let me see what kind of mood he's in. Hopefully he'll be out of here soon," he said, stepping onto his walk. "You guys follow me but hang back."

With that he fixed his sweatshirt, dusted himself off, and headed toward his porch. I caught the guys in black across the street checking us out. They knew 'Zo lived here, so hopefully everything was cool. Hopefully.

The gated door slammed shut as we stepped inside, making Lorenzo's father call out from the kitchen, "Who's there?"

The three of us grabbed a seat on the couch while 'Zo headed toward the voice.

"It's me, Pop."

We looked at each other and leaned our ears in toward the kitchen.

"Lorenzo? Boy, didn't I tell your fat, lazy behind to take out the trash this morning? I told you we gone get maggots and flies up in here."

"Yeah, Pop. Sorry. So what you still doing home?"

"Whatchu mean 'What you still doing home'? This is *my* house last time I checked. I can do whatever I want."

"I meant, don't you have work today?"

"Of course I do—what's wrong with you? I gotta work every day—something you know nothing about, boy. My lunch hour started late because one of the guys was sick. Pissed me off, my boss giving *me* more work this morning. It ain't like I don't work my behind off as it is. Shoooot . . . I wish I had time to be sick, but no . . . I gotta feed your hungry behind." Cabinets creaked open and slammed shut to emphasize his emotions.

"Boy . . . you eat the leftover neck bones?" The refrigerator squeaked open. "Ain't nothing in this fridge." *Slam!*

Creak. "Ain't nothing in these cabinets. We ain't got no leftovers . . . no sweet rolls . . . nothing! There ain't nothing to eat in this house . . . DAMN!"

We raised our eyebrows at each other and leaned in closer.

"I'm out there working my butt off every day to feed your fat behind, *and* your lazy-ass brother, and y'all eating me out of house and home! I come home for lunch and what do I find? *Nothing!* You and that knucklehead brother of yours are gonna start earning your way in this house, you hear?"

"Yes, sir."

Trent mimicked 'Zo's "Yes, sir" with a whisper that broke into a snicker. Andre shushed him from his spot on the couch sandwiched between me and Trent, then grabbed a *Jet* magazine from the coffee table. He almost jumped out of his skin when 'Zo's dad boomed again: "Look here, Lorenzo, pretty soon you'll be old enough to earn your own money, and when that day comes, that's exactly what you gonna do. . . . Matter of fact, what are you doing here?"

The louder he got, the more we hunched into the small couch, our bodies already squeezed together.

"Umm. I'm with my friends. . . . We was thirsty."

A cabinet door slammed with the reply, "Thirsty? You was THIRSTY? What . . . you think this house is your own personal filling station, boy? Huh? You think you can just bring your friends all up in here to eat or drink whatever you please, whenever you please? HUH? Boy, I swear . . ."

The voice trailed off and the house grew silent — too silent. Andre held up the *Jet* beauty for inspection. Me and Trent leaned in to check it out.

"Miss Jacqueline Price — Virgo," Andre read.

"Just like me," Trent said.

"Loves horror movies, jazz, and making quilts," Andre continued.

"I'd love to lay on a quilt with her," Trent chirped.

The conversation in the kitchen bubbled back up.

"So where are your little hoodlum friends?"

"They in the living room. But they ain't hoodlums, Pop."

"Don't you back-sass me, boy!"

Andre dropped Miss Jacqueline Price — Virgo, and the three of us sat up straight, thinking 'Zo's dad was about to come in. The coast seemed clear, so we picked up where we left off.

So did 'Zo's dad: "How many of you is it?"

"Four, counting me."

"And not one job between the four of you?"

Silence.

"No, sir."

Trent mimicked him again. And snickered again.

"I told you, Lorenzo. You hang out with three losers and you'll be the fourth."

Andre mouthed the question "Loser?" and raised his eyebrows. We answered by doing the same.

"But, Pop, we aren't—"

"I know your hungry mouth is not talking back to me."

"Sorry, Pop."

"There's gonna be some changes around here, you hear me, boy? I don't work hard to not be able to eat lunch in my own damn house!"

"Sorry, Pop."

Slam!

"Boy . . . sorry don't feed me. Look at this. A grown man

eating a sorry peanut-butter-and-jelly sandwich with the butt parts of the bread!"

The word "butt" triggered snickers from Trent and 'Dre and popped a green picture of Marisol into my head.

Rough work boots rattled the linoleum floor and our nerves, making our snickers disappear.

"I'll deal with you later. . . . Right now I gotta get back to work."

'Zo's father rumbled out of the kitchen and into the living room, a tiny sandwich jammed in his fat paw. The speed of his breeze almost knocked us over as we stood to acknowledge him with our best teeth-baring smiles.

He replied with a grunt, paused, then turned back to his son. "What you need to do is look for a job. Your 'hanging out' days are numbered. You hear me? Numbered. I ain't coming home to no peanut-butter-and-jelly sandwich again. No sir! Things gonna change around here, Lorenzo . . . OH, YEAH . . . THINGS GONNA CHANGE!"

He thrust the sandwich in Lorenzo's face, smearing a spot of peanut butter near his mouth. 'Zo licked it off as quickly as it went on.

The door opened fast and slammed faster, and the hurricane was gone.

Lorenzo stood in his living room, numb, and mumbled, "It's some Kool-Aid in the fridge. Help yourselves," before heading back into the kitchen.

Trent got up to follow. Me and Andre looked at each other, shrugged, and did the same. Three cups clapped on the counter, interrupting the silence. The clear cups became red as we poured ourselves cool drinks.

Lorenzo stepped outside for the trash when Trent asked: "'Zo, you got any ice?"

Lorenzo gave his reply as he stepped back through the door. "First I'm the garbage man, now I'm the ice man?"

"I'm just asking . . ."

Lorenzo's arms crossed and he exhaled. "Where is ice usually, Trent?"

Me and Andre shook our heads at Trent as he went for the fridge. 'Zo huffed toward the living room, then returned a minute later, sitting down to pour himself some Kool-Aid.

We joined him at the table. Ice clinked in Trent's glass as he took a sip.

"You put ice in there?" Lorenzo accused Trent.

"Well . . . yeah . . . I . . ." Trent said, putting his glass down and pushing it away like he'd gotten caught trying to steal.

Lorenzo shook his head and remained silent. His father just threw a blanket of clouds over the sunshine of our day, making his son, our friend, silent — painfully silent. No talking about girls. No talking about food. No jokes. No "Oh, God's." And no bags.

"What should we do now?" I asked.

Andre swallowed the rest of his drink, stood up, and said, "Let's go play some ball. I haven't whopped up on you in a while, so let's go," he added, shaking Lorenzo's shoulder.

"Yeah, MLK ain't too far," I said.

Trent stood and the three of us hovered over 'Zo, waiting

to go. He just sat there swirling his empty glass in a slow, rhythmic circle.

Trent stepped closer to him, folded his arms, and said in his strongest voice, "Ya Mama so black, her blood type is gravy."

Me and Andre raised our eyebrows to each other, then burst into laughter. Trent's attempt at stealing Lorenzo's bag came out so wrong, it was hard not to.

Lorenzo stared at Trent in silence. His once-swirling glass was now still. An unreadable look covered his face. Then he shook the look away and slowly smiled. The smile bubbled into a laugh as he sniff-sniffed the air, stood tall, and said, "I don't know *what* that was, Trent, but it sounds like somebody wants to get bagged up."

EIGHTEEN

WE STEPPED OUT of the calm of Lorenzo's house onto a chaos-filled block. Taunting shouts replaced the once-bumping music and hovered over a mix of old men in feathered fedoras, young women with babies on their hips, old women in house-dresses and stocking caps, and young men in stocking caps sipping forties.

"What's going on?" Andre asked.

Face after face popped out of the shadows, asking the same thing. When we got here earlier, the guys across the street were the only ones hanging out. They were still there, but they weren't hanging out on the porch anymore; they stood in the center of the storm, and one of them was exploding full force.

He was the biggest and oldest brutha by far: thick arms swung on his wide torso, creased black Dickies covered his tree-trunk legs, while his black sweatshirt stretched across his basketball-shaped belly. Black Stars on his feet completed the package. All black? In the summer?

A shower cap on his head reflected the sun into my eyes, making it hard to see. Through all the bodies and noise and commotion, I saw him swinging a baseball bat and heard him shout something. Part of me wanted to get closer to hear, but mostly I wanted to run the other way.

"What's he saying?" Trent asked.

"I don't know and I don't care. Let's get out of here," I said.

Lorenzo poked his head out over the crowd and got drawn into the storm. He stepped past an old man perched on a cane and a woman in a bright pink housedress, then stopped and got on his tiptoes.

"Awww, that's just Crazy Ray. He must be dusted again," Lorenzo said.

"Dusted?" I asked.

"Yeah, you know . . . on angel dust . . . PCP. That stuff make him crazy all the time. That's why they call him Crazy Ray," Lorenzo said.

"If it make him crazy, then why he keep doing it?" Andre asked.

"Why do you keep playing ball? Because you can. Same as him. He likes to sprinkle a little dust into his weed . . . puff-puff and that's it," Lorenzo said, his feet flat and now staring at us. His heels rose again and his head with it as he said, "Somebody must've said something to set him off though."

"Like what?" I asked.

"Shoot . . . when you dusted, it could be anything," 'Zo said, making his way to the center of the storm.

"Lorenzo . . . don't you think it's a bad idea to approach somebody on dust swinging a bat?" I asked.

It seemed like a logical question, but he waved me off and walked closer. Andre and Trent trailed close behind. Feeling like an idiot on the driveway alone, I joined them in the street. The crowd grew by the second. Andre clutched the ball at his side, but Trent bumped him and the ball dropped.

"Dang, Trent . . . I dropped the ball. Y'all see it?"

I saw it. I reached down to grab it, but the crowd shifted and a female foot kicked it away. Shoot.

"It's over there . . . rolling," Lorenzo said cool and calm, before shouting with excitement, "Oooooh, shoot . . ."

The ball rolled through the crowd, headed for Crazy Ray. His thick, wooden bat sliced the air as he shouted at the top of his lungs: "It's game time, bay-bay! Who wants to play?! Who want some of what I got, HUH?"

The crowd egged him on:

"Go 'head, Ray!"

"Grand slam, baby! Grand slam, Ray!"

"Knock it out the park!"

Ray didn't notice the ball rolling his way, but our eight eyes did.

"Shoot, man, it's right there. What we gonna do?" Trent asked, hopping with anxiety.

The crowd focused on the bat and the big crazy brutha

swinging it, not the basketball rolling his way. One of his friends kept shouting, "Cool out and swig this forty, Ray," but he wouldn't.

"We gotta get the ball and get outta here," I added.

Ray's friends gave up and watched the show like everybody else. The crowd wisely gave him space. The ball rolled to a stop behind him, resting alongside the wheel of a beat-up brown truck on the driver's front side. The bed of the trunk was filled with a bunch of lawn stuff, and Ray swung his way backward into what looked like a lawn mower. The top of the mower poked him in the back, making Ray swing around.

He spun and screamed at the mower, "Whatchu want? HUH? Whatchu want? You ain't taking me out! It's game time, podna! Game time! YOU WANT SOME OF THIS . . . HUH!?"

He marched to the front of the truck.

"You ain't taking me out! It's my time . . . GAME TIME!" he shouted, fire blazing in his eyes, as he raised his bat to the sky to swing on the front windshield.

He brought his arms back and with his right foot took a step backward—right onto our ball. Everything sped up like a scene from *The Flash*: The ball rolled forward—he fell backward—the bat flew in the air—the ball rolled from the front wheel to the back—Lorenzo and Andre sprinted for the ball—me and Trent did the same—the bat crashed to the ground, just missing me and Trent's heads as we ducked—two guys in black went for the bat—two more in black went after me and Trent, fists raised, arms cocked, ready to swing.

"They cool—they cool—they cool!" Lorenzo shouted.

He stood just a few feet away, but the two formed a wall of black and blocked us. The left side said, "They witchu, 'Zo?"

"Yeah . . . we just wanted our ball." He held up the ball like a rescued flag. "See?"

The wall separated and they left to check on Ray.

"Let's get out of here, man!" Andre said.

"You ain't got to tell me twice," Lorenzo agreed.

The crowd moved in on Crazy Ray, so we headed out. Fast.

"Where'd that ball come from?" popped out of the commotion and put more pep in our step.

We hot-stepped to the end of the block, looked back, and saw the crowd still there. We were glad we weren't.

"Man who *was* that?" Trent asked.

More like *what* was that?

"I told you—Crazy Ray," Lorenzo said matter-of-factly. "My oldest brother said he went to Marshall when he was there, but he never finished. That's 'cause Ray loved him some weed. He got thrown out of school when his baseball coach caught him passed out in the dugout with an empty forty bottle dangling from his hand and a bag of weed under his head. Ever since then, anything related to baseball seems to put him over the edge—especially if he's dusted."

"He must be already on the edge if that's *all* it takes," I said.

"Yeah, but see, when you dusted, you ain't you—you somebody else. My brother said Ray got bored with straight weed, so one of his boys hooked him up with some dust and that was it. When he hit that stuff, he got all pumped up . . . like he was a superhero."

Our sneakers were on autopilot headed for MLK. We paused at an intersection, waiting to cross. Andre bounced a rhythm that Trent followed with each button push. I looked toward the intersection but kept looking back, expecting to turn around and find Crazy Ray slicing the air with his bat.

"You think this was something? Shoot . . . one time he was down at this market over on Wilmington, right, and he just started eating stuff right off the shelf: boxes of cereal, cookies, candy, chips . . . you name it. So the manager comes out and says he's gonna call the cops. But by this time Ray is in the fruit section, grabbing oranges and squeezing the juice out of each one like it ain't nothing into his wide-open mouth. Juice is everywhere—dripping all over his hand, his mouth, down his white T-shirt and stuff, but he didn't stop there. Then he grabs some big ole cantaloupes and starts crushing them one at a time with his bare hands."

"Talk about orange crush." Trent laughed.

"Then what happened?" I asked.

"Then an ambulance rolls up with a couple of cops following. Four guys jump out and wrestle him onto one of them things with wheels to take him away. His body kept jumping around, so they had to strap him down, and they strapped him down, all right—arms, legs. They even had to shove a mouthpiece in his mouth so they could strap his head down. By the time they were done, he couldn't move nothing!"

Green light. We crossed. Andre led the way, with me and Trent on either side of 'Zo.

"Then what happened?"

"Dang, Shawn . . . what am I . . . the news? After that, I

don't know. I'm sure it couldn't have been too good if he got taken away by an ambulance and some cops, with his whole body strapped down."

MLK was up ahead, but the image of fire-filled eyes and a bat kept popping into my head.

"How many times you think that happens?" I asked.

"I don't know. Stuff like that only seems to happen on county day. Today *must* be county day. Shawn. . . . Didn't we walk past a bunch of long lines today?"

"I don't remember. Probably."

"Your watch can tell what date it is, right?"

"Yeah, why?"

"Betchu it's the fifteenth!"

I glanced down at my Timex runner's watch. A quick press of a button proved Lorenzo right.

"Yup—the fifteenth."

"I knew it. Crazy stuff like that always happens on county day. Most people get they checks and pay bills or buy food or clothes or whatever . . . but some people get they checks and lose they mind. I'm telling y'all," he said, shaking his head, "anything can happen on county day."

NINETEEN

WE'D BEEN TO MLK plenty of times since our run-in with the Pirus, but every time I stepped from the sidewalk to the grass, the taste of dust coated my tongue and my back tensed up.

I scanned the park. The court was hopping with a game—mostly older guys, possibly high schoolers. A group of girls double-Dutched near the courts chanting:

"Mama's in the kitchen
cookin' rice.
Daddy's outside
shootin' dice.
Baby's in the cradle
fast asleep,
and here come Sister
with the H-O-T.

With each letter in "hot," the rope whipped the air and concrete harder, in between swings, barrettes bouncing in intricate braids. Voices from the rec room floated out toward us between skips.

"Looks like M-L-K is the place to be to-day," Lorenzo sang out, headed for the courts. Andre bounced with him while me and Trent hung back, checking out the sights and sounds MLK had to offer on this hot, sunny day.

"Ay, Shawn, ain't that Black Bruce over there?" Trent asked, nodding his head left.

I looked in the direction of his nod and found a tall brutha dwarfed by a tree. His long, lanky body moved in an all-black kung-fu suit with white tassels tied in front. The outfit looked like a Chinese waiter's uniform. Each long leg thrust out to the side in a kick. First the right leg — *kick*. Then the left — *kick*. Again. And again. With each kick, his mouth moved, but no sound came out.

"That could be him . . ." I said, focusing in on the face. "It's hard to tell 'cause he's so far away."

"Let's go check him out," Trent said, starting in that direction.

"Maybe we should just hang back. He's obviously alone and over there for a reason."

"You probably right." He paused, then aimed his vision at the court. My eyes looked onto the court as well. Andre grabbed the ball from 'Zo and walked over to the game in action. He exchanged words with a shirtless baller.

"Does Andre know him?" I asked.

"I don't know. Let's go see," Trent said.

Our question was answered as we got closer to Andre and heard: "Wuzzup, little brother? Where you been?"

The game was over and Andre's brother stood shirtless, slapping five with Andre and giving a "What's up" to 'Zo. Me and Trent walked up, and Andre introduced us: "You remember Shawn and Trent?"

His brother nodded and gave us a soul clap. Then 'Dre asked, "You guys remember my brother, Randy, right?"

We nodded, even though we only saw his brother once in a blue moon. I think that's the first time he ever told us his name.

"So, Randy . . . what you been up to since you got home?" Lorenzo asked, poking Andre in the side with an elbow and a wink.

Trent snickered. I sighed and looked to the court. A group of guys were playing 21, and one of them was shooting a free throw. He didn't bend his knees and he didn't flick his wrist, so I knew what was coming before he even shot the ball: a brick. And there it was, clanging off the rim and bouncing out of bounds in terrible form. Dad always told me: bend your knees and spring into your shot. Release with a flick of the wrist and follow through. This dude did none of that. I felt sorry for the backboard.

Randy laughed and said, "You know what I was doing."

He eyeballed Lorenzo and Andre, then added, "And I know y'all was still there even when I told you to leave."

His arms folded and he stared the four of us down. Was he pissed or just giving us a hard time?

The free-throw bricker tapped Randy on the shoulder and

said, "Ay . . . y'all wanna run? We wuz about to run a three-man, but y'all got four so we can run a full."

Randy raised his eyebrows at us as if to say, "Wanna play?"

We looked at each other, then at the other players. They were all big. Much bigger than us. Our hesitation made Randy say, "Come on, y'all. Don't be scared—we just ballin.'"

But we were scared. And it showed as we stepped onto the court. Andre, usually talking smack to whoever guarded him, stood silent as the bricker stood next to him on D. Trent and 'Zo were on one team, and me and 'Dre were on the other team; 'Dre's brother was with us. Me and Trent guarded each other, but 'Zo got stuck guarding this big brick-house of a brutha.

Randy tossed the ball into Andre. "Straight to fifteen," he said as Andre brought the ball up.

Everybody on the other team stepped up to guard their man. Bodies flew around the court with each bounce of the ball. Sneakers shuffled left to right—right to left.

"I got li'l man right here," popped out of Bricker's mouth.

Andre was greeted on the other side of the half-court line by Bricker's crouching spiderlike body and almost turned the ball over. Almost.

In the blink of an eye, 'Dre pulled out his between-the-leg spin move and spun right past him. Bam-bam, cross, spin right . . . gone—just like he had been doing all day. When 'Dre spun, I escaped Trent and ran to my favorite spot on the court, the right elbow of the free-throw line, where Andre was headed.

We've done this play on 'Zo and Trent so many times, I knew what was coming next. A body stepped up to help out on 'Dre. I got open and he hit me with a crisp chest pass. Bricker hustled past Trent to help guard me as I caught the ball. Uh-oh. I pump-faked him into the air and watched his body sail right past me.

Shoot the ball: bend your knees, spring into the shot, sign it with your wrist, and follow through . . . just like Dad taught you — swish.

"Nice shot, Shawn," Andre said, slapping me five as I made my way up the court.

Randy pushed his little brother on the back of his head and said, "Somebody been practicing," then shouted, "One-zip, us."

Bricker pointed in my direction and said, "Ain't go be no mo' of them, homey," then pointed at Trent and said, "Lock him down," talking about me.

Now, I been playing with Trent for a while, and he can't guard me. Plain and simple. That's not trash talk; that's just a fact. Out of all of us, Trent is the weakest. He plays hard and he tries, but the three of us are just better than him. I don't know why — that's just how it is. I felt bad for him right now, though, because if I torched Trent during this game, he might get bawled out by this dude who can't even make a free throw. I didn't want that. But I also didn't want to lose.

The next batch of points came fast and furious: a dunk by 'Dre's brother here, a dunk from the other team there, a jump shot by 'Dre here, a layup by 'Zo there. The four of us and Randy were playing pretty good—even Trent managed to make a few jump shots. I didn't take it easy on him; I just didn't hound him on D like I do when I play Andre.

Throughout all of this, Bricker still had that look in his eye. After I made another jump shot, he yelled at Trent, "If that's your man, get up on him!" Then he rushed Trent to show him, knocking him down in the process.

But that was just the beginning.

If somebody dropped a pass: "Catch the ball, PLEASE!"

If he dropped a pass: "Why you throwing it over there when I'm over here?"

If a teammate missed an open layup: "Can somebody PLEASE make a layup?"

If he missed an open layup: "It slipped off my fingers."

He seemed to forget about all the open jumpers he missed and all the times he went one on five as he said this to his teammates. This wasn't lost on me or Andre as we tried to encourage our friends on the other side; we been playing together for so long that it was hard seeing some knucklehead all in our friends' faces. Randy tried to shut this clown up too. More than once he splashed in Bricker's face, shaking his head and staring at him while backpedaling up court. But guys like that only get more upset. They take it personal, then they take it out on somebody else.

Andre brought the ball up, and Bricker met him on the other side, swiping at Andre's face like a cat to distract him. I came over to help, but he tried to jump up on me too. I weaved left, then right, then Andre threw the ball over his head to me. I threw it right to another teammate. Randy raced up court, pointed to the rim, and caught a quick lob for an easy dunk. Sweet.

I slapped high five with Randy as he ran back, but my smile disappeared as I turned around and saw Andre on the ground clutching his stomach. Randy saw it too. He ran over to his little brother and said, "'Dre, what happened?"

Andre clutched his stomach as he pulled himself up and said, "I'm cool, just caught a forearm."

Randy rushed Bricker, stuck his finger in his face, and said, "Ay, man, keep yo' hands to yo'self."

Bricker held up his hands as if to say, "What did I do?"

Randy backed off, his eyes burning into Bricker, and shouted, "Game point—our ball!"

One point and we'd win. Andre was standing but still clutching his stomach. He didn't look good.

"'Dre . . . you cool?"

"Yeah, Shawn, why don't you bring it up."

I didn't want to bring it up, especially if Bricker was going to be swiping at my face. But I had no choice. I wiped my palms off on the bottom of my shoes and took the ball out. I tossed it into Andre, who tossed it right back. Bricker jogged up slow, following 'Dre, then he darted back over to me. The instant he broke for me, I lobbed it over his head to Andre, who pushed the ball up court. I raced to follow but then . . . *BLAM!*

Blue sky. Purple sky. Yellow clouds. Red birds. Green sun. Blue sun. White shadow. Black shadow. Voices. And pain.

"Shawn."

Mama waking me up.

"Shawn."

Auntie calling for ice.

"Shawn!"

Marisol running up behind me.

A cough. My cough. Inhale. Cough-cough. Exhale.

"Shawn . . . you all right?"

I blinked the colors away and stared up at four tall shadows. The tallest blocked the sun from my eyes. It crouched down and the sun broke through.

"You all right, man?"

Randy?

The light struck me in the eyes and pierced pain into my brain. I exhaled.

"Catch your breath," the voice said.

I sat up. My head throbbed, my chest felt like an elephant had stepped on it, and everything looked and sounded fuzzy. A loud voice cut through, "If li'l man can't stand the heat, he need to stay out the kitchen!"

Bricker.

Randy jumped up, knocking the fellas in the process. "What I tell you?" he said.

I tried to stand but couldn't catch my breath.

"Don't get up too quick," Andre said, adding, "He got me too."

What's he talking about?

"You took a forearm to the chest," Andre said.

Trent added, "And I think you hit your head when you fell."

I ran my fingers across the back of my head and didn't feel any blood. Good.

"Still game point. Check ball," Randy said.

"Well, let's go," Bricker replied.

Yeah, let's go.

"Shawn . . . you sure you cool?" Andre asked as I tossed the ball back to him after one dribble.

Inhale. "Yeah. Let's go." Exhale.

I shook the cobwebs away with each pass of the ball. My lungs were working overtime. Bricker was *not* going to win. Somebody needed to shut him up, but who?

I caught a pass and scanned the court. Where was everybody? Trent crowded closer. Where was Andre? There he was, moving down low. I quick-flicked it to him in the corner. Bricker saw this and yelled out, "Trap!"

He and a teammate rushed over, but Andre was ready for the trap. He tossed a high pass behind them to Randy, swooping in from the right. Randy caught it, came down, and bounced back into the air in one quick motion. Bricker backed off Andre. Instead of rising with Randy, Bricker got under him and took out his legs, flipping him over and onto his back.

We rushed him.

"AY, MAN! What's wrong witchu?"

That was Andre.

Once again Bricker threw his hands in the air, all innocent, and said, "What?"

Andre got up in his face, even though Bricker was a good couple of inches taller than him, and said, "What's your problem?"

Bricker hovered over Andre and said, "Ain't no problem, homey. . . . You got a problem?"

Andre stepped in close enough to smell Bricker's breath.

"Yeah, I got a problem. I got a problem with you acting like this is football."

Andre? Is that you, my brutha?

His eyes were locked on Bricker's.

"I got plenty mo' where that came from," he said, lunging at Andre, but he was held back by his teammates.

Me, Lorenzo, and Trent rushed over and formed a wall between Bricker and Andre. Randy lay behind us, sprawled on the ground in pain.

"What y'all gone do now? Huh? Yo' brother cain't help you now! Look at 'im . . . holding his back, crying like a bitch!"

We just stood there as Bricker grinned and laughed. What *are* we gonna do? I wasn't about to swing on him, and if Andre did, then he's even crazier than I thought. Instead, Andre bent down to check on his brother, who managed to sit himself up.

"Randy, you all right?"

His legs wobbled but he got on his feet. "Yeah. I'm cool."

"Our ball," Bricker shouted.

"I don't think so," Randy said.

"You turned it over when you dropped it," Bricker said.

Was he serious?

Randy shook off the pain and stepped up to Bricker's face, hovering inches over him.

"I dropped it 'cause you pulled that bullshit bridge move, taking my legs out from under me—that's a foul. So I'm callin' it. Our ball," Randy said, cool as ice, grabbing the ball.

All Bricker could do was raise his hands and say, "All right, all right."

Randy twisted and turned his torso a few times to stretch, then shouted with more spring in his step, "Ball's in."

He flipped it to Andre. Andre brought the ball up, with Randy trailing behind him. I ran near the baseline. Right to left. A teammate set a screen, and I ran left to right as 'Dre dribbled up top. Bricker jumped out to guard him and swiped at Andre's face, but 'Dre stayed cool. He kept his body between Bricker and the ball, then turned around to talk smack, his eyes focused on Bricker's like Master swinging his chain, about to chop some heads.

"Game's 'bout to be over," he said, dribbling the ball in circles between his legs like we've seen him do so many times.

"Oh, is that right?" Bricker said.

Andre replied with the ball. Bang-bang between the legs. Right to left—left to right, spin, and . . . gone. Again. Straight to the basket. Faster than I've ever seen. Past Bricker, past Lorenzo, past two more players, flicking the ball up and over the brick-house brutha's tree limb of an arm like a balloon . . . higher and higher and higher and higher.

Time stopped ticking. Sneakers stopped squeaking. Mouths stopped speaking as silence filled the park. The whisper of a breeze gave way to the whisper of net cords caressing the ball in a *swish* as it dropped back to earth.

Andre's eyes followed the ball into the basket until it dropped. When he landed, his momentum carried him in a circle, back to where Bricker stood. He stopped, stood tall face-to-face, and said the only thing he could say: "Game."

TWENTY

"CHECK YOU OUT . . . talking smack and backing it up!" Randy said, draping his arm around Andre's shoulder and shaking it.

Bricker was long gone and the court was now empty.

As good as Andre is, none of us have ever seen him do anything like that before. I slapped him on his back and said, "What got into you, 'Dre?"

He shrugged. "I 'on't know. I just did it. I kept thinking about the pain in my stomach and seeing you on the ground and seeing Randy on his back and . . ."

His words dribbled into space as his eyes did the same; the movie was replaying in his head.

Randy snapped him back into reality. "So you going out for the team?"

"I was planning on it."

"You keep playing like that and you'll be on the varsity no problem," Randy added.

"Really? I was just hoping to make freshman or JV, but hey . . ."

"You too, Shawn. I'm telling you . . . both of y'all . . . in the back court . . . man . . . you guys will be killing it."

Then Randy grabbed *my* shoulder and shook it. That was the first time I imagined myself running on the same court with Andre—freshman, JV, whatever. If we played like we did today, who knows?

"Yeah, maybe so," I said.

The five of us took over a couple of benches and stretched our exhausted bodies. Lorenzo sprawled on his back as usual while Trent sat on the top of the same bench next to him. Andre and Randy took over another bench, spreading their arms like wings and extending their legs like landing gear. I stretched my limbs across the cushy green grass in front of both benches and exhaled; that last game wiped me out.

"Y'all play down here a lot?" Randy asked.

"Yeah . . . but not just here," Andre answered.

Lorenzo added, "Sometimes we go over to DuBois or Carver. Depending on . . ."

I knew what he was gonna say and I'm sure Trent and 'Dre knew too, but nobody wanted to finish the sentence. Randy got the hint and finished it for us.

"Depending on where the Crips and Pirus are, right?"

"Yeah," Andre said.

Our heads dropped as we nodded.

"Man, I hear you. You guys haven't had any problems, though, right?"

Again we looked at each other. Our silence spoke louder than words.

"What happened?"

Andre told his brother what happened last year with the Pirus in this very same park near this very same court. As the story trickled out, my eyes darted around the park. The four Pirus choking weed smoke reappeared on the court we were just victorious on, and my mouth filled with the taste of dirt. Andre got to the part about his brother's shorts, and Randy's grip tightened on the bench.

Bloodred smeared my brain when he mentioned the golf club swinging on him. And me. BAM. My back tightened so I stood, stretching my arms east and west. When he finished, it was silent among the five of us. At last Randy spoke: "Man . . . I didn't know about all that."

"How could you? You weren't here, so . . ." Andre said, fading into silence. A few breaths later, he finished, "It ain't nobody's fault, though. That's just how it is."

Lorenzo sat up wide awake in his seat and added, "Yeah, that's why we have the color check."

"The what?" Randy asked.

"The color check. Before we go out anywhere in the morning, we just make sure none of us is wearing blue or red," 'Zo said.

"It's funny you say that because I'm in my navy shorts. Y'all realize that?" Randy said.

Actually, we didn't. At least I didn't. And I usually catch everything.

"Things change as you get . . . bigger," he added with a flex of his chest.

I hadn't realized how much bigger he was until that moment. Our bodies, except for Lorenzo, were tall but all skin and bones. Randy was not only taller, but filled out with muscles.

"In time you guys will see that too," he continued.

"I don't know, Randy, I'm the biggest one of all of us, and that don't change a thing," Lorenzo offered.

"Yeah, you big but . . . not in a good way . . . know what I mean?" he said with a sly laugh.

Me and Trent laughed too, Trent's laughter bubbling louder than mine.

"I'm sorry, Lorenzo, man," Randy said. "I'm just saying . . . being big and being strong are two different things. On the ship, I play ball, lift weights, run, and do other stuff to stay in shape. But see, I been doing that since high school."

The four of us nodded as Randy went on.

"When I was your size, Andre, I had a hard time keeping up with other guys on the court. I was skinny and quiet and always getting pushed around, but the taller I got, the more I hit the weights to fill out my frame. The bigger I got, the better about myself I felt," he said, running his hands over his upper body. "I didn't want to be *all* muscles . . . just get a six-pack and some guns to show off," he added, flexing his arms with a grin.

We laughed.

He continued, "Anyway, I know how it is, bro, and I wish there was something I could do for you, but you gotta do it yourself. When it comes to getting picked on, you gotta be confident in yourself and believe that nobody can mess with you."

"So . . . this was my fault?" Andre said, tossing the ball back and forth.

"I ain't saying that at all. What I'm saying is . . . some targets are easier than others. You guys are still young, so that right there makes you a target. But you take the target off your back when you . . . when you got that look in your eyes that says, 'I ain't afraid of nobody,' ya know?"

"Now Randy, that's all Kool and the Gang . . ." Lorenzo started.

"Cool and the what?"

"Kool and the Gang. You know, like the music group. You ain't never heard that? Man, you been at sea too long," Lorenzo said.

Randy laughed as 'Zo went on. "That's just something we say. Anyway, just because I think somebody ain't gonna beat me up doesn't mean they won't. Right?"

"Right. Right. But . . . you guys are all big, growing boys. . . ."

"Some of us are bigger than others," Trent said, rubbing Lorenzo's belly like a Buddha. 'Zo smacked his hand and sucked his teeth.

"So, Randy . . . what's it like living on a ship? Don't you go crazy being cooped up?" I asked.

"It's cool, for the most part, but sometimes you find

179

yourself staring at the sea, ready to jump in," he answered with a laugh.

"What y'all do for fun?" Lorenzo asked. He eyeballed Andre and winked.

Randy didn't take the bait. He leaned forward with his answer. "I told you . . . play ball and work out mostly. I read a lot. A bunch of us play cards: spades, whist, poker, whatever. A couple of guys got bands and stuff. There's a lot of people on the ship, so we have plenty to do. It gets boring when you go out on the deck and all you see is ocean every which way you look. It's cool to relax and think, but, man . . . sometimes you feel like you on an island. And you are—it just moves."

"Any fine ladies on that island? Maybe wearing bikinis?" Lorenzo asked.

Randy settled back into his seat and spread his arms across the bench.

"Of course we got girls on the ship, but those ain't the ones to go after," he said, sitting up and hunching forward in his seat. A grin crept across his face as he threw in, "The ones you go after are in port. And, man . . ." he said, settling back into his seat, "do we go to a lot of ports: the Philippines, Japan, Hawaii, Thailand, Guam . . . shooooot!"

Lorenzo's face lit up as Randy ran down the ports. My dad had mentioned a lot of the same places from his time on a ship, but hearing Randy say them made me think more of the girls than the places themselves.

"So what happens when y'all get into port?" 'Zo asked.

"We get leave, a couple of days to do whatever we want. And let me tell you . . . a bunch of sailors cooped up on a ship for three months arriving into port for leave is a dangerous thing."

We all laughed.

"Usually we hit a bar and get some drinks in us first—some of us more than others. I can't stay in one bar for too long, but some of the guys find a spot and shut it down. After that, me and some friends hit a couple of clubs and dance until the sun comes up."

Lorenzo did a little dance on the bench, waving his hands in the air side to side. The bench shook and groaned under his weight, making Trent smack him in the leg.

"So that's where you meet the ladies?" 'Zo asked.

"Shoot . . . there, the bar, the street, wherever. When you on leave, time is short, so you don't waste it."

Lorenzo stopped his little dance and came down from his stage to ask, "So how you do it?"

"Do what?" Randy asked, folding his arms with a confused look covering his face.

Lorenzo spoke slower and lower. "You know . . . how do you get the girl to go with you to . . . you know?"

"You been wanting to ask that since y'all left the house, right?" Randy laughed.

We joined him. I sat up straight to hear his answer. We all did.

"Well . . . it ain't no thang. You just gotta talk to 'em, listen to 'em, tell 'em what they wanna hear. You know, like . . . 'Girl, you so fine, how could I not say hello . . . you sitting here with all this sweetness and me with a sweet tooth.' You know . . . stuff like that."

"You say that?" I said, raising my eyebrows.

"All the time. At the very least it gets me a smile. And that's all you need. Once you get 'em smiling, the door is open. Just don't say something stupid to slam it shut," he said, standing up. "See, the thing with women is, they know we want it, so they play hard to get. But don't let that throw you off. All women want it just as bad as we do — they just try to play it off like they don't."

The last sentence caught my and Lorenzo's attention, making both our eyes wide. It always seemed like we were the dogs chasing the helpless cat, but I guess the cat likes to be chased.

"Yeah, but . . . how you know when it's time to . . . you know?" Andre asked, rubbing the ball and wiggling his body to say what words couldn't, making all of us laugh in the process.

"You ain't ready for that, baby bro!"

"I'm just saying . . . it's one thing to be talking to a girl you just met in a club one minute, then the next minute be . . ."

Lorenzo finished the sentence with soft "yeah-yeah-yeah's" and "Oh, God's," making Andre and Trent crack up. Even I had to laugh. Lorenzo's big body jerked each time a sound came out. His hands clawed at his shirt, and his head shook side to side as he got louder and louder.

"OK, I get it," Randy said, cutting him off. He made his way over to his little brother, threw an arm around his shoulder, and said, "You'll know when it's about to happen. But right now? I told you . . . you ain't ready for that!"

He snatched the ball from Andre and headed toward the

court. Lorenzo tried to ask another question, but Randy cut him off again. "Come on, let's play some ball."

We broke into teams: me and 'Zo versus Randy and Andre. Trent took a seat on the grass for a second, then disappeared into the park.

"Straight to eleven," Randy shouted, flipping the ball into Andre.

The game began and so did the questions.

I asked, "So what do you do on the ship?"

"I fight fires."

"What?" Lorenzo said, stopping his dribble. "You joined the navy and then took a job doing something you could've done right up the street?"

Bank shot from Randy. Rebound to Andre.

"Yeah . . . but I didn't wanna stay here. As much as I love Compton and this knucklehead"—he nodded toward Andre— "I wanted to get out and see the world, man. I mean . . . if you had your choice, would you wanna fight fires here in Compton or on a ship that sails the world?" Pass from Andre to Randy. Pump fake on Lorenzo. Dunk.

Good point.

The game went on and so did the questions, until Randy ended it with an alley-oop from Andre.

"That was a good one. Let's run it back," Lorenzo said.

That was closer than we thought. They only beat us by two, and we were ready for more. Andre started shooting free throws, but Randy said, "Sorry, boys, but I gotta get to the gettin.'"

"The what?" 'Zo asked.

"Hey . . . you say what you say, and I say what I say, and what I said is: I gotta go. I gotta take care of a few things before I go out tonight."

"Who you going out with?" Andre asked.

Randy scratched his head and hesitated before he answered. "Ummm . . . you guys kind of met her already."

That got 'Zo chanting, "Go, Randy! Go, Randy!"

Trent joined us on the court as me and Andre joined the chant. He stared at us confused but chanted anyway.

"Go, Randy! Go, Randy! Go 'head! Go 'head!" echoed across the empty court and throughout the park.

Randy shook his head, grabbed his shirt off the bench, and took off, waving with his back to us. Our chant followed him out of the park.

"All right . . . why we saying, 'Go, Randy'?" Trent asked.

"My man is gonna make some more noise tonight," Lorenzo answered.

"*Your* man? Last time I checked, Lorenzo, Randy was *my* brother."

"You know what I mean, 'Dre. He's one of us now; he balled with us and everything."

"Maybe he'll tell us all about it," Trent added.

"I doubt it. He barely talked about it, even though Lorenzo kept pestering him," Andre said, bumping 'Zo in the side.

"Ay . . . I'm just trying to *educate* myself," Lorenzo said, emphasizing "educate." "All I know is . . . soon that's gonna be me getting ready to go out on a Friday night," Lorenzo announced for the park to hear.

We traded standing on the court for a seat on the bench. Trent and 'Zo took one bench; me and 'Dre took the other. The park was still hopping, but some of the characters had changed: the double-Dutch girls had been replaced by a group of kids playing kick ball, and Black Bruce was nowhere to be found.

"So, Trent, where'd you go while we were playing?" I asked.

"I just went for a walk around the park."

"A walk around the park?" Lorenzo said, jerking up as he reclined. He gave Trent the evil eye and asked, "Where you walking to around the park?"

"I wanted to see if anybody from school was here. And then I ran into Black Bruce."

"I told you to leave that dude alone, Trent. I'm sure he don't wanna be bothered. Especially by you," I said.

"Relax, Shawn. He was cool. I saw him practicing and we started talking."

"What'd he say?" Andre asked.

"I asked him how long he been doing what he's doing . . . what color belt he is . . . stuff like that."

"So what'd he say?" I asked.

"First of all, he kept calling me 'young blood.' You know, 'young blood' this, 'young blood' that . . ."

'Zo cut him off, his back now flat on the bench. "All right, 'young blood,' just tell us what he said."

"Anyway, he said he's been doing the kung-fu thing for about ten years now. Said it keeps him young."

Lorenzo bolted upright to face Trent. "How old is he?"

"I wondered the same thing, because he looks kinda young, but get this: dude said he's fifty-two!"

All our mouths flew open.

'Zo: "What?"

Andre: "For real?"

Me: "Are you serious?"

"Yup, and he still does competitions. Said he likes to practice here, under the big tree, so 'young bloods' like myself can check him out. I told him how we like watching Bruce Lee flicks, and he said that's his main man—he loves to see him in action too."

"So . . . this dude fights?" Andre asked.

"Yup. And he's won more than he's lost. He taught me a few things too. Here. . . . I'll show you something."

Trent jumped off the bench. His face got all serious as he planted his right foot in front of his left foot. A high-pitched "KIII-YAAAI" leaped from his mouth as his legs leaped into the air. I think he was trying to kick, but his body flailed like a shocked scarecrow instead.

"What is that supposed to be?" 'Zo asked, his eyebrows arching up like he just saw an alien doing the hustle.

"I didn't do it as good as he did, but that's called a butterfly kick."

"Why? 'Cause you kicked a bunch of butterflies out of the way?" Lorenzo asked.

"He showed me a few other things too. . . ."

Trent got ready to do something else, but 'Zo stopped him. "That's all right, Trent, we trust you."

Trent ignored him and just started punching and kicking

the air. My legs were more tired than I thought, so I settled back into the bench and scanned the park. Folks were disappearing one by one. My thoughts drifted from the park to the weekend and Dad. It's been almost a month since I saw him because he missed his last visit. Dang . . . school had still been going on! Shoot, today had been more interesting than all of last summer combined. Randy and his "date" had taken care of that.

TWENTY-ONE

THE SCALP-SOOTHING BREEZE blew Marisol into my thoughts. Her hair brushed across my face as I swiveled my head around the park. Everywhere I looked, there she was: next to a tree in pink, sitting on the grass in yellow, drinking from a water fountain in turquoise, shooting caroms in purple, eating ice cream in white, double-Dutching in green, playing kickball in orange.

I wonder what she's up to this weekend.

"What you guys up to this weekend?" I asked.

"Same ol,' same ol.' Just listen to my dad chew me out as usual," Lorenzo said.

"Nothin' much," mumbled out of Trent's and Andre's mouths.

"What about you, Shawn? Which house you gonna be in this weekend?" Trent asked, making the three of them snicker.

They know I bounce around a lot: Auntie's on weekdays in Compton, Mom's on nights and weekends in Carson, and Dad's every other weekend in Santa Monica. Three houses. Three adults. One teenager.

Dad called this morning before Mama dropped me off, so at least I knew where I would be tonight.

"I'm going to my dad's."

"I said it once and I'll say it again: I don't know how you do it, Shawn. All that going back and forth from here to there . . . I'd go crazy," Lorenzo said.

"It ain't that bad. It keeps me on my toes because it keeps things interesting. Usually we play a little ball, and then, depending on how he's feeling, we do something else. Last time I saw him we went to the La Brea Tar Pits. That was right before school let out."

"Dang!" in three-voice stereo.

"Feels like school got out a long time ago now, huh?" Andre asked to the wind.

We nodded, then stared in silence—Lorenzo at the sky, Andre at the ball in his lap, and me and Trent at our sneakers.

Images of the past were replaced by visions of the future: me and Andre playing ball in junior high PE turned into me and Andre running the break on the b-ball team; me and Trent slap-boxing after junior high turned into me and Trent doing kung-fu moves in gym; me watching 'Zo solve complex math problems turned into me listenin' to 'Zo bag on somebody at lunch; me and Marisol talking once in a while between classes turned into me and Marisol kissing in the back of Spanish class . . . hopefully.

Are we even gonna be in the same class? Marshall is a big school.

"How many people you think go to Marshall?" I asked.

"My brother said there was like five hundred people in his class when he got out so . . . four times five hundred is . . ." Andre started.

Lorenzo finished, "Dang! Two *thousand* people?"

"Yup, that sounds about right. But the school is spread out, so maybe it won't feel like that many people are there," Trent said.

"I don't care how it *feels*—I just wonder how much we gonna see each other, especially if we don't have the same classes," I said.

Silence. I think this was the first time any of us even thought about that. In junior high we had most of our classes together, so we saw each other all the time. But with our class about to double in size, who knew what to expect?

"There's always lunch," Lorenzo said.

"Don't they have, like, three lunch periods?" Andre asked me.

"You asking the wrong person."

"We'll see each other one way or another. I mean . . . at the very least we'll be in the same school. Right?" Trent joked. Everybody nodded, but nobody laughed.

Lorenzo looked at the bright side. "That just means more girls! Speaking of which, Shawnie-Shawn"—he rubbed his big mitts together—"wuzzup with you and Marisol?"

Where did that come from? I didn't wanna talk about

Marisol, because whenever I do, I say stuff I don't wanna say, so I said, "Nothing."

That got a laugh from everybody and a "Yeah, right. Shawn, you know you got a thing for her!" from Trent.

"I don't have a 'thing' for her," I said, shifting on the bench and staring at the court.

That got another laugh.

"Come on, Shawn, we *know* you got a thing for her," Andre said, before Lorenzo interrupted with, "And I *know* you wanna show it to her, right?"

He rolled off the bench howling with laughter. Andre slapped five with 'Zo as he stood, and Trent chuckled under his breath. I sucked my teeth and shook my head.

"Suck your teeth all you want, Shawn, but Marisol is fine. And with all them guys at Marshall, if you don't make a move, I guarantee you," 'Zo said, suddenly serious, "somebody else will, brutha man. Know what'm sayin'?"

I did. He had my attention, but I tried to hide it.

"I'm just saying . . . you better do something."

"Yeah, Shawn, 'cause if you don't . . . I will."

Who said that? Trent?

"Just kidding. You my boy, Shawn"—he slapped my back—"but at Marshall she's gonna be fair game."

"And that's a game *many* bruthas are gonna wanna play," 'Zo added, with a devilish look in his eyes.

The thought of him picturing Marisol in his head made me shift on the bench. "I get the picture, Lorenzo. Can we talk about something else now?"

"We could, but this is too much fun. Every time we even say her name, your head goes all up in the clouds and your eyes get all twitchy like Master in kung-fu flicks," Trent said.

"Look at you . . . squirming in your seat," Andre observed.

Am I?

"I'm not squirming; my legs hurt."

"Yeah right, and Lorenzo hates food," Trent said.

Lorenzo sniff-sniffed the air and faced Trent.

"What's that smell?" 'Zo started.

"Oh no, here we go," Trent muttered.

He dropped his head into his hands and stared at the peeling paint on the wood bench.

"Ah-um . . ." Lorenzo cleared his throat. "Ya Mama is so dirty . . . pigs tell her to use a bib!"

"OOOOOOOOOOOOOHHHHHHHHHH!"

Me and 'Dre fell off the bench, slapping our legs.

Trent stuck his feet out and folded his arms in angry silence while Lorenzo's Buddha belly jiggled at his own bag.

"He got you good, Trent," Andre said, then shouted, "A bib!" and stomped his feet. He snatched up the ball and headed toward the court. "Y'all coming?"

"Nah," me and Trent said.

"Not me. I'm done for the day," Lorenzo said. "My legs are tired and I'm hungry."

"So what else is new?" Trent shot back.

Is he really that dumb?

"That's all right, Trent. I already bagged you up. You not

even worth sharpening my blade," Lorenzo said, making his way over to a spot on the grass near the court.

Andre shot free throws as Trent and I shot the breeze on the bench.

"Shawn, listen, Black Bruce was telling me how he's had his black belt for a few years now, and he said that if we worked at it, we could earn ours in about four years; that's how long it took him. He said we could—"

"Hold up . . . what's this 'we'? You wanna get a black belt in kung fu?" I asked, turning to him. "Are you serious?"

"Why not? Even if it takes four years, we'd have it by the time we graduate Marshall."

Images of Trent snapping kicks, punching boards, and shouting, "WAAAAAA-TAAAA" leaped into my head, and as strange as it was, I could see him doing that, maybe even me. But when the words "graduate" and "Marshall" were mentioned together, I couldn't see us doing that.

What then? We had a hard enough time figuring out how to spend our summer days. Now, hearing Trent talk about having a black belt by graduation reminded me that four years stood between me and my future.

"Shawn, what time is it?" Lorenzo shouted from his spot near the court.

"Time for you to get a watch!" I said without shouting.

"What?"

"I said it's about four."

"Dang! That mean you gotta get to steppin' soon, huh?" Trent said.

"Boy . . . what you doing here?"

"We was playing ball," Lorenzo said, nodding toward Andre, who still had the basketball. "I could ask you the same thing, but I can see that with my own eyes," he added, folding his arms across his chest and looking at his big brother like a parent catching his kid stealing from the cookie jar.

"Ain't no thang but a chicken wang" came Dayshaun's reply.

He tried to stand, but a downpour of giggles tumbled out of his mouth as he slid back to earth. The Crip to Dayshaun's left got passed the joint and took a long drag, making the lit end turn bright red as he inhaled.

"Dang, Tyrone . . . take two and pass. Two . . . and pass," the bookend on the left said.

Tyrone held the smoke in his lungs, closing his eyes as it traveled down to his toes and out of his mouth. His eyes and mouth opened as he soaked me and Andre, standing inches away, in a thick cloud of stinky smoke.

We coughed and took a step back.

He laughed and thrust the joint at us. "Y'all don't toke?"

"Nahh, I'm cool," I said.

"Me too," Andre said.

The smell made my stomach hurt.

"So what you doing here, little brother?"

The bookend who told Tyrone to "take two and pass" started cracking up. He shook his head and said, "Ain't nothing little 'bout yo' brother, D."

That squeezed a snicker from me and Andre.

'Zo sucked his teeth and said, "I already told you: playing ball."

The joint made its way down the line as we stood there watching like idiots.

Lorenzo lingered over his brother. "I hope you ain't planning on going home for a while. Pop was mad earlier when he couldn't find no food in the house. And I know he won't be happy to see you all—"

"What? Shoooot. I 'on't care. I ain't even thinking about him," Dayshaun interrupted.

"You better hope he don't find out you on that stuff," Lorenzo said.

"What you mean 'that stuff'? It ain't like I'm tappin' my veins like a fiend. It's just weed, little brother. Shoot, I been doing this longer than a minute, and Pop ain't found out yet."

The three of us looked at Lorenzo. He broke through the smoke with "Dayshaun, you got any money? We hungry."

Dayshaun filled his lungs with smoke as the question floated his way. His answer came out in a slow, high-pitched puff aimed to the blue sky: "You lucky it's county day; otherwise I wouldn't have squat. How much you need?"

"How much you got?" Lorenzo pounced.

"Boy, how much you need?"

I held up five fingers. 'Zo had other ideas.

"Ten bucks."

"Thas it? Ten? Hol' up," he said.

Again Dayshaun tried to stand, this time holding on to the wall for dear life as he staggered to an upright position.

"Wooooo, I'm high as a mug." Dayshaun laughed, rubbing his scalp and shaking his head.

He punched a paw into his black Dickies and pulled out a thick wad of bills rolled up and squeezed tight by a rubber band.

We rushed him to take a look.

"Dang, where you get all that money from, Day?" Lorenzo asked.

"Bag on up. Y'all don't worry 'bout this here," Dayshaun said, pushing us back with his words and his arm as he thumbed through his roll. He went through it twice and couldn't find a ten or even a couple of fives.

"It's your lucky day, little brother; the smallest I got is a twenty." He peeled one off and thrust it at Lorenzo.

Our eyes lit up. Dang! Twenty bucks? Why didn't we find him earlier? We could've eaten like kings.

Lorenzo palmed the bill and shoved it in his pocket. Dayshaun did the same with his wad of bills and slid back to the concrete, taking the roach of a joint between two fingers, holding it like a tiny bug.

The bookend on the far right coughed out a cloud and said, "Ay, what about Tameka? Over on Stockwell? She gotta big ole Jell-O booty I wanna make jiggle!"

Our laughter echoed off the walls and into the park.

"Yeah . . . but that face! UGGH! That's a double-bagger right there," Dayshaun said, puckering his lips like he just ate a sour lemon.

The four of us looked at each other as if to say, "Double-bagger?"

But our unspoken question was answered when the five of them said in stereo, "One for her and one for you!" Soul claps and a downpour of giggles followed.

We laughed too but didn't know what we were laughing at. A voice called out from the park, ending the joke.

"Who dat?"

Nine heads spun around and before anybody could speak, a pair of Pirus were running onto the handball court.

Uh-oh.

Me, Andre, Lorenzo, and Trent looked at each other and froze. None of us was in red or blue. Still . . . Crips plus Pirus equals . . .

"Let's go!" Lorenzo shouted.

Two more Pirus ran up from the other side, and before we knew it, red was chasing blue off the handball court and onto the center of the basketball court. We hustled behind the rec room — the perfect place to see but not be seen.

"Aww, man! This ain't cool! What we gonna do?" Trent said, bouncing around.

"I 'on't know. But I do know we got to get out of here before somebody sees us," I said.

Before we could say another word, red rushed from the left, blue from the right, but unlike paint, together they didn't make purple. A cut-down golf club held by red swung down upon an L.A. Dodger blue cap, knocking the owner to the ground. More fists and clubs followed, bringing blood and agony. The brutha we just watched blow weed smoke and talk about getting together with Kendra from Grape Street was throwing wild punches at a short, squat, plug of a brutha dressed in black khakis and a red tank top. My vision zoomed out from the ridges on his red tank top to a wide shot of red-and-blue chaos. Silver beams of light shot through the color as cut-down clubs gleamed in the sun like sparks flying when metal scrapes metal.

My lungs released hungry breaths. My heart pulsed my sweat-soaked gray T-shirt against my chest as my legs rattled with nervous energy.

"Lorenzo, you seen yo' brother?" Trent said.

Lorenzo shook his head, then ran to look out the back of the rec room and saw nothing. Trent and Andre raised their hands to shade their eyes as they stepped out of our hiding place to get a better look.

"What y'all *doing*?" I whispered.

They were a good step in front of me and could easily be seen.

"Somebody's gonna see us."

"Relax, Shawnie-Shawn, we just gettin' a better look. They ain't even thinking about us," Andre said.

He tossed the ball back and forth in his hands as fast as he could. I guess I wasn't the only nervous one. Lorenzo ran up from the back to get a better look, except—

"Dang, Lorenzo . . . see what you did?!"

What Lorenzo "did" was bump Andre, making the ball bounce out of his hands and roll onto the grass, about a free throw away from the court.

Andre ran out to get the ball as tires screeched to a stop in front of the park. He hustled back as five Pirus jumped out.

The four Crips were now outnumbered by nine Pirus with cut-down clubs.

"What we gone do now?" Trent said.

"Lorenzo . . . ain't that your brother?" I said, pointing in the direction of two Crips and a dude in black beating down the short, squat Piru.

"Shoot . . . Dayshaun!"

The words leaked out of Lorenzo's mouth as we watched Dayshaun get yanked up by two Pirus. In slow motion, four hands grabbed him, lifted him up, and raised him high into the sky. Then everything sped up as they rammed his back down into the blacktop, squeezing the air out of his lungs and making him scream, "UNNNGHHH!"

"Y'all see that? They ain't playin'! Who knows what they gonna do to him. We gotta go help him out."

"Lorenzo, are you crazy? Those are Crips and Pirus beating the crap out of each other on the court. Did that escape your vision?"

"I don't care, Shawn. I ain't go stand here and watch my brother get beat up," he huffed. "That's my BROTHER!"

With that, Lorenzo rushed out to help Dayshaun.

"Lorenzo, what's wrong with you?" I yelled.

"Lorenzo, are you crazy?" Trent shouted.

Andre turned to me and Trent and said, "We can't let him go out there alone."

Andre looked at Trent. The two of them looked at me. They seemed to have their minds made up. I didn't and they could see the fear in my eyes as they waited for me to join them. I felt like I was standing on a cliff about a mile high and had to jump. No ifs, ands, or maybes; I *had* to jump. I couldn't turn around; there was no other way down. I didn't know what to do, but they were like my brothers, and like Lorenzo said, I couldn't stand there and watch my brother get beat up, so— I leaped.

We raced out of the calm of the rec room into the chaos on the court for Dayshaun and Lorenzo. As my sneakers scraped the blacktop, I counted all the bodies and we were even: nine on nine. Their nine had clubs, but at least we had nine bodies. The ball watched from the grass as we rushed over to help 'Zo pull the Pirus off his brother. Their red sneakers sent swift kicks into his body as Dayshaun lay on the ground trying to cover himself. Each swing of a shoe brought rib cracks and meaty thuds. 'Zo reached in to grab his brother, but one of the Pirus got ahold of him from behind while another Piru slammed a punch into 'Zo's gut, dropping him like a sack of bricks to the ground. Me, Trent, and 'Dre rushed in to help Dayshaun too; a club swung down on Trent's back, Andre took a punch to the face that knocked him down, and I reached in for Dayshaun's legs but my right eye caught a punch. Stars danced in front of me, and it felt like my eye was being pushed back into my brain. A club swing to my gut came next and laid me out on the blacktop like everybody else. Cough—can't . . . breathe.

"This don't concern y'all!"

Two Pirus grabbed Dayshaun again. The sound of muscles being tenderized pounded our eardrums and then . . . silence. The swinging stopped. The clubs stopped, and finally the fists stopped. A Jheri-curled Piru shadowed Dayshaun and crouched down over his beaten body.

"It's county day, podna! I know you got somethin' for me . . . right?"

He jabbed his hands into Dayshaun's front pockets and pulled out the wad of bills. The same wad that at one time held the twenty that was now in Lorenzo's pocket to get us some food.

I tried to catch my breath from the heat of the blacktop. Everything was blurry in my right eye, but my ears worked fine and heard:

"I tole you 'bout coming up on my spot. Ain't no poaching going on here, podna . . . YOU HEAR ME!"

He stuffed the wad of bills in his front pocket, then raised his knee to the sky and smashed his foot down onto Dayshaun's right wrist, crushing the bone into the blacktop like a cockroach beneath a heel. A horror-movie scream leaped from the bottom of Dayshaun's lungs and pierced our ears with his pain.

"Yeah, we'll see how you sling with a broken wing, PODNA!"

From my snake's-eye view with my one good eye, I inched my head up to see what happened. Bloodred bled over blue bandannas and blacktop as nine scattered souls littered the court like trash. The hyenas cackled into the distance, and in the blink of a swollen eye, they were gone.

TWENTY-TWO

"WHAT HAPPENED?"

Who said that? My ears heard the words before my eyes were open to see the face. Slap!

"Hey!"

"I was just trying to get you up, young blood."

Who's slapping me in the face? I tried to blink my eyes open, but only my left eye moved. I tried to sit up, but my stomach was in a world of pain and held me down.

"Do I know you?"

All I could make out was a big shadow hovering over me with a hand reaching for my right eye.

"Wooo! That's a real shiner you got there!" the voice said. "You don't know me, but I see you boys playing ball around here all the time."

I coughed as I rose, then reached to touch my eye. The hand stopped me.

"Don't touch it. It ain't pretty, but you'll be fine. Just your standard-issue black eye, young blood," the voice said.

Young blood? I've heard that before. My memory kicked into gear and flicked back to Trent: butterfly kick . . . young blood . . . Black Bruce!

"Black Bruce?" snuck out of my lips.

"Is that what y'all call me?" He laughed.

I was embarrassed to say that to his face.

"Hey . . . I can dig it. Y'all must like Bruce Lee. I get it. Name's Herbert—you can call me Herb. One of your boys was watching me practice earlier. I came back to get in a little more work before the sun went down and saw all you young bloods just lying on the court." He pointed around the court. "What happened?"

"Crips . . . Pirus . . ." tumbled out.

"Say no more."

He helped me to my feet. Pockets of pain filled my stomach. I stumbled as I tried to focus out of one eye. I was the last one up. The sounds of pain hovered over us as I saw everyone clutching at different body parts. Dayshaun sat on the grass nearby, cradling his wrist like an infant, his black leather belt balled up and clenched between his teeth to fend off the pain. His eyes had that look like Master's right before he went on his revenge-filled rampage.

Lorenzo stood, hunched over and holding his stomach. His breathing could be heard a mile away. Trent lay silent on his back on the grass, staring at the sky. Andre sat inches away, carefully wiggling his jaw back and forth with his hand. The four Crips sat silent on the court. Two of them covered their noses with bandannas and held them high to keep more blood from spilling onto the court. The other two dabbed at different spots on their faces, cursing each time the bandanna touched a wound.

"Man, what them 'rus run up on us fo' like that?" one of the Crips said, jamming his bandanna into his back pocket as he stood.

"I 'on't know, but somebody gone catch one for this. Oh, yeah! Payback is a bitch!" another Crip said, lowering his head to spit clots of blood.

I felt my way to the grass with Black Bruce—I mean Herb—following close behind.

"You young bloods better get to the hospital or something, 'cause it looks like a train just ran over all y'all," he said.

"Man, who are you?" one of the Crips asked, lowering the bandanna over his nose pointed to the sky.

Trent gave the reply: "Thas Black Bruce."

Herbert laughed but corrected him: "My name's Herb. I found all you guys laid out on the court here."

All eyes focused on him and nodded thanks.

Lorenzo stood upright and approached his brother. "Dayshaun, you gotta go to the hospital, man. I heard that bone crunch all the way from where I was. We could call an ambulance or . . ."

Dayshaun spit the belt out of his mouth and groaned, "No ambulance! Pop's gonna kill me if he finds out. I'll handle this myself."

His breath came in quick bursts as he gathered himself up and inched his way over to the Crips. "Let's go."

He turned back to Herbert and said between teeth clenches, "Thanks for your help, chief, but I'll take it from here. They got a car." He paused in pain and finished, "I'll have 'em take me and just drop me off." A grin crept across his face as he said, "It's a shame I broke my wrist playing basketball."

"Look here, young bloods," Herb said, turning to watch Dayshaun and the Crips hobble away, "it ain't nunna my business, but what y'all doing hanging out with Crips?"

My right eye was swollen shut and it was still hard to see with one eye, but I noticed that a gray beard graced his face and gray streaks ran through his short-cropped hair. He was tall: Kareem Abdul-Jabbar in *Game of Death* tall. And skinny. A dark brown tracksuit hung over his frame with a large black Chinese character peeking out from a white T-shirt showing beneath the jacket. His feet sported black kung-fu slippers.

"My brother . . ." Lorenzo started, "he was the one in black, and he knew the Crips that were with him. Unfortunately" — he hung his head — "I guess he knows some Pirus too."

Herbert echoed the words we've all heard over the years: "Pirus plus Crips equals trouble. Y'all know that, right?"

"Yeah, we know, we know," Lorenzo said, pausing before he finished his train of thought, "but Dayshaun, my brother, was getting beat down, and I couldn't just stand there and watch."

"I can dig it. I can dig it," Herbert said, stroking the long gray strands in his beard before adding, "That takes guts — mixing it up with the Crips and Pirus like that."

Andre added, "We couldn't let him go in alone, so we jumped in too."

"You know why your brother was catchin' a beat-down?" Herbert asked.

Lorenzo stood up, pulled the twenty out of his sweatshirt pocket, and said, "This."

"Twenty bucks? You jiving me."

"No, not just this, he had a big wad of bills rubber-banded together, and this was the smallest." Lorenzo stared at the bill. "I got it 'cause we were hungry and broke. One of the Pirus took the roll and said something like 'Wasn't gonna be no poaching goin' on.' Then . . ."—Lorenzo hesitated—"he stomped on my brother's wrist."

Herbert flinched. 'Zo continued: "That's why he was holding his hand like that."

What do you say after that? The only sound to be heard was our heavy breathing as we tended to one wound or another, seen or unseen.

"You boys gonna be all right?" Herbert asked, shattering the silence.

"Yeah . . . I think so. They weren't after us, but we each took a hit. Lorenzo took one to the gut. Andre took a punch to the face, and I got clubbed on the back," Trent said, then nodded in my direction. "But Shawn got it the worst; he took a fist right in the eye and a club to the stomach."

Trent paused. "You all right, Shawn?"

All eyes zoomed in on me. I felt like crap. My eye hurt like crazy, I was hungry, and whenever my stomach growled, the pain got worse. "Yeah . . . I'm cool," I said, hiding the pain.

And for the most part, I was. Considering that four fourteen-year-olds stepped into what looked like World

War III, and survived, was big. We didn't want to go in, but we did and we lived to tell about it. I guess that's the bright side — we survived.

"You guys had each other's back. That's good. That's what friends do: they look out for each other. Big man here saw his brother getting beat down, so he jumped in. Y'all didn't want big man to get beat down, so y'all jumped in too." Herb scratched his beard and looked at me. "You lucky it wasn't worse." He glanced down at his watch. "I gotta go. It looks like you guys gonna be fine, but try to stay out of the middle of all that nonsense. That's a place you definitely don't wanna be. You made it through this time, but next time might be a different story," Herb said. His long, brown frame disappeared into the park, getting smaller with each step.

"You should have seen the look on your face, Trent, when you got clubbed. I thought you were gonna scream like a baby," Lorenzo taunted.

Here we go.

"Look who's talking! Who's the one that dropped like a brick with one hit? Huh? One hit!"

"What about you, Andre? You looked like you were about to cry when you got tagged in the eye!" Lorenzo said.

"I know you ain't talking to me, mister one-hit-and-then-play-dead. I saw you lying on the ground with your eyes all closed, peeking one eye open every once in a while to see if they were gone," Andre said, reaching for the ball.

"I wasn't playing dead. My stomach hurt so bad, I had a hard time keeping my eyes open." Lorenzo rushed Andre and got in his face. "You callin' me a punk, Andre? 'Cause I'm the

The fellas stood. "We'll go with you," Trent said.

"I'll be cool. I gotta rush home to clean up and figure out what I'm gonna tell Mama. She's gonna kill me when she sees my eye like this!"

"Shoot, when my pop finds out about this . . ."

Lorenzo didn't have to finish his sentence because after this morning, we knew exactly how his father would react.

Our sneakers were back on autopilot, carrying us out of the park. A bounce of the ball from Andre got us chattering again.

Trent started with "Man, that was something, wasn't it? We got into it with the Crips *and* the Pirus!"

The way he said it, you would think he was talking about a vacation at Disneyland or something.

"And here we are. Still standing," he said, before cupping his hands around his mouth to shout to the sky: "I'm still standing! What y'all think about that, blue and red?"

Andre whacked him on his head. "What's wrong with you, man?"

"Ay . . . like Herb said, we was in the mix and here we are," Trent said, thrusting his arms out and dusting himself off like he just survived a major earthquake without a scratch.

That got the three of them talking, or shall I say bragging, about being in the mix. Talking about who took the hardest hit or who did what when they got hit. Like Trent said before, I got it the worst, but it was nothing to brag about. Especially since I now had to explain to Mama how I got a big ol' black eye. She's always talking about how bad the fellas are, and this is just the excuse she needs to keep me from hanging out with them. My ears popped back into reality when I heard, "Ain't that right, Shawn?"

"What?"

"At least we got a good story for when we start school," Lorenzo said.

Is he serious?

"Yeah, Lorenzo, we can tell everybody how we each took one hit and then hit the ground," I said, with some laughter flowing into me.

"No, no, no, Shawn. See you looking at it all wrong. Nobody saw it but us and the red and blue. We can be as bad as we wanna be. I think I'm gonna say I nailed a Piru in his eye before he punched me in the gut," Lorenzo said, but then he paused. "You know what? I don't have to say I got hit at all. Yeah, I'll leave that out. Maybe I'll even add that I beat up a couple of Pirus. That might sound good."

Andre and Trent started forming their versions of what happened, and I worked on my story for the only person who mattered: Mama.

"What you gonna tell your Mama, Shawn?" Trent asked.

"I don't know, but I know I gotta make it good. Otherwise, y'all may not be seeing too much more of me this summer." I wanted to laugh, but I couldn't. It was the truth.

Their heads dropped for a hot second, knowing it could happen. Andre shook the ball at me. "We ain't going nowhere, Shawnie-Shawn. We'll be right here. I know we gonna see you Monday, so don't even sweat it."

Lorenzo slapped me on the back and whispered, "Thanks for having my back. You still my brutha from another mother."

He spun me around to inspect my eye. "Put a steak on that—it'll help. My brother's had a few of those, and that's what he always does."

I looked at him sideways. "I know you love food and everything, 'Zo, but . . . a steak?"

"I'm serious, Shawn. You ain't heard that?"

Trent and Andre nodded in agreement, Trent saying he'd seen that in the movies and Andre saying his brother did the same thing.

We gave each other soul claps and said good-bye as we left MLK behind.

"Have fun with your dad this weekend. We'll see you on Monday," Trent said, "same bat-time, same bat-channel."

Lorenzo called out as I stepped away, "Don't forget about the steak. I'm serious, Shawn. . . . It works!"

We scattered in four different directions. I rushed off to clean myself and come up with a believable story. Mama would be home any minute. It was already after five. She usually worked later on Fridays, but, still, she would be at Auntie's soon. Speaking of Auntie, what am I gonna find when I step through her door today? She said she had a lot to do this morning. That don't matter, though—she always has time to drink.

Before I knew it, I was on her block, waving "hi" to Miss Johnston while hiding my eye and ignoring Miss Bricknell. I stepped through Auntie's door and was greeted by the scent of gumbo. My stomach grumbled in hunger and pain. I needed some food. Bathroom first, food second. I glided past the blaring TV and Auntie's empty spot on the couch to look at my eye. I stepped in front of the mirror and heard, "Shawn . . . is that you?"

"Yeah," I shouted, and got to work. Dang . . . I looked like the creature from the black lagoon. A puffy, purple ring surrounded my half-shut eye. I grabbed a washcloth and dabbed it at the raw meat, flinching each time cold water touched it. Blood dripped from my hands, and dirt and blacktop pieces fell from my face, spinning down the drain with any confidence I had of explaining this to Mama. A torn sneaker was one thing, but a black eye was something else.

I gotta hurry. Shoot, what am I gonna tell her? Think about that later. First, I gotta find a steak. I headed to the kitchen. Still no sign of Auntie. Where is she? I heard her stirring around the house, but I haven't seen her. I cracked open the fridge, found some half-thawed meat on a plate, and ripped open the packaging. The slab of flesh was slick with blood, but I stabbed it onto my eye anyway, dripping meat blood on the floor in the process. The fellas were right: the steak felt good.

"Boy . . . what you doing with my cube steak? And what happened to your eye?"

Auntie! Shoot. Think fast. Keep it simple. Be cool. Basketball . . . "Ummm, it happened during a basketball game. I went up for a rebound and somebody elbowed me in the eye."

Yeah, that sounded good and believable.

"Boy, put my steak down and put some ice on that. You ruining my dinner for tomorrow," she screamed, adding, "And clean up that mess," on her way to the living room.

It figures; the one time I hoped Auntie would be passed

out, she's wide awake. That don't ever happen. She run out of "juice" or something?

I stood there for a few minutes, pressing the meat to my eye, letting the cold of the flesh seep in. With both eyes closed, I almost drifted off to sleep until I heard *beep-beep!*

Shoot . . . *Mama's here!*

I put the steak back on the plate, tossed it in the fridge, and headed to the sink to clean the blood off my face. Be cool. Stick to the story. If she finds out everything, you can kiss your summer good-bye, Shawnie-Shawn.

Mama's jangling keys announced her presence as she stepped through the door to kiss Auntie hello. "Shawn . . ." she called in her usual voice. Auntie whispered something to her, and she called again in a voice I haven't heard since my last whipping a couple of years ago, loud enough for the whole neighborhood to hear: "Shawn Christopher Williams . . . get yo' behind in here RIGHT NOW!"

TWENTY-FOUR

"**YOU TRYING TO TELL ME** you got that black eye playing basketball? You expect me to believe that?"

Mama stood just inside the doorway with her arms folded and her right foot stuck out at me. I stood a few feet away between her and the TV. Her head cocked to the side and her eyes focused on mine. Hard.

I know that look. The one that said she didn't believe me. But instead of talking my way out of it, I stayed quiet. It's hard to beat Mama at that game, though, 'cause she'll just stand there and eyeball you until you talk—which, I did.

"Yeah. I told you—we were playing ball with some older guys at MLK and there was a lot of bangin' goin' on when I went up for a rebound. I reached in for the ball as this big dude tried to protect the ball by swinging his elbows out. One of 'em caught me dead in the eye and knocked me to the ground."

I could feel her eyes burning into me as each syllable escaped my lips. She stepped in my face, sticking her hand near my eye.

I flinched. "Whatchu doin'? That hurts!"

"I'll bet it does. I wanna see how bad it is." She stepped closer.

Why does everybody wanna do that? My eye is puffy and purple. Of course it's bad.

"Now, Shawn . . ." she started.

Here it comes.

"Lemme ask you a question."

I looked past her. "Yeah."

"Do I look like a fool to you? I mean — look at me, boy — do I look like I just fell off the turnip truck or something?"

"No, Mama, I . . ."

"Look here, boy, I KNOW you didn't get that from playing no game. Now are you gonna tell me what happened, or am I gonna have to get the strap when we get home?"

The strap? What does she think I am, a kid? Shoot, I haven't gotten a whippin' since she found that note with all the bad words on it. That was a bunch of inches ago. Now I'm bigger than her!

"I ain't no little boy, Mama. I'm gettin' ready to go into high school, so you can't treat me like a child."

I stepped back and folded my arms. Two can play this game.

But she stepped up. "I KNOW you didn't just back-sass me! Now, did you? I SAID I wanna know what happened, for real! Not some BS story about you playing ball."

Auntie pulled herself off the couch. "Sis, y'all want some gumbo to take home with you? I got a fresh pot."

Mama nodded. In the kitchen drawers slid open. Auntie placed a large plastic container on the table with the hot food, then disappeared out of view. Ice cubes tinkling into a glass was followed by the *crack* of a bottle opening—like a baseball bat hitting a home run.

Should I tell Mama about the fight? Maybe I should—get it out of the way and let her see her boy ain't no baby no more.

"All right, it didn't happen in a game." I hesitated. "It happened . . . in a fight."

Her eyes narrowed on mine, but I stood taller and finished. "Lorenzo's brother was getting beat up, so we jumped in to help him."

There, I said it. Just like when I jumped in to help Dayshaun, there was no turning back now.

Auntie strolled in with her "juice" and plopped back on the couch to watch the news. She didn't realize she had real news going on right there in her own living room.

"We jumped in to pull him out, but each of us took a hit."

Silence. MUTE flashed on the TV screen. Auntie's tinkling ice mixed with Mama's heavy breathing. She took a swallow from her glass and asked, "Sis, you all right?"

More silence. Mama's deep breath let me know a storm was coming. In a low voice, she said, "I'm fine."

She sat in the easy chair and stretched her legs out. "Now, Shawn, who was beating up Lorenzo's brother?"

I wanted to sit too. But I didn't.

"Some Pirus. They came out of nowhere. We were playing ball and . . ."

"*And* what?"

"He was hanging out with"—I hesitated; if I said "Crips," then all hell would break loose—"some guys, and they were over on the handball courts when we found them."

"Brenda, what's he talking about?" Auntie said.

"Well, it seems that Shawn's black eye didn't come from no game, just as I suspected. Matter of fact, I think he's trying to run a game on me. Aren't you, Shawn?"

Man, I'm getting tired of this. I only did what my friends would have done for me. She wasn't there; she don't know what happened.

"No. I told you . . . Lorenzo jumped in to help his brother, and we jumped in to help him."

She sucked her teeth and stood up. I wasn't finished.

"They would have done the same for me if . . ."

"If *what*, Shawn? If *you* was in a fight? You probably right. Your friends probably would help you—they're your friends. But I know you: you don't get into fights. At least, you didn't before. But see . . . this don't make sense. There's something you ain't telling me, Shawn. What's missing?"

I wasn't gonna tell her everything: the Crips, the weed smoke, the wad of money—uh-uh. She hears all of that and there goes my summer.

"Ain't nothing missing. That's it. We were helping our friend."

I stood tall, crossed my arms, and looked down on her.

"Liar!"

Smack! Right on my cheek.

"Brenda!" cried Auntie.

My head jerked around. The Piru got my right eye, and now Mama got my left cheek.

"DANG, MAMA! What you do that for?" I rubbed my cheek and got in her face. "I AIN'T NO LITTLE BOY!"

I flung the front door open and rushed down the steps and into the car. I'm tired of hearing her voice. Tired of her telling me "who I am." I *know* who I am. Does she? Does she know the stuff I gotta deal with every day out here? *Hell no!* She thinks I'm still a kid. Kids don't get into fights with Crips and Pirus. Kids don't talk about having sex. Kids don't hang out with dudes getting high. Kids don't do nunna that.

"I'm a let your father deal with you on this. I lost my patience with you, boy," she said, thrusting the container of gumbo in my lap before heading home.

The ride went quickly, and my anger got stronger with each mile traveled. I know I ain't grown, but I'm fourteen years old and can take care of myself. Mama only saw what she wanted to see, and what she saw was a child. So that's how she treated me.

Still . . . if she found out everything that went down today, she would freak out and shackle me to Auntie's, where I'd be doomed to lazy days of slurred words, drunken moans, and boring soap operas.

When we got home, she put the gumbo on the counter and went straight to her room. She closed the door, but I heard her talking on the phone, probably to Dad. I couldn't wait to see him. He would understand. When it came to stuff like this, it was a dad thing and definitely not a mama thing.

I couldn't think about that now, though. My stomach's been growling since before I got hit, so I jumped on the gumbo. Mama swooped back in and busied herself around the kitchen, trying to avoid me.

"Put this on your eye. It'll help."

She flung an ice pack on the counter toward me and disappeared again. The purple fire surrounding my eye cooled as I pressed the pack into action on my way to my room to work on the gumbo. The latest *X-Men* sat on my bed, so I flipped through it as I blew on the hot, bubbling stew. Nightcrawler and Wolverine were racing to save Professor X when the doorbell rang.

Dad.

Mama didn't leave her room, so I got the door.

"Boy, what happened to you?"

Mama walked in before I could answer.

"Yeah, Shawn, tell your father what happened. Minus all the lies and game playing of course."

Awwww, man . . . here we go.

We went into the living room. Mama and I took our spots on the couch. Dad remained standing, hands in pockets.

"You not gonna sit, Dad?"

"Shawn, tell me how you got a black eye."

I told him the same thing I told Mama, after the whole game lie. I played up the fact that I was helping a friend. Since he's a guy, I thought he would understand where I was coming from. His hands stayed in his pockets, jangling change, as he listened. His eyebrows didn't dance. His head didn't shake. His arms didn't fold and unfold. And his eyes looked at me; they didn't burn through me.

"So let me get this straight. . . . You guys were playing ball and you ran into Lorenzo's brother?"

"Right."

"Then, out of nowhere, some Pirus came and started beating him up."

"Right."

"And that's when you and your three friends jumped in."

"Right."

He was cool about it, like he is about everything, until his hands emerged from his pants and he crossed his arms.

Uh-oh.

"Why did Pirus just start beating him up? Were they Crips?"

Uh-oh. Stick to the story. You mention the Crips, Shawn, and . . .

"Why you hesitating, Shawn?" Dad said, his eyes questioning everything I just said.

"Yeah, Shawn . . . why you hesitatin'? Thinkin' of another lie?" Mama accused, shaking her head.

I hated when she did that. Think fast.

"To tell you the truth . . . I don't know who they were." I scratched my head and tried to believe it myself so it came out right.

"See that, Shawn, I don't know what to do with this boy. I can't believe a word out of his mouth." Mama threw her hands up to Dad, who has my name—I mean, I have his name.

They were quiet. The whole room was quiet. Maybe they believed me. I hope so. I didn't wanna keep lying, but I didn't wanna lose my freedom. Dad tapped his foot on the carpet like he always does when he's about to make a decision.

Mama spoke with her hands, "I mean . . . between the lying, the back talk, the scrapes . . ."

"What scrapes?" Dad asked.

"Take a look at his sneakers and ask him."

Dad sighed and finally took a seat. "Shawn, lift up your feet."

I was about to, but Mama beat me to it, jerking my sneaker into the air to show him. When Dad acknowledged it with a shake of the head and a pursing of the lips, she dropped it. OUCH! Lucky's fangs reappeared.

"I just don't know what's gotten into him lately. Maybe you can talk some sense into that hard head of his," Mama said.

She rose from the couch and went into the kitchen. Dad asked me about the sneaker, and I told him the same story I told Mama, only I left out the whole "lowrider" thing.

"Shawn"—he pointed—"I know something's going on that you ain't tellin' me, but you *and* your mother seem a little stressed right now, so we'll talk about it later."

Mama strolled back in with a big bowl of gumbo and reclaimed her seat.

"See, I think it's them boys he been hanging out with." Chew-chew. "Lord knows what you guys do during the day." Chew-chew and a point with the spoon. "I don't know how much more of them you'll be seeing this summer."

"Now hold on, Brenda, the boy is a teenager. That's half

of it right there. You can't just not let him see his friends any-more," Dad said.

Thank you, Dad. I knew he would see things my way. I knew he would . . .

"But still, Shawn . . ." He reclined back into his seat and rubbed his goatee. "I can't help but think you might need a change of scenery."

Mama jumped in. "Whatchu mean 'a change of scenery'?"

Her spoon dropped into the bowl and she eyeballed Dad.

"I mean, Brenda, look at the situation. You got Gertie watching him and . . ." He knew better than to bring that train into the station, but he kept going. "He's gotta deal with this gang stuff, and . . . I don't know, maybe a change of sce-nery would . . . help things."

"So what are you trying to say?" Mama asked, sitting a little straighter.

This was getting good. But what was Dad talking about, "a change of scenery"?

He stood and made his way over to the fireplace. Pictures of me through the years sat on the mantle. He plucked up one of me missing my two front teeth and stared at it as he spoke: "Y'know, he *is* about to start high school." He put down the picture. "Maybe he should go to school here."

Mama's eyes jumped when Dad finished. Her head was already shaking as she put the bowl down, "Uh-uh. No. I don't think so. You see how this boy is right now, Shawn? I couldn't trust him in this house alone."

Me go to school here? No Crips . . . no Pirus . . . no Auntie . . . no pink slip? Shoot, I could get with that.

"Brenda, listen, you gotta face the fact that Shawn ain't a child anymore. He's *our* child, yes, but he's no longer *a* child."

Tell her, Dad. Wait a second—that would also mean no Lorenzo, no Trent, no Andre . . . and no Marisol. *Dang!*

Mama sighed and settled back into her seat. She tapped her foot as Dad finished.

"Now, Brenda, I know I'm not here all the time, and I don't get to see Shawn the same way you do. But you and I both know that we raised Shawn the right way and that he's a good kid. You gotta trust that."

Dad looked me straight in the eye. "We know he ain't no man yet. But we gotta let him grow."

Tell her, Dad.

Mama finished off the bowl, put it on the coffee table, and stared at Dad. "So what should we do with him?"

He sat back down, sighed at me, and said, "Maybe it's time he started making a few decisions of his own."

He leaned back into the seat and put his arms behind his head like he was ready to do a sit-up. "I mean, that's what being a man, or an adult for that matter, is all about: making decisions"—then he leaned in for emphasis—"and dealing with those decisions."

What? I looked at Mama. Did she think this was a good idea?

"Wait . . . what are you talking about, Dad?"

Mama stood, then jumped in.

"I hate to say it, but your father's right: you need to start making some choices on your own and dealing with the results.

I know we raised you well, Shawn, but sometimes, boy . . . that mouth of yours writes checks your behind needs to cash."

I was lost. "What are you guys even talking about?"

"What your father is trying to say is we should let *you* decide where you go to high school. I knew the day would come sooner or later that Gertie wouldn't be watching you; I just didn't think it would be today."

She stepped into the kitchen to let Dad finish.

"So what do you think, Shawn? You wanna go to high school here, or you wanna go to Marshall? You get to choose. Me and your mother will talk about when you need to make your decision by, but ultimately the choice is yours."

Hmmm. Go to school at Marshall with my friends and deal with Crips and Pirus, or go to school here and avoid the gangs but leave my friends behind?

Shoot, I thought I wouldn't have to deal with stuff like this until I was out of high school, not before I even started.

TWENTY-FIVE

CARSON OR COMPTON? Freedom or friendship? That's what it comes down to. Freedom from the Crips and Pirus, freedom from Auntie, freedom as a teenager or . . . friendship; friendship with the fellas and friendship, hopefully more, with Marisol.

But it wasn't all about Marisol. Now that me and the boys have been talking about high school, I've gotten excited about what the school year holds for the four of us: playing ball with Andre, listening to Lorenzo's bags, and watching Trent and Passion go at it. At the same time, thoughts of . . . something different, something new, appealed to me. Especially when I see my puffy eye in the mirror and I'm reminded of how it happened.

This wasn't gonna be easy.

"So, Dad, what we doing this weekend?"

"I was thinking we could go to the boardwalk or Venice. Something like that," he answered.

"Cool."

"And you know we'll be going to church on Sunday, so I hope you got your clothes."

"You know I wouldn't forget that."

Downtown L.A. blurred before my eyes as we sped toward the freeway. Dad hummed to a Temptations song on the oldies station. It wasn't one of my favorites, even though I like the Temps, so I stared out the window and rewound back to this morning and how the day began: the dream—Marisol and Janine. And oh, yeah, sticky sheets. I should've known it wasn't my day when I woke up with sticky sheets.

Man, it felt like the dream happened last year—the whole day did as Carson and Compton disappeared in the rearview mirror. Randy rockin' the bed, Crazy Ray swinging his bat, Lorenzo's dad chewing him out, Master of the flying guillotine, the drunken Master, Marisol's hair—her birthday . . . I wonder if she'll invite me to her party. I hope so.

The Crips smoked out, a fist to my face, blurred vision, Dayshaun's wrist crushed beneath a bright red All Star— *ouch!*

Dayshaun's scream echoed into my ears as one of the Temptations hit a high note and held it. I squirmed in my seat until he was silent again.

"What's wrong with you?" Dad asked, eyeballing me like I had turned into an alien.

"Nothin'."

Should I tell Dad everything that happened with the red

and blue? I don't have to mention the smoking, but maybe I should mention how the fight got started in the first place. Actually, maybe I *should* mention the weed smoking. I mean, it's not like I smoked. He'd be proud that I didn't. Mama wouldn't see it that way, though. She'd freak out, thinking I'm trying to hide something from her, like she always does. Dad don't think like that, though. At least he listens. Maybe I should tell him everything. Then I won't have to worry about what I did and didn't tell him.

"Ummm, Dad . . ."

"Yeah."

I told him everything. From the moment we finished the game and smelled the smoke to the moment I got to Auntie's and put the steak on my eye. No sense in leaving anything out.

Dad's body language changed moment to moment as the story unraveled. His eyes widened when I mentioned the smoke; he exhaled when I told him I passed on the joint offered up. His head shook when I described how we all got hit at least once, me the only one to get hit twice. His nose squinched up when I described Dayshaun's wrist getting crushed. He nodded when I mentioned Herbert, then he laughed when I told him we called him Black Bruce. His body did a lot of things, but his mouth never said a word; he just listened until I was done.

"Now you see why I didn't tell Mama everything?"

He nodded and let out a sigh. The freeway was long gone as we wound our way up the hill toward his house. This was always my favorite part of the drive. The sun was setting over the ocean just below us as another picture-perfect California day disappeared into dusk. I imagined me and Marisol sitting on the beach with her in my arms, watching the sun dance on the waves. I brushed her hair out of my face and sniffed the scent coming from it. Flowers? Strawberries?

Dad jumped into my dream. "Now, Shawn, I understand why you didn't wanna mention all this to your mother, but you gotta understand why she's worried. Hell, I almost flipped out when you opened the door and I saw that black eye," he said, shaking his head.

His eyes darted between me and the winding road. "I understand what you're saying, but I understand where she's coming from too. You may not agree with how she reacted, but she's still your mother and you still have to respect her."

"What about me? She treats me like a kid and doesn't always respect me."

"Boy, are you serious? Don't you ever disrespect your mother. Ever. You hear me? I know she can be hard on you, trust me, I know, but she does that because she loves you. She sees all the knuckleheads running around doing dumb stuff, and she doesn't wanna see you go down that path, and neither do I. And believe me, Shawn, it's easy to go that way. You fall in with the wrong group or make a bad decision, and—boom—your life changes before your eyes: one minute you're shooting baskets; the next you're shooting a gun."

He shook his head after "gun," then continued: "Personally, I hope you decide to go to school in Carson. I worry about you too, but I know you're not a kid anymore. I know we raised you to do the right thing . . . like telling me the real story behind your black eye." His eyes looked into mine. "I'm proud of you for doing that."

We turned onto Dad's street and made our way to his house. End of the block. Yellow house. On the left, 100 on the mailbox.

"But make no mistake, I'm still your father, and while I'm not too thrilled to see my son sporting a black eye, at least it was to help a friend," he said as we pulled into the driveway. He shut the car off and added, "That took courage."

We got out and started our weekend together. I grabbed my bag from the trunk and took it into my room.

Ever since he and Mama got divorced, Dad's lived in some tiny places over the years. Most of them were little one-bedroom apartments, so I always had to sleep on the couch. I remember he had this one bed that I absolutely hated. It was cheap and the springs were forever sticking me in the back. One time I jumped on it and it folded itself up—with me in it. Dad came and got me after I screamed my head off, but both my ankles were messed up for like a month after that. I knew I shouldn't have been jumping on it, but he still felt bad because he knew the bed was cheap in the first place.

A few more small apartments and cheap pullout beds later, and he got this place: his first house. He asked me where I thought he should live about five years ago, and next thing I know, here he is—on top of a hill, overlooking the ocean. Just like I answered.

At first I thought it was weird that he would ask his son, who he only saw twice a month, where he should live, but then I realized it didn't matter to him because he travels all the time and is hardly home. Even though I wasn't gonna live with him, he was still thinking of me; I'll never forget that. The fact that he got a house big enough for me to have my own bedroom was Kool and the Gang too.

"Dad, what's for dinner? I'm starvin'," I asked in the kitchen as Dad banged through assorted pots and pans.

"Didn't you eat before you left your mother's?"

"Yeah, Auntie made some gumbo and it was good. But I'm still hungry."

"Oh, yeah, I forgot—you're a teenager."

"A hungry teenager."

"Is there any other kind?"

He pulled the skillet out of a cupboard and put it on the stove, then opened the fridge and pulled out some ground beef and shredded cheese.

"Let me guess: tacos."

"See, I knew you were smart."

Dad's tacos. The only thing he knows how to make. I take that back: the only thing he knows how to make well. But I live for Dad's tacos. The sound of the meat sizzling, the corn tortillas frying up into a big bubble in the hot oil, the cheese melting on the meat when I sprinkle it on, the cool tomatoes on top, and the hot sauce finishing it off perfectly.

"You got Cholula, right?"

He reached over to the stove top and grabbed a small bottle of the spicy sauce. "Always got Cholula."

"I feel like I ain't seen you in ages, Dad. Where you been? You bring me anything back?" I said, pulling up a stool.

"The paper sent me to Mexico to photograph Mexican

wrestlers, called *luchadores,* and I had a good time—a real good time. I wish you could've been there, but you were still in school at that point. I didn't forget about you, though. . . . In the living room, on the table, there's a bag of stuff I got you."

I hustled off the stool, into the room, and returned with the bag. There wasn't much, but what was in there was pretty cool: a funky yellow face mask with black rings around the eyes, a wooden doll with colorful marks on the face and a sinister smile, a deck of playing cards with a bunch of masked wrestlers, and a tall, skinny bottle filled with brownish-yellow fluid with a worm floating in it.

"What's this?" I said, holding up the bottle and looking at him through it with the worm between us.

"That's mine. It's called mescal, and it's like tequila."

"Is it alcohol?"

"Of course it is."

Auntie popped into my brain.

POP—Auntie cracking open a bottle. POP—ice tinkling in brown liquid. POP—Auntie sprawled out on the couch. POP—an empty glass shaking at me.

"I didn't know you drank, Dad."

"I am an adult. A lot of adults do."

I stared at the worm. Is it alive or dead? I'm sure it's dead if it's in there, but it moved in the bottle like it was alive.

"What do you do with the worm?" I said, spinning the bottle, making the worm knock into the side.

"You drink it."

I gagged but I couldn't take my eyes off the worm, floating

this way and that, as images of Auntie continued to float this way and that through my head.

On the other side of the bottle, Dad said, "Not everybody drinks the way your Auntie does, you know."

How'd he know she was flashing through my head? One by one the images changed from Auntie into Dad.

POP—Dad cracking open his worm-filled bottle. POP—Dad shaking an ice-filled glass at me. POP—Dad sprawled out on the couch. POP—Dad screaming at the top of his lungs.

"Shawn! Don't you hear me? I'm standing a foot in front of you and you still can't hear me?"

"Sorry, Dad. I was thinking."

"Well, stop thinking and set the table."

"Can we eat in front of the TV? The Dodgers should be playing tonight, right?"

"Probably. Why don't you go check the *TV Guide* and see. Otherwise we'll sit at the table."

I checked and, sure enough, they were. I flipped on the TV to the game.

"Top of the second. The Giants are up to bat. No score yet," I shouted to the kitchen.

I set up the TV trays side by side and headed back to the kitchen.

"How many tacos you want?"

"Four."

"Four? Boy, you're gonna eat me out of house and home."

"I told you I was hungry."

"You can have three. Get some salad too. Dressing's in the fridge."

Dang! Three tacos, Dad? I'm hungry. What, does he think I can't eat all four?

He handed me my precious platter of tacos fixed just how I like them: cheese melting and tomatoes cooling. A few shakes of Cholula on each one finished them off. I fixed my salad, grabbed a soda, and headed into the living room. Dad had already polished off one taco as I took my spot on the couch. Happy food sounds came out of his mouth, and pretty soon all you could hear was crunching and chewing from us and stadium sounds from the TV. Vin Scully was finishing an ad about Farmer John sausages when the Dodgers scored the first run of the game.

"How's your eye?"

My eye! Shoot. I was so focused on getting some food in my belly that I forgot all about it. It still stung and I couldn't see out of it much, but otherwise it felt fine.

"Not too bad."

"Put an ice pack on it when you're done. There's one in the freezer." He swallowed a bite and added, "What about your stomach?"

"That's fine. It only hurt right after it happened." I crunched a bite. "The food helps."

He stood. "You need anything?"

"I'm good."

Another Dodger sent a homer over the fence as Dad left for the kitchen.

Crack!

Auntie passed out.

He reappeared with a beer and cracked it open. The crack of Auntie's bottle sounded off in my head again.

I glanced over at the beer more than a few times, making Dad say, "What's up?"

"Nothin'."

He looked at the beer and then at me. "What, you think I'm turning into an alcoholic?"

My mouth was full, so I shook my head, then chewed out a "Naw, Dad."

He finished off his last taco and wiped his hands and mouth with the napkin. The grease turned the white napkin bright orange.

"Plenty of adults drink without it being a problem, Shawn." He took a sip. "Your Auntie has a disease."

Before he could finish, I interrupted him.

"Everybody keeps saying she has a disease. I mean we learned about that in health class. But if that's the case, how come everybody that drinks doesn't get this disease?"

He sat back in his chair and thought for a moment.

"Well, alcoholics don't necessarily drink a lot because they love the taste of it. Matter of fact, the stuff she drinks — whiskey, I think — is pretty nasty when you come right down to it."

He took a sip of his beer, sat back, and continued.

"Most alcoholics drink to escape something; something could be weighing on their mind, and they start using the alcohol to help them forget their problems. The problem is, before they know it, the alcohol isn't there to just help them forget, but to help them live. When that happens, their body needs it like you and I need air to breathe."

He took another sip of beer.

"Take me and your mother. We drink what we drink because we enjoy the taste and social aspect of it. We both like to relax with a beer, play cards, dominoes, whatever. But when I wake up in the morning, I'm not thinking about having a drink and neither is your mother. But a lot of alcoholics do."

I nodded, chewing a mouthful of meat and tomatoes.

He leaned in and ran his fingers through his goatee. "I know that can't be easy for you, having to deal with that every day."

It wasn't. Yeah, I got used to it over the years, but it was never easy.

I wiped my greasy lips with a napkin. "I'm usually gone during the day anyway, but by the time I get back to the house, she's usually passed out somewhere. Like yesterday . . . she was passed out on the kitchen floor. I had to pick her up and put her on the couch." I sat back and added, "That happens a lot."

Dad shook his head.

"And most of the time, when I put her down, she starts shaking her cup at me for something to drink. And not water."

I almost mentioned the slurred words, crying, and everything else, but I was tired of even thinking about it, so I stopped. Dad must have known, because he sat in silence. His eyes were glued to the screen, and so were mine . . . at least one of them was. I needed some ice for my eye.

"You want anything?" I asked before heading to the kitchen.

"I'm good."

I hunted through the fridge for dessert. Dang Dad, you ain't got squat for food. Hold up . . . what's this? Bingo! Some Neapolitan ice cream. I opened it and only strawberry was left, my favorite. I dished up a huge bowl, then grabbed the ice pack and headed into the living room.

Loud snoring assaulted my ears as I stepped into the room. Dad was passed out as the game played on. I took a sniff of his beer, squinched my nose, and shook him awake.

"Dad!"

He rubbed his eyes. "This game is putting me to sleep. Why don't you see if there's a movie on."

Cool. I grabbed the remote and flipped through the channels. When it comes to movies, Dad is all about science fiction. I need variety.

"Oh, man!" I said to the TV, pausing on a Bruce Lee flick as Chuck Norris got his leg broken.

"*Game of Death*! Let's watch this!"

"I think I'll pass," Dad said, rubbing his eyes.

Dad had seen *Game of Death* so many times, he knew it word for word just like I did. It was one of my all-time favorites, so of course I was gonna watch it.

"Man . . . I'm tired." He stretched. "I'm gonna clean the kitchen and go to bed. You can stay up as long as you want, but when I say it's time to get up in the morning, you better get up. Understand?"

"Yeah, Dad."

"I'm serious, Shawn, none of that 'five more minutes' nonsense, you hear?"

"All right, Dad, I'll get up."

"And clean up your mess before you go to bed."

He shuffled into the kitchen, ran some water, clanged some plates, rattled some pans, and soon the light was off and he was shuffling off to his room. A "good night" and the door closed. I was alone with Bruce.

I threw my legs onto the couch and put the ice pack on my eye. The stinging was gone, but I still couldn't see out of it so good. On-screen, Bruce broke bones and smashed limbs as my worn-out body was devoured by the couch. I pulled up my shirt to inspect the nasty purple welt on my stomach left courtesy of the cut-down club. It had the weirdest shape to it. Kind of like a half-moon stretched into a tiny island. A few more "WAA-TAA's" and "KIYAI's" from Bruce, and soon my eyelids were heavy and I was out. Hissing static opened them back up. I flipped the TV off and dragged myself to bed. Unlike at my house, my bed here is bigger and the sheets are newer. I just hope I don't wake up to find them sticky.

TWENTY-SIX

"**SHAWN, GET UP.** Time to cut them raggedy naps."

Awwww, man.

"What time is it?" I mumbled.

"Just after nine. I wanna get to the barbershop early so we don't have to wait."

I rolled over.

"Five more minutes, Dad. It's Saturday."

"What'd I say last night about that 'five more minutes' nonsense? I know it's Saturday, but you're not gonna laze the day away in bed."

I groaned and pulled the sheets up.

"Come on, we'll grab some donuts on the way."

That got me up. I threw on my clothes and brushed my teeth, and we headed out. No sooner had I sat down in the car than Dad started sniffing the air.

"What is that smell?"

He sniffed over at me.

"Ughh! Boy, when was the last time you took a shower?"

I sniffed my underarms and, yeah, I was pretty ripe.

"I 'on't know . . . a couple of days ago, I think."

"A couple of days, Shawn? You gotta handle that funk. Ain't no ladies gonna wanna talk to you smelling like that."

He pointed at my head. "And look at your hair."

I flipped down the visor mirror and saw that my fade had faded out.

"Speaking of ladies, you been talking to any?"

"Dad!"

"What? Come on, Shawn, you're a teenager now. I was your age a long, long time ago, and that was all I could think about. You gonna tell me no girls have caught your eye?"

Dang! I knew I would have to tell him about Marisol sooner or later, but like Mama said when it came to me leaving Auntie's, I didn't think it'd be today.

"Well . . . there is this one girl. Her name is Marisol and . . ."

"And what? She got one leg, no arms, no lips . . ."

I laughed. "No, Dad, she's Mexican."

Why'd I say she was Mexican? He don't care.

"Mexican? Is she cute?"

"Is she cute? What do you think? I do have good taste, you know." I patted my chest with pride.

"You better. You are *my* son, after all. So tell me about her. Is she cute? Or is she fine?"

We had a rating scale when it came to describing women,

and "fine" was a perfect ten. "Cute" was in the middle, and "all right" was down at the bottom with "has a nice personality." Marisol was right at the top and, to me, off the charts.

"Oh, she's fine . . . with a capital *F*. She's got this really long hair and . . ."

Do I tell him about the butt? Nahh. Hold off on that. He'll ask me about it, and I don't feel like describing her butt to my Dad.

"She's a little younger than me and a little shorter too. She's got these big brown eyes, and her smile . . ."

Her smile popped into my head, glowing like yesterday's pink sunset over the ocean, and warmed my face.

"Wait . . . she's younger than you? How young?" He eyeballed me.

"Just a couple of months. Matter of fact, her birthday is coming up in a few weeks."

He exhaled.

The ocean glittered beneath a bright blue sky as we made our way down the hill. The California breeze had the palm trees swaying, so I cracked my window open to let my funk out.

"So what's going on with her? You talkin' to her or you just admiring her from afar?"

He emphasized "afar" like a Shakespearean actor.

"Since school got out, I haven't seen much of her, but when I do, we always talk."

Should I tell him about the fellas embarrassing me in front of her? Or her showing me her butt?

"The fellas think she likes me too. They said she's always standing real close and touching me when we talk."

"Really? What do you think?"

"I don't know. I know what I think of her, but I don't know what she thinks of me. Ever since they said that, I been thinkin' back to little things like that."

"Well, I'll do what I can to help you. But you gotta help yourself by taking better care of your appearance. You're lucky me and your mother love you, because right now you don't look like no child of mine." He laughed and shook my head. "I'm just messing with you. But seriously, first thing we gotta do is take care of your nappy head."

He laughed again as we wound our way to the donut shop. Half a dozen donuts and a slight stomachache later and we were at the barbershop: Smitty's House of Style.

"Flash. Junior" greeted us as the bell clanged open to Smitty's and announced our presence.

"Whooooaaa! Junior, what happened to you? That eye is so black, it looks like a hole!" Smitty said.

Shoot, my eye. I was able to see out of it much better than last night, so I almost forgot about it. Almost. There was no way I could forget about it now.

"He just got into a little scrape," Dad said. His arm draped over my shoulder and he shook it.

All eyes focused on me. My eyes looked at the floor.

"A *little* scrape? Shoot! I'd hate to see a big one." Lester chuckled, snipping his scissors in the air to clean the clumps of hair out of them.

Laughter from the barbershop congregation brought the room to life. All the usual suspects were here: Smitty, the owner and the most requested barber—a big barrel-chested man with a glowing bald dome; Lester, his skinny sidekick with a gray goatee and a short salt-and-pepper natural; and David, the youngest barber — a big fullback-looking brother with a close-cropped cut and an earring in his left ear. David had the nickname "Pretty Boy" because of that earring, whether he liked it or not. And seated on the sidelines, as always, heads waiting to be cut, some I've seen before mixed in with new ones. The older heads flipped through issues of *Ebony, Jet,* and *Sports Illustrated* as the TV shouted assorted animated sounds to the younger heads. I was the only teen in the shop. And the only one with a black eye.

"How long, Smitty?" Dad asked.

"You got three in front of you," Pretty Boy said.

"Was he talking to you?" Smitty snapped.

Pretty Boy rolled his eyes and ran the clippers through the natural in front of him. We grabbed a pair of seats and waited for the barbershop talk to heat up. This was always my favorite part when it came to getting my hair cut — trash talk and street preaching from men of all shapes, sizes, and ages. This was the barbershop. I always listened and never spoke, like most of the youngsters, but Dad liked getting into it and wasn't afraid to jump into the fire. Most of the guys had seen Dad's pictures in the *L.A. Times;* that's why they called him "Flash." Sometimes they busted on him because of some of the assignments he got — ugly dogs, fat politicians, beauty queens — but they all showed him respect because he was doing what not too many people, let alone black men, were doing: making a living doing what he loved.

"So what's the good word, Flash? You been taking pictures of any wars or stuff like that?" Lester asked.

"Nahh, I'm cutting back on all that traveling, Les. They got me doing a lot more local stuff. I wanna be around to see this one grow up." He shook my head.

"Yeah, he's growing all right. I bet he's eating you out of house and home, huh?"

Why does every parent say that . . . house *and* home? Aren't they the same thing?

"Oh, you know that. Don't let his skinny legs fool you — the boy is a human garbage disposal."

I crossed my arms and stuck my legs out. I hate when adults talk in front of me like I'm not even there.

"At least Junior is skinny. My grandson is about the same age, and he's already bigger than me! I told his Mama she better get that boy on a football team or something and put that weight to work."

An "I hear that" came out of nowhere, followed by "Y'all remember that one big kid who used to come in here? Had a lightning bolt scar on his forehead? What was his name? . . ."

And so it went. Names got recalled, stories retold, laughter bubbled from bellies, and "I hear that's" were sprinkled throughout. All while scissors snipped and hair was clipped. It was sunny outside and there was noplace I would rather be. Everything was Kool and the Gang. Until . . .

"So how'd it happen?"

"Huh?"

"Your eye, Junior . . . how'd it happen?"

Smitty motioned his clippers toward his eye as he dusted

off his freshly cut customer. I didn't know what to say, so I looked at Dad. We spoke low, mouth to ear.

"Go 'head. Tell him."

"The whole thing?"

"No, just how you were helping a friend."

Why did I have to do that?

"Umm, I stepped in to help a friend"—I glanced at Dad—"who was getting beat up."

There, I said it.

"Well, how 'bout that, Flash? Junior's getting down with the get-down," Smitty said with a hearty chuckle that got a laugh out of Dad.

"At least you was helping a friend. Ain't nothing wrong with that. Shoot, I know guys who got beat up because their 'friends' took off when they needed them, or set 'em up in the first place."

"That ain't no friend," a voice chimed in.

"If that's a friend, I'd rather have more enemies," another added.

And so it went.

I sat up taller in my seat as my black eye made me the center of attention . . . in a good way. When I jumped in to help 'Zo, it felt like I was doing the right thing, but hearing these men, all of whom look like they've seen their fair share of scrapes over the years, say they would've done the same let me know I did do the right thing, even if Mama disagreed.

Smitty finished off another head and called me to his chair. Cool. I liked all of the barbers, but Smitty always hooked me up extra nice.

"You know what I'm gonna do for you, Junior? I'm giving you the special. I've had a few shiners in my life, and I know how it feels—it hurts like hell. Yeah, I'm a give you a little something that'll make the girls look at you, not your eye."

Smitty snapped the sheet and placed it over me and tied the neck in the back.

Dad chimed in, "What's that, Smitty? A Caesar? A quo vadis? A DA?"

"Naw, Flash, that was your time. This is a whole different time, and different times call for different cuts. I'm a trim it down and style it nice—you'll see. You gonna be beating the girls off with a stick, Junior."

The clippers whirred, and my hair started falling in fat clumps. I hoped he wouldn't give me a baldy like he has. I kept my eyes closed and head down. I didn't see any results until Smitty held up the mirror for me to look at the end. And when he finally did, I felt a smile grace my face and I heard my voice say, "Cool."

Smitty was right. The first thing I saw was the pencil-thin sideburns curving down my cheeks. I didn't even know I had enough hair for sideburns. The hair on top was cut in half and shaped to my head. It took a while before I even glanced at my eye. It felt much better and looked much better than yesterday, but you could still tell somebody punched me.

As Smitty moved the mirror around my head, I stepped outside of myself, and for the first time in my life, I saw me: Shawn Christopher Williams. I saw my father's jawbone announcing its presence. I saw my mother's nose, flaring, as I admired my cut. I saw eyes staring back at me that belonged to someone who has seen a few things in life — less than a man, but more than a kid.

Images of the past replayed themselves in Technicolor 3-D, subtitled with words flashing across my mental movie screen: me rushing in after Lorenzo — COURAGEOUS. Me slapping Trent's back — FRIEND. Me helping Andre off the blacktop — TEAMMATE. Me laughing with the fellas — BROTHER. Me making a basket — CHAMPION. Me listening to Randy — DREAMER. Me reading books — INTELLIGENT. Me helping Auntie off the floor — COMPASSIONATE. Me talking to Marisol — LOVER.

Yeah, I nodded to Smitty, I liked the cut. But now I admired the face it framed.

"Nice, huh?" Smitty said, smiling with me in the mirror. He dusted me off, slapped me on the back, took Dad's cash, and sent me on my way.

Dad was already waiting at the door, his goatee not as scraggly as when we walked in. A wave from our hands, a doorbell clang, and another episode at the barbershop was done until next time.

TWENTY-SEVEN

"**IT'S GETTING CLOSE** to lunchtime, and I know you're probably hungry, so why don't we head down to the pier," Dad said in the car, looking at his watch.

"Sounds good."

The mirror had my full attention again as I reinspected my new sideburns. They were very fine and framed my face like a picture. I turned my head this way and that, keeping my eyes glued to the mirror. I looked closer at my upper lip and noticed a wispy patch of fuzz.

"I'm growing a mustache."

"You are not."

"You can't see it. But it's there."

"Whatever you say, Shawn. Just try not to look at yourself so much. Girls like it when you look at them."

I flipped up the mirror and stared out the window, taking in the street sights as we wound our way through Hollywood.

The oldies station played Dad's favorite Earth, Wind and Fire song, but when a commercial came on after, he said, "Umm, Shawn . . . your mother wanted me to talk to you about something."

My belly rumbled as we passed an In-N-Out burger. My eyes darted from the yellow letters on the sign to Dad's mellow face in the car.

"About what?"

If it has something to do with Mama, it could be anything.

He flicked the radio off.

Uh-oh, this is serious. He never turns the radio off. He may change the station, but he never turns it off.

I sat up straight.

"You remember waking up with wet sheets recently?"

Wet sheets? Of course I remember that. It was just yesterday. How could I forget?

"Yeah, why?"

"Your mother wanted me talk to you about what happened."

"I know, Dad. . . . It was an accident. I drank a lot of water before bed that night and . . ."

"I know it was an accident, but . . . it wasn't what you think it was."

What other kind of accident is there? I guess number two, but that's just nasty.

His left hand scratched his goatee as he said, "It's kind of weird having this conversation again because we had it just a couple of years ago."

"You mean the . . ."

"Yeah, that one. We talked about it in general before, but now it's time to get specific."

"Specific?"

He hesitated, but the confused look on my face made him push on.

"I had a hard time talking to you about this last time, and I'm having a hard time now," he said more to himself than to me.

Both hands clenched tight on the steering wheel, and his eyes stared straight ahead at the road. Red light.

"There's no easy way to do this, so I'll just say what I have to say."

He inhaled, exhaled, then spoke easier. "What you had the other night was called a wet dream."

I turned my head. "A what?"

"A wet dream," he said loud and clear.

I knew I was too old to pee my bed.

"The medical word is — *ahem* — 'ejaculation,' but plain and simple it means" — his eyes searched outside for the right words — "now you can make a baby."

A baby? I don't want to make a baby. At least not for a bunch of years . . . a whole bunch of years!

He exhaled another deep breath. "You remember our talk right?"

"The Talk." Even though it was a couple of years ago, I remember it like it was yesterday. More than anything, I remember Dad tripping and stumbling over his words before he caught his footing. We had the talk because he wanted to find out what I knew. I had heard some things in school, so we started with that. He laughed half the time and shook his head the other half, then broke down what was true and what wasn't:

No, you couldn't get a girl pregnant by rubbing her behind all night.

No, you couldn't make your thing longer by pulling on it.

No, malt liquor didn't make your thing longer either.

No, you couldn't get a disease from kissing a girl.

No, you couldn't get a disease by sitting on the toilet.

Yes, girls have a separate hole for peeing and pushing out babies.

Yes, it takes two people to make a baby.

Yes, there were things you could do to not make a baby. But, no, having the girl wash herself afterward was not one of them.

Stuff like that. I can't even remember all the stuff I believed or told him, but I do remember thinking that the guys who gave me the info in the first place—namely, Lorenzo and his brothers—didn't know as much as they thought they knew.

"A wet dream is one of the first times semen comes out. That's what fertilizes the woman's egg to make a baby." He looked from the road to me. "Remember?"

I remembered a few things, but that wasn't one of them. After we talked about what I'd heard, we talked about what different parts on the man and woman were called, where stuff was, what did what. It was all kinda . . . scientific . . . and boring. I know I missed a few things, because after a while my mind wandered off.

"If you don't remember anything else, remember this: your pistol is now loaded. So be careful." His head nodded in the direction of my lap as if a gun were resting on it.

I laughed. "Why you call it a pistol?"

"'Cause a pistol ain't a toy, and it can be dangerous if used in the wrong way," he said, looking me in the eye. "Understand?"

"I think so."

I was just getting used to my sideburns. Then Dad tells me I can make a baby. Now all I could think about was the gun in my pants.

My lap felt heavy while a baby's voice bounced through my skull: screeching, screaming, crying—loud. I tried to shut it off but couldn't find the switch. It disappeared when Dad said, "Your mother brought it up to me the other day. She thought I should be the one to talk to you about it"—he looked me in the eye again—"not her."

I didn't know what to say, so I said nothing. I looked out the window and noticed mothers pushing babies in strollers. Some were older. Most were young. I tried to imagine me and Marisol walking on the pier pushing a stroller, but that was one image that didn't want to appear. Thank goodness.

The street sights were replaced by parked cars as we searched for a spot in a garage.

"So what happened in your dream?"

"Huh?"

"Your dream? Wet dreams usually happen when you're dreaming about a girl, and you're . . . you know . . ."—he bumped my shoulder—"doing your thing."

"Oh . . . I don't remember."

"Come on, Shawn, you can tell me."

"It's not that. I wish I could remember what happened, but I can't. I spent all day yesterday trying to piece it together, but the harder I tried, the more it disappeared. The only thing I remember is that Marisol and Janine were in it."

"Janine?"

"Yeah, Janine. She's the older sister of my friend Trent, and she starts UCLA in the fall on a track scholarship."

It felt like we were driving in circles looking for a place to park, but I was ready to get out of the car.

"You never mentioned her."

"Yeah, that's 'cause she's older than me and way out of my league. The other day she came into the living room in these bright yellow short-shorts and this tank top . . ." I couldn't even finish the sentence without getting tight in the shorts.

"She have nice co'ners?"

"Nice what?"

Dad laughed. "Corners. Hips. Most black women have nice hips; that's how they're built. But the real nice ones have a unique shape to them . . . like, rounded corners."

His right hand let go of the steering wheel, and he traced a curve in the air that brought Janine's *S* shape to mind.

"Anyway, all I remember was her and Marisol. I don't even remember what they were wearing."

A car pulled out and we took the spot. Dad grabbed his camera from the backseat, and we headed toward the pier.

"All I can tell you is if either one of 'em appears in your dreams again, be prepared. Put a towel down or something . . .

because that was just the first time. Trust me, there's plenty more where that came from. Just you wait. That pistol in your pants is gonna start talking to you, telling you what to do, how to act, and it's gonna shut your brain down. Especially when you see a pretty young thing strolling down the street in a silky skirt."

Dad directed my eyes at a beautiful dark-chocolate woman of college age standing a free throw away at the light. She was about my height, and her shoulder-length hair danced in the California breeze. A smooth peach skirt clung to her peach-shaped bottom, and her chocolate-brown legs plunged toward the gray concrete, ending in a pair of peach flip-flops that showed off her toenails painted the same color. My heart beat faster.

We crossed the intersection, my eyes glued to the skirt swaying in front of me and nothing else. The only sound that mattered was the rustling of silk brushing against her peach skirt as she swished her hips to the other side. The rhythm of her rear had me hypnotized.

On the other side of the street, Miss Chocolate Peach disappeared into a flesh parade of female bodies — tall, small, black, white, in-between, older, younger, long hair, short hair, but mostly beautiful.

My eyes bounced around the bodies like a pinball. Red bikini here — pink bikini there — polka-dotted one-piece here — tiny orange two-piece there — corners swinging this way and that. And legs. Legs, legs, legs . . . everywhere!

My mind drowned in a sea of female flesh. A million ants raced through my body, touching each nerve. Too many girls.

Too many boobs. Too many butts. Too many legs. I couldn't take it. All the blood in my body rushed to my midsection. Breathe. Breathe. With each breath my shorts got tighter, like they were taking my blood pressure.

"Shawn . . . Shawn! You there, brutha man?" *Finger snap!* Dad snapped through the haze.

"All these exposed bodies made you deaf. I been pointing out places to eat and asking where you wanna go for a few minutes now, but you haven't said a word. Just remember: you control it; don't let it control you."

When it came to food, all I remember is wolfing down a couple of fish tacos in the midst of all the eye candy. It was a picture-perfect L.A. kind of day, the girls were out to play, and food was the last thing on my mind.

Dad mostly snapped pictures of the sights on the pier. He even let me take a few, but every time I pointed the camera at a particularly cheeky butt in front of me, he took it away. "What'd I say about control?"

Just minutes after he said that, I got a crash course in "gun control." I was checking out a pack of three women, possibly fresh out of high school, all of them in tiny bikinis and popping out of their tops. I turned my head as they walked past, and they all had corners; the one in the middle especially. She was dark-skinned but not black—like a cross between black and Mexican—and she had long, thick, curly black hair that draped halfway down to her butt. I swiveled my head to watch her hips sway in a see-through blue sarong. The only thing in the world that mattered at that moment was those swinging hips—or should I say "co'ners"—swaying. Side to side.

TWENTY-EIGHT

"YOU GOT ANYTHING to eat, Dad?"

"Don't tell me you're still hungry? You just ate a bunch of hot dogs not long ago."

"Yeah but that was a while ago. I'm hungry again."

"There should be stuff for a sandwich in the fridge."

Dad disappeared into his room. I stepped into the kitchen and found some ham, cheese, and mustard but no bread. Dad reappeared with his chessboard.

"You up for a game?"

"Yeah, let me just finish making this. Where's the bread?"

"It should be in the basket near the microwave. If it's not there, then I'm all out."

Sandwich fixed, cut, and ready to be eaten, I joined Dad in a game of chess. He taught me when I was little, but I never quite figured out the whole "thinking a couple moves ahead" thing.

"Black or white?"

I took a big bite out of my sandwich and chewed. "Black."

Dad plucked my pieces off the board one by one with ease, taking my queen before I was even halfway through my sandwich, on his way to swift victory—as usual. By the second game, my sandwich was gone, so I tried to take my time and go slower, but it didn't matter—new strategy, same result. In one move he handcuffed my knight, bishop, and rook and blocked my queen so she couldn't get through to help.

"How'd you do that?"

He scratched his goatee.

"I know what you like to do, so I just thought ahead of you. I knew you were gonna move your knight here to try and get my queen, but that was just a setup by me the whole time. When your knight couldn't do anything, you brought in your bishop to help, and that's when I went for the kill. Basically . . . I played you." His hands went behind his head and he said, "Check."

Dang! I moved my king around a few times, but I knew it was only a matter of time before he would say "checkmate." And four moves later, he did.

"Let's play something else. Something a little easier, where I can hold my own."

He got up to go to the fridge. "You want something?"

"Yeah, I'll take a soda," I said, smacking my lips from the sandwich.

I put the chess set away and grabbed the cards. "How 'bout some spades?"

He got up and grabbed two cans from the fridge: a beer for him and a soda for me.

"Sounds good to me."

We took a seat and popped our cans.

"You wanna shuffle?"

"Of course."

My eyes bounced back and forth between my shuffling hands and Dad's beer. He noticed and said, "You wanna taste?"

"Of your beer?"

"Yeah. You keep looking at it."

"Nahh . . . I took a smell of it yesterday."

"And?"

"It stinks," I said, turning up my nose.

"Shawn, you should taste it . . . to see what you're dealing with."

Truth is, I did want to taste it. If lots of adults drink it, then it must at least taste good, even though it didn't smell good. Right?

"All right."

I pulled the can up to my lips and took a sniff; it smelled like sweaty armpits. I closed my eyes and took a swallow, then gagged. "Ughhh."

"I was hoping you would say that." He laughed as I tried to wash it down with my soda.

"How do you drink that?"

"It's an acquired taste," he said, taking another sip.

The sight alone put the taste back onto my tongue. I took another sip of soda.

"Dad, I'm confused. You said last night that alcoholics drink to forget their problems, not for the taste. But what about you? That tastes terrible, and you're still drinking it?"

"You're right. Like I said, beer is an acquired taste, and I've had years to get used to it. The fact is, Shawn, everybody drinks for different reasons. Most people drink because it helps them relax . . . after work, watching a game, playing cards." He nodded at our hands. "The problem is, if you drink too much, you don't just get relaxed—you get drunk, and I don't have to tell you what that looks like."

POP—Auntie on the couch. POP—Auntie slurring words.

Yeah, I know what that looks like.

"I know my limit, but some people don't."

I threw down a five of spades and took his jack of hearts.

"You been playin' with your mother? 'Cause you finally seem to have gotten the hang of this."

"A li'l bit."

Dad got up and returned to his seat with a can of Beer Nuts.

"So how is your mother these days . . . aside from you guys fighting and stuff?"

"She's fine. Just the other day I asked her about going to school in Carson because of Auntie, and she didn't even want to think about it."

I dealt a new hand.

"Well, the offer is on the table now, so . . . the choice is *yours.*" Dad popped some peanuts into his mouth after popping open the can.

"You gonna play any sports when you go to school?" He tossed down a five of hearts and added, "Whichever school that may be?"

I sorted my hand between soda sips.

"I don't know. My friend Andre wants me to try out for the basketball team with him. We play well together, and I never even thought about it until he told me that I'm the only one that locks him up on D—and he's the best of the four of us!"

"So your D's gotten even tighter, huh?"

"Yeah . . . you know . . . I don't want anybody scoring on me. I may not score much, but they won't score much on me either."

"All right now."

Dad sorted more cards.

"So what do you think you're gonna do?"

He tipped his can back until it was empty and got up to get another one.

"I don't know. Right now I'm leaning toward Marshall, of course, because my friends will be there. But the other day me and the fellas were talking about how many people go to Marshall."

"How many go there?"

"Something like two thousand!"

"Two thousand? Wow! That's a lot."

"Tell me about it. We were wondering how much we'll see each other with so many people. We thought we'd at least get to see each other at lunch, but there's, like, three lunch periods, so that might not even happen."

I tipped my can back to empty it and started choking.

"You OK?"

I caught my breath. "Just went down the wrong way." Then I cleared my throat and said, "And of course there's Marisol."

"Of course! Girls always figure into the equation somehow. You run any game on her?"

Game? The only game I have is in basketball.

"I wouldn't even know what to say. Most of the time I can't even look her in the eye . . . I get all tongue-tied."

Dad dug out a handful of peanuts and fed them into his mouth one at a time.

"You telling me my boy ain't got no game? I know you're not telling me that. Right?"

I shrugged. "What can I say? I'm only fourteen. You got any suggestions?"

I got up and grabbed another soda.

"Shoot, age ain't nothin' but a number. Game is all about confidence. Now, let me ask you this: When you play ball, you believe you can lock anybody up on D, right?"

"Yeah, usually."

"Usually?"

"OK, yeah."

"Yeah. So when you see her, just bring that thinking to her."

I plucked individual peanuts from the can.

"I don't understand. You want me to pretend like . . . I'm playing D on her?"

Dad laughed.

"No, no, no. I'm saying you gotta believe in yourself that you can do it—that you can talk to her. Try it next time you see her. Your friends are probably right when they say she wants to talk to you."

"What you mean?"

"I mean . . . your friends can usually see what you can't— they can see how she smiles at you, but you can't because you're too busy trying not to look at her. Right?"

"Right."

"See, what you gotta do is talk about *her;* girls love that. A lot of bruthas think they gotta use corny pickup lines and stuff, but listen, all girls really want . . . is to be treated nice— and with respect. Compliment her. Flirt with her a little bit. Get in close and tell her how nice she smells. Stuff like that."

I nodded and remembered Marisol spinning her back to me to show me her hair; I did say something to her about it.

"So does Carson have any chance?"

"Of course. Otherwise my mind would be made up already. Having some privacy after school would be nice. Not having to deal with Auntie or the Crips and Pirus would be nice too . . . real nice."

I pointed to my eye as I plucked more peanuts. Dad inspected it a little closer.

"It looks much better. Swelling's gone down, but it's still a little purple. It should be gone by next week."

Cool. I didn't want Marisol to see me with my eye like this, because she might get the wrong idea; she might think I like to fight or something. Maybe I won't see her again until it's gone.

"I saw your last report card by the way—great job. Especially in English."

I popped more peanuts into my mouth and crunched a "Thanks."

"You keep that up and you can go to any college you want. You know what you wanna do after high school?"

I scratched my head and took a sip of soda.

"I don't know. I was thinking about a couple of things: college, the navy . . ."

"The navy? What made you think about that?"

"You always have good things to say about it, and my friend Andre has a brother who's in the navy now as a fire-fighter. He travels the world, meets lots of girls, *and* he gets paid for it. That's what I wanna do. I wanna travel, see the world . . . do something I wouldn't normally do, ya know?" I grabbed a few peanuts, then added, "I haven't thought about it a whole lot, but the thought did cross my mind. How did you like being in the navy?"

Dad leaned back in his chair and looked to the ceiling. A smile came across his face as he lowered his eyes back toward me.

"I wanted to see the world too, but I didn't have any money. That's why I joined the navy. I was a supply clerk on an aircraft carrier in the Pacific near the Philippines. If you needed something, you saw me," he said, pointing to his chest with pride. "When I finished basic, I wanted to be assigned as a photographer, but a friend of mine told me it'd be easier to take pictures of whatever I wanted if I did something else."

Dad filled his hand with more peanuts, then continued:

"I made some great friends and traveled to places I probably would have never seen otherwise. But for you . . ." — he crossed his arms — "for you . . . I see more."

He took a sip of beer before he looked me in the eye.

"It'd be better if you went to college first. Then you could at least be an officer and have more options. I can see you doing that." He tipped his beer upside down before adding, "Trust me, it's better to give orders than take 'em, and you're a natural leader — smart, courageous . . ." He pointed at my eye.

I reached my hand in for more peanuts but came up with dust, so I sat back in my chair and finished off my soda. Dad got up to clear the table, and I gave him a hand.

"Did I mention I photographed plenty of girls?" he asked, then answered his own question with "Oh, yeah. High school, the navy, and ever since. And you know what?"

I grabbed the cards off the table. "What?"

"They all loved having their picture taken. Every last one of them."

Kitchen cleaned and the clock past eleven, we headed off to bed. As I stepped into my room, Dad came out of his and said: "Matter of fact, that's how I met your mother."

TWENTY-NINE

THERE SHE IS. *Miss Chocolate Peach.*

Catch up to her.

"Excuse me, miss?"

Her head doesn't turn. Did she hear me?

"Miss? Oh, miss! Excuse me. . . ."

She stops. Her head turns.

I run up. She stares at me. A breeze brushes black hair across her hazel eyes.

Pinkish red lips say, "Were you calling me?"

Peach fingernails streak through her hair.

"Yeah, ah . . . yes, I was."

She folds her arms.

Speak up.

"I'm a photographer for the Times, *and I . . . ah, would like to photograph you for a new feature we have called 'L.A. Woman.' Would you mind?"*

Her skirt caresses her sleek legs.

Her lips caress my ears with her answer: "Really? You wanna take a picture of me?"

Click-click, click-click.

"So, ahhh . . . what's your name?"

Click-click, click-click.

There's another one. Catch up to her.

A blue sarong caresses curved corners.

"Really? You wanna take a picture of me?"

Click-click, click-click.

And there's another. Catch up to her.

"So, ahh . . . what's your name?"

Click-click, click-click.

"What about my friends—don't you wanna photograph them too?"

A clinging polka-dot one-piece next to a smiling orange bikini.

"Definitely."

Click-click, click-click. Click-click, click-click.

"We're headed to our apartment down on the beach to get cleaned up. You wanna join us for a little party?"

"A party? Sure why not?"

Pop.

The boardwalk. Me. Surrounded by cops.

"Young man, put down the gun!"

Pop.

"Mister photographer man, come inside. Could you grab us some towels, please?"

Peach. Blue. Polka dot. Orange. Sand on skin.

Pop.

"No sudden movements! Lay down your weapon!"

How many cops? One. Two. Three. Four. Five. Six. Seven. Eight.

Pop.

"Oh . . . what happened to your eye, you poor thing?"

Peach fingertips on purple flesh.

Pop.

Red lights swirl. Blue lights swirl.

A bullhorn: "Young man, put the gun down . . . NOW!"

"You'll never take me alive, pig!"

Pop.

"Ooooohhhh! Your skin is soooo soft."

"And that hair . . ."

"Yeahhhh . . . I could run my fingers through it alllll day."

"Me tooooooo."

Fingers on scalp. One hand. Two hands. Three hands. Four hands.

Pop.

"Young man, lay down your weapon or we WILL shoot."

"I'm not afraid to use this!"

We WILL shoot. We WILL shoot.

Pop.

"Can you help me out of this sarong?"

Fingernails on my face. On my arms. On my chest. On my legs.

A breathy breeze in my ears from four pairs of lips.

Pop.

Gun in my hand. I swivel in a circle. Finger on the trigger.

"You'll never take me alive!"

Twitch.

Bang-bang. Bang-bang. Bang-bang. Bang-bang.

Ahhhhhhhhhhhhhhhhhhhh . . .

Shake-shake-shake-shake.

"Shawn, Shawn! You OK?"

"I didn't do it. I didn't do it."

"Didn't do what?"

Dad?

I blinked my eyes open and sat up. Where am I?

"What happened?"

The clock blinked nine o'clock as the alarm buzzed the room. Dad turned it off.

"Your alarm went off and you started screaming at the top of your lungs. You all right?"

Morning lit up the room and billowed the curtains open. Everything looked normal. Under the sheets I touched my body to make sure all my parts were there. Aww, man! Not again; my pajama bottoms clung to my crotch. I scooched under the covers and pulled the blanket up to my neck.

"Yeah"—my heart raced—"must've been a bad dream."

"You remember what happened?"

POP: Sand on skin.

"Not really."

"Well, come on, get up. Time to go to church."

Dad left the room. I closed my eyes. Dang!

I peeled the blanket off and checked the sheets; they were dry. Thank goodness. I must have been sleeping on my back when it happened. Dad popped his head in the door as I ran my hand across the sheets. I jumped up when he said, "Come on, Shawn, get dressed."

Shoot. I had to clean myself up without him noticing. Unlike our house, Dad's house is on the small side, so it's harder to hide when stuff like this happens. I poked my head out the doorway and saw him in the kitchen with his back to me. Now's my chance. I tiptoed into the bathroom and locked the door. The smell of bleach filled the bathroom as I peeled the sticky pajama shorts off. Is that me? I twitched my nose and glanced into the mirror. FLASH. Peach fingertips on purple flesh flashed over my brain, disappearing as fast as the image appeared.

"Shawn, you better be up, boy!" Dad called from the kitchen.

"I'm brushing my teeth."

I tiptoed back into my room and got dressed. A few bowls of cereal and we were out the door.

Dad said, "I see you combed your hair this morning," as he started the car.

"Of course."

A blue sky greeted us as we stepped outside. The air hung still and hadn't heated up yet as we wound our way to the bottom of the hill. A right turn here. A left turn there. One stop sign. Another stop sign. A right turn and we were there. Church—our Sunday basketball game. B-ball is our religion, and this is where we celebrate it. Dad's been bringing me here ever since he moved in, so we've become regulars. There are about twelve to fifteen players that always show up, but I've always been the youngest and still am.

Since Dad has been out of town and missed my last couple of visits, he hasn't seen how much better I've gotten in the last few weeks. Playing every day with the fellas since school got out did that.

I still remember my first game here. Dad told the guys to treat me like everybody else — no special treatment just because I was young. At first I was mad and scared because I was much smaller than everybody else. But Dad said, "As long as you can pass the ball and play D, guys will always wanna play with you, no matter how young or small you are."

His words bounced into my head as we exchanged soul claps with the guys on the court. I've gotten bigger and better since that first game and can now hold my own on the court no problem.

"The two Shawns. Number nine and ten. Let's do this!"

That was House. The biggest and oldest player on the court. A honey-colored brutha built like a cinder block, he was good to have on your team. I don't know exactly how old he was, but he had all kinds of braces on his body and huffed and puffed hard whenever he played. Get him down in the low post, though, and he was a monster — tricky, sneaky, smart, strong. He used everything he had to win, but he always played clean and was the unofficial leader of the game. I guess you could say he was "the preacher."

"Ball getting too boring for you, Li'l Shawn?" House said, pointing to my eye. "Now you taking up boxing?" he added, eclipsing the sun.

"Nah, I, ah . . . It's a long story." I shrugged.

"Say no more — we all got one of them. So look here. It's

gone be you, Darryl, George, J.J., and me. Big Shawn, you running with the other squad."

In the barbershop I'm Junior. Here I'm Li'l Shawn. I'm not so little anymore, but as long as me and Dad have the same name, I'm always gonna be called one or the other.

"Take who takes you," House shouted as he handed the other team the ball at the top of the key. Everybody lined up on their man according to size, and I ended up guarding Dad. Dang!

Usually we play on the same team because the guys thought it was more fair that way. Not anymore. Me and Dad were now closer in size. I was as tall as him but not as strong. But still, he hasn't seen me play in a while, and I have a few tricks up my sleeve.

"You ready to be taken to school?" Dad said.

Sneakers scraped the gray concrete as the ball got tossed into action. He might have been bigger and stronger than me, but Dad wasn't nearly as fast as Andre, who I'm used to guarding all the time, so when a pass got tossed in his direction, I stepped in front of him and snatched it up. I pushed the ball up the middle of the court with George on my right and J.J. on my left. House's husky voice boomed behind me: "Trailer! Trailer!"

George is the high-flyer of the three, so I dished it off to him, and he floated in for a reverse layup.

"Y'all see that? Lord have mercy . . . Li'l Shawn's got some skills! One–nothing, us."

House's voice thundered over the court as he, me, and George slapped five. I raced back down to pick up Dad.

"So your D is even tighter, huh?" Dad said as he moved into the post.

I shrugged. "You know."

The ball flew around the court. Dad danced between the blocks. I hated playing him down here because he had so many moves. I couldn't let him touch the ball. I waved my hands side to side to deny him the ball, but he caught a lob thrown his way anyway.

Shoot. I knew what was coming next. His body swung from the right baseline into the lane, and his right arm rose into his patented hook shot.

"One up," someone shouted as we ran up court.

"Don't worry 'bout that, Li'l Shawn. Ain't nothin' you can do to stop that," House said.

I brought the ball up. Dad picked me up at half-court. I passed it off to George on the right, then cut left. The ball flew into House, who whipped a pass across the court to J.J. "Jump shot, J.J." His wrist flicked the ball into a perfect arc and splashed through the net. I was still focused on J.J.'s flicked wrist as House shouted, "Get back! Get back!"

Dad had taken off downcourt, and a long pass got hurled over my head. He caught it like a football receiver and converted the easy layup with nobody on him at the other end. He winked at me as he ran back up court.

Come on, Shawn, you gettin' lazy! You know better. I threw my hands up. House tossed the ball in to me, and I yo-yoed it up the court. House made his way to the left blocks. George was on the right. Darryl ran from the left baseline to the right, while J.J. clapped his hands at me for the ball on the right side of the key. I dribbled near House on the left and lobbed a pass in to him. Dad got up on me with his arms out. I faked left and cut right, headed for the basket. Hard. House dropped a no-look bounce pass that I caught and converted into a layup with Dad nowhere near me.

That must've got Dad going, because he scored a few more points over me with his hook shot and there was nothing I could do. House tried to get me a few easy shots, but his man kept dropping over to help Dad crowd me, so I threw up a couple of bricks.

My teammates passed me the ball less and less. At one point I felt like I was just running up and down the court for no reason. What's the point of playing hard if I'm not even touching the ball?

I lifted my eyes to the sky and noticed a lone white cloud swirling in the sea of blue. I blinked and a white bikini appeared. A blue belly button in the middle winked at me. Peach fingernails circled it like the breeze swirling the cloud.

"Li'l Shawn, come on, get your head out the clouds. I said switch on D. You on Darryl's man now," House said.

Dad had punished me all day with his hook shot and was the only consistent scorer on his team. I knew they wanted to get him the ball, so I spied on him while guarding my man, who spent most of his time standing around waiting to shoot a jumper. He hadn't hit one yet, so I had a feeling I could leave him to double down on Dad. My man backed up to give Dad room to work, so I dropped off him and dropped down on Dad as he went into his move, but instead of shooting the ball, Dad tossed it over my head and back to my man, who hit a wide-open jumper. Of course.

"Point up. Come on, Li'l Shawn, get in the game," House said, tossing the ball in to me.

I glanced up high to the ocean-blue sky, and the bikini-shaped cloud had been stretched into what looked like a lightning bolt lying on its side, thin and skinny with a crick in the middle. I brought my eyes back to earth and eyeballed all the players on the court. I was the youngest by a whole bunch of years. I'll bet I was also the fastest one out here.

I focused my eyes on the basket. Like a mustang held captive for years with the gates to freedom finally thrown open, I ran. I ran without the shackles of fear dragging me down. I ran with the freedom of youth at my back. I ran with the energy of a lightning bolt and flashed past a defender as he tried to step in my path. My right hand crossed the ball to my left as all sound disappeared. My eyes focused on the rim and nothing else. A body stepped in front of me. Another one. A dribble to the left. A dribble to the right and the rim rose in front of me. I lofted my feet off the ground and rolled the ball off my fingertips with a grand flourish.

The ball never had a chance. A hand extended out of nowhere and sent it back in the direction I had just come from. A member of the opposing team caught it, spun, and dribbled in for an easy layup.

"DANG!" I shouted on my side of the court as "Game!" leaped out of a mouth on the other side.

My teammates dropped their heads in unison, and three pairs of eyes burned through me. The fourth pair belonged to

House, who towered over me and said, "Million-dollar move with a ten-cent finish."

I stood alone under the basket as everyone else hit the water fountains. I lifted my head to the sky and saw the cloud that had drifted into my thoughts was now scattered across the sea of blue in cotton-candy-like wisps. My eyes tilted from the blue of the sky down to the gray of the concrete. Dad's sweat-drenched arm draped a stain on my shirt as we walked off the court toward the sideline.

THIRTY

"CHIN UP, SHAWN. That was just one game."

Yeah. One game I wish I had back. We plopped onto the grass, and Dad said, "Whew! I'm sittin' the next one out. My time off the court is catching up to me. I need to get back in shape." He slapped me on the back and added, "But you keep playing . . . I'll watch."

"We got next" came from a pair of lips at the other end of the court. I counted nine bodies. Dad's team picked up George, which meant the new team needed one. I had to play. I couldn't leave the court like that. The same lips shouted, "We need one."

House collapsed on a patch of grass next to Dad as J.J., Darryl, and me circled the free-throw line, awaiting our turn to take a shot to get into the next game. Darryl bricked his shot left. J.J.'s shot went in and so did mine. He shot again

and missed. I shot again and hit nothing but net. Cool—
I'm in.

"Let's do this!" the same lips shouted.

"So it's me, you, Stick, Wiz, and High-Top," the voice said
before adding, "I'm Jamal."

Stick? Wiz? High-Top? What kind of names are those?
Stick was skinny like one, but Wiz and High-Top didn't match
their names much. Wiz was short and squat and didn't con-
jure up any images of a wizard. High-Top was all arms. Maybe
they call him that because he can dunk.

Me and Jamal slapped five. Me and the other guys nodded at each other. I looked at each one to make sure I knew
who was on my team. This was a younger squad than my last
one—these guys looked like they just got out of high school,
and they looked like they could ball.

Jamal tossed the ball in to High-Top, who dribbled for
what seemed like five minutes, then clanged a jump shot off
the backboard. Stick pounced on the rebound and tried to put
it back but threw the ball up way too hard. His man on D
grabbed the rebound and threw the ball downcourt to a wide-
open teammate who scored the first point of the game. Are
you serious? These guys can't ball. They just wannabes.

We exchanged baskets but were still down by two. Finally,
Wiz passed me the ball when the double team came. From
my favorite spot, I leaped off the ground and flicked the ball
out of my hand, into a slow spin, and through the rim with a
clean *swish*. Dad and House showed their appreciation with
applause.

"Yeah, Li'l Shawn. Give that youngster the ball!"

I smiled as I jogged up court because House said what I was thinking: give the youngster the ball. But nothing changed. I got myself open, but Wiz looked over at me, then looked the other way and tossed it to Stick. The pass was too low and got stolen. My hands slammed onto my waist, and my eyes burned through Wiz. He looked away. Dang, where's my boys when I need them?

I walked over to Dad and House on the sideline. "Can you believe this?"

"That's what happens when you get a bunch of kids on the same team—all style, no substance," Dad said. He and House laughed, then Dad said, "You need to say something."

I wanted to say "What?" but Jamal stood near me as Dad ended his sentence.

My "teammates" continued to ignore me, so I finally said something to Wiz as we headed up court. "You didn't see me wide open in the corner? That's a couple of times now."

"We real ballers out here trying to do our thing. What you gonna do? You just a kid." He laughed before heading up court.

What am *I* gonna do? I'm *just a kid.* At least I can play. Who do they think they are? Real ballers? Please! Not even close. Doing their thing? Puh-lease. I gotta do something. Feels like it's nine on one because not only did I have to keep the other team from scoring, but I had to convince my team to let me even touch the ball.

Jamal tossed the ball in to me and said, "Right back."

I don't think so. As soon as the ball touched my hands, I

pushed it up court. My man jogged up the court slow, so I hit overdrive. I zigged left, zagged right, and darted into the lane where two defenders stood. I rose and floated a teardrop over the taller of the two, and the ball splashed through the net. I eyeballed my teammates as I hustled back on D. That's right, I scored. Again.

"I told y'all . . . GIVE THE YOUNGSTER THE BALL!" House testified.

Dad shook his head. Why'd he do that?

I've scored every time I've touched the ball, and these wannabes still don't show me respect. I glanced over at the sidelines and saw Dad standing now with House next to him, whispering in his ear. My eyes caught Dad's as he pointed toward the action. My man had the ball. He faced me up and dribbled slow. Real slow. And low. I can rob him. Watch the ball. Right. Left. Right—snatch. I poked the ball away and took off downcourt. As soon as I took off, Wiz ran up on my right, clapping for the ball. I looked left and saw Stick running hard too. Jamal was nowhere to be found, but when I heard "Trailer, trailer!" I recognized his voice.

Should I pass it to either of these guys? They hadn't passed it to me, and when I got knocked down, they didn't help me up—they laughed.

Forget them. I took it myself. I knew where I was going. I crossed half-court and looked right and left to make it seem like I was trying to figure out who was gonna get the ball, but when I reached the free-throw line, I crossed the ball from right to left between my legs and laid the ball up with my left hand, my off hand. I kept my eyes on the ball and, as I landed, saw Jamal grab the rebound and put it back in one smooth motion.

"Eight up!" he shouted.

I glanced over at Dad again, and he stared me in the eyes, his arms folded and an unhappy look on his face—probably because he knows I'm better than the clowns I'm playing with.

Stick threw up a couple more bricks and Wiz stayed silent on D, but High-Top and Jamal brought the score to game point. Hard to believe we didn't get blown out, playing the way we played and continued to play. Another one of Stick's air balls had to be retrieved on the far court, so I headed over to the sideline to talk to Dad.

"Can you believe these guys?"

He unfolded his arms. "Them? I can't believe you! What happened to passing the ball? Looking out for your teammates?"

"What are you talking about? Don't you see them not passing it to me? Didn't you see two of 'em laughin' when I got knocked to the ground?" I said, throwing my hands in the air. "Are you even watching the same game as me?"

"As a matter of fact, Shawn, I am. I know they're not passing you the ball and not giving you much help on D, but trying to do everything on your own is not the right way to play. You know better than that. You gotta speak up for yourself, but . . . two wrongs don't make a right."

I wanted to say something else, but I turned around to see Jamal bringing the ball up. I was open and surprisingly he flipped a quick pass to me. I held the ball to figure out my next move. I pointed to the left block, and High-Top, who was closest to me, set a screen where I pointed. As soon as he got into position, I took advantage of the screen and drove to the right. When his defender left him to guard me, I dropped a pass to him as he cut to the basket—a perfect pick and roll.

"Game," High-Top said as the ball dropped through the net.

I looked over to the sideline, and Dad was slapping five with House, who then cupped his hands over his mouth to broadcast in his thunderous voice, "Y'all see that? The youngster does it all! THAT BOY HAS BEEN TOUCHED BY THE HAND OF THE LORD!"

THIRTY-ONE

CHURCH ENDED when the congregation collapsed on the grass in a collective breath of exhaustion. Me and Dad said our good-byes and headed back to the car for our post-church ritual: a burger spot of my choice.

"So, superstar, where you wanna eat?"

We waited at the stop sign while I made my decision. To the left: Fatburger. To the right: In-N-Out. Straight ahead: Tommy's.

"It don't matter — I'm starving. Which is closest?"

"Fatburger it is!" Dad said, turning left.

Of the three spots, In-N-Out was at the top and Tommy's was at the bottom, but they were all my favorites, just for different reasons. In-N-Out had great simple cheeseburgers, but it was drive-thru only. Tommy's had sloppy chili burgers, but it was also drive-thru only. Fatburger was cool 'cause not only could I sit down; I could also get whatever I wanted on my burger. And usually what I wanted was bacon, barbecue sauce, and jalapeños. Dad always got the special—with egg on top. Yecch!

The park disappeared behind us, but the games didn't. Our sweat-drenched bodies filled the car with funk, so I rolled my window down.

"Looks like you got a little better since we last played," Dad said, staring straight ahead, adding, "I take that back—you got a whole lot better. If we were keeping stats, you would've filled up almost every category: points, rebounds, assists, steals."

I stretched my legs out as he asked, "How'd that happen?"

"Just from playin' with my boys, I guess," I said, shrugging. "So, Dad, why you always abusing me with that hook shot? You know I can't stop it."

"That's why I use it. You use whatever you can to get the job done, especially when you get to be my age. You were the fastest out there today, so you used that. House is big and strong, so he uses that. But you know, Shawn, basketball isn't just about how fast you are or how big you are or how nice your J is." He took his right hand off the steering wheel and touched his index finger to his temple as he said, "More than anything, you gotta use your head."

A purple skirt caught my eye as I glanced out the window. Dad brought my attention back to him when he said, "That's what you need to work on."

Here we go.

He continued, "If you wanna play on a team, you gotta

go beyond that. I know you were mad that your team wasn't passing you the ball, but you gotta show them you deserve it."

"But, Dad, you saw how they didn't pass me the ball, even after I scored a couple of baskets. You saw how nobody helped me on D, even when I seemed to be the only one who cared about defense. You saw—"

"Shawn, Shawn, Shawn. Yes, I saw all that. And for the most part, you're right—you played well. But I also saw you throw the ball away a few times. And I saw how you wanted to do everything all by yourself more than a few times."

"That's 'cause I didn't think I'd ever get the ball. I only did what I thought I needed to do so we could win."

Dad spun the steering wheel into the parking lot and we parked. Before we got out, he said, "Just like in chess, you gotta think ahead. Most of the time, the best move isn't the obvious one."

"So . . . I'm supposed to let guys just walk all over me and leave me out of the game?"

We got out and approached the entrance.

"No. But you do need to speak up." He pulled me in close. "And I don't just mean with your words. Actions speak louder than words."

He flung the door open, and the scent of burgers tickled my nose and stomach awake. As we stepped inside, my vision narrowed in on the girl behind the counter. Short and curly brown hair framed a sweet, round, peanut-butter-colored face. Almond-brown eyes fluttered lengthy black eyelashes. Her lips were nice and full and uncolored by lipstick. Her name sparkled in script on a gold necklace just below her chin and just above her uniform-covered breasts, but I couldn't read it. Her skin had a nice glow to it—probably from the grease.

The line was a few people deep, and we stood at the end of it. Instead of looking at the menu, I watched Almond Eyes struggle with a big jar of onions in one hand, while the other hand wiped tears from her eyes. She turned around, and I caught a glimpse of her bouncing behind in her tight black uniform pants. Oh, man. My eyes bounced back and forth between her and the menu over her head. When we reached the counter, I got a better look at her name tag: Yvonne. How do you say that? E-vonne? Or Ya-vonne? Dad elbowed me in the ribs before I could answer my own question. He leaned in from behind and whispered, "I see you're hungry for something other than a burger."

I whipped my head around and shushed him. He bumped me and whispered, "Talk to her."

"Dad, we at Fatburger."

"So, she's here and so are you. You could practice up for . . . what's the Spanish girl's name again?"

"Marisol. And she's Mexican."

"Sorry. Yeah, Marisol. What's Burger Queen's name?" he nodded toward Yvonne, peering in at her name tag.

"Ya-vonne?" he said.

The line moved up by two people, and one person stood between me and the fine Burger Queen.

"You sure it's not E-vonne?" I asked.

As the person in front of us finished giving their order, Dad said, "I don't know. Let's find out."

I backed up behind him and grabbed his arm. "Dad, don't . . ."

"Welcome to Fatburger. Can I take your order?"

We gave our orders without a hitch, and I thought I was home free, but as Dad reached for his wallet, he said, "Ummm, one other thing . . . We were wondering, how do you pronounce your name? I say it's Ya-vonne, but my son"—he pushed me in front of him—"Shawn here, says it's E-vonne. Can you help us out?"

I can't believe Dad is doing this. My heart throbbed in my throat. My mouth watered, and my hands became slippery with sweat. I rubbed them up and down on my shorts. I looked out the window, over at the trash can, above her head, down at the bacon, over at the onions, behind her at the soda fountain; my eyes looked everywhere but at her.

Once her fingers punched everything up, I crept my eyes back in her direction.

"It's E-vonne," she said, moving some curls out of her eyelashes with her right finger before adding, "so I guess your son is right."

Her eyes harnessed mine. Shoot! Why did Dad do this? I don't even know this girl. I don't even live near this girl. I don't know what to say. I don't even know what to do.

Breathe. Inhale. Exhale.

"What was your name again?" she asked, peering at me as I tried to hide behind Dad. He got slick and stepped over to the mustard and ketchup, leaving me all alone in front of her. There was nobody in line behind us, and her coworker stood near the grill making the burgers.

"Ummm, Shawn. My name is Shawn."

"OK, ummm-Shawn." She giggled, and her laugh lit up her face.

Think, Shawn, think. What to say? What to do?

"So . . . E-vonne, that's a pretty name. Where's that come from?"

Dumb question. Why'd you ask her that?

"My mom." She laughed again.

"I mean, any particular reason she chose that name?"

Don't insult the girl's name, Shawn.

"It's the same as hers," she said.

"Oh. That makes sense."

Oh, that makes sense?

Her necklace shimmered at me as she leaned forward on the counter and said, "What about you? Where does your name come from?"

"Number 242," her coworker shouted. He handed Yvonne the tray, and she handed it to an older white dude as he handed her his ticket. Shoot, you better get on the ball, Shawnie-Shawn, before more people come in; the girl *is* still working.

"My Dad. He has the same name," I said, nodding at Dad sitting near a window watching us.

"So I guess we have something in common, huh?" she said, twirling a finger into a short brown curl.

"Yeah, I guess so."

"Number 875" was called out, and a pair of very large, very dark-skinned brothers came up and grabbed two very full trays.

Yvonne grabbed a washcloth and a spray bottle and started cleaning a stack of trays in front of me. She doesn't wanna leave?

"So, Shawn, you live around here?"

"Sort of. My dad lives a couple blocks away, but I live in Carson. I see him twice a month . . . on the weekends."

What are you doing? That's too much information. What did Dad say? Ask about her.

"What about you? You live around here?"

Of course she lives around here. Stupid question, Shawn.

"Number 243" was called, and a young white woman and her toddler of a daughter came up. The mother looked at her tray, pursed her lips, then said, "Where's my drink?"

Yvonne looked at the woman's receipt, then grabbed a large cup and filled it with root beer. I glanced over at Dad, who sat with his hands behind his head, smiling.

"What'd you say again? Where do I live?"

I nodded.

"Right up the street—close enough to walk."

She finished her trays and started filling the containers with assorted toppings. She excused herself for a second, and I watched her disappear into the back. A big bag of lettuce was in her hands as she emerged from the refrigerator. She reached under the counter and plunged a knife through the big bag. Ask about her.

"So . . . you go to school here?"

"Yeah, I'm gonna be a junior at Uni High. What about you?"

Go, Shawn. Go, Shawn. Check you out, talking to a junior—a *fine* junior. But what do I tell her about my school? I don't even know what *my* school is gonna be. Should I make something up? Nah, she may know somebody at either school.

"Well . . . I'm just getting ready to start high school, but I haven't figured out which one."

Her blade paused in the plastic as she heard my answer.

"For reals? You mean you not even *in* high school yet?" she said, choking back a laugh.

I knew it. I knew I shoulda lied about my grade. I blew it. Stop talking. Just stop talking, Shawn. You gonna mess it up if you open your mouth again.

Her knife started moving.

"Well, you sure don't look like no freshman," she said, smiling, then added, "But what you mean you don't know which high school you gonna go to? How can you not know? You moving or something?"

"Number 876" was called, and Dad came over and took the tray away. Shoot! I gotta go. I was just getting going too.

"Not quite. It's kind of a long story," I said, brushing my fingers across my sideburns. Maybe that's why she thought I was older.

I dropped my head and was about to follow Dad when she said, "Maybe next time you come in, you can tell me all about it."

Next time? Tell her all about it? Dang—she wants to talk to me again? The words slid from her lips as she leaned on the main counter, about waist high. The second button on her polo shirt popped open. Her gold YVONNE necklace swayed back and forth like a watch swung by a hypnotist . . . and I was hypnotized—*Pop.* A picture of her snapped into my memory as I tried not to stare.

I excused myself, and me and Dad headed to our table. My head swiveled around, and my eyes bounced with Yvonne's bottom as she disappeared into the back. *Whew!*

Yvonne. Pronounced E-vonne. Named after her mother. Lives close enough to walk to work. A junior at University High. Wants to hear *my* long story. A junior! That's like . . . sixteen. Go, Shawnie, go, Shawnie, go, Shawnie-Shawnie-Shawn-Shawnie!

Dad and I sat in silence except for the sound of burger bites, fry crunches, and soda slurps. Yvonne must have taken a break because she didn't come out of the back for a while, but when she did, she tickled a wave at me. Just like Marisol.

Marisol. I hadn't thought about her much this weekend. I mean, between the black eye, the haircut, and ball, I had other things on my mind. But Yvonne had made her pop back into my head: same height; skin color and eye color about the same too. The main difference was the hair; Yvonne's was short and curly, and Marisol's was long and straight. Yvonne's body was also a little more, uh, filled out than Marisol's too. A little more up top and little more in the corners department too.

I kinda wish the fellas were here to see this. They won't believe I had the guts to talk to a girl as fine as Yvonne. But I know if they were here, they'd say something like they did the other day in front of the Hut. All them sounds and stuff . . .

makes me mad just thinking about it. If they did that, Yvonne would definitely know I wasn't in high school. It don't matter now anyway, 'cause they aren't here. I am. With Yvonne. Lorenzo was right about one thing though: life is good when girls are smiling at you, and Yvonne smiled a lot—a *whole* lot. At me. Even when she found out I was gonna be a freshman! I wonder if Marisol thinks I don't look like a freshman? She knows how old I am, so it might not have even crossed her mind.

From now on when I come to Dad's, no more In-N-Out or Tommy's; strictly Fatburger on Sundays after church. Hallelujah! Too bad I'm only here twice a month. I wish there was a way I could see more of Miss Yvonne. Wait . . . what if . . .

"Dad?" I chewed.

A splash of bright yellow egg yolk squirted out of his burger and onto a fry as he took a huge bite. Ugh.

"What?" He chewed.

"It's my decision where I go to school, right?"

I crunched a fry.

"Yeah."

"Well, what if I went to school out here"—I crunched another fry—"and lived with you?"

He was about to take another bite of his mess of a burger but paused. "Why? Because of Miss E-vonne?" He nodded back toward the counter.

"Come on, Dad. You saw how she was talking to me." I leaned in and whispered over the hot food. "Did I tell you she was a junior?"

He sat back in his chair and crossed his arms. "Really?"

He sounded more surprised than me when I heard her say that. But that didn't keep him from saying, "Now, come on, Shawn. Do you really wanna leave all your friends behind and everything you know in Compton *and* Carson to go to high school out here because of some girl you just met at Fatburger?"

His left eyebrow arched up as he took another bite of his burger.

"What if this girl has a boyfriend?" He chewed. "You ever think about that?"

Shoot. I didn't. I figured that since she was talking to me, she was free as the breeze. It don't matter anyway. I just think it'd be cool to live with Dad. I only see him once in a while, and we always have a good time. Lately me and Mama just been butting heads left and right. She's constantly on my case and jumping to conclusions. Like with my black eye. The fellas in the barbershop treated me like a warrior coming home from battle. But Mama? She treated me like a 'banger-in-training.

"True, true. But what about me and you . . . living together?"

I bit into my burger again.

"I don't know, Shawn. Don't get me wrong. I love spending time with you, I really, truly do. But we see each other on the weekends; it's easy. I don't have to work. You don't have school, and we can just hang out and do whatever we want. But when I'm working . . . I'm on the run and not home a whole lot."

He bit into his burger, then took a big slurp of soda, adding, "Besides, your mother has you officially until you're eighteen."

"What do you mean 'has me officially until I'm eighteen'?"

"Well, when we got the divorce"—he chewed to a stop—"she got custody of you until your eighteenth birthday. I'd have to go to court to change that."

"And you don't wanna do that?"

"Listen, Shawn, everything is cool the way it is right now and—"

"But it's not cool, Dad. Mama's always on my case. She don't trust me. She don't like my friends. And, to top it off, she still treats me like a child."

He sat forward and clasped his hands on the table.

"Shawn, I know it's hard with just the two of you right now, but a drastic change like that is just not gonna happen. That would kill your mother—you're all she's got. I know it doesn't always seem like it, but she loves you more than anything in the world, and to pull you out of her life right now would be . . . it would be a big deal to her. A really big deal."

I glanced up toward Yvonne, only to find her chatting with another guy who looked older than me. And her. I put up my burger up to hide my face.

"Besides, the only person you know out here besides me is Burger Queen. And you don't really *know* her."

Good thing Dad couldn't see Yvonne going through the same motions with this new guy like she did with me.

Smiling—like she did with me. Laughing—like she did with me. And leaning on the counter—DANG!—just like she did with me.

I'm glad Dad didn't see her; I'd never hear the end of it. I can see it now: an endless stream of "I told you so's" and jokes about how well I *know* her. I finished off my last few fries and sucked up my last swallow of soda. We threw our mountain of napkins onto our trays and gathered up our trash before standing. My arms stretched east and west and caught Yvonne's attention. I looked at her and she looked away. How many other "Shawns" has she talked to since she's worked here? Hey, I can't be mad at her. A girl as fine as she is probably gets talked to all the time—at least she talked to me in the first place. I guess she *is* free as the breeze.

Dad and I made our way to the door just as Yvonne's new "friend" was getting ready to leave. Dad held the door open behind me. The "friend" stood in front of me and couldn't see me. The "friend" waved 'bye to Yvonne first. I couldn't help it—did the same. She tickled a wave good-bye. To both of us. Dad saw it all—and laughed.

THIRTY-TWO

WHEN WE GOT HOME, Dad jumped in the shower. I stretched my back across my bed, kicked my shoes off, and stared at the ceiling. Yvonne — sigh — Yvonne . . . a junior. I still can't believe a junior was talking to me — li'l ol' Shawn Williams from Carson. Future freshman at . . .

I sat up. I couldn't finish the sentence. What was I gonna do? I wanted to hang with my friends at Marshall, but I wanted to give Carson a chance too. But what would I get out of going there?

I'd be the new guy. That could be a good thing. Or a bad thing. Girls would wonder who I was and how old I was. Guys would wonder if I'm any good at sports; that could be good — my b-ball skill could sneak up on them. I could take classes at Carson they probably don't have at Marshall. Like French. And I wouldn't have to worry about any of my classmates stabbing the teacher. Or me. That would definitely be good. I wonder what kind of people *do* go there. I know there's blacks and Mexicans, but what else? Carson has a lot of Samoans — we have four families on our block alone — so I'm sure I'd see plenty of them. But what else? I wonder if Carson is smaller than Marshall. I should find out. Now that I was finally thinking about it, I had more questions than answers.

I plopped back onto the bed. It'd be hard to leave my boys. And Marisol. Could I really leave her behind? I don't know, but after talking to Yvonne today and seeing all them bikinis yesterday . . . it's a wide-open world when it comes to girls. Man, Dad was right: girls always figure into the equation somehow. This wasn't gonna be easy.

"Shower's all yours," Dad said, poking his head into my room with a towel around his waist.

The clock ticked two; just a few hours to go before Dad would take me home. It felt like forever since I was home or saw the fellas. If they could have seen me this weekend . . . man! Andre would have gotten a kick out of seeing me on the court today. Lorenzo would have gotten a kick out of seeing me talk to Yvonne — if he didn't try to talk to her himself. And all of them would have gotten a kick out of being surrounded by all those bikinis on the pier yesterday — a *big* kick.

As the water washed over me in the shower, I closed my eyes and opened my mental movie screen. Kaleidoscopic images collided in crystal-clear colors: peach fingernails . . . blue sarong . . . orange bikini . . . bright smiles . . . dark skin . . . light skin . . . Yvonne . . . Marisol . . . Carson . . . Compton . . . Lorenzo . . . Trent . . . Andre . . . Auntie . . . Mama.

The once-hot water was cool and turning colder by the second. Dang, Dad used all the hot water! I hurried to rinse the soap off my lathered-up body. By the time my wet feet stepped onto the cold tile, I was shivering.

Dad knocked at the door. "I'm gonna take a nap. If I'm not up by four, wake me."

"OK," I yelled.

Four? That's almost two hours away. What was I gonna do until then? I combed my hair and moved closer to the mirror to inspect my sideburns; they were already getting darker. The hair on my upper lip was getting darker too. Cool. I should have a full-blown mustache soon. I wonder what the fellas will think. And Marisol. I hope I see her soon. With summer, you never know. Sometimes you see somebody every day for a month, then you don't see them again until the first day of school. I hoped I would see her before that.

I backed away from the mirror and patted my hair. It looked good. I touched my less-black eye. It looked good. I rubbed my cheeks. My sideburns looked good too—shoot, I looked good. Don't fall in love with yourself, though, Shawn. Remember, Dad said girls hate that.

I rubbed on some deodorant, got dressed, and went back to my room. I sat on my bed, twiddled my thumbs, and stared into space. What now? I took a walk around the house, looking for something to do and found myself standing in front of Dad's bookcase—or should I say bookcases. Dad and Mama have always loved to read; maybe that's where I got it from. Mama loves romance, horror, and mysteries. Dad loves pretty much everything else: old stuff, new stuff, fiction, nonfiction, history, travel—you name it. He's had bookcases in every place he's lived, but over the years he's added more books to his collection, so he's needed more shelves . . . way more shelves.

Five cases towered in front of me. All about the same height; a little taller than me with five shelves on each one. I scanned the titles: *Soul on Ice* . . . *Miles* . . . *Think and Grow Rich* . . . *The Godfather* . . . *Cane* . . . *The Fire Next Time* . . . *Roots* . . . *Cotton Comes to Harlem* . . . *Mumbo Jumbo*—*Mumbo Jumbo?* . . . *The Autobiography of Malcolm X*—*The Autobiography of Malcolm X?* Didn't that professor recommend this to Mama for me? I tugged it out. A picture of Malcolm X stared at me from the cover and "As told to the author of *Roots*" blared below the title. I snatched it and headed outside.

When Dad asked what kind of house I thought he should get, in addition to mentioning that it be on a hill overlooking the ocean, I also said it would be great to have a hammock. So, on my first visit a few years ago, we went and picked one out together: bone-colored with big holes to let the breeze in. We hung it under two trees, and it's gotten plenty of use ever since.

I positioned myself in it and got comfortable. The warm California breeze caressed my scalp as the ocean glittered in the distance. The neighbor's palm trees leaned over to sneak a peek at what I was reading as I stretched out and cracked open the world of Malcolm X.

The book caught my attention from the first sentence when it opened with him talking about the KKK knocking on his mother's door while he was still in her belly, and it only got better as his unbelievable life unfolded before my eyes. I was surprised by the things that happened in his life, but it wasn't until he talked about eighth grade that I completely identified with what he was going through. He was one of the top students in his class and elected class president. He was also one of the few black students in the school, but back then he wasn't called black—he was called a Negro half the time and a nigger the other half. Dang.

Anyway, Malcolm's English teacher called him in after school to talk about his future before he went to high school, just like this teacher did with all the other students. Malcolm and two of his classmates shared the highest grades in the school, but when he mentioned to his teacher that he might want to be a lawyer, his teacher, who had given him some of his highest marks, laughed in his face and suggested that Malcolm "stay in his place." He then suggested that Malcolm do something more realistic for a nigger, like be a carpenter, because he was good with his hands. Never mind the fact that he told the other students with worse grades than Malcolm that they could be anything they wanted. Dang!

Eventually, the name-calling and poor treatment he got for being black drove him from the detention home he stayed at in Michigan to his half-sister's home in Boston. His half-sister was a very dark yet proud member of the black race, unlike many of the other blacks he encountered at the time: those who bowed to whites, those who dismissed other blacks as inferior because of their dark complexion, and those who were content to make a living as a shoe-shine boy or waiter at the local country club. None of that was for Malcolm. He asked his half-sister, whom he'd only spoken to in letters, and she took custody of him. He looked forward to something in Boston that didn't exist in Michigan: the chance to dream.

He was fourteen, just like me, when he made that decision. I don't know if I could've done that, but times were different back then, and he saw an opportunity for change and jumped on it. He didn't know what would happen in Boston, but he knew it had to be better than staying in Michigan. I'm not in the same exact position, but I don't know what's gonna happen either way. His decision was a little easier: stay in Michigan and be called a nigger while he worked as a shoe-shine boy or carpenter, or take the first train to Boston and start over. The details of his move faded as my eyes drifted into sleep, and the image of Malcolm on the page was replaced by Dad standing over me, blocking out the sun and shaking me awake.

"Go get your stuff. We're leaving soon."

I rubbed my eyes awake.

"Already?"

"Whatchu mean already? It's a quarter to five."

I sat up. "A quarter to five? Shoot. I forgot to wake you up."

"That's all right. I needed the rest."

Dad eyeballed the book as I dog-eared the page and got out of the hammock.

"*Malcolm X?* I was wondering when you'd find that book."

We stepped into the house, me bringing up the rear.

"Whaddyou mean 'when'? You knew I was gonna read this?"

He rubbed his goatee.

"I didn't know exactly when, but I had a feeling you'd read it sooner or later," he said.

"Well, there wasn't much to do when you took your nap, so I grabbed a book. I do like to read, you know."

"I know you do. That's why I kept most of my old books. I just didn't expect you to read today. Shoot, I thought you would've walked down to Fatburger to talk to Miss Thing again." He laughed.

"Ha-ha. Very funny!"

"Go get your stuff so we can leave."

I held up the book. "Can I take this with me?"

"Of course."

I got my stuff together and threw it in my bag. My pajama shorts crunched when I folded them up. Gross. Mama's gonna know it happened again. I hope she doesn't give me a hard time about it.

"Ready."

We hopped in the car, and the yellow house at the end of the block with 100 on the mailbox and the hammock in the backyard disappeared behind us, not to be seen by my eyes for another couple of weeks at least. My mind wandered back to Malcolm and his move: Michigan to Boston. The segregated Midwest to the wide-open Northeast. That's a pretty big change. Especially for that time. Especially at that age.

"So, Dad, when did you read that book?"

Dad swung his head over at me as we got on the freeway.

"What? *Malcolm X?*" He paused. "Shoot . . . I read that a while ago. I gotta think way back for that."

His eyes ran through a range of emotions, ending with surprise.

"Actually, it was right before you were born. I was driving a cab, and I read it while waiting for fares at the airport. It blew my mind. I had heard about what he had done when I was a lot younger, but I didn't know much about him as a person." He looked over at me and asked, "How far did you get?"

"I fell asleep just after he moved to Boston." I paused. "He was fourteen, you know."

That turned Dad's head my way.

"Really? I read it so long ago, I don't remember all the details. I remember Boston, but where was he before that?"

"Michigan."

I ran the story down about his English teacher and why he left Michigan, and Dad shook his head the whole time. He sat up straight and said, "I guess he proved his teacher wrong."

I nodded. Skyscrapers shadowed the car as we wound our way through downtown L.A. I thought about Malcolm at fourteen and Malcolm as an adult. I'm glad times have changed. Yeah, things happen here and there, but it's not like it was. If I was at the top of my class and my teacher suggested I stay in *my* place, Mama *and* Dad would give that teacher an earful and make sure he no longer taught me or any other student ever again. I'm sure plenty of black parents felt the same way, but what could they really do? Especially in a time when if a black person talked back to a white person, he could find himself beaten up or, worse, strung up in a tree like a piñata.

Malcolm hoped Boston would be better for him, but he didn't know what was gonna happen. When he was on that bus, was he scared? Excited? Which did he think about more: his past in Michigan . . . or his future in Boston? Was there a girl who made the decision to leave harder for him? My decision wasn't quite the same, but it was still a big one. I had no idea which school would be better for me. I'm sure Malcolm had no idea either, but like Dad said, we know what he went on to become. Did that decision have anything to do with it?

Malcolm stayed in my thoughts right up until we pulled into the driveway. That was fast.

"Look at you. Eye looking bad. Hair looking good," Mama said, opening the door.

"And what's this?" She ran her fingers along my face, then turned my head left and right to inspect my sideburns.

"I'm starving. We got anything to eat?" I said as I kissed her and entered the kitchen.

"Glad to see you too, Shawn," I heard from behind.

"How you doing, Shawn?" Mama asked Dad as he stepped in the door.

"I'm good, Brenda. You have a good weekend?"

Mama made her way into the kitchen, and Dad followed.

"Yeah, I was finally able to clean this house from top to bottom. Speaking of which . . . Shawn, your room looks like a cyclone hit it, so I left that for you."

Here we go.

Dad took a seat at the kitchen table. Mama joined him. I hunted through the cabinets and fridge for something to eat.

"What's for dinner?"

"There's a roast in the oven. It should be done in a few minutes."

I found a fresh bag of tortilla chips and some salsa and joined them at the table. Everybody started crunching chips.

"So?" Mama said.

"So, what?" I crunched.

"So how was your weekend?"

"It was cool." I chewed.

"You guys do anything special?"

"We went to the Santa Monica Pier yesterday, hung out, took some pictures, but today was more mellow." Dad crunched.

"That reminds me . . ." I got up to get the book. "Look what I found." I tossed it in front of Mama.

She held up *Malcolm X*. "Yeah, I remember this book. Your father got it right after we got married, read it, and started wearing dashikis and black leather jackets." Mama laughed toward Dad. "Talking about 'Black Power' and stuff."

Dad rolled his eyes and folded his arms. "That was a while ago."

"Really, Dad? Did you wanna be Malcolm X or something?"

"Not quite, but no other bruthas had said what he did, and I connected to a lot of it."

"So you read any of it, Shawnie?" Mama asked.

"He just started today. Tell her where you are," Dad said.

"He just moved to Boston from Michigan." I crunched. "At age fourteen."

"Is that right?" She chewed. "You learn anything that might help you?"

"I learned I ain't Malcolm X."

Me and Dad laughed. Mama crossed her arms. "Shawn, I'm serious."

"I'm just messing with you, Mama. I learned I have a tough decision to make that could affect my future."

"Could?" Dad said.

I rolled my eyes. "*Will* affect my future."

Mama got up. She opened the oven to check on the roast, and the scent of seasoned meat snaked up my nose. She stirred the potatoes, carrots, and peas around and closed the oven door. Ohh, that smelled too good.

"When we gonna eat?"

"In a few minutes. You want stay for dinner, Shawn?"

Dad paused to finish chewing his chips, then said, "Thanks, but I gotta run. I gotta catch up on some work before tomorrow."

Chips crunched around the table until Mama said, "I'm glad to see you taking this decision seriously."

Yvonne snapped into my head. If only Mama knew about the conversation me and Dad had about Miss Thing, aka Burger Queen.

"So how long do I have to make it?"

I looked at the two of them. Dad looked at Mama.

"Well, I was going through your registration papers for Marshall, and final registration is about two weeks before school starts. That's about a month away."

She dusted her hands off. "So I would say a month from today. That should give you plenty of time to figure it out."

A month? I guess that's not too bad.

"There you go. One month. That's four weeks to decide where you wanna spend the next four years of your life," Dad said.

Dang. Why he say it like that? A month sounded much longer than four weeks. It's gonna be here before I know it.

Dad stood. "I gotta run, but I'll see you in a couple of weeks, all right?"

I stood and we gave each other a hug and slaps on the back. Dad whispered in my ear as Mama pulled the roast out of the oven, "Remember what I said? You control *it*—don't let *it* control you."

Yvonne popped into my head. Mama wiped away the image of Yvonne leaning on the counter with "Dinner's ready."

I loved hanging at Dad's, but I was glad to be eating Mama's home cooking again. Most of the stuff Auntie makes Mama makes too, but Mama gets a little exotic sometimes, making stuff like Japanese sukiyaki, enchiladas, Chinese food, Italian food, and all kinds of other stuff. Dad makes great tacos and . . . well, he makes great tacos. I'm glad I can eat whatever I want when I'm at his house, but Dad doesn't cook much, so by the time I see Mama on Sunday, I'm ready for some real food.

And that's what Mama made: real food. A typical Sunday dinner: pot roast with carrots, potatoes, peas, and hot rolls. The rolls were my favorite. I took the bread, split it open, spread butter inside, and jammed it with wedges of tender pot roast, eating it like a sandwich. My mouth exploded with flavor as Mama spoke.

"So . . . did your father talk to you about anything in particular?"

My mouth chewed the mini sandwich until I was able to speak.

"Yeah. A few things."

She scratched her fork across her plate.

"You talk about your eye?"

"Yeah, we talked about it," I said before plunging a forkful of carrots in my mouth.

"And?"

I put my fork down and took a sip of water.

"*And* what? We talked about it, and that was the end of it."

"The end of it?" She put her fork down and brought her hands up to rest her chin on them. I felt her eyes on me as I mashed the peas on my plate. I hate peas.

"I mean . . . we talked about other stuff related to that too."

She ripped into a fresh roll. "What kind of other stuff?"

"Oh . . . you know . . . how it'll affect my decision."

She sawed into her meat. "I see."

We sawed and chewed in belly-filling silence for a good couple of minutes. I hadn't eaten anything except chips since

Fatburger, and this was hitting the spot. Hard to believe that was just this afternoon; it felt like years ago now.

"Dad got to see how good I am at basketball today," I said.

"Did he think you weren't good?" She rubbed her roll around her empty plate, sopping up the gravy.

"He knows I can play, but he hasn't seen me in a while. He was surprised at how good I got in such a short time." I bit into my potatoes and smacked. "I'm pretty good, you know."

"You better be, as much as you play."

I pointed a forkful of meat at her. "So what about you, Mama? Please tell me you did something else besides clean the house this weekend."

Her plate was empty, so she sat back.

"As a matter of fact, I did."

I stabbed more meat to work on.

"You gonna tell me, or you gonna leave me hangin'?"

She hesitated.

"I went on a date."

I dropped my fork and drank some water.

"A date? With who?"

She spun her plate around.

"Professor Hopkins . . . from school."

"I knew it! I thought you said there wasn't anything going on between you two?"

"There wasn't—until Friday. He asked me to a jazz festival this weekend, so I said why not?"

She got up and scratched her slippers toward the sink.

"I wouldn't even call it a date."

I finished my food and carried my plate over. "I would."

"Oh, hush, boy. It was a nice day, so we had a picnic and listened to some jazz. He dropped me off when it was over and that was it. We didn't even talk about going out again."

"Why? You scare him away?"

She flicked water my direction as she rinsed the plates off.

"No . . . we had a good time."

She paused and put her head down. "He just didn't ask me."

Did she wanna go out with him again? Maybe that would mellow her out. All she really has is me and Auntie to hang with. And she don't hang with Auntie. Maybe Dad was right. If I left . . .

"Well, I'm sure he'll ask you again." I slung my arm around her and got in her face. "I mean, who can resist this face?"

I grabbed her cheeks and stretched them like taffy.

"Shawn, stop!" She aimed the sprayer at my face and squeezed.

I ducked and dodged and did what I could, but she got me good.

"Come on, Mama. My shirt is getting soaked."

"All right, all right. I'm done anyway. Why don't you go put your stuff in your room?"

I headed to my room as she called out, "And clean it while you're in there."

I peeled off my soaked shirt, threw it to the floor, then plopped on my bed and stretched out. So Mama had a date this weekend? Good for her. For real. I couldn't be here by myself all weekend — alone — with nothing to do but clean the house. I wonder what this "Professor Hopkins" dude is like. Is he black? White? Tall? Short? What? I bet he's black. All the books he's recommended so far have been by black authors. I wonder what he looks like. Hopkins. Sounds like a nerd. Hop . . . kins. I bet he wears glasses. I can just see him in one of them brown tweed jackets with the patches on the sleeves, puffing on a pipe. Wearing his glasses. Big, thick, Coke-bottle glasses that you can see China with.

I got up. What time is it? Seven thirty. Still early. Dang! My room *was* a mess. I might as well clean it. It'll give me something to do and give a fresh start to the week.

I unpacked my bag and unfolded my crunchy shorts. Ughh. I almost forgot about them. I grabbed my wet shirt off the floor and rolled it into the shorts so they would both be moist. I'm sure she knows "my accident" is gonna happen again, but at least she won't know it happened this weekend at Dad's.

I stepped around the room, plucking piles of clothes from the floor and furniture. A white T-shirt here. A gray T-shirt there. Black shorts here. More black shorts there. It wasn't until I peeled a pair of purple shorts off my bed did I realize I didn't have much color in my wardrobe. That wasn't necessarily by accident. Whenever we went shopping and Mama held up anything blue or red, the only thing I could think of was the Crips and Pirus, so I always passed on what she picked out.

I sat down on my bed. Exhale. I'm tired of thinking about them. I'm tired of thinking about what colors I can and can't wear. I'm tired of always trying to figure out which park I can or can't play ball at. My heart began to race. Now I know the anger Malcolm felt. The Crips and Pirus are black just like me, but they might as well be white and I might as well be living in the segregated South, because as far as I'm concerned, if you can't wear what you want or go where you want, when you want, then you ain't free. Plain and simple. In Compton you gotta watch your back, because if you young like me, at any moment you can find yourself facedown with a mouthful of dirt and a foot pushing you down simply because a bunch of 'bangers are bored.

My anger pulsed through my blood and brought me to my feet. I put it to use by finishing my room. Every plain white T-shirt and basic black pair of shorts I picked up added fuel to my fire. No red clothes. No blue clothes. No color. No control. No freedom.

The safest I ever felt was with my boys. And even that was starting to change, with Dayshaun getting his wrist crushed. Who knows what'll happen next, now that we mixed it up with the knuckleheads. If Dayshaun's dad ever found out about that, he might not even let 'Zo hang with us anymore; he already thinks the four of us are a gang. Most people do. They think I don't see them watching us. I know what they see — they see what they wanna see. They see four of us walking down the street and think we wanna rob them. They think we want what they have when we not even thinking about them at all. Why can't we just be four young black kids? Better yet, why can't we just be four teenagers? Not four suspicious characters. We aren't characters. We real — I'm real.

Flesh-and-bone real. Having-two-parents real. Basketball-playing real. Book-reading real. Cracking-jokes real. Stealing-pomegranates real. Kung-fu movie–watching real. Daydreaming real. Girl-watching real. Bikini-loving real. Untrusted real. Getting-smacked-with-fists-and-clubs real . . .

"I'M REAL!"

I slammed my clothes against the wall like paint splashing a blank canvas.

My chest pumped anger through my nose as my heart slowed its beat. I stared through the wall in front of me, then at it like I had never seen it before.

My green T-shirt from junior high dangled from my Bruce Lee poster. All my other clothes lay in a big pile against the wall. I reached out for the shirt. And thought of Marisol. And her smile — bright as the sun, soft as green grass.

The sun of her smile blew my blues away.

She made my heart race. She made my palms sweat. She made my nerves buzz. She made my nose twitch. She made my mouth water. She made my tongue twist. She made my eyes wide. She made me look to the sky. She made me dream. She made me see the beauty of life. She . . .

She made me feel real.

THIRTY-THREE

MONDAY CAME and I hit the ground running. When me and the fellas met in front of Pop's, they all got a kick out of my new haircut and sideburns—especially my sideburns.

"I didn't even know you had sideburn hair," Trent said, inspecting them up close.

"Neither did I," I replied.

Lorenzo told us Dayshaun had a huge cast on his wrist, and as far as his dad knew, it happened playing basketball.

I told them about Yvonne, and Lorenzo said, "See, Shawn, you ain't ready for that. I should've been there. I would've handled that like a real man."

To which Trent replied, "You ain't no man."

"I see your black eye is almost all gone too," Andre said, inspecting my eye.

"Yeah, I did the steak thing when I got to my Auntie's on Friday, and it did feel good, but mostly I just kept putting ice on it over the weekend."

"I told you steak works," Lorenzo said.

"Dang, Shawn . . . sideburns, almost no black eye — it's like you a whole new man," Trent said.

"HAH!" Lorenzo burst. "Like Trent said, 'He ain't no man.'"

We teased as usual. Joked as usual. Laughed as usual. Messed around as usual. And played ball as usual. But I never mentioned the decision I had to make. I would tell them only if I decided to go to Carson; no use in saying anything unless I had to.

The days ran into each other as summer tumbled faster toward the first day of school. Our basketball games ran longer. Our movie watching became more frequent. And Auntie made more bottles crack open and disappear. Mama went out with Professor Hopkins a few more times and loosened up on me a bit. Dad cut short a visit because he got called away to a major earthquake. I wanted to go with him, but he said natural disasters are great for pictures but not much else. It was just as well because a weekend at home gave me a chance to pick Brian's brain on my possible future high school in Carson.

"How many people go there?"

"About five hundred per grade, so . . . about two thousand."

"How many lunch periods you have?"

"Two."

"You guys have a pink slip?"

"A what?"

I broke down the pink slip and, just like Mama, he didn't believe me, so I said, "That's what I've heard."

"Nahhh, we don't have anything like that because we don't need it. I can't believe they let him do that."

"The Crips and Pirus do much worse."

He nodded. "I guess so."

"You got a school paper or anything like that?"

"Yeah. A good one too. There's also the yearbook."

"What about sports? How you guys do in sports?"

"Our football team has gone to the state finals ever since I been there, which is a couple of years now. That's because of the Samoans. We got a whole bunch of 'em, especially on the offensive line. As big as they are, you or I could run behind them without getting touched." He laughed.

He looked to the sky for a moment. "What else? Oh, yeah, our basketball team is good. I know a couple of guys who got recruited by UCLA, Cal State Dominguez Hills, USC . . ."

"So what kind of people go there?"

"You mean what color?"

"Yeah."

"Oh, you know . . . we got a little bit of everything—mostly black and white. Some Mexicans. A few Chinese. And of course, Samoans. We got a lot of them *and*"—he bumped my shoulder—"we got plenty of fine girls."

That got my attention. The bikini parade on the pier a few weeks back popped into my head. So did Miss Yvonne. So did the guy she was talking to after me.

"That help?"

"A little bit."

"So what you gonna do?"

"I don't know, Bri. I still don't know."

About a week before I had to make my decision, I ran into Marisol. Me and the boys were cooling off at the Tamale Hut when she breezed in. My back was to the door, so Lorenzo kicked me when he saw her.

"Shawn . . . turn around."

"Why?"

"Just turn around."

Trent glanced back, then knocked my shoulder. "Check it out. It's your hot tamale."

He grabbed my head and spun it around for me, but I swiveled it back before Marisol had a chance to see me. Andre waved at her to come join us, making me slide down into my seat.

"What's wrong with you, man?" I whispered.

"What's wrong with me? What's wrong with you? Look at you, trying to hide from her. This ain't hide and seek. . . . You better talk to her," he said, sliding out of his seat.

He nodded at Trent and 'Zo to join him outside, and they followed, but not before Lorenzo said, "You better handle that, Shawn. Because if you don't . . ."

"Will you get out of here, 'Zo," I said as Marisol started over. Ivy was with her. Marisol whispered something to her, then left her, near the counter.

All right, Shawn. Just like last time with Yvonne. Remember what Dad said: Look at her, talk about her, compliment her, pay attention to her, don't —

"Hey, Shawn. I haven't seen you in a while," she said, taking a seat facing me.

Come on, Shawn. Don't be nervous.

"I been around. Me and the guys just been hanging out as usual."

Not bad. Not bad. Ask about her.

"How's your summer been?"

She flicked her braid to the back. Oh, man. That hair. Those eyes—

"So far so good," she said with a smile. "How 'bout yours? You do anything special?"

"Not really."

Not really? Come on, Shawn, you can do better than that.

Her chin rested in her palm, her arm propped straight up on the table, as she looked me in the eyes. Uh-oh. Look away. No. Don't look away. Come on, Shawn. Relax. Remember Yvonne. What did Dad say? Talk about her.

I looked at her bare arm glowing in front of me, beneath her chin. "Are you a lefty?"

She raised her head. "Yeah, how'd you know?"

She looked surprised. I hope I didn't embarrass her. I pointed at her arm on the table and said, "Whenever I do that, I do it with my right hand because that's what's comfortable for me. You're using your left, so I thought . . ."

"You thought right," she said with a big grin.

I put my hands on the table and thumb-wrestled in silence. She surprised me when she reached across and touched my hands. She barely touched them, but she did touch them.

"I almost forgot . . . I'm so glad I ran into you. I never got to officially invite you to my birthday party." She let go, then said, "It's this Saturday. You think you can come?"

Huh? Her birthday? Hey now! Go, Shawn! Hold on. Calm down. Be cool. But not too cool. Hurry up and say something before she thinks you don't wanna go.

"I think so. Lemme check with my mom to make sure we not doing anything," I said, knowing full well that Mama would probably just clean the house.

"Here," she said, pulling a pen and a tiny heart-shaped notebook from her purple purse, "let me give you all the information."

She scribbled on the pad. "Here's the address and my phone number in case you get lost." She pushed the paper across the table. "It starts at seven."

"Really? Seven?"

"Yeah, my brother got a DJ and everything. I hope you can come."

Me too.

Ivy came over as she stood. "I gotta go, but I hope I see you this weekend."

Her pale purple sundress leaped just above her knees as she flounced out. Her long black hair, tied into a braid with two yellow bubbles, swayed like a horse tail over her purple-covered butt. Hmmm . . . purple and yellow. I wonder if she likes the Lakers. She flipped her braid aside and gave a wave good-bye as she stepped back into the heat of the day.

The bell on the door clanged when she left, then again when the guys came in. The heart-shaped paper with her address and phone number sat on the table as they walked over. I better hide it or I won't hear the end of it. Lorenzo saw me reaching for it and grabbed my hand. "What you got there, Shawnie-Shawn?"

He snatched it.

"Gimme that!"

"I just wanna see what it is." He held it above my head and waved it around.

"Come on, Shawn, let us see," Trent said.

'Zo sat down and placed it on the table.

"SHAWN! You got them digits! AND her address?"

He bumped my shoulder.

"And what's this?" He pointed to the time. "You gonna meet up for a little . . ."

I snatched the paper back. "It's for her birthday, fool. Her party is this weekend, and she invited me."

They jumped up and whaled on my head.

"Shawnie-Shawn got a girlfriend. Shawnie's got a girlfriend," they sang for the whole Hut to hear. I tried to put my head down, but Trent held me up while Andre and Lorenzo each sang into an ear.

"Come on, y'all. Stop! Get off me!"

I broke free and rushed out the door. They followed and ran up in front of me to make me stop.

"So you going?"

"What you gonna get her?"

"Can we go too?"

I stopped and looked each one in the eye.

"To answer your questions: probably, I don't know, and I don't think so."

"Aw, come on, Shawn. That's cold," Trent said. "At least tell us if you going or not; you know you want to."

Lorenzo jumped in. "Of course he's going. He's a fool if he don't. And he better take us with him." He slapped me on the back and shook me.

"She invited me, not you guys."

Should I bring them? It would be cool if they could go, but I know they'll do something to embarrass me.

"Don't worry about us, Shawn. You better get her something nice, though. I hope you got some money," Andre said.

Shoot. Money. Something I didn't have much of. Dad's still out of town, so I have to ask Mama for some. I didn't care if she knew about the party because she's gonna have to take me. I just didn't wanna tell her about Marisol; she'll try to get all in my business.

The day ticked away, but Marisol stayed in my thoughts. Her purple dress. Her yellow bubbles. Her long black hair. Her bright brown eyes. Her tanned brown legs. Her butt pushing the dress out in the back. Man! The heat got hotter the more I thought about her.

I turned onto Auntie's block and sketched a picture of Marisol on the empty sky: purple straps on her shoulders, her brown eyes peeking out, sparkling like stars. I was just about to sketch her smile when I bumped into someone.

"Oh, I'm sorry, chile," a little brown lady said.

"No, excuse me."

Black covered her from head to toe. She pushed aside her net-veil-covered face to dab an eye with a white handkerchief. Dang . . . who died? I blinked my surroundings into focus and realized I was standing in front of Miss Johnston's house. A pair of long, black funeral limousines were parked in front. Miss Johnston wasn't on her porch, and a stream of folks shuffled in and out of her house. This can't be good.

I approached the woman I bumped into. "Pardon me, ma'am, but . . . is Miss Johnston OK?"

Her wrinkled hand touched my smooth arm. "Oh, chile, I'm sorry to be the one to tell you, but Nettie . . . has gone home."

"Gone home? You mean . . ."

"To the Lord. She passed on the other night. In her sleep — praise Jesus. He took her in peace." Her head dropped into silence.

What do you say to that?

Her head raised up and a thin finger moved her veil aside. "And how did you know Nettie?"

"Oh, I, umm, my auntie lives right there," I said, pointing. "I pass by here every day during the week. Ever since I was a kid."

Miss Johnston passed before my eyes as I recalled her old brown hand waving at me, her warm smile and cheerful voice singing out, "I'm just enjoying the light of the Lord on another glorious day."

"She always had a kind word for me." I dropped my head, searching for something else to say. I came up with "It was always good to see her. She always asked about me and my auntie."

"Well, she's in a better place right now and" — she looked to the sky — "I know she's smiling down on us all."

She waddled away but turned back to say, "We just getting back from the services if you wanna come inside."

"Thank you, but I have to get going."

"Well, you take care of yourself, chile, and you tell that auntie of yours we all said hey."

I walked away, my eyes no longer focused on the blue of the sky, but the gray of the concrete. Dang, Miss Johnston is . . . I can't even say it. She's . . . I won't ever . . . Dang.

Pictures of Miss Johnston painted themselves on the concrete as I hung my head low to remember her. Always outside. Always in a housedress. Always smiling. Always nice. To everybody — not just this person or that person — everybody. Mama's been bringin' me here for a long time now, and I've seen her out on that porch every day since the first time I walked to school. She was old then and only got older. I guess it was a matter of time. Hard to believe I won't ever see her again. She was part of my day as much as my boys were. I saw her on the way to see them, plus I saw her on the way back. Dang, Miss Johnston — I mean Nettie — I'm gonna miss you.

Miss Bricknell was watering her lawn as I strolled by. Does she always have to be in her garden when I pass by? I wish she would have died instead of Miss Johnston. Why did God have to take her when this old hag would have done just as well?

"You need to tell that auntie of yours . . ." she started.

"Why don't YOU tell her?" I shouted.

Shawn! Where'd that come from? In all the years she's shouted at me and Auntie, I never said a word. But not today. I didn't know Miss Johnston that well, but I knew her well enough that whenever I passed her house, I felt good. I got the exact opposite feeling when I passed Miss Bricknell's.

"What did you say to me, boy?"

I stomped past her into the house, leaving her jaw open to catch flies. Silence greeted me as I made my way around the house searching for Auntie. Not again.

"Auntie," I called out.

Nothing in the house was on. No TV. No radio. Not even the stove. What the heck was she doing? A box of old pictures lay scattered across her spot on the sofa. But no Auntie. I checked the kitchen and there she was, sprawled on the floor.

"Come on, Auntie, get up."

I scraped her limp limbs from the floor and spied yet another empty bottle looming over her from the counter.

"Avery? Baby . . . is that you?"

Who was Avery? "Auntie, it's Shawn. Come on, we got to get you up."

I helped her up, and we staggered into the living room. I cleared the pictures on the sofa for her to sit. She plopped down with a groan and tilted to the side. I caught her before her head hit the lamp on the end table.

"Come on, Auntie . . . sit up."

I propped her up so she sat straight, then got her some ice water. I tinkled the ice-filled glass in front of her, making her eyelids flutter. "Whas this?"

"Drink it—it's good for you."

Her eyes noticed the clear fluid in the glass, and she smacked it to the floor, scattering ice and soaking the carpet. I picked up each individual cube. Fine. Let her take care of her own self. I glanced at the pictures on the sofa and saw what looked like a mini Mama; I had seen a few pictures of her as a child before, so I knew what she looked like. The photo was brown and white, and she stood next to an older girl with an older couple behind them. Auntie . . . Grandma . . . Grandpa? I grabbed the pictures and sat down with them on the other couch. Auntie's head swayed side to side, and when she finally did hit her head on the lamp, she snapped awake. I jumped up to help her, but she waved me off.

"I'm OK . . . jes need some . . ."

She tried to stand but plopped backward against the wall, making the picture hanging over her fall with a loud *thunk*. It just missed her head by a couple of inches. She's gonna hurt herself.

"You all right?"

"I'm fine. I jes need my . . . jes need a . . ." She paused to hiccup, then held out her hand to help her finish. "I jes need my cup . . ."

She tried to stand but got the same result as last time. I flicked the TV on.

"Auntie, you wanna watch anything special on TV?"

Her head bobbed in my direction, then swung back toward her clock.

"Wha time is it?"

"Almost five? Why?"

"Awwww, no! I missed my stories." Her fist flew up to rest beneath her head, and two long sighs later, she was asleep.

Oh, well, I tried.

I clicked the TV off and flipped through the pictures. Most of them were in black-and-white or brown-and-white, and a lot of them had people I had never seen before. I recognized what had to be Mama in a few of them. A bunch of others had just Auntie. What looked to be Grandma and Grandpa were in most of them too. They died when I was little, so I don't remember a whole lot about them, and the few pictures that Mama has shown me are of them when they were old. Some showed Grandpa holding just Auntie. Some showed him holding just Mama. Some showed all four of them. And most of them looked like they were taken in Louisiana, because they didn't look like any place around here. Auntie had a silly face or a big gap-toothed grin in most of her pictures, while Mama looked serious in hers. Looking at Auntie passed out on the couch across from me, it was hard to believe she was ever a kid. Or ever had a grin on her face.

The photos were in the box without rhyme or reason — just one big pile of pictures stuffed in a box. One image stopped me in my tracks. It was black-and-white and the largest in the box. It was a guy and a girl, and the girl looked like Auntie. The guy was a dark brown soldier dressed sharply in an army uniform, holding a trumpet. The girl was about college age in a white dress that dropped to the tops of her black-and-white shoes. Their arms were around each other, tight. Her head was nuzzled into his neck, and they each had a big smile on their face. I flipped it over, and in faded black ink I was able to make out *G & A Forever.* G & A, huh? The G was probably for Gertie, so the A must be for . . . Avery? I'll bet it was. Finally a name. Who else would it be? I held the picture up and shifted my vision between Auntie passed out on the couch and Auntie smiling in the picture. My eyes bounced back and forth between the two for a while. What happened to that smile from the picture? I put it down and stared at her. Where did that Auntie go?

Her head slid off her hand and she jerked awake. She blinked a few times and smacked her lips. "I need some water."

I got up and got her some. She straightened herself and took it in her hands carefully. Her nap must have helped.

"Put the news on for me, Shawn."

She wiped the drool from her mouth and scooched down into her seat. A soft breath escaped her lips as she took a sip of water. I began putting the pictures away when she noticed me. And the box.

"Whatchu got there?"

She must have forgot that she had pulled them out.

"Some pictures." I hesitated. "They were on your sofa when I came in."

I held on to the picture of her and "A." I wanted to ask her about it but didn't want her to get all crazy on me. I'll play it cool.

"I didn't know you had all these pictures of you and Mama and Grandma and Grandpa."

She took another sip of water. "Yeah, thas all of 'em."

I held up the big black-and-white to make sure she saw me looking at it.

"You know who this is?" I stood and handed it to her.

She took the glossy yet worn photo from my hand and exhaled as she examined it. I didn't know what to expect, so I took a seat on the couch and waited.

"Where'd you find this?" she said, shaking the memory at me.

"It was in that box." I pointed. "It was already out when I came in."

"Thas nunna ya business!"

She hoisted herself off the couch, tossed the photo down, and shuffled into the kitchen. So much for finding out about "A."

She shuffled back in and plopped on the couch, this time careful not to hit her head on the wall. Her eyes zoomed in on the weatherman on TV giving the five-day forecast.

"Did you hear about Miss Johnston?"

"What?" she said, not taking her eyes off the screen.

"Miss Johnston—I don't know if you knew this, but she, ahhh . . ."

Dang—how do I say this?

"She . . ."

"Come on, Shawn, say what you gotta say," she said, irritated and focused on me.

Just say it.

"Miss Johnston passed away the other day." There, I said it. "Her relatives are over there now saying good-bye, and one of them told me on the way here just now."

The words hit her ears like a hammer on a nail, and her expression changed from irritation to disbelief in a short breath. Her eyes fell to her lap and stayed there. Her body rocked back and forth, slow and steady, as moans vibrated from her throat. Uh-oh. I disappeared into the bathroom, and when I came back, her seat was empty. Shoot. Where'd she go? I swung my head around and saw the front door open. I stepped outside and there was Auntie staggering out of the gate. Aww, man. Where you goin', Auntie?

"It ain't right! LORD, YOU KNOW IT AIN'T RIGHT!" she shouted, clawing at the air.

Miss Bricknell came out of her house. Shoot, I got to get her back inside.

The words trickled out of her mouth as she staggered on. "Why, Lord? Why you hafta take such a . . . such a . . . sweet . . . such a sweet, sweet, heart? HUH?"

I ran after her. "Come on, Auntie, let's go in the house."

"Let GO of me!"

Bodies appeared in front of each house as she staggered across the sidewalk toward Miss Johnston's. She pushed me off and screamed each time I tried to grab her. The sight of Miss Bricknell slowed her down. Uh-oh.

Auntie leaned on Miss Bricknell's fence and pounded her chest. "Whatchu want, Josephine!? Huh? Whatchu got to say t'me today? HUH? Whatchu got to say? You don't like me, do you, Josephine? I KNOW you don't like me. I know that— I know. But you know what? I don't like you neither—never have. Whatchu think about that? Huh? Whatchu think about that, Josephine? Huh? Wassamatter—cat got your tongue? You ain't got nothin' to say to me? HUH?"

Miss Bricknell crossed her arms and glared at Auntie and

me—especially me—in silence. I returned her evil eye, and she went in her house. I didn't have to turn my head to feel every eye on the block on us. This is crazy. I got to get out of here.

"Come on, Auntie, we causing a scene. Let's go back in the house."

I felt helpless as she staggered on, still pushing me away. "LET GO OF ME! I got somethin' to SAY!"

Her right hand pointed a finger to everyone watching her. "I see y'all lookin' at me—I see y'all lookin'. I know whatchu see—I know whatchu see." She dropped her hand and swayed, trying to stand still. "You see a drunk—thas whatchu see . . . an old drunk."

Her eyelids flickered as she pointed back to Miss Johnston's. "But not her. Not her. No . . . she saw a . . . woman. A woman wit a . . ." Chest-heaving sobs pumped out her words. "A woman wit a . . . broken heart."

Why is she telling all these people her business like this? They don't care. Matter of fact, most of 'em are laughing. Or smoking. Or drinking. But all of 'em are watching; like we some kind of bad soap opera or something. I wish she would stop.

I reached for her again, and again she pushed me off. The swaying ship of her body steadied for a moment as she shouted, "SHE SAW A WOMAN! Not a"—she choked—"not a drunk!"

She threw her fists to the sky. "And you took her away, Lord! You took her away. It ain't right. You shoulda taken me! Why didn't you take . . . me?"

She collapsed to the ground in a flurry of tears. I struggled to pick up her heaving body, but I was no longer alone. "Come on, Sis, let's get back inside," Mama whispered to Auntie's buried head.

"Shawn, you get that side. I'll take this one."

We looked at each other, and I could tell Mama did not like seeing her sister this way, especially with everybody laughing, staring, and shaking their heads. We shuffled her into the house and placed her on her spot on the couch. I closed the front door. Some of the bodies on the block had gone back inside, but a few looky-loos remained, laughing and wondering what they had just seen.

"Drink this," Mama said, handing Auntie a new cup of ice water.

"I need a real drink," Auntie said, not smacking the cup down but still pushing it away. Her head nodded back and forth as she moaned, "Nettie . . . Nettie."

Mama pulled me aside. "So what happened this time, Shawn?"

"Let's go into the kitchen."

We left Auntie to her sobs. I broke down everything for Mama from the beginning. She clutched her chest when I mentioned Miss Johnston.

"And that's when she lost it—I mean *lost it,* Mama. I've never seen her that way. I come here every day and find her on the floor, but that's the first time she ever went outside like that."

I pulled out a chair and sat down. Mama stood, staring out the window.

Why Auntie do that? She must have known Miss Johnston better than I thought. Or she was so drunk, she didn't know what she was doing.

"I can't take this no more, Mama. You know how embarrassing that was?"

She touched her hand to my neck. "I know, baby."

"But what kills me the most is how everybody just stood there watching us like . . . like we was a TV show or something. You shoulda seen them—laughing, pointing, and poking at each other like . . . like she was a clown or something."

Mama pulled up a seat and covered my hands with hers; they were nice and cool and not shaking like mine. We sat in silence, the two of us looking at the sidewalk outside of the window.

"Mama, I wanna show you something."

I stood and poked my head out the kitchen door to check on Auntie. She lay sprawled across the couch, passed out and snoring to her heart's content. I signaled Mama to follow me into the living room, and we sat on the couch. I pulled out the box of pictures and picked up the photo of Auntie and "A."

"You ever seen this picture?"

She took it in her hands and held it up.

"That's Sis and her boyfriend."

"Her boyfriend? You know his name?"

"I don't know—that was a long time ago."

I showed her the back.

"Ummm, Aubry . . ."

"Avery?" I said.

"That's it. Avery. How'd you know?"

"That's the name she said when I picked her up off the floor," I said, staring into the eyes of the soldier with the big smile and gleaming horn. "She ever talk about him before?"

Mama dropped the image on the table, then leaned back in her seat. "Nope. She never did." She sighed.

I held the worn, faded photograph up, staring at Auntie's young, smiling face, then lowered it, revealing her worn, faded body, passed out on the couch.

"After today, Mama . . . I don't think she ever will."

THIRTY-FOUR

"**I WANT YOU TO STAY HOME** with Gertie tomorrow."

I knew Mama would say that. After what happened today, I'm surprised she didn't ask me to stay home with Auntie the rest of the summer. I felt sorry for Auntie, so when I said "all right," I meant it. I didn't wanna walk in the door after being with the fellas all day and find her dead instead of passed out — especially after hearing her say she should have died instead of Miss Johnston. I'm sure she didn't know what she was saying, but I didn't tell Mama; she would freak if she heard that. And anyway, at least I'd get to finish *Malcolm X*.

But how was I gonna tell the fellas? If I didn't show up at Pop's first thing in the morning like I always do, they might come looking for me. That wouldn't be good. I had to think of something, but I didn't want to think about it now. I wanted to get the last part of the day, with Auntie, out of my head and think about the first part, with Marisol and her party.

I flicked on the radio to break the silence. Mama tapped her hand to the beat and said, "What do you want for dinner?"

"We eating at home or going out?"

"We can go out. We can either eat it there or get takeout."

Hmmmmm. We only eat out once in a blue moon; she must be worn out. I know I was. Takeout would be good, but from where? The Tamale Hut popped into my head. Followed by Marisol sitting in front of me . . . smiling.

"How 'bout Mexican? There's that El Pollo Loco near the mall."

"Fine," she said without turning her head.

Back at the house, I tore into half a chicken while Mama picked at her beans and rice.

"I suppose your decision got easier today," she said.

Tortilla chips crunched in my mouth, making it hard to hear. "What?" I stopped chewing. "What'd you say?"

"I said, your decision probably got easier today—you know . . . after what happened with Sis and all." She punched her fork into her beans.

I finished chewing before I spoke again. This might be a good time to tell her about Marisol.

"Actually . . . it got harder."

She put her fork down. "Oh. Why's that?"

"As far as Auntie goes—you're right, I am tired of dealing with her. But . . . that wasn't the only thing that happened today."

I didn't want her to get the wrong idea, so I cut her off

before she could jump to one of her conclusions. "And no, it wasn't anything bad."

Dang. How do I tell her about Marisol? She's always teasing me about girls, and now I have to tell her about the one I like? How do I do that? I guess if I could tell Auntie about Miss Johnston . . .

"Ummm . . . there's this girl . . ."

"A girl?" Her ears perked up and a grin graced her face.

I lowered my head and pushed my beans around my plate. "Her name is Marisol. She invited me to her birthday party on Saturday."

Whew—I said it.

"Mary-sol? Tell me about this Marisol. She don't sound black."

"Does that matter?"

"Now, Shawn, you know I don't care. I'm just trying to imagine what she looks like."

Shoot. Every time I think about what she looks like, the first thing that pops into my head is her body and her butt— especially her butt. I can't tell that to Mama, though.

"Well . . . we've been friends since we started school together. She's Mexican. Has real long hair. What else? . . ."

The day I ran into her after the movies flashed across my brain. Dressed in green. Smiling. What else do I say?

"Ummm, she's real nice . . . a good student . . ."

Mama put down her fork and laughed. "Now, Shawn . . . she's real nice? . . . a good student? Come on. That's it? Tell me about this girl. I see you smiling when you say her name. She has a hold on you; I can see it on your face. And that's good, baby. I'm happy for you. I am. But come on . . . she's a *good student?* Shawn, please! Tell me something real about this girl."

The smile I hadn't seen on her face in a while reappeared.

"Anyway, like I said, my decision is harder now because . . . when I think about Marisol and going to her party . . . it's like the whole scene with Auntie never even happened. You know what I mean?"

She slurped her soda. "Oh, I know what you mean. I was like that with your father when we first met. I got a smile on my face and didn't have a care in the world. . . ."

She stared at her plate, probably thinking about the good times. But the thought of Mama thinking about Dad that way was . . . weird.

"Wait . . . is that why you wanted Mexican?"

I tried to play it off by stuffing chicken in my mouth, but her "mmm-hmm" choked me up.

"So how long you been in love, Romeo?"

"I'm not in love!" I coughed.

"Uh-huh . . . right. Hey, if she makes your 'gray skies blue,' then that's love, baby," she said, singing the words "gray skies blue."

I guess she was right. When something bad happened, I thought about Marisol and forgot all about it.

"Anyway, Marisol is as much a part of my decision as Auntie is, and you know how big a part Auntie is."

"I do." She sighed.

Her hands clasped together as she looked me in the eye.

"You know, Shawn, I gotta say . . . you really do a good job with Sis. Considering how long you been dealing with her whole . . . situation — how much you've put up with her over the years — particularly today . . ."

Her eyes blinked down at her plate, then focused back on mine. "I don't think I ever told you how much I appreciate you taking care of her. Thank you."

"Why you gettin' all wishy-washy on me, Mama?" I joked.

She shrugged. "I'm just saying . . . I don't envy your decision — it's not an easy one. You have any idea what you wanna do? You know you only have until Sunday? Which happens to be the day after this party."

Shoot. I knew the date was coming up, but I didn't realize it was the day after the party.

"I still don't know. And today didn't make it any easier. Between Marisol, the Crips, the Pirus, Auntie, Marshall . . ."

"Marshall? What about Marshall?"

"You know, the pink-slip thing. Plus, the fellas told me that a few thousand students go there and we might not even see each other."

"*A few thousand?* That's a lot of folks."

I put my fork down and wiped my mouth.

"I know. On the other hand, at Carson I'll have my freedom. I just won't know anybody except Brian — and he'll be a junior. He told me about the school and it seems cool, but . . . I don't know. I just don't know, Mama."

She finished her soda and stood with her picked-over plate in hand.

"Well, the clock is ticking. Whatever you decide, just make sure you're happy with it a hundred percent. Ain't nothing worse than second-guessing yourself."

I cleared my plate and joined her in the living room when the dishes were done. She curled up in her usual spot on the love seat, so I grabbed a pillow and collapsed on the couch. I didn't tell her what time the party started, and I still hadn't mentioned the gift.

"Can you take me to the party on Saturday?"

She flipped through the channels. "What time does it start?"

I hesitated. "Seven."

Her finger paused on the remote. "Seven? Ain't that a little late for a party?"

"Now, Mama, she's turning fourteen, not four. She said her brother's gonna have a DJ and everything. What'd you think it was gonna be? Cake, punch, and pin the tail on the donkey?"

"And what time is this party going to end?"

I never thought about that.

"I didn't ask. How long can I stay?"

She flipped through a few channels like she didn't hear me, then said, "You can stay until eleven—no later. If it ends before that, call me."

Eleven? Heyyyy! That's the latest she's ever let me stay out. Probably because I never go anywhere. Kool and the Gang.

"You all right, Mama? Can I quote you on that? Should I get that in writing in case you forget?"

She rolled her eyes. Now I gotta get some money for the gift.

"You know, Mama, it is a birthday party. Which means . . ."

"What?"

"I need to buy her a gift."

Silence.

"I know you heard me."

She put the remote down but kept her eyes on the TV screen. "Yeah, I heard you. But I ain't hearing you."

"What?"

"I won't have any money, Shawn, until I get paid on Friday. And even then, I still got bills to pay. I can't help you right now, so you might wanna try earning a little something on your own before Saturday."

On my own? Awww, man! How'm I gonna do that? I only have a few days, and unlike Lorenzo, I don't have a big brother to borrow it from. Plus, who knows when Dad'll be back. Shoot. What am I gonna do? Better yet, what am I gonna get her? At least that'll tell me how much money I need.

"What do you think I should get her?"

Mama stopped the screen on *Wheel of Fortune*. A new puzzle was about to start. A phrase. Five words.

"How old is this girl gonna be again?"

Vanna turned around three *T*'s on-screen.

"I told you: fourteen."

She was silent until the wheel stopped spinning. When $350 appeared, she said, "Well, let me ask you this: do you want her to know you like her?"

I do. No, I don't. Wait. I do. No, no, no. I don't.

"I don't know. I guess so."

Vanna flipped around two *H*'s.

"You guess so? You may not see this girl ever again after this party and you guess so? This is your chance, baby. You better jump on it."

"I know. You right."

Next, $1,000 appeared on the wheel.

"N. Ask for an N," Mama shouted to a little old white lady on-screen, trying to decide which letter to call next. She called for an L and two appeared. She bought an E, and Mama said, "I hate when they buy vowels. Such a waste of money."

"Speaking of money . . . my gift? You got any ideas?"

"I'm sorry, Shawn. I'm trying to solve this puzzle. You know what she likes?"

"You mean what she likes to wear?"

The wheel on the screen clicked to BANKRUPT.

"No, just what she likes in general. You gotta start somewhere."

I stared at the puzzle on the screen as Marisol danced through my head. Wait . . .

"The writing on the wall!" I shouted.

"What?"

"The puzzle. I solved it."

She looked to see if the spaces matched the words, then shook her head. "You did it again."

"See . . . I should try to get on when they have Teen Week again. One–nothing, me. Now what was I saying? Oh, yeah, Marisol. The only thing I came up with is green. And pink. And purple."

"What are you talking about? Green? Pink? And purple what?"

"I always see her in one of those colors. Pedal pushers. Hair clips. Whatever."

"Now we're getting somewhere. You know any of her sizes?"

The blank look on my face and my shrug answered her.

"I didn't think so. You mentioned a hair clip. And you said she has long hair. Right?"

"Yeah, it goes all the way down to her butt." Oops.

She frowned at me and lowered her eyebrows.

"What? I'm just saying — to let you know how long it is."

A new puzzle appeared on-screen. "Around the House" was the category.

"Maybe you could get her a nice hair clip."

"A hair clip? That sounds kind of, I don't know, cheap?"

A young white guy clapped on the screen shouting, "Big money . . . big money." The wheel clicked to a stop at $500, and he shouted "N." Nothing came up.

"Cheap? Not necessarily. A nice hair clip, a real nice one, can go for as much as fifty bucks. Some even more. I wouldn't spend that much on one for myself, but if somebody gave me that as a gift . . ."

A hair clip? I don't know. Seems so . . . small.

"But the best part is, she'll think of you whenever she puts it on."

Ahhhhh. I didn't think of that. That *would* be cool. Real cool. But fifty bucks? That's a lot of money. Especially when you don't even have a dime. Dang! I knew this wasn't gonna be easy.

A young black woman on the screen clapped as Vanna

flipped around three *D*'s, two at the end of the first two words. The puzzle only had three words, but I had no idea what they might be.

"A hair clip, huh? That's a good idea. I can't afford fifty bucks though."

"They don't all cost that much. I'm just saying, that's about how much a real nice one is. It don't matter how much you spend, but how much it looks like you spent."

She curled her legs onto the couch and stared at the screen.

"Polished hardwood floors!" she shouted.

"Awww, man. I had no idea what that was."

"Big surprise. The category *is* 'Around the House.'"

The white guy asked for a *T* and nothing appeared. He had no idea either.

"Speaking of which, what are we doing this weekend? I hope we not gonna just clean up 'around the house,' you know?"

The white lady on the screen shouted out the answer after Vanna flipped around two *H*'s.

A grin crept across Mama's face. "Well . . . I might be seeing Aaron."

I turned in her direction. "Aaron? Who's Aaron?"

"You know him as Professor Hopkins—Aaron is his first name. I thought I told you that."

I swung my legs in her direction. "No, you haven't told me anything about . . . Aaron. Y'all gettin' serious?"

"No, we are not getting serious. He's divorced, like me, and neither one of us wants to travel that road again. We just like doing stuff together: going to the movies, bowling, listening to music. You know, just having a good time. It's good for me to get out once in a while."

"I heard that!"

She flung the pillow in my direction. "Oh, hush up."

I threw the pillow back at her. "I'm just glad you doing something on the weekends besides cleaning the house. Just don't forget about the party—Saturday at seven. OK?"

She waved me off. "I got it, I got it."

"Speaking of Professor Hopkins," she said during a commercial, "you know he asks about you all the time."

"He does? Why?"

"Well, he does teach literature, and you like to read, so we talk about that. Matter of fact, last time we spoke I told him you were reading *Malcolm X* and how it's helping you with your big decision."

I jumped to my feet. "My decision? You told him about that?"

"Calm down. We talk about lots of stuff."

I sat back down, still facing her. "But he don't know me."

"But he does know *me*. So calm down. He was impressed that a fourteen-year-old was reading that book already—very impressed. A lot of the students in his class haven't even read that book yet."

"Really?"

"Oh, yeah. When I mentioned some of the other books you've read in the last couple of years, he said he teaches some of them in his course."

"For real? In college? Which ones?"

She looked to the ceiling. "The one that stands out most is *Invisible Man*. Probably because you read that not long ago, right?"

"Yeah, late last year."

Her eyes rolled from me to the screen as *Wheel* came back on.

"He teaches freshman literature, so his students are fresh out of high school—eighteen, nineteen. He said you keep reading books like that and you'll have no problem when your SATs roll around."

"My SATs? What's that?"

"That's the test you take to get into college. There's an English section and a math section. The higher your score, the better chance you have of getting into whatever college you want. You have thought about college, right?"

I've thought about my future—in high school. Not college.

"A little bit."

Her hunched back straightened. "Just . . . a little bit?"

She didn't sound thrilled. What could I say?

"College just seems so far away. This whole high school thing is right in front of me, so that's what I've been focusing on."

She settled back into her seat. "Anyway, I told Aaron you're a smart kid; sometimes too smart for your own good"—she laughed—"and you're gonna go far in life."

"You said that?"

Her eyes bounced between me and the screen.

"Of course I did. You're my child. I didn't raise no dummy."

The white guy was back on the screen clapping and shouting, "Big money . . . big money."

The $5,000 spot on the wheel clicked to a stop, and he just about lost his mind.

"S, fool, S!" Mama shouted at the screen.

He called for a B and nothing appeared. Who calls for a B with only two letters on the board? This guy is clueless. What's the category? "On the Menu," huh? That's right up my alley.

Mama stared at the puzzle, trying to figure it out when I shouted, "Garlic mashed potatoes. I got it again! That's two for me, one for you."

"I told you I didn't raise no dummy," she said, whacking me with the pillow before heading into the kitchen.

A few spins later, the young black woman finally solved it, winning $8,250.

Mama's right; she didn't raise no dummy. Shoot, if I was on *Wheel of Fortune,* I'd have enough money to buy Marisol a hundred hair clips. But I'm not. So I can't. I don't need a hundred anyway. Just one. All I need is money for one.

Hopefully tomorrow I'll figure out how to solve that puzzle.

THIRTY-FIVE

"I NEED YOU TO CLEAN the backyard today so I can start a garden," Auntie said the moment I stepped into her house the next morning. "I'm sick of paying for wilted vegetables at the grocery, so I'll grow my own . . . like I used to."

The backyard was one big mess. This was gonna take time. Oh, well. Not like I have anything better to do. Especially with Auntie watching her soaps inside. I was mad I didn't get to see the fellas to tell them I wouldn't be around for the day, but they would just wanna come over and hang out anyway. I didn't want that.

By lunchtime, my shirt clung to my body, sweat-soaked from the heat. I wanted to get a little more done before I ate because I didn't know if I would want to come back out again. I got most of the junk cleared out and was ready to start on the garden itself. A square patch of dirt about the size of two of me lay framed by a bunch of wooden stakes and string. The patch of dirt sprouted plenty of weeds and didn't look like it was ever a garden. The heat finally took my breath away, so I went inside for a break and found Auntie watching her stories on the couch. She sat cool and calm—no swaying, no moaning. Her glass of "juice" was nowhere nearby. I wondered when it would come out.

I guzzled a tall glass of apple juice myself, the only drink besides water in the fridge, and hunted for something to eat.

"What you got to eat, Auntie?" I yelled to the living room.

"There's some leftover dirty rice and crab in the fridge," she hollered back.

Dirty rice? Mama made some one time, and I didn't like it. Dang. I don't like crab either. What else is there? I flipped through the cabinets and settled on a basic peanut-butter-and-jelly sandwich. I found the bread and the jelly no problem, but not the peanut butter.

"Where's the peanut butter?" I yelled.

"In the fridge. Behind the lard," she yelled back.

The fridge? Who keeps peanut butter there? I pulled it out from behind the big red bucket of lard and stuck the knife in. I tried to spread it, but it was so hard, it ripped the bread to pieces. Dang! I'm hungry!

"You got anything else to eat, Auntie?"

"Boy, this ain't Burger King. You can't have it your way."

Now I know how Lorenzo's Dad felt. I didn't buy the food in this house, but I was mad there was nothing to eat, especially after working so hard outside. After hunting through the cabinets and fridge again, I tracked down some lunch meat and made a sandwich. Auntie's familiar big bottle sat on the counter in the corner and held my attention as I chewed my food. It hadn't been cracked open. Yet. Hopefully it won't. And hopefully I won't have to scrape her off the floor later.

About an hour later, the rest of the backyard and garden were done. I dragged my tired body inside and collapsed on the couch with *Malcolm X*. It was good reading but, just like at Dad's, before I knew it, I was fast asleep. Ambulance sirens jerked me awake. Huh? Oh, just the TV. I went into the kitchen for some water and saw Auntie's bottle on the same counter, in the same corner, staring me in the face, half empty. Dang! How she do that so fast?

My stomach rumbled, so I tracked down some donuts and went to town. The clock read 2:15 — still three more hours before Mama gets here. I strolled back to the couch and found Auntie sitting in her spot — still cool, still calm, and still watching her stories. Isn't there anything else on besides soap operas? I grabbed *Malcolm* and went out to the porch. The fresh air felt good. Now I see why Miss Johnston liked sitting outside every day. Maybe I'll do the same when I'm old.

My thoughts drifted from Malcolm's life to Marisol's birthday gift and how to pay for it. What else can I get besides a hair clip? What are other people gonna get her? Andre said to get her something good, but what does that mean? Maybe I could talk to Janine and ask her. Yeah, right. Trent probably won't even let us back in his house if she's there.

Speaking of Trent, I wonder what the fellas are doing right now. Probably playing ball somewhere. DuBois? MLK?

Maybe they at the movies. Or the Tamale Hut. Maybe Marisol is there. I wonder what she's wearing. Purple? Pink? Green? Lorenzo better not be talking to her.

Miss Bricknell was nowhere to be found, so I went and got a closer look at her roses. Picture-perfect pink, yellow, white, and red petals dotted the sea of green in front of her house. How could such beautiful flowers grow from such an evil woman? I should snip a few off and give 'em to Marisol. Nah. That sourpuss Miss Bricknell would know it was me. She already thinks I'm a thief. No use in proving her right.

I stepped back in the house to find cool and calm Auntie replaced by passed-out Auntie. She's sneaky with that bottle. At least she's passed out on the couch and not the floor. Hopefully she'll sleep it off there. I stepped back outside on the porch and looked in the direction of Miss Johnston's house. Her chair sat lifeless and alone. How much stuff had she seen on the block? Auntie's little episode was one for the books, for sure, but Miss Johnston, old as she was, must've seen stuff that beat that by a mile. Shoot, I've seen a few things here myself over the years.

One time, there was this woman across the street who pulled a shotgun on her husband after he beat her one too many times. It was late in the day and I was waiting for Mama on the porch when this big dude comes running out of his house in nothing but striped boxer shorts, his fat belly bouncing. This tiny little woman in a ripped shirt and dress chases after him, carrying a big ol' shotgun. He's screaming and shouting for her to put the gun down and then — get this — he gets down on his knees and begs, straight-up *begs*!

He's crying and praying and carrying on to her the whole time, but then, not only does she lower the gun — I couldn't believe this — she starts saying she's sorry. *She's* sorry! He snatches the gun out of her hand, punches her in the eye, and says for the whole neighborhood to hear, "Bitch, you EVER do that again and I'll kill you. You hear me? I'LL KILL YOU!"

I guess what Mama said is true: every pot has its lid.

The Cali breeze tickled the trees, and, like one of Auntie's soap operas, I felt young and restless. I took a walk around the outside of the house just because, and when I got back to the porch, I saw three bodies approaching from the direction of the Wrights' house — opposite the way I usually come. They were different sizes and didn't look familiar, but when I saw a basketball bounce between them, I knew who it was.

Shoot. What are they doing here? I stepped inside, and Auntie was still passed out. When I stepped back onto the porch, they were in front of the fence shouting my name.

"What y'all doing here?" I asked as we exchanged soul claps across the waist-high fence. I stood on Auntie's green grass on one side; they stood on gray concrete on the other.

"You wasn't at Pop's this morning, so we wanted to make sure you was all right," Andre said.

"How'd you guys find me?" I said, trying to hide my surprise.

I never even told them where Auntie lived.

"Glad to see you too, Shawn," Trent said.

I was glad to see them — real glad, but they gotta go. If they see Auntie passed out . . .

"We ran into Passion at the Tamale Hut and asked her if she knew where your Auntie stayed. She knew the street but not the house," Lorenzo said. "Good thing you was outside. Looks like nothing but old folks live on this block."

Yeah, good thing I was outside. Lucky me. They went to the Tamale Hut?

"We saw Marisol," Andre said.

"Looking fine as ever in some little short-shorts," Lorenzo added.

I folded my arms and stared at him. "So?"

"So, you know you in love with her, Shawn," Trent answered.

"I am not. But what you doing looking at her shorts, 'Zo?"

"See? I told you," Lorenzo teased. "We just messing with you, Shawnie-Shawn. She wasn't even there. Passion was there with one of her sisters."

Why he always do that?

"It's too hot out here. Ay, Shawn, can we get something to drink?" Andre asked.

They must have just finished playing ball, because their shirts were soaked. Shoot. I don't wanna let them in the house, but I don't wanna be rude either.

"Of course. My auntie was sick yesterday, so Mama had me stay with her today to make sure she's cool. She's sleeping on the couch now, but we can hang out here on the porch. We just gotta keep it down so we don't wake her."

Auntie was still passed out on the couch as I stepped inside. I *really* hope she don't wake up anytime soon. But if she does, maybe she won't be drunk anymore. That would be good. I still can't let them in the house, though. The last thing I need is for them to see her laid out.

I brought out three tall glasses of ice water. Lorenzo looked at his and said, "No Kool-Aid?"

"You lucky you got water, 'Zo. At least I put ice in it."

He shook his head and took a seat on the lowest step. Trent took the step up from him, and Andre sat next to me on the top.

"So what y'all do so far today?"

"The usual. We just finished playing ball over at DuBois. It wasn't the same without you as our fourth. I had to take turns beating up on these two in one-on-one," Andre said.

"Black Bruce was there too. He showed me a few more moves. I think I'm gonna take kung fu," Trent said.

"Is that what you was doing? Looked to me like you was having a fit, Trent," Lorenzo said.

"How you know? You was sleeping on the bench," Trent shot back.

"It's hot, man. I was resting my eyes," Lorenzo said.

"And your belly," Andre added.

"Don't make me break out the bags!" Lorenzo shouted.

"Keep it down, 'Zo. I told you my auntie's sleeping."

"Sorry." Lorenzo sipped.

"So, Shawn, you figure out what you getting Marisol?" Andre asked.

"And how you gonna pay for it?" Lorenzo added.

Their six eyes zoomed in on me. Do I tell them what Mama said . . . about the hair clip?

"Not yet. My mother suggested I get her a . . . a . . ."

"What, Shawn? Your Mama said you should get her a what?" Trent said, knocking my knees.

Do I really wanna tell them? It sounded all right when Mama told me last night, but now, sitting in front of them . . . I don't know. Hey, if I could tell Auntie about Miss Johnston . . .

"A hair clip. I told her Marisol has long hair and always has a hair clip pulling it back, so she suggested I get her one— a nice one."

All right. Let the arrows fly.

"Shawn, Shawn, Shawn."

"A hair clip?"

"Aren't they, like, real small?"

"I said the same exact thing, but Mama said whenever Marisol wears it—get this—she'll think of me," I said with pride.

"But what if she *don't* wear it. Does that mean she *won't* be thinking about you?" Lorenzo said, shaking his empty glass at me.

"Shut up, Lorenzo," Trent said.

"How much they cost?" Andre asked.

"She said there's all kinds, but they could go for as much as fifty bucks."

"Fifty bucks!" the three voices said.

"For a hair clip?" Lorenzo shouted.

"Shhhhh. I told you . . . keep it down."

I poked my head into the door and Auntie was still out.

"Where you gonna get fifty bucks?" Andre said.

"Yeah, that might as well be a million bucks," Trent added.

"I know how you can get it," Lorenzo said, standing. He stretched his arms to the sky and his belly button winked at me.

"Dang, Lorenzo, can't you wear something longer to hide that thing?" I said, pointing to his eyeball of a belly button.

"What you doing looking at it?"

"It was winking at me!"

I got into my chair on the porch.

"All right, Lorenzo, where do I magically get fifty bucks?"

Lorenzo sat down on the steps and lowered his voice when he spoke.

"My brother's been asking me to drop off these packages for him around the neighborhood. He said he'd give me fifty bucks for each one. I did it one time a while ago, but the house had all these Pirus hanging out, so I didn't do it anymore. He gave me the fifty bucks and said he had work for me whenever I needed cash."

"Are you crazy, 'Zo? You do remember your brother's wrist getting stomped on, right? I'm sure them 'packages' had something to do with it," Trent said.

"I know. I know. I'm just saying, you do it one time and — *boom* — nice new hair clip," Lorenzo said.

"Yeah . . . if he's still alive," Andre said.

"Or with nothing broken," Trent added.

"Hey, at least I made a suggestion. I don't hear y'all speaking up."

He's right. Nobody else said anything. I thought about delivering the package for one hot second, but the sound of

Dayshaun's wrist being crushed echoed back into my ears and vibrated through my body. That wiped that thought from my head.

"Shawn, look, you ain't gotta spend fifty bucks. Shoot, you ain't even gotta spend a dime. Does your mama or auntie have anything that you could give as a gift?" Lorenzo said.

"Listen to you, cheapskate. You'd give free cheese as a gift if you could! Don't listen to him, Shawn. Yeah, you don't have to spend fifty bucks, but you still got to buy her something," Andre said.

We moved from the gift to who might be at the party when Miss Bricknell called to me over the fence. I ignored her, but she got loud: "I know you hear me, boy! That crazy aunt of yours got the whole neighborhood talking. Everybody saw her drunken self staggering around out here and carrying on. She planning another show anytime soon?"

The fellas raised their eyebrows at her. Then me. That brought me to the fence.

"What is it, Miss Bricknell?"

She flipped her sun hat up to eyeball me and wagged a glove-covered finger in my face.

"I don't appreciate Gertie speaking to me the way she did yesterday. You tell her I'll be waiting for an apology whenever she's ready."

Is she serious? An apology? I know she don't expect Auntie to apologize, let alone talk to her.

"Is that it, Miss Bricknell?" I said, as calm as possible.

"No, that's not it. You and your little hoodlum friends need to keep it down."

Unlike yesterday, I kept my mouth shut and walked away; she wasn't worth the spit from my mouth or the headache in my head. I turned around to join the guys when the front door flew open. Oh, no.

"Shawn, what's going on out here?" Auntie yelled.

The flying door hit Andre in the back, making him jump.

"And who are these boys?"

Shoot. This ain't good. This ain't good. I ran to the bottom of the steps.

"Ummm, these are my friends, Auntie. The ones I usually hang out with . . . after Mama drops me off. They were worried when they didn't see me this morning, so they stopped by to make sure I was cool. Ummm . . . that's Andre, Trent, and Lorenzo."

She grumbled out a hello, then turned around to go inside when she heard, "Gertie! . . . Gertie! . . . I know you hear me!"

Auntie turned back around in her wrinkled housedress and staggered over to the fence. Aww, man, this is getting worse by the second. She looked fine right up until she staggered. Not good. I gotta get the fellas out of here.

"Ahhh, guys, maybe you should go."

"Come on, Shawn, this looks like it's gonna be good," Trent said.

Yeah, good for everybody else to see. Bad for me.

"Come on, let's go in the house and get some more water," I said, nodding toward the house and stepping inside.

I led them into the kitchen. I hope they don't see the bottle on the counter.

"You got ice?"

"What's with you and ice, Trent?"

I twisted some cubes from the tray into their glasses. Lorenzo hunted through the fridge while Trent and Andre stared out the window at the commotion.

"You got any food in here, Shawn?"

"Yeah, 'Zo, here." I handed him a jar from the fridge. "Try making a peanut-butter-and-jelly sandwich with ice-cold peanut butter."

"Mannnn, my grandmama keep her peanut butter in the fridge too. Why old folks do that? It ain't like it's gonna go bad."

The door slammed shut and I heard, "What's this?"

I didn't have to turn around to know what he was holding.

"Ayy, Shawn, your auntie and that lady really going at it," Andre said from the window.

He and Trent each held a side of the curtain open. The window framed a picture of Auntie and Miss Bricknell yelling in each other's face.

"Stay right here," I said, rushing out the door.

Auntie was wagging her finger in Miss Bricknell's face when I stepped in to pull her away.

"Let go of me, Shawn!"

The fellas came out onto the porch with glasses in their hands and shock in their eyes. I couldn't look at them. My worst fear was happening right before my eyes. In a big way.

"You need to mind your business, you old HAG!" Auntie screamed in her face. She stormed past me and the fellas and into the house, slamming the door behind her.

"And you need to put down that bottle, you old DRUNK!" Miss Bricknell cackled with all her might.

She sucked her sourpuss at me, narrowed her beady little eyes, and went back to her precious roses. I watched her while the fellas watched me. I can't believe this just happened. The moment I hoped would *never* come just went. One minute I'm talking about hair clips and a birthday party, the next I'm pulling my drunk aunt off her crazy old witch of a neighbor. What do you say after that? I didn't know what to say, so I said nothing.

The fellas came off the steps and surrounded me. I felt their presence, but I couldn't lift my head. The patch of grass under my feet held my attention as I searched for four-leaf clovers. I did that as a kid when I waited for Mama to pick me up. Maybe if I found one, my luck would change.

A hand touched my shoulder. Then another. Then another.

"We better go, Shawn."

That was Andre.

"Yeah. But we'll see you tomorrow, right? Same bat-time? Same bat-channel?"

That was Trent.

I nodded.

"Yeah, Shawn. We'll be there."

That was Lorenzo.

He shook my shoulder. "Just like we always are."

THIRTY-SIX

"**SHAWN, I ALMOST FORGOT** . . . I got something for you," Auntie said, disappearing into the kitchen while Mama waited in the car.

What now? She returned holding a five-dollar bill.

"What's this for?"

"It's all I got, but you earned it . . . for cleaning out the backyard. It looks great. You got rid of all that junk and weeded the garden too! I can't wait to get some collards into the ground. Maybe some sweet potatoes and tomatoes too," she said, thrusting the bill at me with a smile.

I don't think I've ever seen a smile on her face except in her old photos. I held the bill up. Can she afford to give me this?

"I can't take your money, Auntie. You should keep it."

"No, no, no. You earned that. My new garden will more than make up for it. Take it." She pushed the bill into my hand. "You know what I'll do with it." She laughed.

A laugh? Where'd that come from?

I thanked her and raced out the door. I got in the car and showed Mama the bill just as she was about to start the car. She let go of the key. "Where'd you get that?"

"Auntie gave it to me."

"What I tell you about lying to me, Shawn?"

I knew she would get like this.

"I'm not lying. You think I would show it to you if I was lying? I cleaned out her backyard today because she wants to start her garden back up, and she gave me this as I was leaving."

She started the car. "Sis can't afford that. You should have given it back."

"I tried, but she said I earned it—and I did. I worked my tail off in the hot sun today. But that's not all. She put the bill in my hand then said, 'You know what I'll do with it.'"

That turned Mama's head. "She said that?"

"And then she laughed! Go ask her."

Mama shook her head as we pulled away.

"My sister. Your auntie . . ." Mama laughed.

I stuffed the bill in my pocket and enjoyed the radio and the view on the way home. I didn't have the heart to tell Mama what happened with the fellas, Auntie, and Miss Witch; it would only upset her. As bad as it was, it could have been worse if Auntie was more drunk. At least she didn't cry and moan. Maybe that's why she gave me the money. Maybe she felt bad about what happened yesterday. And today. Maybe not. Maybe she don't even remember yesterday. I don't know. I do know I worked my butt off today. And now I have five dollars more than I had yesterday.

"So you gonna help me out with some money when you get paid tomorrow?"

"I should be able to."

"Should?"

"I still have bills to pay, Shawn. Remember? I gotta go grocery shopping, and you're not exactly a light eater, you know."

"But, Mama, you said . . ."

"I never promised you anything, Shawn."

I turned away from her toward the window.

She touched my knee. "I can't promise you much, but I can promise you twenty dollars."

"Twenty bucks? That's it?"

"Hey . . ."

"I know, I know, 'I'm lucky to even be getting that,'" I said in my best impression of her.

"Don't be smart, Shawn. There's plenty you can get for twenty-five dollars." She turned my way. "You could also clean out a few more backyards or do some yard work for folks. I'm sure somebody would pay you."

My shirt felt sweaty just thinking about working under the hot sun again.

"I don't think so. It's too hot. I was dead tired by the time I was done!"

"I'm just saying, twenty-five could grow into fifty or more with a little hard work."

I thought about Lorenzo and Dayshaun's offer to make a quick fifty. If Dayshaun could afford to give Lorenzo fifty bucks to deliver a package, then I wonder how much he's making. The crunch of bone on blacktop followed by a soul-piercing scream erased that question. The memory of Dayshaun snaking on the ground shifted my butt in my seat.

"You all right?"

"Yeah, I'm fine."

I would love to have more money—not just for the gift, but for me too. I'm tired of relying on the fellas for money. Especially now that I know where Dayshaun's money comes from. Maybe I can do some more work to earn some money for myself. But I can't think about that now. Right now, I gotta focus on what I'm getting *Marisol.* Maybe me and the fellas can look around tomorrow as something to do. They've been cool about it so far, not messing with me or giving me a hard time. Plus, they didn't make a big deal out of Auntie, which they could have easily. Maybe they won't embarrass me after all. It would be good to goof with them at the party. A lot of my classmates will probably be there, but it won't be the same without them. Now I wish they could go. I'll ask them.

When we finished off yet another game of basketball the next day at DuBois, that's just what I did.

"So y'all wanna come to the party?"

Our four bodies were spread across our two usual benches. Me and Trent on one, Andre and 'Zo on the other. Trent stretched his legs out while I hunched forward to catch my breath. The sun made my neck blacker by the second. Andre stood to dribble, giving Lorenzo space to lie down across the bench. My question pulled him up.

"You serious, Shawn?"

"As a heart attack."

"I thought you said we weren't invited," Trent said.

"You weren't. By her. But I'm inviting you—y'all wanna come or not?"

Andre stopped dribbling. "What time it start?"

"Seven."

They all said, "Seven?"

"Now that's a party," Lorenzo said.

"Yup. She said her brother got a DJ and everything."

Lorenzo got up to steal the ball from Andre.

"I can't believe you, Shawn. Going to a party with a DJ, and you wasn't even gonna invite us? That's just wrong. We your boys," Lorenzo said.

He was right. It'd be weird to not have them at the party with me after all we went through this summer, our last before high school.

Lorenzo gave up on stealing the ball and plopped down next to me on the bench, pushing Trent aside.

"Watch it, big boy," Trent said.

"Don't make me bring out the bags."

Trent got up to join Andre.

"You're right. So y'all wanna go or not?"

"Of course."

"You kidding me?"

"What do you think?"

"Cool. Remind me to tell you where it's at before I leave today."

"So what's up with your money situation? You get her anything?" Andre asked.

"My sister said you should get her a candle. A big one that smells nice, like flowers or the ocean. She said girls love that," Trent said.

Lorenzo started, "Speaking of your fine—"

"Don't start, Lorenzo."

"Fine. But . . . a candle?"

"I was thinking we could go look at some stuff over on Wilmington before I go today. We still got some time. My auntie gave me a five yesterday for cleaning out the backyard, and my mama's giving me a twenty tonight. That's plenty for a gift. I could at least get some ideas."

Andre picked up the ball. "Well, let's go."

We started out of the park, but Andre and Lorenzo stopped.

"Is that . . . ?"

"Yup."

"With a . . . ?"

"Yup."

Me and Trent brought up the rear, so I couldn't see what they were looking at.

"Why y'all stop?"

I stepped out of Lorenzo's shadow and blinked twice. POP. POP. My eyes zoomed in on Marisol laughing and leaning against Black Bruce's tall practice tree, next to . . . who is that?

Blue tank top. Creased blue jeans. White boxers glowing. Blue bandanna hanging out the pocket just above black croc-a-sacks. A Crip? You gotta be kidding me!

It looked like he was alone with her.

"Aww, man, Shawn," Lorenzo said.

"What should we do?" Andre said, turning to me.

"Let's just go the other way," Trent said.

"It don't matter which way we go, Trent, she still talking to a Crip," Lorenzo said.

I took a step back. Breathe, Shawn. What you gonna do? Should I keep walking and just ignore her, or turn around and go the other way?

"What you gonna do, Shawn?"

"Maybe she don't even like him."

"She sure ain't acting like it."

I watched the villain in blue press close to her while she laughed and pushed her hair out of her eyes—just like she did with me. Just like Yvonne. I knew it, these girls are all the same!

Lorenzo faced me and whispered, "Forget her, Shawn. There'll be plenty of girls at Marshall . . . fine ones too."

Or Carson.

We stood there. Just far enough to see but not be seen.

"We can't stand here forever, Shawn," Trent said. "What you wanna do?"

What do I wanna do? My nose picked up the stench of our sweat. My ears picked up bass-rattling cars bumping in the distance. Is this what Spidey sense feels like? My hand slid down the back of my sweat-covered neck. My mouth became dry as the desert. My eyes took snapshots of the tall jet-black 'banger in a dark-blue tank top and Marisol in yellow pedal pushers and a blouse to match. She laughed and tilted her head to the ground. Just like she did with me. I caught a glimpse of the butterfly clip in her hair — the one she wears the most. Mannnn . . . forget her, her hair clip, and her party too!

I stepped past the fellas and continued walking in the same direction. I didn't care if she saw me. I'm tired of hangin' in the background, blending in. I wanted to stand out. Like Malcolm said, sometimes you gotta stand up and be counted.

Andre ran up behind me. "Shawn, where you going?" The guys followed.

I kept silent and kept walking. Marisol was about a three-point shot away on the grass. She's so up close and personal with the blue 'banger, she probably don't even see me, probably don't even care. I held my head high and stared straight ahead. Just like Malcolm did when he stared down a bunch of cops in Harlem.

"So . . . what we doing, Shawn?"

"We leaving, Trent."

The three of them followed in silence, staring straight ahead as we strolled past the lovebirds, still close, under the tree. I wanted so bad to look at her, but I couldn't stand the sight of her with someone else — especially a Crip. Just the thought of her with someone else twisted me up inside. Worse than the Piru stepping on my back. Worse than getting punched in the eye. Worse than getting forearmed in the face. Worse than getting clubbed in the gut. Worse than pulling Auntie off the sidewalk in front of the whole block.

Man, girls. . . . They smile in your face, laugh and flirt with you like they love you, and then turn around and do the same with another dude. I thought I knew her. What was I thinking? Did I really believe I was gonna go to her party, give her my little gift, get showered in kisses and thank-you's, and live happily ever after? Please. My anger pushed me faster out of the park.

"Shawn, slow down."

What? That don't sound like Andre, Lorenzo, or Trent. I turned around. Marisol. The guys let her in the circle, then backed up. I folded my arms and looked down on her.

"Didn't you hear me calling you? I said your name a few times."

"No."

I looked over her head. It was easy to look away.

Her voice was warm. "Where you going?"

Mine wasn't. "We was just leaving."

"To where?"

"What do you care? You got somebody to keep you company."

I nodded over at the blue 'banger. He eyeballed both of us, especially me. She glanced back at him and laughed.

Her voice dropped. "You think I'm with . . . him?"

"That's what it looks like to me."

She covered her mouth and laughed. "Please! He's gotta be like twenty-something, and I'm barely fourteen. Ughhh!"

The ice in me melted as I looked into her eyes.

"I ran over here to get away from him," she whispered in close. "I was on my way to Passion's, and he stopped me and started talking to me. I'm all alone, so I got nervous and didn't leave — I couldn't."

I turned back to the guys and smiled; everything *was* Kool and the Gang. I turned back to Marisol and found myself eye to nose with the Crip. Two wide nostrils flared out over me as his face screwed itself up.

"Can I he'p you, cuzzzz?"

Forty-ounce fumes filled his words and singed my nose hairs. Dang! Marisol had to breathe that up close. What was I thinking? I should've known she wasn't with this clown.

"Nah, I'm cool."

His face pushed closer.

"Nah, you ain't cool. Why you talking to my girl here? Y'all know each other or something?"

His girl? I glanced back at the fellas. Their eyebrows raised as high as mine.

"Yeah. Ahhh, we go to school together."

He stepped in closer. His body funk pushed me back.

"Yeah, well . . . school's out, cuzz. So you best be gettin' on . . . SCHOOLBOY."

Marisol inched closer to the fellas. "I have to go. I'm already late to see my friend."

He swung his torso toward her. "Uh-uh. I ain't done talking to you."

I had to say something. "She said she had to go."

He swung back on me. "SO!? What YOU gone do, SCHOOLBOY? Huh? Look at you. Who you gone hurt with them . . . BIRD-ASS arms? You couldn't hurt a fly." He laughed, lifting my arms and slamming them into my sides.

"Huh, cuzz . . . what YOU gone do? Wit' yo' . . . BIRD-ASS chest." He pushed a finger into my chest, making me stumble backward.

"See that? One finger and I pushed yo' BIRD-ASS back. And I got nine more where that came from, cuzz'n." His hands balled into fists.

Lorenzo stepped up.

"What, FAT BOY? You want some of this too? I'll lay you out like a casket, cuzz."

Lorenzo stood still. Andre and Trent stepped up. The four of us focused on him. We weren't moving. Four of us to one Crip. The odds were finally in our favor.

"Y'all want some too? I got plenty fo' all y'all," he said, tightening his fist and flexing his muscles.

Marisol tried to creep her way out of the park. The Crip tried to follow.

I stepped in his way. "She said she had to go. Just let her be on her way."

"Boy, you better get outta my way." He threw me aside.

The fellas stepped up and we formed a wall between him and Marisol.

"Y'all kidding, right? It ain't no thang to lay ALL y'all out right here."

He jerked his arms up like he was gonna swing.

We flinched.

He laughed. "See? I ain't even swing and y'all bitch up."

My heart pulsed in my ears. Marisol watched from the far side of the fellas.

I crossed my skinny little arms and waited. I've been tagged purple in the back and socked black in the eye from red Pirus, but I'm still here. What color was this blue 'banger gonna put on me?

He eyeballed the four of us, then sucked his teeth. "Mannn, y'all ain't even worth the sweat on my sack. It's too damn hot out here!"

He pushed past us and walked away. But not before yelling out, "Go on wit' yo' schoolboys . . . STUCK-UP LITTLE WETBACK!"

I walked over to Marisol.

"You all right?"

Her back was to me, so I couldn't see her face. Her yellow butterfly clip smiled in a sea of black hair. What now? Do I touch her? Hold her? She spun around to reveal a pair of glassy eyes. Dang . . . she gonna cry? I glanced back at the fellas. Lorenzo made a walking motion with two fingers and pointed at me and her. Andre and Trent did the same. What . . . walk her to Passion's?

"Ummm, Marisol, listen, if you want, I could . . ."

I glanced at the fellas again. They walked in a circle with their arms around each other.

"I could walk you over to Passion's if you want."

She smiled up at me. "No . . . you with your friends. I don't want you to go out of your way." Then she touched a finger to each eye. "It's so bright out here. My eyes are watering."

"It's not outta my way. Matter of fact, before all this, we were about to . . ." Go pick out a gift for you. "We were on our way to Lorenzo's to get something to drink. His house is this way."

"It would make me feel a lot better. I walk through here by myself all the time, but that's the first time that's ever happened. I got scared. He was bigger than me. . . . I was alone. . . . I laughed at his jokes to be nice, but before I knew it . . ." Her eyes dropped to the ground.

"Well, he's gone. I'm here now."

She smiled. "Yes . . . you are."

We headed out. I looked back at the fellas, and they were slapping on each other, screaming, "Go, Shawnie! Go, Shawnie!" without making a sound.

The park and the guys faded behind us as I walked next to Marisol. Alone.

"You talk to your mom about the party?"

"Yeah, she said it's cool. She was surprised to hear it's gonna start at seven."

"Really? When did she think it was gonna start?"

"I think she thought it was gonna be a cake-and-punch party with pin the tail on the donkey." We laughed. Then silence.

I peeked at her when she turned her head, which she did a lot because the street was so active. Her butterfly clip smiled at me every time she looked away — two smiles for the price of one. I wanted to get closer, but I was thrilled just to be alone with her. We were on the DMZ and getting close to Pop's. The fellas popped into my head. I would've never thought to walk her over to Passion's. As usual, they were looking out for me.

I snuck a peek at her again and caught her sneaking a peek at me. Our eyes locked for a hot second before she turned away and caressed her hair. I couldn't pull my eyes off her, but I had to; my chest bumped into something—I mean—someone.

"Slow yo' stroll and watch where you goin'!"

I peeled my eyes from Marisol, and a green peacock stood in front of me—mint-green from hat to shoes with the toothpick to match. This dude again? Don't he have any other clothes?

What's his name again? I moved next to Marisol so he could pass. "Sorry 'bout that."

"Yeah, you lucky Larry Luck is in a good mood." He sniffed.

Larry Luck! That's right. I followed his feathered fedora down the street as he went on his way.

"*Who* was that?" Marisol asked, with the same surprised look that graced my face the first time I saw the green peacock.

"Didn't you hear? That's Larry Luck."

"What's with all the green . . . especially the . . ." She pointed toward her mouth.

"Toothpick?"

"Yeah. What's that all about?"

"I don't know, but believe it or not, I bumped into him before and he was wearing the exact same thing—green from head to toe, toothpick and all."

"Really?"

"Oh, yeah."

Silence. Again.

How much farther? I could walk with her forever, but I don't know what to say. What did Dad say? Talk about her.

Ask about her. She must have been thinking the same way because words came out of her mouth first.

"So, you ready for high school?"

She shook my arm when she said "high school." It felt good.

"I think so."

She inched closer and looked up at me. Her eyes warmed my face.

"All those people, though . . . I don't know. I'm a little scared. Aren't you?"

I stopped to face her.

"I was. But not anymore."